Not by Sight

Praise for Kate Breslin

Not by Sight

"*Downton Abbey* meets *The Scarlet Pimpernel* in Kate Breslin's wonderful historical novel set amidst the drama of England's WWI home front."

—Elizabeth Camden, RITA and Christy
Award-winning author

"*Not by Sight* will sweep you away with romance and intrigue to WWI England, where a spirited young woman seeks to live out her patriotism and faith in challenging times. Well researched with captivating characters, Kate Breslin brings us another story that will touch our hearts and lift our spirits."

—Carrie Turansky, award-winning author of *Surrendered Hearts* and *A Refuge at Highland Hall*

"In her sophomore novel, Kate Breslin continues to define excellence in storytelling with complex characters and deeply researched themes, firmly rooting the reader in the vivid landscape of WWI-era Britain. *Not by Sight* held me spellbound by Jack and Grace's emotionally engaging journey from loss and pain to eventual restoration. It's a tender story of love and the enduring power of faith to guide us—even when the road to healing remains unseen."

—Kristy Cambron, author of *The Butterfly and the Violin* and *A Sparrow in Terezin*

For Such a Time

"I absolutely loved this book. *For Such a Time* kept me up at night, flipping the pages and holding my breath wanting to know what would happen next. . . . The story is gripping, compelling, and I dare anyone to close the cover before the last suspenseful page."

—Debbie Macomber, #1 *New York Times* bestselling author

"When I finished Kate Breslin's novel for the first time, I had an urge to flip back to page one and start reading all over again. It's that good. *For Such a Time* is an intimate portrait painted on a grand scale, bringing to life the drama and pain of suffering with the triumph and joy of freedom. This book deserves a wide audience, and newcomer Breslin has a bright future."

—Susan Wiggs, #1 *New York Times* bestselling author

"An engrossing and inspiring story from a talented new writer."

—Sheila Roberts, bestselling author

Not by Sight

KATE BRESLIN

BETHANYHOUSE
a division of Baker Publishing Group
Minneapolis, Minnesota

© 2015 by Kathryn Breslin

Published by Bethany House Publishers
11400 Hampshire Avenue South
Bloomington, Minnesota 55438
www.bethanyhouse.com

Bethany House Publishers is a division of
Baker Publishing Group, Grand Rapids, Michigan

Printed in the United States of America

Library of Congress Cataloging-in-Publication Data
Breslin, Kate.
    Not by sight / Kate Breslin.
        pages ; cm
    ISBN 978-0-7642-1161-4 (pbk.)
        1. World War, 1914–1918—England—London—Fiction. I. Title.
PS3602.R4575N68 2015
813'.6—dc23   2015005742

Scripture quotations are from the Holy Bible, New International Version®. NIV®. Copyright © 1973, 1978, 1984, 2011 by Biblica, Inc.™ Used by permission of Zondervan. All rights reserved worldwide. www.zondervan.com

This is a work of historical reconstruction; the appearances of certain historical figures are therefore inevitable. All other characters, however, are products of the author's imagination, and any resemblance to actual persons, living or dead, is coincidental.

Cover design by Kathleen Lynch / Black Kat Design
Front cover photograph of woman by Susan Fox / Trevillion Images

Author is represented by Hartline Literary Agency

15 16 17 18 19 20 21   7 6 5 4 3 2 1

To Marjorie

A woman who lives by faith,
and a mother who taught her daughter
to become whatever she could dream

For we live by faith, not by sight.
2 Corinthians 5:7

1

CHETFIELD HOUSE, MAYFAIR
LONDON—APRIL 1917

Her father would never forgive her.

Grace Elizabeth Mabry stood in her flowing green costume on the steps outside the grand London home of Lady Eleanor Bassett, Dowager Countess of Avonshire, and clutched a tiny gold box to her chest. She knew the "gifts" she was about to bestow on the unsuspecting cowards inside would ruin Patrick Mabry's hope that his daughter would ever gain acceptance into polite society.

All those months at finishing school, destroyed in a single act.

"Are you ready with your feathers, miss? No second thoughts?"

Grace tightened her grip on the gold box and glanced at the costumed sprite beside her. "I am committed to this cause, Agnes. 'For King, For Country, For Freedom.' Didn't Mrs. Pankhurst say those very words at our suffrage rally yesterday?"

Agnes nodded. "And for Colin?"

Grace smiled. Agnes Pierpont was more a friend to her than lady's maid. "For my brother most of all," she said. "And the sooner we get inside and complete our task, the quicker we'll help to win this war. Then Colin can come home."

And Mother would have been so proud, had she lived. Grace blinked back unexpected tears. The year since Lillian Mabry's death from tuberculosis had been difficult. Colin's enlistment had only aggravated their gentle mother's condition. Yet Grace was proud of her brother. He did his duty for Britain. Just as she must do hers, in any way possible—including today's scandalous act.

Three Rolls-Royce automobiles drew up the street in front of the mansion. Pressing a gloved fist to the bodice of her gown, Grace watched a boisterous crowd of costumed men and women spill out of the cars.

"Ready?" Agnes looked equally anxious. A burst of hyena-like laughter escaped before she could cover her mouth. "I am sorry, miss," she said, blushing. "When I'm nervous . . ."

"It's all right." Grace took a deep breath. "I'm ready."

For Colin, she reminded herself. Thoughts of her twin fighting in the trenches of France lent her strength. Surely God was on her side. Grace imagined herself a modern-day Joan of Arc about to rally her countrymen to battle. She hoped to write and submit an article about the night's experience, especially after having received her latest rejection from *Women's Weekly*.

The partygoers ascended the steps, moving toward the front door. Grace and Agnes clasped hands and rushed to join them, slipping into the house amid the crush. They pressed on through the foyer and then down a lushly carpeted hall to finally arrive at the ballroom.

The rest of the company dispersed while Grace paused with Agnes to ogle the sumptuous décor. Her father, a tea distributor and owner of London's prestigious Swan's Tea Room, ranked among the city's wealthiest tradesmen, yet she had never before seen such opulence.

Four table-sized chandeliers hung from the high-coved ceiling, their crystal drops as large as tea balls and glittering like jewels beneath the lamplight. Along one rich mahogany paneled wall, swags of red velvet draperies showcased enormous windows, each pane the size of the entire glass frontage of Swan's.

Grace barely heard the sprightly notes of Mozart floating over the throng as she gaped at the endless supply of champagne bubbling in delicate glass flutes, carried on silver trays by black-and-white-liveried footmen. Men who certainly looked able-bodied enough . . .

Recalling her purpose, she scanned the room. Lady Bassett was sponsoring the ball, a costume affair, for the British Red Cross Society. Agnes had dressed as a winged wood sprite, the earthy tones of her outfit accentuating her fawn-colored hair. Grace, for her part, chose the fabled guise of Pandora.

Such waste, she thought. Hadn't the dowager seen the posters warning against extravagant dress? It was positively unpatriotic.

Grace glanced down at her own beautiful costume and felt a stab of guilt. Still, the disguise had been necessary in order to gain admittance to the party. She and Agnes had a higher purpose, after all.

The newspaper had reported the benefit would aid wounded soldiers. Several "conchies"—conscientious objectors against the war—would be here tonight, performing their community service by supporting the festivities.

It was the reason Grace and Agnes had chosen this particular event.

Edging open the small gold box that completed her ensemble as the mythical troublemaker, Grace withdrew her contraband and hid it against her gloved palm. "For King, For Country, For Freedom," she murmured to herself.

"Miss?"

She turned to Agnes. "I'll meet you back here when we finish, agreed?"

Agnes pursed her lips and nodded. Grace watched her mill through the crowd toward the opposite side of the room before she scanned the guests on her own side, seeking her first target.

Jack Benningham, Viscount of Walenford and future Earl of Stonebrooke, stood directly ahead. Grace ignored the racing of her pulse, telling herself it was simply nerves as she stared at the tall, broad-shouldered man she recognized only from the photographs she'd seen in the society pages of the *Times*, and from his scandalous exploits recorded in the *Tatler*.

His objections to the war were well publicized, though he certainly seemed fit enough for duty. At twenty-eight, the handsome Viscount Walenford was but eight years older than Colin and herself. He held a long-stemmed red rose and wore black velvet from head to toe. With his clipped blond hair tied off in a faux queue at his nape, he looked every inch the eighteenth-century Venetian rogue, Casanova.

Her mouth twisted in scorn at seeing two women in daring costumes clinging to either side of him—Cleopatra and Lady Godiva. Grace watched as he settled an arm possessively over Cleopatra's shoulder while bending his head to smile and whisper in Lady Godiva's ear.

"Jack Benningham is a playboy, a gambler, and stays out until dawn." She'd heard the gossip, spoken in tones of mixed censure and titillation by several of the young ladies who regularly took tea at her father's establishment. And it seemed true, if Lady Godiva's blush and tittering laughter were any indication.

At the moment Grace didn't care if he was the biggest profligate in London. The only moral flaw concerning her was the fact he was *here* while her dear brother was in France, fighting the "Boche."

Moving toward him, she glanced at the others in his party.

A portly man in laurel wreath and a white toga made the quintessential tyrant, Julius Caesar. The tall elderly woman beside Caesar was Lady Bassett herself, wearing the unmistakable sixteenth-century headdress, ruff collar, and damask gown of Queen Elizabeth.

Hearing a burst of hyena-like laughter rise over the buzz of conversation, Grace paused to glance toward the other side of the ballroom. Agnes must be at work distributing her feathers.

Grace turned back to her quarry and met with Casanova's deliberate gaze. His sudden, teasing smile caused her heart to race a staccato beat to the lively music.

Jack Benningham was a coward, she reminded herself. Yet he was also a viscount, his father an earl of the realm. Grace took a moment to consider the full impact of her actions. Once the deed was done, there was no going back. And Lady Bassett, who happened to be her father's chief patroness at Swan's, would surely recognize her and toss her out.

She thought of her father's reaction. Da might go through with his promise to marry her off or send her to live with Aunt Florence. She wet her lips. Escape was still an option. She could turn around and leave . . .

Jack Benningham stifled a yawn, resisting an urge to check his pocket watch. He smiled, pretending interest as his father's friend, Lord Chumley—Julius Caesar—regaled him with another pointless anecdote.

Patience, he told himself. It was imperative that he keep up pretenses. Although tonight, for some reason, Jack chafed at having to be here. Plucking another flute of champagne from a passing footman, he took a sip, then looked over the rim of his glass at his target. The man standing across the room disguised as the American film star Charlie Chaplin hadn't yet moved.

Surveillance was tiresome. It made one's mind wander, like

musing for the umpteenth time over the latest lecture from his father just hours prior to the ball. It was always the same: Why did Jack continue to embarrass him with his pacifist views? Why couldn't he have been more like Jack's brother, Hugh, God rest his soul, who took up the battle cry when war was declared?

Ironic how, after Hugh's death, it was Jack's power-wielding father who obtained for him a written exemption from the fighting. No doubt a gesture meant to salvage the Benningham line. Duty was paramount to the hard-nosed earl, who had carped on all afternoon about Jack's consummate philandering and irresponsibility, and how he must start thinking about his duty to family instead of himself all of the time.

All the while, Jack could hear his mother's quiet sobs in the background.

"I say, Walenford, you seem a bit distracted tonight. I suppose it's an intolerable bore listening to an old man prattle on when you have two pretty birds beside you, eh?"

"Not at all, Lord Chumley, just feeling a bit stifled in this cape." Jack smiled at the man in the toga before turning to his hostess. "You've managed quite the crowd tonight, Lady Bassett."

"Indeed." The old woman adjusted her ruff, then narrowed her gaze on Caesar. "And I'll have you know, Lord Chumley, those 'pretty birds' you speak of are my granddaughters."

She turned an indulgent smile on Cleopatra and Lady Godiva. "I've employed them at the behest of Miss Violet Arnold, Lord Walenford's bride-to-be. They are here tonight to keep an eye on him while she visits Edinburgh with her father."

"Ah, yes, someone must keep me in check," Jack drawled. Violet's command no doubt stemmed from a wish to avoid scandal rather than any jealousy on her part.

"I do feel for the young woman," Lady Bassett went on. "Miss Arnold has been through so much." She made a *tsk*ing sound. "But a year is more than enough time for her grief." She nodded at Jack. "And you have met the challenge admirably, Walenford. I'm certain your good father the earl is pleased. Stonebrooke will have its young countess, after all. An August wedding will be just the thing."

"Just," Jack echoed with a forced smile. Again he sipped at his glass of champagne. Contrary to his father's opinion of him, Jack *was* doing his duty—in fact, going so far as to take up his brother's place at the altar. When the American heiress, Violet Arnold, first became betrothed to Hugh, money exchanged hands—from her father to his. Hugh would provide a coronet in payment for shoring up Stonebrooke's flagging coffers.

Then his brother had died, leaving Violet unmarried. Without the promised title, the Benninghams owed the Arnolds quite a sum.

It was still difficult to grasp that after months of fighting at the Front, Hugh had returned home unscathed . . . only to drown in a freak boating accident weeks later. A shock not only to his family but also to Violet's. Yet it didn't change the financial arrangement. Jack had no wish to marry; however, he knew what was expected. Stonebrooke must be saved at all costs.

Of course, he would have to change his ways, but only for a time. The earl did promise that once Jack married and produced an heir, he could go to the devil if he pleased.

The notion enticed him, as he had little use for a wife. Yet . . . in the back of his mind, disquieting thoughts of settling down had already begun to take root. Jack caught himself thinking less about living in the moment and more about his future.

He discarded the consideration and instead gazed at the beautiful young women on either side of him—off-limits, of course, as he hardly wished to tangle with their lioness of a grandmother.

Still, the scenery was pleasant enough. Raising an arm to rest against Cleopatra's shoulder, he winked at his hostess's look of reproach. Lady Bassett's charming granddaughters served to enhance his romantic guise at the party tonight, without any emotional entanglement.

Movement from across the room caught his eye. Chaplin had left his place by the window. Jack straightened, reminding himself he had a job to do. It wouldn't sit well with his superiors if he failed. Because although he professed to be a conscientious objector, he simply preferred fighting the enemy on his own terms. Unbeknownst to his father, the earl—in fact to anyone but Sir Marcus Weatherford, his friend and a lieutenant at the Admiralty—he was doing his bit for his country without having to set foot on foreign soil.

Jack had become a spy catcher for the Crown.

Espionage, ever present before the war, seemed to have grown to rampant proportions in the past three years. Hundreds of suspected enemy agents were apprehended and tried, with many convicted traitors executed at the Tower. Jack's social reputation allowed him to infiltrate any arena, from dockside brothels to the finest salons, enabling him to make such arrests.

Marcus once said half jokingly that Jack's notoriety as a playboy aided the War Office more efficiently in the boudoirs of London than it ever could in the trenches of France.

He watched as Chaplin moved to another empty spot along the opposite wall. No one had yet approached him.

Jack took the assignment because his section of the British Intelligence Agency, MI5, had received a tip. An unknown German agent was to arrive at the ball tonight and meet with a man already under the Admiralty's watchful eye—the man disguised as Charlie Chaplin. Once an exchange was made, Jack would follow the German from the ball to his lair, where New Scotland Yard could make the arrest.

He lifted his glass to take another sip of champagne. So where was he—?

A shimmer of bright green near the door caught his eye. Jack turned . . . and then forgot everything else.

She was a vision. Jack swallowed as he stared at the exotic beauty only a few yards away. Her cloud of fiery auburn curls looked ready to burst from the green ribbons holding them in place, and her gown, a wispy emerald-green affair, clung to her alluring figure, swaying gently as she turned with a regal air and surveyed the room.

"I say, is that Pandora?"

It took a moment for Lord Chumley's question to penetrate Jack's senses. But yes, he'd already glimpsed the small gold box she held against her lovely bosom.

Cleopatra spoke up. "According to myth, the gods made her the most beautiful woman on earth—"

"To ensnare Epimetheus, the brother of Zeus's enemy, into marriage," Lady Godiva finished. "She would cause him mischief by opening her box and releasing trouble into the world."

"I could do with a spot of trouble," Chumley muttered under his breath.

Jack heard him, and the unexpected rush of anger he felt took him aback. He said nothing, unable to tear his gaze from the auburn-haired beauty near the door.

"Who is she?" Lady Bassett demanded. "I cannot see her clearly from this distance."

Jack's pulse quickened as she started in their direction. "Excuse me," he said, breaking from the women at his side. He ignored Lady Bassett's frown as he moved apart, waiting to catch Pandora's attention.

Halfway across the stretch dividing them, she paused. Only half aware, Jack did so too, holding his breath as she lifted her head to scan the room. When she turned back to him, their gazes locked, and he offered his most dazzling smile.

Immediately she straightened and blushed. Then she frowned

at him, and Jack wanted to laugh. Air eased from his lungs when after a moment she flashed a determined look and resumed her trek.

All conversation stopped when she came to stand directly before him. Jack caught the heady, exotic scent of flowers—jasmine?—as they continued staring at each other. He took in her exquisite features, the porcelain skin and dainty nose set beneath wide emerald eyes. Her full lower lip crying out to be kissed . . .

Ever so slowly, the green-eyed beauty held out a gloved hand. Delighted, he smiled and gently grasped her fingers, bringing them to his lips.

Only when she pulled away did he notice the gift she'd given him.

Grace watched, breathless, as he looked down at the white feather of cowardice. Uncertainty over his reaction warred with the effect his nearness was having on her senses. She discovered he was even more impressive up close. One could drown in those midnight-blue eyes, and his smile . . . sweet heaven, it made her almost giddy.

She had to remind herself again of his cowardice, and as he looked at her, Grace was satisfied to note his smug expression had turned to a look of pure astonishment . . .

Before he grinned and tucked the feather behind his ear.

She glared at him, her moment of righteousness quashed. When he silently offered her his red rose, she set her jaw. Did he think she played some game? Grace had risked her reputation in order to aid her brother and her country. Did this man now think to turn her serious act into a joke? His arrogance was unbelievable! Jack Benningham wasn't just a coward; he was a conceited, overbearing, womanizing . . . turncoat.

Abruptly, he shifted his attention past her and let out a snarl.

Grace drew in a breath at his look of fury. Had the meaning of her white feather finally registered with him? She'd never stopped to consider that her actions might cause violence upon her person.

A scream welled in her throat as he grabbed her by the waist and, with a muttered curse, lifted her easily. Did he intend to toss her across the room?

He set her gently to one side, then strode to the nearest exit.

Dazed, Grace turned to watch him leave. "You!" sputtered the outraged Queen Elizabeth, and then she met with the dowager's look of shocked recognition. "I shall speak to your father, young woman," she promised, before raising a hand to signal a servant.

Grace went clammy with fear, and for an instant she thought to escape. Yet she knew there was no turning back—Lady Bassett could hardly forget the incident.

Colin's image rose in her mind, renewing her determination. Her brother was counting on her! Quickly she sidestepped her hostess and managed to thrust two more white feathers of cowardice into unsuspecting hands before the butler grasped her arm.

Five minutes later, she and Agnes were ejected from the house.

"That was close," Agnes said in a breathless tone. "I handed out my last feather before the butler got me." A burst of hyena laughter escaped her.

Grace grinned, her pulse racing. "I handed out just a few, but one which I hope will reap many returns." She nodded toward Jack Benningham, who was climbing into a cab without a backward glance. "He's an earl's son, a public figure. If he enlists in the Army, I feel certain his conchie friends will follow."

Never would Grace forget the look on his face before he stormed from the ballroom. She'd made her point, and if ruffling the conscience of the arrogant coward might help her brother win the war, she was satisfied.

What she didn't want to think about was Lady Bassett's

threat. Grace knew Da would have the whole story before the kettle was on at Swan's the following morning.

Jack drove off in the cab, barking instructions to the driver as he mentally cursed his own lapse. He'd not only let the German agent slip from his grasp, but now he risked losing Chaplin. His only recourse was to follow him back to his den and interrogate him, perhaps salvage the situation.

Leaning back in the seat, he frowned at the white feather *she'd* given him—the mysterious auburn-haired minx who had caused his distraction.

If his current circumstances weren't so dire, he'd have been more amused *and* thankful for her action. Jack was aware of his enemy's recent surveillance of him. His cover as a conscientious objector seemed dangerously close to being compromised, a condition that also concerned Marcus.

Pandora's feather had done much to aid his deception, yet he doubted the knowledge would please her. Who was she? Jack had been sorry to leave, for she was not only beautiful but seemed to have a mind of her own—a novelty among the women he normally associated with.

He smiled, recalling the passion in those angry green eyes. And her lips, so tempting to kiss, particularly when she frowned at him.

Jack looked out at the fading twilight toward the docks ahead. His humor waned. He'd made a mess of things tonight. Only by staying focused could he possibly minimize his losses.

Still, he allowed himself another smile as he raised the white feather to his lips. Whoever she was, he would find her, his Pandora—and get that kiss.

2

Surely being banished never felt so good . . .

With the smallest twinge of guilt, Grace jotted the words into her journal, then raised her face to the brisk summer breeze blowing in through the open window of the cab. She marveled at the pastoral beauty of the Kent countryside. It seemed unsullied and tranquil compared to town. Thatched-roof cottages and rustic barns lay interspersed among groves of alder and plane trees, the fading white flowers of the rowan in sharp contrast with the bright red berries of the buckthorn.

Relieved at being away from her father's watchful eye and Lady Bassett's censure, she couldn't have asked for a more pleasing exile. It was the perfect setting for her next story.

"We're almost to Roxwood, miss!"

Grace turned from the window and smiled at her maid's excitement. "Have you grown tired of all the traveling, then?"

"Not at all," Agnes said. "Since I came to this country, I've never stepped outside of London. In the past two weeks we've been to Norfolk and all the places in between." Her brown eyes widened. "I didn't know Britain was so grand."

"Yes, it has been a whirlwind," Grace said. "I can hardly believe we left London just this morning." Now they were traveling the last leg of their journey to Roxwood. The Kent estate apparently encompassed an enormous amount of acreage between Canterbury and the town of Margate and would be their home for the next few weeks as she and Agnes began their service in the Women's Forage Corps—WFC—harvesting and baling hay for the cavalry horses overseas.

"It was good of your father to hire us a cab."

"There wasn't much choice, since the trains don't run on Sunday. It wouldn't do for us to be late reporting for our first day of work." Grace added in a low voice, "Anyway, likely Da paid the driver to report back on my behavior."

Agnes shot her a sympathetic look. "Yes, he's been very . . . attentive toward you since the costume party."

"I suppose 'attentive' is a nice way of putting it," Grace said with wry humor. Lady Bassett followed through on her threat, and Da had been furious over Grace's "white-feather stunt." He'd railed for days, alternating between threats to bring Aunt Florence from Oxford or marry Grace off to his American protégé, Clarence Fowler. Then he forbade her to attend any more suffragette meetings with those "brazen Pankhurst women." Finally, heeding the advice of his chief patroness who warned him to "keep an eye on that one," he'd restricted Grace to the upper offices at Swan's, preparing tea care packages for the soldiers while he decided what to do.

"I knew the risks of attending the ball that night," she went on. "And I have no regrets, despite my being confined." She cast her maid a meaningful glance. "Not while my brother fights in France and others are allowed to shirk their duty."

Like Jack Benningham. Grace shifted her gaze toward the

window while again her mind replayed her thrilling encounter with the tall, handsome, blue-eyed Casanova. As always, the memory of his seductive smile, and the way his midnight gaze held hers in those moments they stood facing each other, had the power to make her pulse leap. They hadn't spoken a word that night, yet she'd sensed a connection between them. It was a feeling she didn't particularly care for, not only because of his scandalous reputation, but because he *was* a coward. Grace hadn't seen him again after the ball, but she'd read in the *Times* days later about a fire at his London townhouse. Rumors buzzed through Swan's of how after a night of substantial gambling losses, a drunken Jack Benningham had accidentally set the place ablaze. Apparently the damage was minimal, with him sustaining minor injuries, but she still hoped the ordeal had changed him enough to quit his squandering and do something useful for his country.

"Anyway, I'm free now," she said, turning back to her maid. "And we'll be doing more for the war than simply packaging up tea bags." She leaned to nudge her maid affectionately. "All thanks to you, dear Agnes."

Agnes's face turned pink. "It was luck I found the Women's Forage Corps leaflet."

"More like a miracle." Grace had chafed at being hemmed in at Swan's, and as more letters arrived from her brother, the desire to hurry up the war and bring him home gnawed at her. "Especially since Da wasn't keen on me working at a munitions factory or driving an ambulance back and forth from the field hospital."

"And you do look sharp sitting behind the wheel of a motorcar," Agnes said. "But I think he worried about the danger. Remember the Silvertown accident?"

Grace nodded. The *Times* had reported the munitions factory explosion killed scores of women workers. "All the more reason I'm grateful you suggested he let me join the WFC," she said, then laughed. "Honestly, I'd actually given up hope Da would let me out of his sight, let alone agree to my traveling to Kent, yet here we are."

"I think it might have to do with the recent bombings," Agnes said.

Grace shot her a glance, all humor gone. Countless enemy air raids over London during the past three years had resulted in hundreds of innocent deaths. In June, a single bombing by the Germans had killed over 150, and she and Agnes had left on the heels of another, just days before, that struck down dozens. "Da may not be pleased with the idea of my working in the fields and getting dirty, but you're right, he believes I'll be safer in the country."

But would her father be safe? So far there had been no attacks in the area around Swan's or their home in Knightsbridge, yet the threat was ever present. Another reason the war must end, she thought. Taking a deep breath, she tried to shake off her unease. God had preserved them so far, and she would pray He continued to do so. "You know, Agnes, despite our troubles in the city, Da never would have allowed me this venture if you hadn't agreed to come along," she said. "I want you to know I'm grateful."

"Oh, miss, I am eager to be away from London, as well." A shadow flitted across her features before she smiled. "And anyway, with my pay from the WFC, I hope to save enough to open the small dress shop I've always dreamed of."

She laid a gloved hand over Grace's. "Since I've met you and learned of the suffrage movement, so much seems possible again." Her brown eyes misted. "When I think back to the day you found me and came to my aid . . ."

"Forget the past." Grace squeezed her maid's hand, hoping Agnes wouldn't brood again over that cowardly husband of hers, Edgar Pierpont. "Think instead of your dress shop, or more important, the marvelous experience we shall have safeguarding a vital asset to the war. Cavalry horses are in precious demand, Agnes, like my Nessa."

Filled with emotion, Grace paused. She'd cried when Da sold her mare and Colin's bay gelding, Niall, to the Army. But the need for horses was still great. "Keeping them fed is critical," she continued. "We can be proud in knowing our value to the war effort. 'For God, King, and Country.'"

"Oh, miss, when you talk that way about your country and patriotism, you sound like Mrs. Pankhurst," Agnes said.

"Don't forget Britain is now your country, too."

Agnes nodded. "I do want to be a loyal citizen."

Grace eyed her with compassion. "Soon you'll have the chance—oh, we're here!"

The cab gave a lurch as it rounded a corner, where a large wych elm spread its leafy green branches over a weathered wooden post that spelled out ROXWOOD in white lettering. Passing through an opening in the gray stone, they followed a narrow cobbled road into the heart of the small village.

"What a quaint little place." Grace noted the various shops shouldering upper apartments along either side of the street. The myriad colors and textures only added to its charm. Tall burnt-brick storefronts squeezed in beside painted gray, blue, or green stuccos. Several had neat, white-framed windows above, displaying bright gingham curtains. As the cab drove along the main thoroughfare, she observed four unpaved side streets, and at the end of the village a church's spire rose into the sky. The driver pulled alongside what looked like a community hall at the center of town. A few shopkeepers clad in work aprons emerged to gawk at the newcomers.

"There's someone from the WFC." Agnes pointed to a matronly woman standing beside a long cart drawn by a pair of draft horses. She was dressed in the same khaki trench coat, green breeches, and hat that Grace and Agnes would be wearing during their stay.

With the cab's fare already paid by her father, Grace and Agnes collected their luggage and disembarked. "Miss, you don't think they'll have a problem with my . . . being your maid, do you?"

"Don't fret." Grace offered a reassuring smile. "We agreed you don't work for me at all while we're here, remember? I plan to pull my fair share. And you must call me Grace. Look, here she comes."

"Welcome, ladies, and right on time," the round-faced matron called out as she met them halfway. "I'm Mrs. Ida Vance, the gang supervisor at Roxwood." Mrs. Vance seemed quite a bit older than her and Agnes and offered a pleasant smile as she extended a hand to each of them.

"Nice to meet you. I'm Grace Mabry, and this is my—" Grace paused, glancing at Agnes—"my friend, Agnes Pierpont."

"We're pleased to have the extra help." Mrs. Vance led the way back to the cart. "How was your trip?"

"It's been a remarkable journey," Grace said. "Two weeks' training at a farm in Norfolk, a stop back in London, and now we're here."

"Well, since we don't work on Sundays, you can rest up. Tomorrow, be prepared for hard work. More local boys left for France last week, and there's much to be done. The estate covers many acres of land."

"How far is it from here?" Grace asked.

"A couple of miles." Mrs. Vance climbed nimbly up onto the cart's bench seat and took the reins. "Set your bags in back and hop on in."

Once they were under way, she said, "There are six of us altogether, and we billet at the estate's gatehouse. We'll stop there first so you can drop off your luggage, then I'll take you to meet the others. One of the cats had kittens, and they're all down at the barn."

The gatehouse turned out to be a two-story stone building covered in ivy and situated at the entrance of Roxwood Manor. The first floor housed a small parlor and a kitchen with a breakfast nook. Another room off the kitchen contained a laundry area and bathroom. "We're fortunate Lord Roxwood had ordered the indoor toilet installed." Mrs. Vance winked at them. "Especially with so many of us."

"Will Lord Roxwood be overseeing our work?" Grace asked.

"Dear me, no! He's the ongoing mystery of this place." Mrs. Vance had removed her hat, revealing pretty chestnut hair cut short in the latest style. Along with the sparkle in her hazel eyes, Ida Vance didn't look terribly old after all. "No one knows him, because he's never been seen. Some aren't even certain he's in residence."

"Really?" Grace quelled an impulse to retrieve her journal from her bag and take notes. Could this be her story in the making? "Can you tell me more about him?"

"Later." Mrs. Vance led the way upstairs. "Right now I'll show you our sleeping quarters."

A large room encompassed the entire upper floor, with two rows of three beds each. Four housed an assortment of portmanteaus, haversacks, and hatboxes beneath them.

"We're only here long enough to harvest the hay, but it's a place to call home." Mrs. Vance waved a hand toward two empty beds. "Choose between them and leave your bags. I'll meet you back downstairs."

"Well, what do you think, Agnes? Isn't it grand?" Grace said once Mrs. Vance left. She spun in a circle to take it all in. "And this place even comes with its own mystery, the never-before-seen Lord Roxwood. I'll have so much to write about."

"When you're not baling hay, you mean?" Agnes teased, then in a quiet tone added, "Miss . . . thank you for introducing me as your friend. It means the world to me."

"Well, you *are* my friend. And you had better start calling me Grace." She hugged herself. "Oh, I still can't believe I'm here. It will be such an adventure!"

"Mrs. Vance said there's much to do at Roxwood," Agnes reminded her. "I mean, you weren't raised on a farm like me. The work's going to be harder than the chores we did at the practice farm, but with your determination, you'll catch on quickly." Her brown eyes shone with sincerity. "And I'll help you all I can."

Grace sketched a playful bow. "Then I rely on your experience and good sense to keep me out of trouble."

Agnes nodded. "Absolutely, miss."

"*Grace*," she reminded her.

"Yes . . . Grace," Agnes repeated with a smile.

Back in the cart, she and Agnes sat beside Mrs. Vance, who drove the team along an uneven dirt track toward the barn. Roxwood Manor came into view, and Grace leaned out from her seat to try to glean a better look. The two-story brick house was set back from the main road by a long graveled drive. Lacking the tall mansard roof and numerous dormers and columns of Lady Bassett's sumptuous mansion, it resembled more a country squire's home than a palatial estate.

Grace found the manor's unpretentious looks comfortable and pleasing. Rounded stone steps led up to a massive oak door, and the white stone pediment supported by two matching white columns seemed modest enough. For a moment she imagined a family picnic on the front lawn or beside the majestic rose garden blooming with vibrant color.

But there was no family, was there? Only Lord Roxwood, whom no one had apparently seen. Who was he . . . and why was he a mystery? Grace was hard-pressed to contain her curiosity, a natural inclination of writers, she supposed. She couldn't wait until later when Mrs. Vance had promised to answer her questions.

They soon arrived at the barn. The towering structure stood on a gray cobblestone base, with brownish-red siding and a black-slate roof. As the three of them exited the cart, a tall, slightly stooped man of middling years approached. "Mr. Tillman, these are the two new replacements I told you about," Mrs. Vance said.

Grace noted Mrs. Vance's animated tone. "Miss Mabry and Miss Pierpont, meet Mr. George Tillman. He runs the farm for Lord Roxwood and oversees our progress."

Mr. Tillman doffed his felt cap, revealing a thatch of salt-and-pepper hair. His heavily waxed mustache collided with a pair of gray muttonchop sideburns to form a continuous line. "Ladies." He gave a curt nod, then frowned. "You two don't look fit for this kind of work," he said bluntly. "You're going to have to prove yourselves."

Grace stiffened. "We shall," she said, tipping her chin at him. Perhaps he resented women working his fields and getting paid for it, even though the Army Service Corps took care of their wages. She and Agnes were warned about such men during training. "We know what hard work is." She glanced at her maid. "Don't we, Agnes?"

"Indeed," Agnes said, brow puckered. Grace turned to Mrs. Vance, noting her high color as she smiled and stared at Mr. Tillman.

Did her supervisor harbor an interest in the farmer? Grace wondered if there was a Mr. Vance, perhaps off fighting in the war. Or like Edgar Pierpont, maybe he'd left his wife to flee the country and escape conscription. Grace mulled over the possibilities, wondering if this might be her next story, one of unrequited love . . .

"Let's go meet the others."

Jarred from her musings, she walked alongside Agnes as they followed the older pair toward the barn.

Attached to the structure was a lean-to housing several bicycles, where three women in Women's Forage Corps uniforms took shade. Seated on overturned milk cans, they each held a tiny mewling kitten. A box filled with straw sat at their feet.

"Lucy Young, Clare Danner, and Becky Simmons, meet Grace Mabry and Agnes Pierpont, our newest recruits," Mrs. Vance said by way of introduction.

A long moment passed while Grace felt their assessing gazes. She glanced down at her tailored blue traveling suit and wished she'd changed into her uniform before joining them.

A young woman finally rose off her perch and set her kitten in the box. Short, buxom, and apple-cheeked, she was perhaps eighteen years of age and wore her dark hair short beneath her hat. "Hello, I'm Becky, nice to meet you," she said, approaching. Soft brown eyes the color of oolong tea, Da's favorite, studied her and Agnes with interest. "Did you really hire a cab to bring you all the way from London?"

When Grace nodded, Becky crossed her arms, looking impressed. Unhampered by shyness, she quickly told them she was the daughter of a local fisherman, who along with his wife and nine other children lived in a coastal village on the outskirts of Margate.

The next to greet them was a woman comparable to Becky's age and completely the opposite in personality. "I'm Lucy, w-welcome." She spoke so softly, both Grace and Agnes leaned forward to hear her. Pale and oval-faced, Lucy had arresting turquoise eyes, and wisps of mahogany hair peeked out from beneath her hat. As she cuddled her kitten, Grace wondered if her stammer was due to shyness or the same speech affliction her brother Colin once had.

Clare Danner was the last to come forward—or more accurately, saunter into their midst. Tall, willowy, and near to Grace's own age, her ebony locks fell about her shoulders like a black shawl. Having set her kitten back in the box, she nodded at Agnes. "Are you one of the Belgian refugees?" she asked, obviously having caught the slight French accent in her maid's speech.

"Not a refugee," Agnes said, and Grace sensed her hesitation. "I came to your country just before the war."

"Well, it's good to have you helping us." Clare then turned impenetrable gray eyes on Grace. "Take off your fancy gloves and show me your hands, Duchess."

Startled by the woman's rudeness, Grace blinked. Was Clare Danner some woman of rank to make such a demand? Swallowing her retort, she complied and removed her gloves. Holding out her hands, she was conscious of the ink stains on her left hand and the writer's callus on her middle finger.

"Now turn them over."

Grace ground her teeth. Why was she being singled out? Glancing toward the others, she saw they all seemed to wait for her compliance.

She flipped her hands over to reveal her palms.

"Just as I thought. Those hands have never seen a day's work."

"Enough, Danner." Mrs. Vance offered Grace an apologetic smile. "You must excuse her, Mabry. She gets in a dander over anyone connected with the upper classes."

"Well, I'm no aristocrat." Grace turned back to Clare Danner, a mere co-worker after all. "And I have worked, at my father's business." She left off the fact she'd only done paper work, occasionally greeted Da's more affluent customers like Lady B.—and of late, packaged tea bags.

"I'll bet you didn't get your hands dirty once, Mabry," Clare said, reading her thoughts. "Aside from the training farm, anyway. You're a city girl who's never had to earn a living."

"Perhaps," Grace said, struggling for calm. "But I'm here now and ready to do my part."

Clare flashed a catlike smile. "We'll see."

Grace thought the words held more threat than observation.

"All right, ladies. I'm taking Mabry and Pierpont on a quick tour of the farm. When we're finished, I plan to turn some of those Army rations into a nice hot stew for our supper."

Her announcement met with smiles and an eager grin from Becky.

"We'll take a short ride out to the north field first," Mrs. Vance said once the three of them were back in the cart. She surprised Grace by handing her the reins. "Your file says you've signed on to be our horse transport driver, Mabry. Let's see how you do. Just head Merry and Molly over there through the pasture." She indicated a stretch of green bordered by forested hills.

Grace took a deep breath, reminding herself she'd guided Nessa and their small trap through London's streets hundreds of times. She urged the pair of old draft horses forward along a track that cut through an opening in the fence.

The late afternoon sun hovered above the distant tree line by the time they reached the north field. Mrs. Vance called a halt, and they gazed at the endless field of grass shimmering and iridescent in the golden rays of light. Green stalks rustled as they blew against one another, a gentle breeze stirring with the onset of evening.

Seeing the vast acreage, the reality of Agnes's words about

hard work came back to her. Grace wondered if six women would be able to harvest all that hay.

"The harvest begins next week." Mrs. Vance turned to Agnes. "Pierpont, you'll be one of the baling hands."

"Yes, ma'am. I was raised on a farm and know about raking and hauling bales. I may not look it, but I am quite fit."

"Good to hear." To Grace, she said, "You're in charge of the horse-drawn mower and rake, as well as taking the cart to the field each day once the steam baler is running." She paused. "And since you'll be working with the horses, I'm glad to see you're an able driver."

"Thank you, Mrs. Vance," Grace said. "We had a pair of bays stabled in London, before the Army bought them. I can also operate a motorcar—I mean, if there's ever a need."

"It's noted on your application, Mabry. Unfortunately, the Army has confiscated many private vehicles for use overseas, in particular the trucks. You won't be driving around here." Mrs. Vance smiled. "Still, it's good to know you're such a modern young woman. Mr. Vance drove a lorry during the early part of the war, before he broke his hip and got sent home. Once he recovered, the Army deemed him unfit to return. He took a job with the railway, driving a supply truck for the Liverpool Street Station."

Ah, there was a Mr. Vance. "Where is your husband now?"

Grace could have bit her tongue as grief swept across the woman's features. "Killed two years ago, the October bombing at Westminster," Mrs. Vance said softly. "My Robbie liked to stop off for a pint after work at the Old Bell, not far from the theatre." The hazel eyes welled with tears. "Imagine surviving the war, only to die in a pub."

"I'm very sorry, Mrs. Vance." Grace turned to Agnes, and they shared a look, each recalling the recent air attacks on London.

"It's all right." Mrs. Vance wiped at her face with the back of her sleeve. "I just miss Mr. Vance, bless his soul." She smiled through her tears. "I try to take comfort knowing he's in heaven with our Lord while the rest of us must stay here and get on with the task of living."

Indeed they must—to win the war, thought Grace fervently. Once the enemy was defeated, London would be safe again, and her brother could come home.

"We should head back now." Mrs. Vance was composed once more. "It's getting late and I've still more to show you."

When they returned to the barn, she finished with a walking tour of the farm. "When we're not haymaking, we perform other tasks for the Army Service Corps," Mrs. Vance said. "Like mending tarpaulins and making burlap sacks. Before the war, men did it all, but I'm proud to say we ladies are making rather good progress in their absence."

They walked past the barn and outbuildings to an enormous garden of vegetables. Beyond the garden, a chicken coop held a flock of clucking, squawking hens, and a bit farther was a pigpen with two dozen very rotund pigs and their piglets. "We also help with the farm work when there's a need, like gardening or animal husbandry." She turned to them. "Germany's U-boats have been sinking supply ships coming into Britain, and food is becoming scarce. A few months ago the Women's Land Army organized to aid in the crisis through farming here at home. But it may be weeks before they arrive to help at Roxwood. Until then, the WFC will help supply Britain with food, both here and abroad."

"Agnes and I are ready to do our best." She beamed at her maid. They would feed the nation! Grace felt ready to burst with patriotic pride. "Where shall we start first, Mrs. Vance?"

Mrs. Vance chuckled. "Your enthusiasm does you credit, Mabry. I'll assign tomorrow's duties at supper. Speaking of which, let's make haste before I have a starving mob on my hands."

An hour later, the six women sat around a long wooden table that took up most of the compact kitchen. While they feasted on a stew of rations and the delicious bread Becky Simmons had baked, Mrs. Vance gave out Monday's assignment. "Miss Young, you and I will go to the village tomorrow and mend tarpaulins the Army has sent," she said to Lucy. "Danner, you'll take Pierpont and tighten the fence on the west side of the garden." Her gaze swept to Clare and Agnes. "Otherwise the rabbits and deer will soon be devouring our food."

To Becky, she said, "The drainage line along the north field needs to be finished, Simmons. Once we start the harvest, we can't have the hay soaked by rain runoff. You and Mabry have the detail."

Clare Danner snorted with laughter. Grace turned to her. "What's so amusing?"

But the woman ignored her and rose instead to begin clearing the table.

Mrs. Vance scanned the table of women. "Everyone clear on their duties?"

"I very much doubt it." Clare had leaned close enough so that only Grace could hear. A necklace—a painted white flower on a fine gold chain—escaped her duster to swing inches from Grace's face before she hastily slipped it back inside her clothes.

Clare straightened and flashed another smug look before she gathered up the rest of the dishes and took them to a washbasin.

Grace decided to ignore her. Clare Danner seemed full of herself, but she'd change her opinion once she saw how hard Grace could work.

With supper finished and the kitchen clean, the women trooped upstairs to ready themselves for bed. As the hour still felt early to Grace, she chose to remain in her traveling clothes a while longer.

"Are you both from London?" asked Becky, seated on her bed in a white cotton nightgown and eyeing them curiously.

Agnes glanced at Grace.

"We live in Westminster," Grace said. "On Sterling Street, in Knightsbridge. My father owns Swan's Tea Room on Coventry Street in the west end."

"I saw it once, Swan's." Lucy spoke softly from the far corner of the room. "It's q-quite a grand place."

"Then you *are* a high-and-mighty rich girl," Clare said from her bed near Grace's.

Grace forced a laugh to keep from clenching her teeth. "Just because my father is successful—"

Clare cut her off. "How did you two meet?" She turned to Agnes. "And speak for yourself this time, Pierpont."

"Well, I met Miss . . . I mean, Grace, near her father's tea shop." Glancing down at her lap, Agnes added softly, "She gave me employment."

"She's your mistress? I thought as much." Wearing a plain linen nightdress, Clare rose from the bed and turned to the others. "Girls, it seems we have a duchess in our midst, after all."

The others laughed. "I am no such thing, Clare Danner," Grace argued. "I'm just like you."

"No," Clare retorted. "I doubt you're like any of us. But time will tell, won't it?"

Feeling the others' appraising glances, Grace was about to reply when Lucy spoke up and the conversation shifted.

"After church this morning, one of the villagers said he delivered groceries to the manor yesterday and got a good g-glimpse of the Tin Man."

Grace eyed the soft-spoken woman. "Tin Man?"

"The monster living up at the big house," Becky piped up.

"Lord Roxwood. They say he's a hunchback with pointed ears and sharp teeth."

"Such nonsense, Simmons." Fresh from a bath, Mrs. Vance stood in the doorway in a blue cotton nightdress. "How can you think he has sharp teeth?" To Grace she said, "He's called the Tin Man because it's rumored Lord Roxwood wears a metal mask to hide his face."

"But . . . why must he hide?"

"The villagers say he got burned in a fire," Becky interjected. "He's deformed now and has a hunchback. The blaze melted his ears to points, too." She grabbed at the tops of her ears to illustrate.

"Have you seen him?" Grace was enthralled with the idea of the monster from Mary Shelley's *Frankenstein* or Gaston Leroux's Phantom living only a stone's throw away. What a fascinating character for her new story.

Becky shook her head. "They say his lordship never leaves the house. Edwards, his land agent, runs all the errands in town and gives orders to Mr. Tillman about the estate."

Clare fingered the flower pendant at her throat and snorted. "I doubt the Tin Man is even at Roxwood. Likely our lord of the manor sits at his club in London, sipping whiskey and wasting money at playing cards, just like his wealthy friends."

How could such a young, attractive woman be so bitter and angry? "Well, I'd like to see this Lord Roxwood for myself," Grace said.

"And what would you do, Duchess? Invite him to sip Darjeeling with you at your father's fancy tea room?" Clare flashed an evil grin. "Or perhaps you plan to unmask him?"

The women broke into fits of laughter. Hands on hips, Grace opened her mouth to give Clare a good setting down, but then she saw Agnes shake her head. Instead she clamped her mouth shut and fumed. Duchess, indeed!

For some unfathomable reason, Clare Danner chose to be her enemy. Why did she feel it a crime that Grace's father was wealthy? Da had earned every shilling with honest, hard work, and Grace couldn't help the fact she'd never gotten her hands dirty except to cut flowers from the garden.

Becky moved to dim the lights. As all grew quiet in the room, Grace changed into the ecru silk nightgown she'd brought with her, hoping to avoid Clare's ridicule over the expensive garment while the others wore simple cotton.

Once she'd climbed under the covers, she lay there a long while, listening to Agnes's gentle breathing in the bed beside hers, while occasional snores sounded from Becky's direction.

Finally Grace sat up, too restless for sleep. Writing about her first impressions of Roxwood and the mystery of the Tin Man would settle her thoughts.

She retrieved her journal, along with a candle and matches from her haversack beneath the bed. Her gaze darted toward Clare, and for an instant she feared the termagant might awaken and intrude on her most intimate time. Then she tiptoed to the window.

Due to the warm evening, the sash remained open. The night's silence was broken by the chirping of crickets, while a near-full moon illuminated the grounds. Grace lit her candle, then opened her journal.

She'd just begun to write when a shrill cry in the night brought her up short. Grace shivered. Was it a fox? She'd read about them, how the vixen's scream sounded more human than beast. Blowing out the candle, she scanned the grounds below for any sign of the creature. Her attention soon drifted toward Roxwood Manor, and she forgot all about the fox. Even from this distance, the white stone apex and columns of the front porch held an iridescent glow in the moonlight. Her eyes traveled to the rear of the house, where a second-story balcony in the same white stone jutted out . . .

A movement caught her attention. Grace leaned out the window, straining to see.

A man stood on the balcony. Lord Roxwood?

She squinted, trying to make out the hunched back, but even the moon's brightness didn't offer that kind of detail. He did seem tall, at least in proportion to the railing he leaned against. Grace watched him several seconds before another animal's cry sounded to her right, and she instinctively turned.

When she looked back to the balcony, the man was gone.

Had she seen someone . . . or did the moonlight play tricks on her imagination?

Closing her journal, she returned to bed and burrowed beneath the blanket, still musing over the man she thought she'd seen. Then she rolled onto her side, and her thoughts went to Clare and her earlier taunts.

Grace punched at her feather pillow. She was determined to start afresh the next day. She would show Clare Danner she was made of sturdy stock. Despite a more refined upbringing, she could work just as hard as the rest of them.

She thought of all Patrick Mabry had achieved through the sweat of his brow, building up a lucrative tea empire, owning Swan's, and the planned expansion of several tea rooms throughout London. She and her father may have their differences in convention, and both were more strongheaded than either cared to admit, but Grace *was* his daughter. And Mabrys did not give up.

3

Grace had never been so miserable in all her life.

She was sorely tempted to return to the gatehouse and pack her bags for London. She straightened instead, stretching her screaming back muscles, then pulled away her hat to wipe at the perspiration beading along her brow.

Digging ditches hadn't been advertised in the leaflet. Grace recalled her tour of the fields with Mrs. Vance the previous day. Seeing how the sun gleamed against the ripening fields, she'd imagined herself gently leading a horse-drawn team across verdant pastures, feeling the day's warmth against her shoulders. Not breaking her back manning a shovel!

Becky was supposed to have helped her, but she got called away at the last minute to mend fences—Clare's assignment with Agnes. Grace fumed, wondering if Miss Danner had removed Becky on purpose.

She replaced her hat and then removed her gloves. As she flexed her fingers, she noted the blisters already formed against her reddened palms. Her poor hands had never ached so much. The heat beating down on her managed to scorch her exposed skin, and she could feel the sting of sunburn against her nose and cheeks while sweat trailed down the side of her face. And the mud . . .

It covered her from head to toe. Grace shifted, trying to ignore the feel of her dirty, sweat-soaked uniform clinging to her skin. Da would be shocked to see her in this condition, and in fact might not recognize her at all.

She leaned against the shovel and stared out at the acres of grass. This kind of work was a far cry from driving ambulances or packaging tea bags at Swan's, she thought morosely. Soon they would begin harvest. Agnes had warned the workload would be much heavier than at the training farm.

Had Grace been fooling herself to think she could succeed in this endeavor? It wasn't even noon and she felt ready to collapse. She looked at the ditch where so far she'd dug only a few feet of trench. Closing her eyes, she tried to swallow past the knot in her throat. She wanted desperately to do her part, to help Colin, but maybe she *was* completely out of her element.

The mere thought roused her determination. She replaced her gloves and grabbed up the shovel. With her jaw set she resumed digging at the muddy earth, praying for strength with each shovelful. She would do this, she told herself. "For God, King, and Country." For Colin . . .

And because the last thing she wanted was to admit Clare Danner was right.

The next morning Grace thought she might have died, except that Agnes again shook her awake at the unholy hour of five a.m. Rolling over, she groaned with the knowledge she would have to repeat yesterday's dirt shoveling today. Everything hurt. She'd been too exhausted to write in her journal last night, or search out the silhouette of the mysterious stranger standing on his balcony.

Instead she'd collapsed onto her bed in her dirty uniform and fallen asleep.

Agnes gave her another gentle shake. Grace opened her eyes. "Oh, Agnes, I wish Mrs. Vance would let you work with me today. I surely need help."

"Are you all right, miss?" Concern lit her brown eyes. "Breakfast is ready. Shall I bring you something?"

"No, I'm fine, really." Grace rubbed at her eyes. "You go ahead."

"All right, but don't go back to sleep," Agnes warned.

"I'll be down presently," Grace said. Once her maid had left, she rolled over and closed her eyes. Just another minute, she told herself.

She'd nearly dozed off when a voice sounded from the doorway. "Up with you, Mabry, or you'll miss breakfast."

Blinking, Grace sat up as Mrs. Vance entered the room looking spry in her clean and pressed uniform. Self-conscious about her own dirty, rumpled state, Grace swung her feet over the side of the bed, grateful Agnes had thought to remove her boots and her gaiters last night.

The supervisor read her thoughts. "You slept in your uniform," she stated, shaking her head. "You look an absolute fright, Mabry. I hope you plan to change. In the Women's Forage Corps, we take pride in our appearance."

"Yes, ma'am." Grace quickly rose and retrieved her other uniform from the portmanteau beneath her bed. How she longed for a bath! But last night she'd slept through her chance to get clean, as well.

She was smoothing the wrinkles from her fresh garments when Mrs. Vance asked, "Mabry, did you perform any actual field drainage work during training?"

Grace looked up and shook her head. "We received a lecture, with photographs," she said slowly. "Why?"

"Mr. Tillman isn't pleased. He inspected your work last evening. You barely made progress on the ditch, and you left your tools lying half buried in the mud." Mrs. Vance eyed her sternly. "He didn't notice the shovel until he'd tripped over it and took a spill."

Mortified, Grace asked, "Is he injured?"

"His ankle is sprained, but not broken, thank goodness." She took a deep breath. "I'm assigning you a different task today. The Army ordered more sacks, and a shipment of tarpaulins needs mending. Lucy Young is overwhelmed. While I catch up on my reports, you'll work with her." She paused. "You *can* sew?"

Relieved to be excused from digging, Grace recalled many afternoons spent mastering petit point. "Of course," she said, confident she could mend a few sacks. "I'm happy to do it."

The morning air felt chill when, after breakfast, Grace and Lucy ventured into Roxwood where they would do their mending in a back room of the shop owned by Mr. Horn, the village cobbler. Each woman in the WFC had been assigned a bicycle; Grace and Lucy parked theirs in front of the building and went inside.

"Good m-morning, Mr. Horn," Lucy called to the cobbler as they entered.

An aged man in leather apron and black bargeman's cap waved his cobbler's hammer as they continued to the rear of the shop.

The back room was spacious and a bit austere, with a trio of gaslight fixtures mounted above the rustic pine wainscoting. Two wooden chairs and an enormous pile of white tarpaulins took up one half of the room. At the opposite wall stood a treadle sewing machine. A mound of burlap fabric cut into rectangular sheets lay on the floor beside it.

"You'll work there." Lucy pointed at the sewing machine.

Grace chewed on her lip while she studied the contraption. She'd seen one at Selfridges in London, but wasn't familiar with how it worked.

"I'll show you," Lucy said, reading her hesitation. "It's already been threaded, so you c-can start sewing." She moved to sit in the chair facing the machine and retrieved two precut squares of burlap from the floor. Once she'd matched them together, she slipped an edge of the fabric beneath the needle and flipped some kind of metal guide into place.

"Just like this," she said, and began working her feet back and forth against a metal square bracket beneath the machine. The needle came to life, penetrating the burlap. Lucy guided the fabric forward as tiny even stitches followed in its wake. "Now, you give it a try." She rose and made way for Grace to sit down.

Lucy Young had patience in abundance, guiding Grace through the steps until she'd completed her first sack.

"You've got it," Lucy said. Then she crossed the room to begin the task of mending tarpaulins. Companionable silence followed, interrupted only by the noisy treadle.

"Lucy, you mentioned you'd seen my father's tea room," Grace said finally, hoping for a bit of conversation while they worked. "Are you from London, then?"

When Lucy didn't respond, Grace glanced up and caught the woman's wary look. "I'm sorry," she said quickly. "Da's always telling me it's not ladylike to be nosy."

"He's probably right." Lucy softened the rebuke with a wan smile. "We all have our secrets."

Grace's face grew warm. "I'd just like us to be friends."

Lucy's caution eased. "Me too," she said. "I am from London, but I grew up a long way from Sterling Street. In Deptford, near the d-docks."

Grace stared at her while Lucy bent her head to make another perfect stitch in her canvas. Deptford was among the poorest slums in southeast London. "Did you . . . attend school?"

"For a time, but then my mum got sick. I had to g-go to work at the slaughterhouse." She grimaced. "I hated it, but I had six brothers and sisters all younger than me. We needed food."

"What about your father?"

A shadow crossed Lucy's expression. "When he wasn't working, he was at the pub. Those were the good days," she said. "Days he was g-gone."

Grace couldn't imagine feeling that way about her father. They did often frustrate each other, she with her modern ideas and "improprieties" that might jeopardize the tea room's reputation, and he with his conventional views on marriage and how young ladies should comport themselves. Yet Da would never sit in a pub, getting drunk while she starved.

She was grateful he had always taken such good care of her and Colin, even after their mother's death. "Is this your first time away from home?" she asked.

Lucy wet her lips. "No, I left home at seventeen. My youngest brother could f-fend for himself by then. I went to work in the city . . . here and there."

"Did you enter into service?" Grace hoped she wasn't stepping on another verbal land mine as she had with Mrs. Vance about her husband. But writers did have to ask difficult questions in order to gather research for their stories.

"Service . . . yes." Lucy's voice held an edge. "For a time anyway, before I had the chance to get out of the city. M-my health," she added. "I heard they were looking for women to help on farms in the Women's Forage Corps." Her turquoise eyes brightened. "I wasn't sure they would take me, but I'm glad to be here."

"I feel the same way." Relieved to change the topic, Grace noticed Lucy stammered only when she was anxious or upset.

The sewing machine treadle rocked beneath her feet as she stitched another seam and said, "My brother, Colin, joined the cavalry, and I wanted my chance to serve in some way. Since both our horses are now Army property overseas, I'm happy to work with the WFC to make food for them."

"I didn't have such grand ideas," Lucy said. "I just wanted to escape." A desolate look swept across her features and tore at Grace's heart. "I learned early on that women are p-powerless to the whims of the world, and to men. To f-fathers . . ." She bent her head and began to stitch furiously.

While Grace couldn't decipher Lucy's words, she felt their insidious meaning—horrible imaginings that didn't bear contemplation. She must help her new friend. "Lucy, have you ever heard of the suffrage movement?"

"Only on the streets . . . and the pictures of marching women I saw on the front page of the *Times*. I heard men say t-terrible things about them. Why?"

"Because being a suffragette is wonderful."

"You're a suffragette?" Lucy gaped at her. "Do you know Emmaline Pankhurst?"

"I am," Grace said, smiling. "And I do know her. I've attended rallies she and her daughter, Christabel, have held." She added earnestly, "Men don't like suffragettes because they want to keep us under their thumbs."

Grace recalled for an instant Da's desire to marry her off to Clarence Fowler. "They're afraid we'll change the world as they know it—and they're right." She rocked the treadle at her feet and sewed another straight seam, warming to her subject. "Many women work outside the home for a living, but only as domestics or factory workers. Yet we consume goods and make purchases and read newspapers. Why shouldn't we be allowed to vote? The laws of this land affect us as well as men. Once women get the vote, we'll be able to enter colleges, obtain any profession—doctor, lawyer, scientist, veterinarian—even Parliament! One day it will happen, and sooner than you think. We'll wear them down and then we *will* change the world—Ow!"

Grace glanced down and saw she'd nearly sewn her finger with the needle.

"You really believe it will happen?" Lucy asked, blinking. "We'll change the world?"

"And everything in it." Grace nursed her finger, then resumed her sewing.

"At the slaughterhouse I had to butcher animals every day, when all I wanted was to love them." Lucy made another stitch. "When I was a child, we had a cat come around our flat. She was gray and white and had a long ringed tail." Lucy tossed her a wistful smile. "She was also starving, so one day I hid her inside my coat and brought her into our kitchen. I fed her scraps my mum had tossed into the waste bin. Every day the cat came back and I fed her. I even named her Misty, because I'd first found her on a foggy November day."

Grace continued working the treadle. "What happened to her?"

"My father came home early one afternoon and caught me with Misty. I begged him to let me keep her." She raised listless eyes to Grace. "But he'd been drinking."

Lucy tugged hard at the heavy thread to tighten the slack in her stitch. "After he knocked me around a bit, he took the cat outside. I ran after him, but he tossed her into the street, right under the wheels of a passing greengrocer's delivery truck."

"That's terrible," Grace said, frowning. How could anyone have such a cruel father?

"I had other animals." Lucy kept to her sewing. "A dog, a pigeon, even had the old draft horse at the livery on the end of our street. They were pets my father never knew about." She made another stitch. "After Misty, I never brought one home." She glanced up. "When you spoke about women being vet . . . vet . . ."

"Veterinarians?"

Lucy nodded, and her gaze took on a faraway look. "I've always felt more comfortable with animals." She refocused on Grace. "I want to heal them, not hurt them."

"You can." Grace reached for more burlap from the stack. "Don't ever give up on your dream, Lucy. One day you *will* have the freedom to be whatever you want to be."

"I hope so, Grace."

"I know so." And for Lucy's sake, Grace fervently prayed she was right.

∽

Grace awakened the next morning without the aid of Agnes. Because sewing sacks was much easier than digging ditches, she'd had the energy to wash and press both uniforms *and* have a bath in the delightful cast-iron tub the night before. Afterward she'd taken up her place by the window, hoping for another glimpse of the tall stranger at the manor.

He had appeared, pacing along the balcony. Then just as before, the man retreated into the darkness of the house.

Was it Lord Roxwood—the Tin Man? Grace mused as she finished dressing and headed downstairs. And if so, might she request an interview with him for her upcoming story?

She arrived in the kitchen to find the others already seated around the table, tucking into breakfast. Agnes offered her an approving smile.

"Well, look who's arrived . . . and without a wrinkle."

Grace ignored Clare's remark. Taking her place at the table, she spooned a bowl of porridge from the pot and selected a slice of toast and a hard-boiled egg.

"Good morning," she called to Lucy, still buoyed by their inspiring talk yesterday.

Instead of greeting her, Lucy flashed a look of chagrin. Grace paused in slathering apple butter onto her toast to scan the other faces at the table. Each seemed preoccupied with breakfast—except for Mrs. Vance, who frowned at her.

"Is something wrong?"

"We'll discuss it later, Mabry."

Alarmed by the gravity of her supervisor's tone, Grace carefully set down her knife. Had there been another air raid on London? "Please, Mrs. Vance, I wish to know now." She tried to sound composed as all eyes focused on her.

Mrs. Vance said finally, "It's about the sacks."

Grace blinked. "The burlap sacks? But . . . I sewed four dozen of them yesterday."

"A dozen of which you stitched completely closed." Mrs. Vance expelled an irritated breath. "You obviously weren't paying attention, Grace. Now the stitches must be removed, and we simply don't have the time or the resources to fix such mistakes."

Grace heard a snigger of laughter from across the table. Heat bathed her sunburned cheeks. She'd been so consumed with talk about suffrage and turning the burlap under the needle, she hadn't realized she'd sewn a few too many seams. "Let me repair them, Mrs. Vance. I'll work late—"

"No, I'll assign the task to someone else." Mrs. Vance tossed her napkin on the table. "I'm putting you on report, Mabry. I don't like doing it, but every woman must pull her weight." Her tone gentled as she added, "You know, Grace, it might be you're better suited for another purpose. There's no shame in reconsidering your position with the Women's Forage Corps."

"No! Please, I can do this." Grace darted a glance at Agnes, silently willing her help. They had only just arrived, and already she was being asked to leave.

Agnes took her cue. "Mrs. Vance, it's my fault Miss . . . Grace is having a difficult time of it. I promised I'd help her when we got here, but I've done a poor job." She straightened to face Mrs. Vance. "Ma'am, if she leaves, then I feel I should go with her."

Seeing her maid's determined look, Grace felt a surge of affection.

The rest of the women at the table seemed to hold their breath. Mrs. Vance said, "Seems you've got a champion, Mabry. And Agnes does the work of two. One more chance is all you'll get. Make certain you do the job right the first time." Then her supervisor turned to the others. "We work together in this gang, so if Grace fails, we all fail. Understood?"

"Yes, ma'am," they chorused, quickly ducking their heads and resuming breakfast.

"Mr. Tillman tells me the pigs are ready for the butcher," Mrs. Vance said, looking back at Grace. "Since he's indisposed—" she paused, leaving Grace to recall how the farmer had sprained his ankle—"he wants us to take them in the cart to the town butcher."

"Oh, yes!" Grace was eager to redeem herself. "I'll gladly drive them."

Mrs. Vance nodded. "We'll also need to load the animals onto the cart," she said, casting another glance at the others. "I realize it's not what you signed up for, but the WFC will help with the task. Once those new Land Army girls arrive, we can't have them showing us up, now, can we?"

"No, ma'am," said Becky, and the others smiled.

Only Clare sat with arms crossed, wearing a sour expression. "We can thank Duchess here for the extra duty, since she leaves shovels lying about for farmers to trip over." She stared at Grace. "It must be difficult learning to take responsibility for yourself and your belongings for a change."

"Enough, Danner," Mrs. Vance said sharply. "And once you've helped to load the pigs, you can go into the village and begin repairing those sacks."

That drew a huff from Clare. "You're certain you can do

this, Mabry?" Mrs. Vance said, her brow furrowing at Grace. "It's your last chance."

Grace raised her chin. Driving horses was second nature to her. She couldn't possibly fail. "I won't disappoint you, Mrs. Vance."

∞

"Watch and learn, Duchess." Clare held up a long wooden stick for Grace's inspection. Then she wheeled away to join Becky inside the pen. Together the two girls used their sticks to tap at the sides of a large snorting pig, driving the animal up a gangway and into a cage already hoisted onto the back of the cart.

Relieved to simply watch the operation, Grace marveled at their ability. Agnes made her proud as well, working with Lucy to herd and capture five more of the ugly beasts.

Once a dozen pigs were penned, Mr. Tillman hobbled toward Grace on a makeshift crutch. He gave her instructions on how to reach the stockyard of the butcher, Mr. Owen. "He'll unload the pigs, so don't do anything. Just return my cart in one piece after he's finished, understood?"

Grace bristled. "I can do that, Mr. Tillman."

She heard him harrumph as she clambered up onto the cart's bench seat. Mrs. Vance approached as she took up the reins. "Are you comfortable doing this alone, Mabry? I'd send another with you, but the ditch needs to be finished and we've another fence—"

"I'm fine, really," Grace said, adding in a low voice, "and since Clare must take the time to fix my mistake with the sacks, it's the least I can do."

She urged the pair of horses forward, and soon the cart lumbered along the dirt track parallel with the estate. Behind her, the pigs grunted and squealed noisily in their cage. She gripped the reins and focused on the task before her. Occasionally she sucked in a breath as the animals shifted their heavy weight, causing the cart to list to one side.

Roxwood Manor came into view. Grace looked toward the balcony, hoping for another glimpse of the reclusive man who lived there. It stood empty. Her gaze wandered to the lush green lawns sloping gently upward toward the house, and the rose garden filled with clusters of white, red, and orange blooms. Such beauty . . .

As the team rounded the corner beyond a large hawthorn bush, she saw the gatehouse. At the same moment, the pigs jostled the cart and Grace lost her balance. Grabbing at the edge of the wooden bench seat to steady herself, she caught a splinter through her fabric gloves.

"Ow," she muttered and reproached herself for having left her heavier gloves in her haversack upstairs. Pulling to a halt at the gatehouse, she set the brake and climbed from the cart. She turned to the noisy pigs squirming in their cage. "I'll be just a minute."

Her search for the gloves proved fruitless. After she'd rummaged through her own bag, she wondered if Agnes kept an extra pair in hers. Passing by the window, Grace made a quick check on the pigs below—and thought she glimpsed a beige uniform, along with the glint of metal. Was it the brass FC badge they wore on their shoulder strap?

She leaned out to get a better look, but saw nothing except the cartload of noisy animals. Her pulse thrummed. Mrs. Vance would sack her on the spot to find her dawdling upstairs when she should be on her way to the butcher.

Grace hurried to Agnes's bed and grabbed up her maid's haversack. She began searching inside for a pair of heavy gloves when she spied a photograph.

The image took her by surprise. An older woman and adolescent-aged girl stood outdoors beside a barbed-wire fence—a farm, perhaps?—against a backdrop of snowy mountains and thick forests. It might have been winter but for the white flowers in the grass at their feet. Spring or summer then. Both females wore white shirtwaists and light-colored skirts and had the same dark hair and soulful eyes as her maid.

Agnes had never shown her a picture of her family, as these two undoubtedly were.

Feeling guilty for prying, and worried Mrs. Vance might find her here, Grace hastily returned the photograph to the bag and abandoned her search for gloves. Outside, she was relieved to see only the horses patiently grazing on a bit of grass. She walked toward the rear of the cart, wondering what had caught her eye earlier . . .

The sight of the empty cage made her gasp. Grace heard squealing and whipped around to see a dozen pigs tearing across Roxwood's lawn. Panicked, she ran around to the back of the cart and spied the opened latch. The gangway had been let down.

"*Noooo!*" she cried in disbelief—then saw the flower pendant lying in the grass beside it. Realization struck. "*Claaare!*"

Grace scooped up the necklace and glanced wildly about the gatehouse grounds. The woman was nowhere in sight.

By now several of the four-legged demons were headed toward Roxwood's gardens. With a yell, Grace took up the chase, alternately shouting at them to stop and muttering curses at Clare. She envisioned her demise in the WFC. After the others made her a laughingstock, she'd be forced to resign and return to London. Da would follow through on his threat and send for Aunt Florence until Clarence Fowler could return from America to wed her.

A sob tore from her throat as she observed two of the pigs foraging in Lord Roxwood's rhododendrons. Another stood just a few feet in front of her, uprooting one of his prized rosebushes.

"Stop!" she shrieked, and made to throw herself bodily onto the culprit. The pig was faster, causing Grace to slide front first into the mud of a wet garden.

The pig froze for a moment and watched her, the rosebush still clamped in its mouth. Then the animal dashed toward the entrance of an enormous hedge maze several yards away. Grace scrambled from the mud, determined to rescue the plant from the omnivorous thief.

By the time she realized the pig had eluded her, Grace had become completely turned around inside the six-foot-high hedge. Breathless, she stood in her filthy uniform as tears brimmed at her lashes. Now what? She turned around slowly, trying to decide which way to go. She hadn't even known of the labyrinth's existence; a row of tall poplars blocked its view from the road and her window at the gatehouse.

She decided to take a left turn, hoping it would bring her back to the entrance. After several minutes and growing more disorientated, her frustration gave way to stirrings of distress. What if she couldn't get out? She might die of hunger or thirst—

The gurgle of running water caught her attention. Grace walked toward the sound and soon arrived at the center of the maze.

A man in a beige linen suit and wide-brimmed straw hat sat on a stone bench in front of a small fountain. Leaning forward, he cupped his hands beneath the running spout of water.

"Oh, thank goodness!" she cried. "I was afraid no one would know I was here . . ."

He launched from his seat. "Who's there?"

Grace backed away—and bit her lip to keep from crying out. He grabbed for the mask still lying on the bench. "Tell me now!" he demanded, knocking away the straw hat in his haste to retie the covering across his face.

The Tin Man. She caught only a glimpse before he donned

the mask, but long enough to observe his scars: a cruel gash along one cheek, and the angry, serrated flesh surrounding his eyes. Eyes that obviously could not see. Deep blue eyes . . .

Recognition made gooseflesh rise along her arms. She took in his substantial height and the broadness of his shoulders, the blond hair curling about his collar. He'd once sported a faux queue tied at his nape. And in those seconds before he hid from her, she'd recognized his handsome features—the strong nose and squared jaw, his sculpted mouth.

"Jack Benningham?" she whispered.

4

"You know me?"

Instantly he was looming over her. He reached out and grabbed hold of her arms while he barked his question through a veil of steel mesh.

Grace tried looking up at him, then glanced away. He was gruesome. The mask covered the upper part of his face much like a domino mask, except the eyeholes had been filled in with narrow metal strips, making it impossible to see him. Even more ghastly, an attached curtain of steel hid his mouth and the rest of his face from view. Why did he wear such an outlandish disguise? She couldn't help thinking of some eerie, otherworldly being she'd seen in picture books.

"I s-saw you," she said, frightened by his grip. "I recognized you before . . . before . . ." *Before you put on that hideous mask,* she didn't finish.

"Who are you?" His fingers dug into her flesh. "And why did you invade my privacy?"

"A mistake, honestly!" She tried pulling away, but his grip held firm. Her memory of their last encounter returned, and Grace could hardly believe he was the same Casanova who had enticed her with his devilish smile and penetrating gaze. She recalled how that smile had faded to a look of rage after she handed him the white feather of cowardice, and how he'd left the party without a backward glance.

She didn't dare reveal her identity to him now. He seemed angry enough to kill. "I . . . it's the pigs," she said, thinking to appease him with an explanation. "I work for the Women's Forage Corps and was taking them to the butcher, but they got loose. One of them ate your roses and then ran into the hedge."

He must have decided she wasn't a threat because he released her and stepped back. "Wherever the pig's gone, likely it's found a way out by now." His acerbic tone resonated from beneath the mesh. "Yet another instance in which I find animals more intelligent than humans."

Grace felt too relieved at having escaped his clutches to respond to his obvious insult.

"This way, girl." He moved past her, and she followed, her mind still reeling. Jack Benningham was Lord Roxwood, the Tin Man . . .

Not a monster. At least not outwardly, despite his scars. She stared at the powerfully built figure leading her back to what she hoped was the entrance into the labyrinth. Now that she'd seen the mask with its steel veil, she understood why the locals called him the Tin Man. But the rest—the hunchback, pointed ears, and sharp teeth—was the invention of rural imagination.

His moral character was still in question, however. Grace felt certain Jack Benningham's soul must be horribly pocked and scarred with the sins of his past exploits. Yet he wasn't womanizing or gambling now. The sight of him shocked her anew as she recalled the newspaper report of his receiving only minor injuries from the fire. Being blinded was hardly that . . .

"I trust you can find your way back from here?"

Abruptly he'd halted and turned. Grace, nearly colliding with him, quickly stepped back. They had reached the entrance to the hedge maze. Fleetingly it occurred to her that he'd managed to navigate it without being able to see.

"Yes, thank you . . . Lord Roxwood." He was surly and rude, and she was eager to leave his presence. "I'm terribly sorry about the damage to your roses."

She started to walk past him when he reached for her again. She gasped when he latched onto her wrist. "I believe you've forgotten a small detail." His tone held an edge. "You said you recognized me and that you work for the Women's Forage Corps, yet you haven't told me *who* you are. Clearly not some farm girl." His grip intensified. "Too much good breeding in that speech, Miss . . . ?"

He leaned close, the horrid mask inches from her face. Grace thought her heart might stop. She considered lying to him, but to do so would make her as much a coward as he'd been. She wasn't sorry for handing him a white feather at the ball, for unlike Jack Benningham, she was a true patriot of her country. Straightening her spine, she said, "My name is Grace Mabry."

He reared back as if she'd struck him. Releasing her wrist, his breath came rapidly behind the mesh. As Grace watched the agitated rise and fall of his chest, real fear began to take hold. Did he mean to do her harm?

Then just as quickly he recomposed himself. He leaned forward again, menace coloring his tone. "Well, Miss *Mabry*"—he spat her name as though ejecting day-old tea—"I think you've inflicted more than enough damage for one day. Now, get out!"

Grace choked on a cry as she whirled from him and ran all the way back to the gatehouse. Perhaps she'd been wrong and he did have sharp teeth and howl at the moon.

In her distress she didn't register right away that the cart was gone and the pigs vanished. She was too thankful having escaped the man in the abominable mask. She had expected his annoyance, even his anger as he must certainly remember their encounter from the night of the ball. But his loathing, the rage she'd heard in his voice, jarred her.

Shaken, she went inside to change her uniform and wash her face. Afterward she grabbed a bicycle and rode to the barn.

The cart stood out front, the cage empty. Clare must be having a good laugh at her expense, Grace thought bitterly, pulling the daisy pendant she'd found from her uniform pocket. Well, the joke would be on her once Grace offered up proof the woman was responsible.

The barn doors opened and Mrs. Vance stepped outside, hands on hips. Before Grace could utter a word, her supervisor snapped, "Inside."

Grace's heart beat faster. Would she even get a fair hearing?

Inside the building's cool interior, Mr. Tillman stood with the others in a half circle as though waiting for her. The farmer wore a fierce expression and tossed away his crutch as he limped toward her. "You've done it now," he ground out. "The others rounded up the pigs and returned them to the pen, but you . . . you destroyed his lordship's grounds!" He waved his hands to illustrate the chaos she'd wrought.

"Mabry, Lord Roxwood is furious," Mrs. Vance said. "He's already sent word through his steward demanding your immediate removal." The older woman paused, then added, "It pains me to tell you this, but you're dismissed from the WFC, as well."

"The last straw," growled Mr. Tillman. His suffused features loomed over her. "Exactly why women don't belong working on a farm. How could you lose an entire truckload of pigs?"

Grace trembled with anger. Lord Roxwood wanted her gone? Fine, but she wasn't going alone. She glanced at Clare Danner. The woman stood with arms crossed, wearing a smug look. Obviously she had no idea she'd left the pendant behind.

Grace dropped the necklace to dangle by its chain at her side, making sure her nemesis saw it. "It wasn't me . . ."

She fully intended to exonerate herself and name the true culprit. After all, if Danner hadn't been so mean-spirited in the first place, none of this would have happened. No runaway pigs, no encountering Jack Benningham, no getting sacked.

But then she saw Clare's tight-lipped smirk fade, the mocking gray eyes widen, before her features settled into a look of abject terror.

Grace blinked, certain she'd misread the woman's reaction. Then Clare moistened her lips and clasped her hands together tightly as though in prayer, and Grace marveled at the woman's changed demeanor. *"We all have secrets."* She remembered Lucy's words from yesterday.

Did Clare have secrets, too?

Averting her eyes, Grace felt her desire for retribution ebbing. What good would come from demanding Clare's dismissal from the WFC? The woman might be a thorn in her side, but Clare Danner had skills and performed her duties well—unlike Grace, who had proved quite inept. And in truth, Grace likely would have encountered Jack Benningham at some point during her stay at Roxwood, and his attitude toward her would remain unchanged.

She considered Mr. Tillman's sprained ankle—her fault. And the bungled sacks someone else had to fix—again her fault. Perhaps Mrs. Vance was right and she was better suited for another purpose.

"It wasn't my fault. There were unavoidable ruts in the road," she lied, fixing her attention back on the pale-faced Clare. "The lever on the cage must have jarred loose. When I stopped at the gatehouse to fetch my heavier gloves, I didn't notice it, even when I let the ramp down to check on the pigs before I went inside. I returned and found them escaped, running across Roxwood's grounds. I tried chasing them . . ." Her voice trailed off, knowing the concocted story made her sound like a complete muddlehead.

"Pack your things, Mabry. Even if I could change the rules, it's out of my hands. His lordship has ordered you gone in the morning." Mrs. Vance's look softened. "The nearest train is at Margate. I'll take you there myself in the cart tomorrow. I'm sorry, Grace."

Grace glanced at the faces around her, swallowing an urge to cry. Mr. Tillman retrieved his crutch and leaned against it, looking satisfied. Becky and Lucy, along with Mrs. Vance, eyed her with pity. Agnes shook her head and with lips pursed twisted her hands together.

Clare stood near the big double doors, clearly stunned. She spun on her heel and stalked out of the barn.

~~~

"It's done, Edwards?"

"Yes, milord." Jack's steward and land agent cleared his throat and added, "I've informed Mr. Tillman to make certain Miss Mabry leaves in the morning. I believe she'll be taking the ten o'clock out of Margate."

"Good riddance," Jack growled. "Thank you, Edwards. That will be all."

"Shall I call for your valet now, milord?"

"No. Townsend can attend me in an hour. I know it's late, but I don't wish to be disturbed."

"Of course. Good night, milord."

Hearing the door to the bedroom close behind his steward, Jack Benningham—third Viscount of Walenford, heir to the fifth Earl of Stonebrooke, and for his present convenience, second Baron of Roxwood—walked unerringly past the opened French doors leading out onto his balcony.

The marble felt smooth and unyielding beneath his fingertips as he stood at the rail. He knew beyond the sprawling lawns and breathtaking rose garden, or what remained of it, stood the enormous hedge maze planted by his great-grandfather decades before.

This afternoon had been his first venture outside since the accident. Jack congratulated himself that despite his blindness, he could still navigate the labyrinth's twists and turns in order to reach the fountain at its center. Roxwood had been in his family for generations, and he found the simple two-story Georgian-style home a sanctuary against the suffocating attentions of his family, the animosity and revulsion of his fiancée, and the prying, pitying eyes of London society. It was the perfect place to hide . . . until today.

He loosened the ties of his mask, allowing the cool night air to soothe the constant burn of his scarred flesh—and his anger. Patrick Mabry's daughter was here, invading his privacy. Why?

She claimed to be employed by the Women's Forage Corps, yet she'd destroyed his rose garden and tainted his sanctuary. Had she purposely orchestrated the little disaster in order to seek him out, to spy on him for her father?

For the thousandth time, Jack's memory conjured the night long ago when he'd nearly lost his life. At Lady Bassett's costume ball, he had bungled his assignment to shadow the disguised enemy agent when he was pleasantly diverted by a lovely goddess in green, allowing his target to escape.

Jack left the ball then, intent to salvage his assignment with MI5 and follow Chaplin. As he reached the London docks, he'd watched his suspect board the Irish merchant ship *Acionna* as she made ready to weigh anchor. He followed, and while the ship cruised toward the mouth of the Thames, he searched belowdecks for his quarry.

The spy had managed to elude him, but Jack found his lair

with Chaplin's signature bowler hat tossed upon the bed. A thorough search produced a map of the Naval Yards, along with a letter addressed to James Heeren, *Acionna*'s cargo supervisor, and written on Swan's Tea Room stationery. At first, the correspondence seemed innocent—shipping instructions written and signed by Patrick Mabry, the tea room's owner. But then Jack held it up to the heat of the lantern and saw code written with invisible ink and penned in between the lines of the letter.

He'd pocketed the evidence and returned above deck in time to see Chaplin dive overboard. The ship was nearing the mouth of the river, but because Jack had to preserve his newfound proof, he could only watch in frustration while the spy swam for shore. And in the next moment, his world went black.

Jack reached with a finger to trace the still-tender flesh around his eyes, then drew a line along the ragged scar at his cheek. The explosion had knocked him senseless; he awakened in hospital days later to learn he was one of only four survivors. The cargo ship had secretly carried munitions and was torpedoed by a German U-boat.

With his precious evidence destroyed in the blast, Jack was left scarred, blinded, and bitter in the knowledge he'd been lured onto the *Acionna*. Never would he forget Chaplin's backward glance as he boarded her, or his subsequent escape seconds before the explosion.

Patrick Mabry had written the code. Perhaps he and Chaplin were one and the same man. Now his daughter was here . . .

"Milord?"

A faint knock sounded at his bedroom door. "A moment, Townsend," Jack called as he quickly replaced the mask. His household staff was under strict orders never to intrude without first gaining permission. Leaving the balcony, he returned to his rooms.

Whatever her reasons for being at Roxwood, tomorrow couldn't arrive soon enough.

He wanted Grace Mabry gone.

———

"Marcus, we need to talk."

"Jack?" Through the crackling line, Marcus Weatherford's sleepy exhaustion seemed to vanish. "I thought you'd forgotten how to use a telephone! It's been months, man. Good grief, do you have any idea what time it is?"

"Near dawn, I imagine." Jack hadn't slept. Too many questions about Patrick Mabry's daughter and her presence at Roxwood needed answers.

"It's three thirty in the morning." Marcus's tone turned tense. "Jack, what's wrong?"

"Does something *need* to be wrong when I call, Marcus? Other than the obvious?" Jack said irritably.

"At this hour, yes." Marcus sounded exasperated. "Benningham, you've disappeared off the map. No one's heard from you since you left hospital. Even your father calls me. And when I telephone to try to find out how you're doing, I have to speak to that old watchdog, Edwards." He paused. "Is he dead? Is that why you're ringing me at this unholy hour?"

"Edwards is fine. I've called for another reason." Jack relayed to his best friend the encounter with Grace Mabry.

"Mabry's daughter working for the Women's Forage Corps could be legitimate, but you don't think so, do you?" Marcus said.

"And neither do you. As I recall, MI5 doesn't believe in co-incidences." Hesitating, Jack said, "Marcus, I think Patrick Mabry sent her here to spy on me."

Expecting to hear his friend scoff through the receiver, Jack was surprised when Marcus said, "Not good news, old boy."

Jack straightened. "Why?"

"Can't discuss it over the telephone," Marcus said. "Look, I'll verify her application through the Army Service Corps, since they govern the WFC. I'll also do some other checking. It may turn out we're both wrong and her reason for being there has nothing to do with any collusion with her father." He paused. "You've been unreachable for so long, I haven't been able to tell you we finally arrested James Heeren last week. Caught him passing coded information to a known German agent."

"The cargo supervisor for the *Acionna*?" Jack gripped the receiver. "What did he say?"

"Heeren's involved in the same spy ring we've been after for months."

"I knew it! Now, please tell me the code was sent along in one of Mabry's letters?"

"I'm afraid not," Marcus said. "But MI5 still has a man doing surveillance at Swan's and keeping an eye on Patrick Mabry's movements. Unfortunately the trail went cold recently, but Heeren's arrest is a boon. Thanks to you, we know the two men were connected."

Jack's hopes plummeted. "And the proof lies at the bottom of the Thames."

"It might be Mabry doesn't know that." Excitement tinged Marcus's tone. "Look, it's just a theory, but possibly he sent his daughter to snoop around. Can you make certain she stays put? I'll check her story, but it might take time, and those hay-baling crews move around a lot."

Jack bit back an oath. He hadn't thought it through when he demanded her removal. "Get back to me as soon as you can, Marcus. I'll handle things on this end."

"Fair enough. And since we're finally having a conversation, if there's anything I can do . . ."

"Just ring me back with something useful," Jack said before

severing the connection. The last thing he wanted to hear from his friend was anything that sounded remotely like pity.

From the study he carefully retraced his steps upstairs. Like the hedge maze, Jack had spent enough summers at Roxwood to memorize every door and hallway, along with the placement of each chair, potted plant, or other pieces of furniture in the house.

Inside his room, he removed the mask and sat down on the edge of his bed. He needed to figure out a way to delay her departure, at least until Marcus got back to him. Perhaps in the morning Edwards could obtain something useful from the WFC person in charge at the farm.

Jack fisted the steel mesh of his mask. James Heeren's arrest merely confirmed to him Mabry's involvement in the explosion. The idea of his offspring remaining on the property, within proximity of his sanctuary, enraged him. Wasn't it enough he'd been thrown from a burning ship into complete darkness, pocked by scars no woman would ever look at without collapsing into a dead faint?

Except for Mabry's daughter, he thought savagely. She was more callous than he'd given her credit for, especially if she were here to do that traitor Patrick Mabry's bidding.

∾

"Enter," he called to his steward, Mr. Edwards.

Jack stood in his room four hours later, dressed and freshly shaved, the latter only on condition he raise the steel mesh himself just far enough that his valet could get the job done.

At the moment, Townsend was performing the last ritual of grooming, brushing imaginary lint from the back of his jacket.

"Milord, I was able to obtain her file from Mrs. Vance, the supervisor," Edwards said. "Would you like to review it now?"

"Thank you, Townsend. That will be all."

Once the valet departed, Edwards began, "Miss Mabry hired on with the Women's Forage Corps just weeks ago. She recently attended training at Norfolk before being assigned to Roxwood."

"Anything else?" He'd hoped for some kind of substantial proof she wasn't here by accident.

"Very little, milord, though it says she's qualified in driving a horse-transport team, record keeping, and operating a motorized vehicle."

"Perfect," Jack said as an idea began to form. "Arrange a meeting between Miss Mabry and myself immediately."

"Excuse me, milord . . ." The normally unflappable steward hesitated. "I thought you ordered her off the premises."

"Change in plan," Jack said. "With Barnes gone to the Front, I need a driver for the Daimler. Dr. Black suggested I take the country air. Miss Mabry should suit for the task. Tell her I'll pay the going rate."

"Milord, are you planning to offer her a full-time post?"

Hardly, Jack thought. "Mornings only." Since her stay would only be temporary, he could manage two or three hours in her presence each day.

"If it's only part-time work, your lordship, she may not be interested."

Jack hadn't considered that. "Inform the supervisor to keep her on at Roxwood. Miss Mabry must be available to me every day until noon. She can work for the WFC afterward."

"Pardon, milord, but she's been dismissed from service. After the, uh, incident with the pigs. The WFC makes the rules for their workers."

"Then tell them to unmake them," Jack said with impatience. "I undercut the price of my hay and fodder to the British Army more than any other landowner in the district. I hardly think they'll deny me such a small favor. Now see to it, man."

"Yes, milord, immediately."

Once his steward had left, Jack headed downstairs to breakfast. With the skeletal staff he employed at Roxwood, his cook, Mrs. Riley, brought in the meal herself and then left him to eat in privacy.

After removing his mask, he poked at his plate with a fork, satisfied to find the fried kidneys at seven o'clock, two soft-boiled eggs at six o'clock, and a slice of toast and blood pudding at twelve and one. He began tucking into his food. It was the breakfast he had every day and always in the same arrangement. It not only simplified the menu for Mrs. Riley, who had served since his grandfather's day, but it assured Jack there would be no surprises. He found a measure of control in knowing what to expect and when to expect it, a sense of order that the blindness had robbed from him.

Yet he set his fork aside as doubts over his new plan dampened his appetite. He'd been somewhat of a tyrant with Miss Mabry in the hedge maze; she might not wish to meet with him. Jack hoped if she *was* here to spy on him, she would seize any opportunity to renew their acquaintance. If she wasn't, their interview would likely end up being uncivil and one-sided—much like the memory of his conversations with Violet Arnold.

No, Miss Mabry would agree to stay, he felt certain of it. And then . . .

Retribution ignited in him like a flame, illuminating his dark world. While he no longer held the proof she might be seeking, he planned to turn the tables on her, nonetheless. He would use *his* skills to interrogate her during their time together and extract information, enough hopefully to charge and convict the traitor who fathered her and beat him at his own game.

Jack retrieved his fork, seized with new appetite. Surely, God would grant him the justice he deserved.

Frowning, Agnes stood at the door to their bedroom and eyed her mistress. Dressed in her blue traveling suit, Grace Mabry adjusted the straps on her portmanteau and haversack, both packed and lying on the bed.

The look of defeat on her pretty face nearly broke Agnes's heart. She understood the feeling all too well. "You're really leaving then, miss?"

Grace offered a wan smile. "It appears so. I seem to have a habit of bringing about disaster wherever I go, don't I?"

Agnes shook her head vehemently. "Mrs. Vance really should have given you more time. You aren't used to this kind of work like the rest of us." She went to her own bed and pulled out her bags, her heart feeling like lead. She didn't want to go back to London, to the painful memories she'd left there. Still . . . "I'm going with you," she said.

"Dear Agnes, I appreciate your support, but please don't leave on my account. You seem much happier here at Roxwood."

Oh, how true! Agnes felt free here in the country. The air smelled cleaner, the countryside prettier than the dank dirtiness of London's streets. Life here seemed so uncomplicated.

"Where you go, miss, I go," Agnes said, and meant it. Grace Mabry had more than proved her friendship. Not only had she willingly hired Agnes off the streets without so much as a reference, but she'd offered her kindness and respect. Agnes hadn't received those gifts from anyone, including her despicable husband, Edgar, in a long, long while. Not since leaving her mother and sister behind . . .

A wave of emotion seized her, causing unexpected tears. "I won't let you return alone," she said, sniffing, as she stuffed her cotton nightdress into her bag. "I owe you so much."

"Agnes, please don't do this!"

Seeing her mistress's look of distress, Agnes pasted on a smile. "I'll be fine, really," she said, cinching the straps on her luggage. Perhaps Patrick Mabry would decide to send them to stay with Grace's aunt in Oxford. Then they could escape London altogether. The notion lifted her spirits.

"Are you sure you want to leave?" Grace said. "I want you to be happy, Agnes. And Mrs. Vance could use your help here with the others." She sat on the bed and looked down at her lap. "Even if I could stay, Lord Roxwood wishes me gone."

Agnes paused, still curious over exactly what had happened with the pigs getting loose yesterday. Her mistress had told them the ridiculous story of how she'd all but let the animals out herself and then chased them down, but Agnes felt certain something odd was going on.

Like the flower pendant Grace had placed on Clare Danner's pillow last night. And then Agnes and her mistress had taken their meal upstairs instead of sitting with the others. When the rest of the women finally came upstairs and readied for bed, Clare had turned white as chalk dust seeing the necklace. Neither of the two women had explained. Agnes could only wonder at it.

"Well, Mrs. Vance is waiting for us downstairs." Grace rose from the bed and picked up her bags. When her maid did the same, tears burned the backs of her eyes. "Thank you for your faith in me, Agnes. I couldn't possibly imagine a more loyal friend."

She saw emotion return to her maid's expression and tried not to feel guilty about her relief that Agnes would accompany her home. Grace imagined her father's reaction. She felt certain he would send for her aunt and then wire his protégé in New York, forcing her hand in marriage. It seemed she was a complete failure at anything else.

Downstairs, the others sat around the kitchen table, looking as uncomfortable as they had the previous night. Grace was glad at least her last meal at Roxwood had been a peaceful one, with just Agnes for company. Since yesterday's fiasco with Lord Roxwood, tension seemed to be running high in the WFC.

Mrs. Vance rose from the table and came to her. "This is a sorry business, Mabry, but the WFC has strict rules. I hope you understand?"

She offered a hand, and Grace took it. "It's all right, Mrs. Vance. You're just doing your job."

The supervisor looked relieved, then looked to Agnes. "We're sorry to see you go, Pierpont, though your allegiance to Miss Mabry is commendable."

"Miss . . . Grace, has done much for me. I would not leave her." Agnes tilted her chin bravely, and Grace felt a surge of warmth for her friend. Her words also seemed a catalyst, as soon the others rose and came to murmur their best wishes.

Clare was notably absent. Grace recalled the woman's subdued mood last night when she'd found the pendant necklace returned atop her pillow. Well, perhaps she would think twice before picking on any more recruits.

"I'll remember what you told me, Grace." Lucy reached to offer her a hug. "One day I can d-do anything."

Grace smiled, despite the heat against her cheeks. Her own ineptness made a mockery of the words. Even so, she offered, "That's right, Lucy. Never forget it."

"Neither should you, Grace." Lucy shot her a knowing smile. "You just needed a little more t-time, that's all."

Grace nodded. She would miss her new friend. Waving a last farewell, she followed Agnes and Mrs. Vance outside to the cart that would take them to Margate's station.

She gazed at Roxwood Manor for what would be her last time. Jack Benningham's image rose in her mind, and she bit her lip, recalling his hatred. She refused to regret her actions toward him in London, and his behavior yesterday had been reprehensible. Still . . .

Despite what he once was—a playboy, a gambler, and a reckless ne'er-do-well—the scars had undoubtedly penetrated his heart. He was a man no longer himself, but the brunt of local gossip, the wildly concocted Tin Man. Hiding away in his self-imposed prison, shunning the world and all it had to offer.

Even without her good Christian upbringing, Grace might pity him. She sighed. So much for her story about the mysterious "milord." The only one she'd be writing now was about a ninny of a young woman who thought she could work on a farm—

"Mrs. Vance! Miss Mabry!"

Mr. Tillman hurried up the track on his crutch. "Wait!" he cried, wheezing for the effort it took to reach them. "Miss Mabry, the land agent, Mr. Edwards, wants a word." He leaned against the crutch, trying to catch his breath.

Grace's insides knotted. Was she to pay for Lord Roxwood's damaged rosebushes, then? "Did he say why?"

The farmer shook his head. "You're to get up to the house straightaway." His look of vindication breathed life into Grace's fear. She glanced at Agnes, then Mrs. Vance.

"Grace, you'd better go and see what he wants," Mrs. Vance said. "We'll leave when you return."

Taking a bicycle, she pedaled up the long gravel drive to Roxwood Manor. Lifting the door's crested brass knocker, she banged it several times before an aged, sour-faced man in butler's attire finally answered.

His rheumy gaze traveled first to the bicycle, then settled on her. A slight frown formed beneath his beak of a nose. "Milord isn't receiving guests."

Unaccustomed to such haughtiness from a servant, Grace tipped her chin and said, "I am not here to see *milord*. I've been requested to visit with Mr. Edwards."

"It's all right, Knowles," a man's voice called from the interior of the house. "Please allow Miss Mabry inside. Lord Roxwood is waiting."

Lord Roxwood? Grace barely acknowledged the butler as he sketched a bow and stepped back to let her enter. A small middle-aged man in a charcoal suit stood at the foot of the stairs. "Miss Mabry, welcome. I am Edwards, Lord Roxwood's secretary."

Secretary? "You have many titles, Mr. Edwards. I was told you were the land agent, as well?"

"And Lord Roxwood's steward." He smiled. "We accommodate a small staff here at the manor, so his lordship can enjoy the level of privacy he requires." He indicated a part of the house beyond the stairs. "This way, please."

"Wait." Grace hesitated. "Lord Roxwood wishes to speak with me?"

"All in good time, Miss Mabry."

Edwards turned and took the lead. Anxious, Grace followed him down a lushly carpeted hall. Above the dark mahogany wainscoting, red-and-gold fleur-de-lis wallpaper rose along either side. She noticed a trio of paintings—sailboats—each slightly different but obviously intended as a series and cast in ornate gold frames.

"This way." The steward halted beside an open door.

Cautiously Grace entered the room. Clearly it was a man's study. More mahogany paneling lined the walls, and on either side of a stone fireplace stood floor-to-ceiling bookshelves filled with volumes. At the far end sat an expansive cherrywood desk and a pair of leather chairs facing it. Gold drapes covered the single large window along one wall, and the room was dim but for two sconces mounted near the door.

Mr. Edwards moved around the desk and waved Grace toward one of the leather chairs.

"What's this about?" she asked.

The study door creaked behind her.

"Miss Mabry?"

Grace turned and stiffened at the sight of Jack Benningham's towering frame.

"Lord Roxwood," she said, rising. "You wish to speak with me?"

He stepped closer and reached for the back of the chair adjacent to hers. "I understand you're leaving us."

Anger flared in her. He was the one who had all but tossed her out. "Thanks to you, sir. Why have you sent for me?"

"I wish to hire you. I understand you have experience in operating an automobile?"

She blinked. He wanted to hire *her*, the woman who had publicly shamed him at Lady Bassett's ball? "Yes, I can drive," she said slowly.

"Good, it's settled then. Edwards will fill you in on the details. Call for me at nine o'clock tomorrow morning." Releasing his hold on the chair, he turned to exit the chamber.

"Excuse me," she called to him. "You ordered me off the premises yesterday, and now you expect me to work for you as your chauffeur. Shouldn't you at least *ask* me if I want the position?"

Jack Benningham turned around to face her. Grace averted her gaze from the horrid mask. "Well?" His tone held an edge of hostility. "Do you?"

She made herself look at him. He was up to something. His reaction to her name yesterday made it clear he recognized her from the dowager's costume ball. Perhaps it was some kind of trick to exact revenge for shaming him publicly, or he simply wished to humiliate her, making her become for all intents and purposes his slave. "What are your terms?" she asked.

His posture eased. "Mornings you'll spend driving for me. Afternoons, you'll return to your duties with the other workers."

"I no longer work for the WFC."

"Yes, I was told you got the sack." His voice held no mockery. "The problem has been taken care of."

She glanced toward Mr. Edwards, who nodded. Hope rose in her. If she stayed on, she could continue helping in the war effort. She could also remain on her own. Yet if she accepted the terms, she would have to look at the hideous mask every day and tolerate Lord Roxwood's bullying manner.

"Well, Miss Mabry? A simple yes or no will suffice."

She took a deep breath. "I accept." Freedom and helping her brother outweighed this man's arrogance and bad manners.

"Until tomorrow morning, then."

She watched as he swiftly departed the study.

5

She found Mrs. Vance seated at the kitchen table when she returned to the gatehouse.

"Well?"

"I've been hired by Lord Roxwood." Still dazed from her interview, Grace couldn't keep from smiling. Edwards had taken her outside afterward to see the beautiful, shiny blue Daimler parked in the attached garage. "As his chauffeur," she added. "I'm to drive him wherever he wishes during the morning hours each day."

"He's given you a post?" Mrs. Vance looked stunned. "But . . . where will you stay?" Her brow furrowed. "Surely your family won't approve. You should ask your father."

Grace's smile slipped. "I'm to remain in the Women's Forage Corps, where I'll work in the afternoons. At least that's what Mr. Edwards said."

"Hah!" Mrs. Vance puffed up like a tea cozy. "And I suppose he thinks he's in charge of the WFC now?" Her eyes narrowed. "I'd like to know why his lordship would hire you as his driver. Surely he must have a capable servant to perform the task."

Worry clouded her features. "Grace, did something else happen yesterday at the manor you haven't told me about?"

Disturbed at having to tell a lie, or worse, to explain the full truth of her encounter, Grace said merely, "I assure you nothing inappropriate happened."

"Oh, of course not." Mrs. Vance turned the color of rose hips. "I just find this all so odd . . . and very high-handed of his lordship. Please don't take this unkindly, Grace, but you were dismissed from the WFC, and he has no right—"

"Perhaps you'd better see this." Grace withdrew an envelope from her jacket, which contained her employment agreement with Lord Roxwood, along with a letter for Mrs. Vance, and handed it to her.

"It seems I've been outmaneuvered," Mrs. Vance said after reading the contents. "Lord Roxwood has contacted my supervisor in London. Mrs. Stewart agreed to his terms and sanctions his decision." She waved the letter at Grace. "I suppose this means you're staying."

At that moment, Agnes appeared on the steps leading down from their room. "I overheard. We're to remain in the WFC?" Excitement lit her brown eyes.

"If you're willing," Grace said.

"Oh, yes, Miss . . . Grace," she said with a smile.

"I know you didn't expect this turn of events, Mrs. Vance, but surely you're happy Agnes will remain," Grace said. "And I promise to do my best working in the afternoons." She offered her most beseeching smile. "Please, ma'am, I'd like your blessing."

"I won't argue about keeping Pierpont. She's an excellent worker." Mrs. Vance eyed them both. "All right, Mabry, you've got my blessing, so long as you make the effort."

"Thank you!" Impulsively, Grace hugged the older woman. She would try, and with hard work and sufficient time to learn she vowed to succeed—for Colin, and for her own self-respect.

"That's enough now." Mrs. Vance pulled away, again all business. "With your new schedule we'll be a bit shorthanded when haymaking starts. You'll take over Clare's position as timekeeper, recording the harvest. You can work on reports during the morning hours before you leave for the manor." She paused to glance at both of them. "Now both of you, into your uniforms and meet me at the barn. Grace, you and Clare are going to take those pigs to the butcher—and this time no mishaps."

"So, how was your interview?" Agnes asked as they changed clothes upstairs. She was thrilled at the turn of events. They would stay in the country!

Her mistress buttoned up her uniform and said, "Well, of course, you should be the first to know. Lord Roxwood is rude, overbearing, wears the horrible steel mask everyone talks about . . . and we know him, Agnes." She looked up. "Or at least I do. We met at Lady Bassett's ball."

Agnes paused in tying the laces on her boots. "Who is he?"

"Jack Benningham. I gave him a white feather that night."

"He recognized you?" Her hopes fell. Perhaps they wouldn't be staying, after all.

Grace shook her head. "His townhouse caught fire shortly after the ball. The *Times* made light of it, but he received burns to the face. And he's blind now." Her brow creased. "Still, he seems to know who I am."

"I . . . I don't understand," Agnes said. "If he ordered you to leave yesterday, why does he now want you to stay and work for him?"

"I have no idea, except that he decided to retaliate."

Nightmares popped into Agnes's mind as she recalled the night of the ball. "Surely he wouldn't turn us over to the police?" she whispered.

"Of course not," her mistress said. "I'm certain he wishes

only to humiliate me by hiring me to be on his staff. His arrogance in the past proves it."

"You'll tell me, though . . . if it's not, won't you?" Agnes asked. She imagined the only place worse than being in London would be rotting in jail.

"I will, but it's nothing to worry about, really," Grace said, smiling. "And if it means we get to stay, I'll let Lord Roxwood have his fun."

∞

Grace felt relieved when she and Agnes arrived to find the pigs already caged and on the back of the cart. She tried to ignore the little stab of hurt she felt after her conversation with Agnes. Her maid kept the photograph of her family a secret, yet she wanted Grace to share her every thought. Still, it was no reason to be petty. She would just have to earn her maid's trust.

Mrs. Vance hailed Agnes to follow her into the barn, while Grace was left to approach Clare. Expecting the usual caustic remarks, she was surprised when the woman remained quiet as she checked the latch on the cage.

Nor did Clare make eye contact as they both climbed up onto the seat and Grace took the reins, urging the team forward in the direction of the village. Silence continued to pass between them, and Grace grew more uncomfortable. Ignoring the noisy pigs in back, she occasionally glanced over at her passenger.

Clare sat rigid, looking straight ahead. Grace couldn't tell if she was angry or bored. Finally, unable to stand it any longer, she opened her mouth to speak.

Clare had the same idea. "Why did you take the blame for me yesterday, Mabry?"

Surprised at the direct question, Grace realized she'd been called by name and not the hated term *Duchess*. "It seemed the right thing to do," she answered, then shrugged. "I may not have let the pigs loose, but I'll be the first to admit I'm less than fit for this kind of work. And in the barn, when I looked at you, I . . ."

She turned back to the task of driving the horses.

"You what?" Clare demanded.

"I realized we all probably have secrets we don't want others to know." She turned to meet Clare's gaze full on. "And by the looks of it, Danner, your secret seemed dire. Am I right?"

Clare didn't answer. Grace gripped at the reins and concentrated on the road as the cart went over a shallow rut. Then she felt a hand press against her sleeve. "Thanks, Mabry. I owe you."

At Clare's sincere tone, Grace almost smiled. She tipped her head in acknowledgment. "You know, Danner, I didn't make much progress digging a trench the other day. I'm sure there's a smarter way to go about it, but I haven't a clue."

She darted a glance in time to see Clare's smile. The woman was quite pretty when she wasn't making faces. "I can probably help with that, Mabry."

Once the pigs were successfully delivered to the village butcher, Clare and Grace spent the next few hours finishing the drainage line alongside the north field.

"A good day's work," Clare said when they finished. Using the back of her sleeve, she wiped at the grime and sweat covering her face.

"An extra pair of hands helps," Grace said as she leaned against the handle of her shovel. She felt exhausted, her fingers ached, and her soggy uniform chafed at her dampened skin, yet she was proud of her accomplishment. Not only had she pulled her weight for a change, but it seemed she'd formed a truce with Clare Danner.

"You met the Tin Man up at the manor this morning?" Becky said later, reaching across the table for another of the yeast rolls she'd baked. Mrs. Vance had announced Lord Roxwood's latest edict at supper, and the women were pleased she and Agnes would be staying. "Did you scream?"

Grace burst out laughing. "I hate to disappoint you, Becky, but he has no hunched back or pointed ears. Not even a limp. And his howl is more like a bark and quite sharp."

"T-tell us what he said to you, Grace," Lucy said, her eyes rounded like teacups.

"Very little, and he's brusque to be sure. Though he was much more irritated with me yesterday when I chased a pig into his hedge maze and stumbled upon him there."

"You met him yesterday, too?" Agnes frowned. "You didn't tell me."

"But at least I *did* tell you about him," Grace countered. To the others she said, "Considering what happened, afterward . . . it seemed unimportant." She darted a glance at Clare, who dropped her gaze.

Everyone but Becky seemed satisfied. "Well, we're all here now and we want to know everything."

Choosing her words carefully, Grace relayed the events inside the hedge maze.

"I didn't know he was blind," Becky said after she'd finished. "His scars must be horrible."

"Yes, well, the man is formidable with or without them," Grace said, feeling uncomfortable in discussing the intimate details of his wounds.

They volleyed her with more questions. What did the inside of the manor look like? What kind of automobile would Grace be driving? They even insisted on a full description of Lord Roxwood's mask.

"I think you m-must have impressed him," Lucy said at last. "He wouldn't have asked you to be his driver, otherwise."

"Perhaps you're right." Grace didn't share with them as she

had with Agnes her connection to Jack Benningham. Aside from his wish to take a turn at shaming her, she had no idea why he'd changed his mind and hired her.

Hopefully the coming day would reveal his motives.

❧

The next morning, Grace arrived at the manor promptly at nine, anticipating her first day driving the Daimler.

Knowles answered her summons, looking down his beaked nose at her just as he had the day before.

"Is he ready?" she asked.

"You will please await *milord* in the foyer."

Once inside, Grace took the time to observe more of the house. Like the manor itself, the interior décor was tasteful and not too pretentious. Floral carpeted steps ascended to the upper landing, and white-and-burgundy-striped paper covered the walls, accentuating the polished oak banister.

Gray marble floors reflected colored light as the sun penetrated two stained-glass windows along either side of the front door. A brass umbrella stand stood beside one colored pane, and an exotic palm in a Chinese vase beside the other. It was lovely. Having seen Lady Bassett's posh surroundings, she much preferred the elegant simplicity Roxwood had chosen.

"Miss Mabry." His unmistakable voice sounded at the top landing. As he descended the stairs—somewhat arrogantly, she decided—his long legs appeared first, clad in winter-white linen with turnups or cuffs, and brown leather shoes. Next, his lean torso and broad shoulders, garbed in a matching white blazer. Beneath the jacket he wore a brown-striped waistcoat and jaunty yellow tie.

The last of him came into view when she spied his gruesome covering. Grace froze, air trapped in her lungs. While she no longer felt an urge to scream, the sight of the mask with its macabre steel veil still disturbed her.

The man and his scars seemed much preferable to this inhuman-looking creature. "Lord Roxwood," she said, letting out her breath.

The clock in the hall chimed the hour. "And right on time." He continued his descent, then walked unerringly across the marble floor to stand before her. "I had thought you might flee with your life."

"It takes more than a few harsh words to scare me off, sir."

"Milord," Knowles leaned in to whisper. Grace glared at him. She might work for Lord Roxwood, but she wasn't going to call him milord. As a suffragette, she knew equality must start somewhere, and right now seemed the perfect time.

"A brave woman, then," said the towering man in the mask. Grace thought she detected humor in his voice. "I trust Edwards gave you a brief orientation yesterday. Have you brought the Daimler around?"

"It's parked outside."

"Shall we?"

Grace led the way to the car and slipped in behind the steering wheel. She watched Lord Roxwood descend the steps, noting just as she had in the hedge maze how easily he navigated without the use of a cane.

Once he'd reached the driveway, he stood beside the car and waited. With some impatience, he said, "I have done my bit in hiring you as chauffeur, Miss Mabry. Now you must do yours. My door, if you please?"

So it begins. Pursing her lips, she exited to go around and open the rear passenger door.

"I'm sitting in front."

Her annoyance turned to alarm. "But . . . I'm sure it's not the way things are done."

"It's the way I do things." His tone brooked no argument.

Somewhat flustered, Grace complied. She'd only just returned to the driver's seat when he said, "Miss Mabry, I do not wish the car's top down. Who gave the order?"

"Why, no one. I mean, with such a beautiful day, I thought . . ." She'd collapsed the top before bringing the car around from the garage. "I thought you might enjoy the warmth of the sun as we drive."

"In future, you will leave the top intact. Now please replace it and hurry. The morning's nearly gone."

Grace took a deep breath. Was he always this autocratic? She did as he commanded.

"Do you have a particular destination in mind, *sir*?" she asked when she'd finished and slipped back behind the wheel.

"Something close to home, I think." He raised an arm to rest against the back of the seat. "I wish to test your driving skills before we go too far."

"I assure you, I'm quite capable."

"Yes, I haven't forgotten about my roses. Turn right just beyond the gatehouse. We'll travel north along the perimeter road of the estate."

Grace said a prayer for patience as she eased the car forward, making the turn. Soon they were traveling a dirt road with surprisingly few ruts.

"Describe yourself, Miss Mabry, so I can at least envision to whom I'm speaking."

Grace's jaw dropped. Didn't he already know? "I'm . . . of average height for a woman," she said cautiously after a moment. "I've red hair and green eyes and a bit of a pointed chin."

"Truly?"

She glanced over to see him turned toward her. Seized with dread, Grace felt certain he was about to confront her about the white feather she'd given him. Then he would fire her and send her back to London.

"Why are you at Roxwood?"

Jarred by the unexpected question, she said, "I told you before. I was sent here to work for the WFC."

"And your family? Do they live in London? At our first meeting you said you recognized me. Have we met before?"

He didn't know? Grace gripped the wheel and turned to him, recalling the scene of his rage inside the hedge maze. Why, then, had he been so angry?

"Not too difficult a question, I hope."

She wet her lips. "Everyone knows you're Viscount Walenford," she answered carefully. "I've seen your photograph many times in the newspapers. And yes, my father lives in London."

"Is there a Mrs. Mabry?"

Grace shifted. She didn't wish to speak about her beloved mother with this stranger. "Why do you ask so many questions, sir?"

He turned his head slightly. "I have been convalescing in that house for three months without a shred of stimulating conversation. Please, humor me, Miss Mabry."

She swallowed. "My mother died last year of tuberculosis."

"Any other family?"

Why had she expected condolences from him? "My brother fights in France," she said, pride in her voice. "I also have an uncle in Dublin and several cousins scattered throughout Britain." She paused, then added, "My aunt in Oxford."

"You don't sound enthused," he said. "I gather this relative is not your favorite?"

"Aunt Florence isn't a bad person. She's just . . . forthright in her opinions on how young ladies should behave."

"Is she married?"

So many questions! Grace decided it was her turn. After

all, she had a story to write about the mysterious Tin Man. "How long do you plan to recuperate here in the country, Lord Walenford?"

"I'm asking the questions today," he said. "And out here, I prefer Roxwood, if you don't mind. So, is she?"

"Is she what?" Grace asked, confused.

"Married," he said. "Does this aunt of yours have a husband?"

"No, she never married." Grace was growing tired of their one-sided exchange.

"A spinster, then." He dropped his arm from the back of the seat. "I take it the 'behavior' to which she subscribes prohibits *you* from having fun?"

"I beg your pardon. I didn't say—"

"Is she sister to your father or your mother?"

"My father, but I still don't see why—"

"What does he do for a living?"

"Lord Roxwood!" Grace brought the car to a halt. "I understand you've been without company a long while, but this 'stimulating conversation' you seem to think we're having is all on your part. I haven't gotten a word in for all of your questions, none of which has to do with my driving skills." She felt like an insect beneath a microscope.

"I apologize, Miss Mabry. I'm merely curious." He leaned back against the seat. "Your driving skills seem adequate enough. You haven't yet hit a rut to knock me out of the car."

"Thank you," she said with forced politeness.

"Where are we now?"

Grace surveyed the landscape. "There is a grouping of trees off to the right," she said. "They surround a lake—"

"Camden Pond. Look for a dirt track coming up beside a large ash tree. It will take us directly to the water's edge, so remember to brake."

KATE BRESLIN

Grace rolled her eyes. She soon spied the large leafy tree and a wide dirt track beside it. Taking the turn, she brought the Daimler to a stop within a few feet of the bank.

"You didn't answer my question, Miss Mabry. What is your father's occupation?"

She struggled for patience. "He's in the tea business and the owner of Swan's Tea Room in London."

"Is he from London?"

"Dublin, if you must know. He came to Britain when he was my own age of twenty and started working at the docks. He came to know men in the tea import business, and after years of hard work and establishing the right connections, he was able to invest with others in a large tea plantation abroad."

"I imagine he's a rather affluent tradesman, then?"

"If you mean is he wealthy, the answer is yes," she said tersely.

"And when did he open this tea room of his?"

The man was relentless. "Seven years ago," she said wearily. "A few years after my father bought his own tea distributorship. Since he loves all varieties of tea, he opened Swan's as a way to share his passion with others. He plans to expand the franchise and build four more tea rooms across London. Now, sir, do you wish to cross-examine me further? Perhaps you'd like to go to Swan's in London yourself and corroborate my story?"

"Not my sort of place." He spoke with infuriating calm. "I much prefer the club atmosphere. Playing cards and sipping on a glass of twelve-year-old Scotch."

No truer words, she thought, recalling his exploits from the newspaper. Jack Benningham was hardly one to enjoy a proper tea.

"Does your father entertain much?"

Grace felt like screaming. "Swan's keeps him extremely busy. Shall I take you back to the house now?" She felt desperate to be rid of him.

"Perhaps you'd care to get out and view the pond."

His suggestion startled her. "Why, yes, very much. You don't mind?"

"Go ahead and turn off the car."

Grace set the brake and pressed the engine's kill switch. Then she exited the Daimler and went around to open his door.

"You go ahead, Miss Mabry. I'll wait here. There's no breeze yet this morning, so you should find the water smooth as glass."

Stymied at his indulgence toward her, Grace thought he might regret having asked so many questions. "I won't be long."

She walked to the bank and surveyed the pond. He was right; without a breeze, the water stretched outward like a mirror. She could see in it the perfect reflection of the trees, tall and unmoving along the opposite bank.

The mirror distorted as a flock of colorful ducks swooped down to skid along the glassy surface and land with a splash. They ruffled their feathers and swam for a patch of reeds near the opposite shore, quickly acclimating to their new gathering place. She smiled over their antics and turned to call out to Lord Roxwood, intending to share her discovery—then realized he wouldn't be able to see them.

"I heard the ducks," he said when she'd returned to the car. "Are they pochards? The shovelers are common this time of year, as well."

"I have no idea," she said. "They had many of the same colors: browns, creams, a few with green heads. Several were a dull brown."

He crossed his arms. "Miss Mabry, surely you know the difference between a northern shoveler and a gadwall when you see it?"

She sensed his jeering expression behind the mask. "I've lived in the city all my life, sir. Perhaps I could offer you instead the differing species of street pigeons?"

He didn't answer her. Instead he said, "My brother and I sometimes took our small boat out here to fish."

Grace heard his pensiveness, but the mask hid his expression. She imagined two young boys on the water with their fishing poles, each hoping to catch the bigger prize. More than a year ago, the *Times* had reported the drowning of his brother in Serpentine Lake at London's Hyde Park. Hugh Benningham was in a boat then, as well. "Did you spend much time at the estate?" she asked.

"Hugh and I spent our childhood summers here." His voice sounded hollow. "Miss Mabry, I believe I've had enough country air for one morning. You may return to the house now."

"Of course." Using the car's throttle and crank, she brought the engine back to life. He said nothing as she drove the car back in the direction they had come. Lord Roxwood's first outing after being cooped up in the house for so long had doubtless tired him.

His earlier rapid-fire questioning still disturbed her. Grace understood natural curiosity—as a writer, she had it in abundance. Yet he'd seemed insistent, demanding to know as much about her as possible. Why? She felt certain now he had no knowledge of her being at Lady Bassett's ball. Still, he'd asked so many questions, about her father in particular.

Patrick Mabry had never been introduced to any of the Benninghams, nor did he expect to be. Despite the privilege of Lady Bassett's patronage, a self-made Irishman, even a wealthy one, didn't travel in the same circles as an earl of the realm.

Returning to the manor, Grace stepped from the car and was surprised to see the sun almost directly overhead. She checked her watch and saw three hours had passed. She moved around to open her employer's door. "Shall I call for you again tomorrow?"

"It's what I pay you for."

Again his surly self, Lord Roxwood exited and began mounting the steps. "Oh, and Miss Mabry," he called back. "While you work for me, please notify Edwards if you decide to leave the estate. There may be times I request an afternoon outing."

How he enjoyed being lord of the manor. "Very well," she said, holding her temper.

As she watched him continue toward the front door, where the sour Knowles awaited him, Grace reminded herself of the reasons she'd taken the post. She also said a prayer for patience.

Because if her morning with Lord Roxwood was a sampling of the days to come, she would need it desperately.

6

"Jack, you won't believe what I discovered."

"So tell me, Marcus." Jack held the telephone as he sat on the edge of his desk. Since returning from the morning's ride with Grace Mabry, he'd been reproaching himself over his clumsy interrogation. Like a novice, he'd drummed her with so many questions that even the most innocent person might become suspicious. He'd been trained by the best at MI5, and it unnerved him to think he'd lost his edge.

"Patrick Mabry bribed a clerk in the WFC to place his daughter at Roxwood," Marcus said. "It seems your hunch was well-founded. She's obviously there to obtain information for her father. Whether Mabry believes you still have proof against him is debatable. Ordinarily you would already have brought it forward—"

"Except for the fact I'm blind, you mean?" Jack said. "Does he think I perhaps misplaced his letter and now I cannot find it?"

"I *think* if he knows you were on the *Acionna* when it went down, you might have something on him," Marcus countered.

Jack said nothing. Hearing Marcus corroborate his suspicions about Grace Mabry didn't offer the anticipated reaction.

Instead of crowing with vindication, he felt disappointment. He rather enjoyed his sparring match with her today. She'd made her annoyance to his questioning quite clear, her responses seeming impulsive and unrehearsed. Despite her father's bribe to get her here, she certainly didn't fit the profile of a spy infiltrating her target and gaining his trust.

"Jack, my schedule's a bear right now with the spy Mata Hari's upcoming trial, but I can come out after the weekend—"

"No," Jack cut in swiftly. "I need more time with her." He relayed to his friend their employment agreement. "Miss Mabry will tell me what I wish to know."

"Yes, but in light of this new information, I need to come out and meet with her."

"Your presence will only make my fact-finding more difficult," Jack insisted. "She'll become suspicious and the opportunity will be lost. We need information, Marcus, and I feel she can provide it. Right now there's no direct evidence with which to indict Patrick Mabry. We need to prove his involvement with James Heeren *and* the spy ring MI5's been after. I can get names from her, other agents her father's worked with."

"I don't know, Jack. The Admiralty is keen to investigate any suspicious activity. There have been recent developments. If Mabry or his family is involved—"

"She's not going anywhere, Lieutenant." Jack's tone hardened. "I've put my entire staff in charge of keeping track of Miss Mabry's whereabouts. When she's not with me, she'll be working with the WFC." He paused. "I need this, Marcus. I'm the one who's had so much at stake. Please," he said in a low voice, "let me be useful."

There was silence on the other end of the line. Finally his friend said, "You've got a week. Then I'm coming out."

"Thanks." Jack's shoulders eased. "Anything in particular I

should ask her?" He hoped to discover what "recent developments" his friend spoke of.

"No, it can wait, old boy. Just keep me informed."

Once Marcus rang off, Jack returned to sit behind his desk. The Admiralty had information they wanted kept hush-hush. Secrets his friend wouldn't risk talking about over the telephone. And likely it involved Grace Mabry's presence at Roxwood.

Jack thought back to their outing. Despite his inept interview, he'd manage to learn a bit more about her. Red hair and green eyes . . .

Miss Mabry's description had brought to his mind another image—the mystery woman whose delicate lines and features had been committed to memory, his goddess in green. *Pandora* . . .

She was beautiful, her thick auburn curls held captive in green satin bands, her eyes gleaming like emeralds. Her lithe body, swathed in a gauzy Grecian-styled gown, had walked gracefully toward him, the fullness of her lower lip curved upward as she'd offered him her hand for his kiss. Reaching into his vest pocket, Jack withdrew the white feather that had somehow survived the explosion and gently brushed his thumb along its silken softness. He'd never learned her name, but during his weeks in hospital and the ensuing months of darkness, the vision of her had stayed with him, keeping the night at bay, along with the panic he often felt at never being able to see again.

If only he had stayed by her side that night.

Jack pushed himself up from the desk. Wishful thinking couldn't alter the past. He had only the present, and right now he thirsted for justice. His friend had just given him the chance to seek it out.

Excitement coursed through him as Jack returned upstairs to his room. He was back in the game. Already he anticipated his next encounter with Grace Mabry. Ringing for his valet, he mentally prepared the questions he would ask the following day.

He had a week to get his answers. And Jack *would* get them.

∞

The butler answered Grace's summons with the same sour look the following morning. Perhaps it was permanently etched into the craggy features. Determined to be sunny, she made an effort to smile. "Good morning, Knowles."

"His lordship will be with you presently, miss."

"Thank you." She tugged at her gloves. "I'll wait in the car."

Grace remembered to open the passenger door before she moved back around the car and got in. She'd also left the Daimler's top intact. Lord Roxwood would have no reason today for curmudgeonly behavior.

She gazed up wistfully at the clear July sky. With summer in full force and haymaking to begin on Monday, Grace had hoped to join in with the camaraderie of her co-workers, instead of playing driver to a man whose inconsideration stretched the limits of her patience.

He appeared outside the front door. Again wearing his ugly mask, he was clad in a suit of summer linen and wore a brown felt motoring cap. With her initial fear of him gone, Grace marveled anew at his uncanny sense of direction. He seemed to know exactly where he was going without the use of his sight.

"Miss Mabry?" He paused beside the Daimler.

"Good morning, Lord Roxwood." Feeling a bit devilish, she said, "Shall I come around and assist you inside?"

"I am blind, woman, not feeble." He slid onto the seat and closed the door.

Grace felt a moment's triumph at taking a bite out of the man's endless supply of arrogance. "Where shall we go today?" She was eager to drive to another new place.

"Take the first left before you reach the village. There's a post marked Warrenton Road. Travel south until it connects with Isle Crossing, which leads toward Canterbury. We won't go into the city, but there's a lake and a wilderness park not far from the turnoff."

He rested his arm against the back of the seat and turned to her. "And I feel ready to venture a bit farther, knowing you won't run us off the road."

As much as he seemed to enjoy being unpleasant, she vowed she would not allow him to ruin this glorious day for her. Releasing the brake, she eased the car along the graveled drive. They traveled in blessed silence for the first few minutes, and she thought she might get a reprieve from yesterday.

She was wrong. "What are your plans for tomorrow, Miss Mabry?" he asked.

"Well, it *is* Sunday." She glanced at him, hoping he didn't plan to make her drive him about so he could bombard her with more questions. "Mr. Edwards said I would have the day off." A sudden thought struck. "Or shall I be taking you to church? I'm happy to do it. I believe service in the village starts at eight o'clock. I'll fetch you at a quarter till the hour, if you like."

"Miss Mabry, if I ever decide to step inside another church, be assured, I'll summon you."

Didn't he attend church? The news surprised her—until she remembered his reputation in London. Perhaps he felt beyond saving. Her attitude softened. "If you like, I'll speak with the vicar, Reverend Price," she said. "I'm sure he'd be willing to come to the house and talk with you . . ."

The rest of her sentence died with his fit of coughing. Grace slowed the car. "Lord Roxwood, are you unwell?" His shoulders had begun to shake. Was he having some kind of seizure? "What shall I do?" she asked, leaning toward him, alarmed. "Should we go back—?"

"Ah, I'm impressed, Miss Mabry." He sounded winded as he fell back against the seat. "I had no idea when I hired a driver, I'd be getting a missionary in the bargain." His tone held amusement.

He'd been . . . laughing at her? "I merely wish to give you the opportunity to receive the benefit of Christian counsel and comfort," she said hotly. "Reverend Price—"

"Is forbidden to enter my house," he cut in, all humor gone. "As for 'counsel,' you can keep your own in regard to any sermons you might think to impart to me, Miss Mabry, such as those from the good reverend."

Grace clutched at the steering wheel. "So, you don't believe in God."

"What difference would it make? I'd still be blind and have these scars." He turned his masked face ahead toward the road. "I believe in myself. I ask for nothing from God. I expect nothing. A much simpler philosophy and no one suffers disappointment. Now please, just drive."

Shocked by his tirade, she resumed the car's speed. He blamed God for his misfortunes? Grace recalled the townhouse fire, the rumors of his heavy gambling, and his having been drunk when he accidentally set the place ablaze. If he chose to behave abominably and suffer the consequences, it wasn't God's fault.

Such un-Christian thinking, she chided herself, glancing at him. Jack Benningham had more than paid the price for his folly.

She slowed the car as she spied the village directly ahead. The wooden post for Warrenton Road was off to her left. Grace made the quick decision to drive into town first. She'd written a letter to her father days before, but postponed its mailing when she thought her career in the WFC had ended. As she was once again secure in her position, she would post it.

Grace glanced at Lord Roxwood beside her. Surely he wouldn't mind if she took a moment to send it off before they continued their outing.

She eased the car to a halt in front of the post office.

"Why have we stopped?" he demanded.

"I've a letter to post. I didn't think you'd mind. It won't take but a minute."

"You . . . you've brought me into town?"

Her breath caught at his enraged tone. "I promise I'll only be a moment." Then she noticed the knuckles of his left hand whiten as he gripped the frame of the windscreen. His other hand lay fisted against his knee, and if he sat any more rigid he'd be made of stone. She realized her mistake. "I am sorry."

"Get on with it!"

Grace quickly set the brake and exited the car. As she looked toward the cobbler's shop where she'd sewn sacks with Lucy, she thought she saw Clare Danner and someone else—a man—standing together inside.

She started for the shop, intending to find out, before she noticed people staring toward the Daimler. The blacksmith, clad in his leather apron and holding a hammer, emerged from his smithy to gawk at the man in the car. Two older men stood outside the butcher's shop, and a woman with her young daughter paused in front of the greengrocer's, parcels in hand, each gaping at the Tin Man in his mask. As if he were some kind of monstrous curiosity they'd never seen before.

A dog barked in the distance, then yelped, and Grace saw the cur tuck its tail and run behind a building for shelter. The woman selling bread actually left her cart in the street to walk toward the car, staring.

Seized with righteous indignation, Grace tucked her letter back inside her uniform. How dare they look at him that way! She marched back to the Daimler and slid behind the wheel.

Removing the brake, she swung the car around and headed back out of town.

"That was quick." With the car's motion, Lord Roxwood's hand relaxed against the frame.

"I forgot to bring money," she lied. "I'll post my letter another time."

"Ah, the freak comes to town and everyone has to stop and stare, is that it?"

Darting a glance at the mask, Grace wondered if she was being too harsh on the villagers for their reaction. To someone who had never caught sight of him before, the image he presented was frightening.

"I understand," he said when she didn't answer. "It must have been a very busy day in the village of Roxwood."

Despite the light remark, Grace heard his bitterness. "More like busybodies," she muttered. She slowed the Daimler, making the turn he'd indicated.

They began heading south on a well-maintained graveled road. "They're just simpleminded folk." Oddly she felt a need to assuage his pride. "When I first met you, I was a little surprised, but I've discovered you're not a monster."

"Ah, so that's the current rumor they're spreading."

Why couldn't she govern her tongue? "Such silliness," she said.

"What else are they saying?"

Grace didn't think it wise to reveal the outlandish things she'd heard. "You know how people talk," she said vaguely.

"Tell me."

She froze as he leaned closer to her.

"Now, Miss Mabry, unless you'd like to tell me more about yourself and your family?"

Grace needed no further prompting. "If you must know, I was told you had pointed ears and a hunched back, that you limp, which of course you don't, and that you howl at the moon."

The same choked noise—laughter—emerged from behind the steel mesh. "They say all that, do they?" he said finally. "I suppose it does make me a monster."

He turned to the open window. Grace refocused her attention on the road. Plane trees bordered the pastureland to her left, while beyond lay an endless stretch of valley, dotted with majestic oaks and a body of water much larger than Camden Pond. "I see a lake, coming up on the left."

"Harmon Lake."

She glanced at him. "Did you fish there, as well?"

"Rarely," he said. "Most of the time we took Grandfather's small sailboat and crossed back and forth between shores. Harmon Lake is quite large."

Indeed it was. Grace tried to imagine a small boat traversing such a body of water.

"Turn right just before the lake at Isle Crossing. Follow the road for about two miles until you reach the first hill."

She did as she was told, and when they began to ascend the mild incline, he said, "Pull over at the crest. There should be a semicircular patch on which to park."

Grace saw the place he'd described and marveled anew at his sense of direction and his powers of memory. Once she parked the car, he turned to her. "I'd like you to cross the road and walk about five hundred yards. You'll know when to stop."

His request surprised her. He must have sensed her hesitation. "The view is not for the simpleminded, Miss Mabry, therefore I think you'll enjoy it."

She blinked. He'd just given her a compliment. Was it due to her earlier defense of him? She thought to ask, but her curiosity to see a place he deemed worth looking at won out. "I won't be long."

Exiting the car, she traveled a short distance through woods scented with ferns and painted with a splash of white roses and purple orchids. The faint, sweet smell of honeysuckle reached her nostrils as she came to a stop before a precipice overlooking a valley.

It was the same verdant stretch she'd seen earlier. To the east, the sun cast a pink glint against distant clouds, while below her the sparkle of water—a river—meandered like a shiny piece of ribbon across the vale floor. Forests rose in the distance, in varying shades of green, with red-berried hawthorn and the white catkins of sweet chestnut adding their touches of color.

Grace admitted the pastoral scene was unlike any she'd viewed in London, and much more beautiful. She wondered if Ireland might be like this. Da had often talked of his homeland. She'd heard the love in his voice and seen the wistful look in his eyes when he spoke of Uncle Brian's farm outside Dublin. He had told her and Colin there were more shades of green to be seen on the island than in any other part of the world. If it was anything like this view, then she wanted to visit one day.

"Well?" Lord Roxwood demanded when she returned to the car.

"Magical." Grace heard the wonder in her own voice. "I felt as though I were looking at a painting."

"I call the spot Eden," he said. "Who could not wish to paint such a paradise?" He tipped his masked face down. "The view was one of the most impressive I've ever seen."

Was. Compassion seized her, and for the first time Grace saw his guise as the infuriatingly arrogant employer begin to crack around the edges. He'd given her a gift, sharing with her a place once so beautiful to him, now lost forever. "Thank you," she said. "I'm sure I will never forget it."

He nodded, and Grace heard the rustling chink of metal. *Trapped from the beauty of the outside world.* "Shall I drive on?" She didn't wait for his agreement as she set the car back in motion. Again she considered his kind gesture, and her mood lightened. Perhaps they might begin anew and enjoy being in each other's company for a change.

"When we first met in my hedge maze, you said you worked for the Women's Forage Corps. How did you come to be at Roxwood in particular?"

Her optimism faded. "I went where I was assigned. Why?"

"I was curious to know if you could choose your posting. Is your father affiliated with the WFC?"

"Of course not," she said with impatience. "It was my choice to join up and do my part to help my brother and others in the cavalry by working to feed their horses."

"Yes, you told me he's in France. The BEF—British Expeditionary Force?"

"Yes, Colin is in the Second Cavalry Division."

"Have you or your father attended any of the war aid benefits held in London? I ask because at one time I frequented several, doing my bit for our boys overseas."

Grace's mouth twisted in scorn. "Doing his bit" meant drinking, womanizing, and hiding out from the war.

"In fact, the last benefit was held at Lady Bassett's home in April," he said. "Perhaps we met there?"

She gripped the steering wheel tightly. Was he baiting her? Had he known all along she was at the ball? Grace's mind raced. While she disliked being evasive with him, telling the truth would get her banished from Roxwood. "I believe I told you yesterday, my father stays too busy with his tea business to attend parties," she said truthfully. "And while Lady Bassett remains his chief patroness, we are in trade, sir. Neither I nor my father have ever received such an illustrious invitation." She omitted the fact she'd shown up at the ball without one.

"I'd like to know why you persist in these questions," she said, taking the offensive. "In our brief time together you've been more than a little keen to know about my family, my father in particular. Please tell me why."

"I'm merely making polite conversation while we take in the country air."

His interrogation was hardly polite. "I'll make you a bargain," she said as inspiration struck. "You can ask me a question, then I'll ask you one. Does that sound fair?"

She could tell her terms annoyed him. He turned to face the open window, his fingers tapping against the doorframe. "All right," he said finally, swinging the mask back around to face her. "I'll go first. Have you and I ever met before? Prior to you chasing a pig into my labyrinth?"

The fine line she was treading seemed ready to snap. "We were never introduced, but I have seen you before," she said with as much honesty as she dared.

"Aside from my photograph in the newspapers?"

"That's two questions. I believe it's my turn now. What kind of mask do you wear?"

"You'll answer my question first." His implacable tone resonated from behind the mesh. "Well? Yes or no?"

Grace chewed on her lower lip as she weighed how much to tell him. "Yes, aside from the newspapers, I did see you. You were getting into a hired cab," she said, recalling his swift departure from Lady Bassett's ball.

He snorted beneath the mask. "That could be any one of a thousand places." He leaned back in his seat. His voice turned wistful as he added, "There was a time when I was always on my way somewhere."

"I believe it's my turn," Grace said again, longing to change the subject.

He let out a deep breath. "It's called a splatter mask. The metal slats over the eyes and the steel-mesh curtain across the mouth are designed to protect the wearer from metal and paint flakes shearing off inside a tank during shelling." He paused. "Tell me why you decided to join the Women's Forage Corps."

"It wasn't my first choice. I wanted to become a munitionette at one of the factories in London, or drive a field ambulance with the First Aid Nursing Yeomanry, but Da—my father—wouldn't allow it. He said it was far too dangerous."

"Yet he approves of your baling hay for horses in the fields."

"My turn," she said. "Why do you wear the mask?"

She jumped when he leaned toward her and snapped, "Isn't it obvious? I believe you got a good look the other day in the labyrinth."

"I . . . I did," she admitted. "But why wear such a macabre disguise?" She glanced at him. "The mask makes you look positively frightful."

His shoulders eased as he retreated from her a safe distance. "It protects my face. My burns are still healing, and direct sunlight is bad for the skin, or so my physician tells me. As to why I wear this particular covering, well . . . what else would a monster wear?"

Hearing his bitter tone, she looked down to see his hand fisted against the seat.

"Well?" he said.

"I suspect my father allowed me to join the WFC because he was concerned over the recent bombings in London and wanted me safely away," she said quietly. "And he also happens to be Irish."

"I understand the first reason, but why does being Irish matter?"

She smiled. "Everyone knows the Irish love the land. Aiding the war effort in this way is both noble and relatively safe, so Agnes and I signed up and were sent here to Roxwood."

"Agnes?"

Grace tired of keeping track of whose turn it was. "She's

my maid from London." She looked at him. "Do they hurt? The burns, I mean."

"I'm very tired, Miss Mabry. If you'd turn the car around at the first opportunity, I'd like to return home."

Apparently his scars were off-limits. Grace did as he asked and soon had the car heading back toward the manor. When she parked the car and made to exit, he surprised her by opening his own door. "Until Monday," he said, hauling himself from the Daimler.

"You're certain about church tomorrow?" she called to him. Oddly, the notion of his staying at home alone bothered her. The villagers might see him as less frightful and more God-fearing if he at least attended services with them.

"Good day to you, Miss Mabry." He turned his back on her and mounted the steps.

Watching him, Grace felt a jumble of sentiment: irritation at his demands and his constant barrage of questions, but also compassion, as she felt driven to defend his privacy after seeing how others looked at him. Then later, when he'd shared with her the place so very special to him, Eden . . .

Grace felt her insides flutter. He'd complimented her, allowing her to see a side of him rarely revealed to anyone else. It felt intimate in some way.

As she drove the Daimler to the garage, she considered that despite the few answers she'd received from him today, Jack Benningham was an even greater mystery to her now than before.

7

"It's about time you got here." Clare Danner stood at the barn doors with a handful of burlap sacks and a shovel. "Lord Roxwood kept you longer than usual?"

Grace climbed off her bicycle. "Yes, now that he knows I won't crash the car, he actually let me drive him beyond the estate. We headed toward Canterbury."

"Canterbury?" Clare straightened. "What did you see there?"

"We didn't go into the town, just as far as Harmon Lake. The scenery was delightful." She noted Clare's pale expression. "Is something wrong?"

"No," she said quickly, then added, "Come with me. You and I are making chaff for the horses." Carrying her supplies, Clare stepped into the barn through its big double doors. Grace was left to follow.

Inside the dimly lit interior stood a mountain of dried hay, and beside it, a metal stand waist-high with a large cutting wheel and crank handle.

Beneath the stand sat a wooden crate. "Did you make chaff at the training farm?"

Grace shook her head, relieved Clare's question held no mockery.

"This is last year's straw, mixed with a bit of hay. You'll feed it into the chute"—Clare pointed to a metal trough on the opposite side of the stand—"while I chop it with the cutting wheel. Once we've filled the crate, we'll bag it." She dropped the burlap sacks to the ground. "With hay and oats in short supply, the cavalry uses it to bulk up the horses' feed. All right, let's get started," she said with a nod.

Grace pulled on her gloves and began feeding the straw into the chute. Clare cranked the wheel, and the blades sliced it into bite-sized chunks that fell into the crate.

"Have you been to Canterbury?" Grace asked after a few minutes.

Clare's head shot up. "No. Why?"

"You just seemed a bit surprised when I mentioned the town." Grace pushed more straw through the trough. "I thought you must have been there, that's all."

"Well, you're mistaken." Clare's tone was curt. "Did you go anywhere else?"

"We made a quick stop in the village." The memory sparked Grace's ire all over again. "They apparently don't get too many visitors in blue Daimlers."

Clare stared at her. "And having the Tin Man seated inside wasn't a curiosity?"

"They give *bumpkin* a new meaning," Grace said, frowning. "Scads of them stopped in the streets, gawking like he was the bogeyman come to run off with their children." She shoved another wad of straw into the machine. "It isn't as if he can help the way he looks."

"That doesn't stop people from being cruel."

Grace glanced up, surprised at Clare's bitter tone. Ironic when the woman herself had been mean-spirited toward Grace when she first arrived. "Ignorance and fear can breed that sort of attitude," she agreed, not wishing to strain their fragile bond.

"You've got the hang of it." Clare nodded approvingly. "We'll switch off after a while. Making chaff by hand definitely tires out your arms."

Grace beamed. Clare's praise felt like a balm, easing her guilt at being only part-time help to her co-workers. It also felt good to know she was helping her brother and their horses, even if it was in a small way. The sooner the war was won, the sooner Colin could come home. She longed to see him and tell him how proud she was. She prayed she would have the chance.

Oh, Lord, please keep him safe. Her heart squeezed as fear and doubt shoved their way into her thoughts. If something happened to him in France . . .

"Mabry, what's wrong?"

Clare's voice reached her. Grace looked up, shaking off the dark mood. "I'm fine." She reached for another sheaf.

"Are you sick?"

Grace shook her head. She didn't often experience this clairvoyance with her twin: only twice before, once when Colin contracted a serious fever during an expedition with his British Boy Scouts, and another time when she and her brother went out riding together. That time, Colin failed to duck for a low-hanging branch and fell off his horse, breaking his arm.

Now she was having that same impression again. "Have you ever felt a sense of impending doom . . . about someone close to you?"

Clare's pretty features formed a scowl, but Grace caught her look of pain. "Why do you want to know?"

"My brother is at the Front, and I have a bad feeling. Colin could be wounded." She hesitated. "Or worse."

"Grace, you can't let your emotions prey upon you." Clare's tone was hard. "Your brother will come home to you. We can't give up hope. . . ." Her voice trailed off as she began cranking the wheel harder.

"Are you also waiting for someone to come home?"

Clare stopped her work and seemed to consider Grace a long moment before she said, "I suppose I can trust you. After all, you did tell that outrageous story about the pigs." She took a deep breath. "I do have someone," she said softly. "She's not fighting in the war overseas, but I won't give up until I find her."

"Who?" Grace asked gently.

Clare pulled off a glove and reached beneath her uniform for the flower pendant. "Daisy." Her gaze, normally like flint, gleamed with unshed tears. "My daughter."

Grace felt too surprised to speak. Finally she said, "Her father . . . ?"

Clare made a face, but the sadness lingered. "The son of a viscount. His family seat is in the north. I was an upstairs maid with grand dreams and little sense." She gave the chaffing wheel another turn. "Once he learned I carried his child, he wanted nothing more to do with me.

"I was a good girl." She cast an imploring look at Grace. "I loved him and I thought he would be honorable. He made me all sorts of promises, you know, before . . ." A shuddering sigh escaped her. "His mother had me sent off to a Magdalene House. After I had the child, they took her from me, my little girl. I managed to leave the place. His lordliness must have felt guilty. I left the city then. I wanted to change my life, and the WFC offered me that chance. I hoped to earn enough money to hire someone to find my Daisy and bring her back to me."

"I saw you this morning," Grace said. "You spoke to a gentleman inside the cobbler's shop."

Clare nodded. "When you mentioned Canterbury, I nearly fainted. He'd just told me of a report that Daisy is being fostered by a family there. I won't know for certain until he makes more inquiries."

Her face crumpled with tears. "A miracle brought me here, working in this place so close to her. But we'll only be here a few weeks. I can't bear knowing she might be less than an hour from me and yet I might lose her again."

"Oh, Clare." Grace came around the machine and hugged her. She'd been shocked at first by the confession, but her compassion won out as she realized Clare had lost a child. And if Grace had learned anything from women's suffrage, it was that men were generally full of vainglory and enjoyed manipulating women to their whims. "I'm so sorry for what you must be going through," she whispered. "No wonder you dislike aristocrats so much."

Clare looked up teary-eyed, and both women began to laugh.

"I've shared my secret, Grace," she said once they'd sobered. "I hope you won't judge me too harshly, not after the way I've treated you."

"Nonsense. It's in the past." Grace smiled. "Now, please, let me know what I can do to help. I'll even drive you to Canterbury when the time comes to go and get your little girl. How old is Daisy?"

"A year," Clare said. "Her birthday was the eighth, the day you arrived." She put a hand on Grace's shoulder. "I was so upset. I shouldn't have taken it out on you."

"No, you shouldn't have," Grace agreed. "But we're friends now, right?"

Clare squeezed her shoulder. "Friends."

"And besides, look where I landed. After the pig fiasco, I'm still with the WFC *and* I get to drive Lord Roxwood all over creation." She winked. "Not bad for a day's disaster, is it?"

Clare flashed another smile. Grace said, "You should do that more often, you know. You're very pretty, Clare Danner, when you're not scowling at the world."

"And you are quite the worker." Clare indicated the bin now full of chaff. "You've also learned to dig proper ditches, and Becky told me yesterday you did a good job helping with the new fence. The fact is, Grace, I think you're finally one of us."

∞

"Grace, how was your m-morning with the Tin Man?" Lucy reached for a slice of Becky's delicious barley bread and dipped it into her bowl of vegetable soup. "Is he still asking lots of questions?"

"We take turns now." Grace stirred at the hot broth in her bowl with her spoon. The fragrant aroma of celery, onions, and leeks rose to greet her hungry senses. "He asks me a question, then I ask him one. Since he dislikes my prying into his life, I believe it's helping to curb his curiosity with mine."

"What kinds of things do you ask him?" Becky paused in buttering her fourth slice. "If he only howls at the full moon?"

Laughter erupted around the table. "Of course not," Grace said, grinning. "But I did ask about his mask."

That got everyone's attention. "Well?" Becky seemed captivated, spreading butter on her fingers instead of the bread.

"A splatter mask," Grace said. She then relayed his explanation and reasons for wearing it.

Lucy asked, "Did he say how he g-got burned?"

"No, but the accident was in the papers months ago." She told them about his townhouse burning but withheld details of how the blaze got started. No reason to sully his reputation further by telling them he was reported to be quite inebriated when it happened.

"So the Tin Man is also the heir to an earldom?" Becky stared at her, wide-eyed, wiping her buttery fingers on a cloth napkin. "Did you know him from London?"

Grace hesitated and turned to Agnes, seated a couple of

chairs away. She concluded from her maid's slight shake of the head that neither of them wished to share how Grace first met Jack Benningham.

"What does it matter? He's an aristocrat," Clare said. Her new friend grabbed an apple from the bowl on the table and winked at Grace. "And I for one do not wish to sit here and listen while she bores us with his list of lordly titles and estates."

Grace offered an appreciative smile, knowing Clare had purposely diverted everyone's attention from broaching the subject further.

"Let's eat up, girls. We've got church early in the morning."

Mrs. Vance rose from the table with her empty kit and took it to the sink to wash it. "I think Mabry, Danner, and Pierpont get first crack at the tub tonight."

Grace sighed. A hot bath! Later, after she'd scrubbed away the day's grime and bits of straw accumulated beneath her uniform, she donned her nightgown and climbed into bed. Before one of the girls dimmed the lights, she grabbed up her journal and thought about her next outing with Lord Roxwood. She determined to start writing down all the questions she could possibly think to ask him.

Grace had to admit that despite his prickly nature and his questions, she looked forward to a new adventure each day. And he had shared that lovely view with her . . .

Perhaps he was undergoing a change of heart toward her, after all.

8

"Well, ladies, today is the day we begin to make hay!" Mrs. Vance stood beside the breakfast table and made the announcement to a round of cheers.

Grace leaned forward in her chair. Though she anticipated today's outing with Lord Roxwood, their excitement was contagious.

"Young will hitch up the team and the mower blade and start cutting a section of the north field." Mrs. Vance addressed Lucy, then turned to eye Agnes and Becky. "Pierpont and Simmons, you'll walk along behind the mower with rakes and spread the cuttings out to help them dry."

"Lucy, shall I help you with the horses?" Grace asked.

"No need," Mrs. Vance spoke up. "Lucy will do just fine. You go along and drive your Lord Roxwood around."

"He is not *my* Lord Roxwood," Grace insisted, blushing. Lucy and Becky smiled at her, while Agnes pursed her lips and Clare wore a mischievous expression.

"I don't know, Grace. You've been d-driving him around for days. I'm surprised you aren't wearing Roxwood livery by now," Lucy said.

"Yes, then she can come out to the pasture and bale hay in her jodhpurs, jacket, and fancy cap once she's finished with him in the mornings," Clare said with a wink.

Peals of laughter broke out around the table, including Agnes, who flashed a wide grin.

"That's enough, ladies." Mrs. Vance said to Grace, "You'll get your chance at haymaking later today, Mabry. Once you finish at the manor, grab a rake and join the others in the north field." Her hazel eyes sparkled. "And wear your WFC uniform, please."

Grace hid a smile as she rose from her chair and left the kitchen to more howls of laughter. She realized how much she enjoyed their camaraderie, even the teasing. It meant they had accepted her. She had indeed become one of them.

"Shall I ask the first question today?" Grace steered the Daimler in a northerly direction once they passed the gatehouse, per Lord Roxwood's instruction.

"How did you find the good reverend's sermon yesterday?"

He spoke as if he hadn't heard her. Nevertheless, she was determined to keep her patience. "Inspiring," she replied.

Quickly she veered the car to avoid hitting a rut in the road. The track wasn't nearly as smooth as the other roads they had traveled. "Reverend Price spoke about faith and how life's difficulties can undermine our Christian belief if we allow it."

Grace thought she heard him scoff behind the steel mesh. "It's true, though, isn't it?" she said. "Look at the calamities of the world we read about in the newspapers. So much theft and murder, even I find myself doubting the so-called 'goodness of men' and wonder how God allows such things to happen. But Reverend Price says that's the time we must stand fast. When bad things occur, it's the devil working to shake our belief. We have to look to our hearts for the truth and not at what the world does. 'We live by faith, not by sight.'"

As she spoke, Grace failed to miss the next large rut. The car gave a lurch as they drove over it.

"I appreciate your enthusiasm, Miss Mabry, but please keep your eyes focused on the road instead of heaven. Because if you plan to hit each and every pothole from here to Scotland, my breakfast will soon make an unplanned reappearance. Now, let us change the subject."

Grace stiffened. "You did ask."

"To my utmost regret," he muttered.

Forgive him, Lord. Truly she'd never met such a disrespectful man. "All right, we'll begin again with my question." She had decided to start with a less personal one to draw him out. "How long has your family owned Roxwood Manor?"

From the corner of her eye she saw him turn to her. "The estate has been in our family for generations. My great-grandfather, Stonebrooke's third earl, received the estate from Queen Victoria as a reward for some personal favor." He paused. "What shade of red is it?"

"What?"

"Your hair," he said. "Is it red like fire . . . or like a carrot? Or is it the color of rust?"

Grace hadn't thought much about it. "It's just . . . red."

"You must do better than that, Miss Mabry. I cannot see it, so therefore you must tell me." He leaned toward her. "Well?"

Grace thought a moment, then brightened as an image came to her. "It's like a fresh cup of steaming Assam."

"I beg your pardon?"

"Assam tea. Just after it steeps and is poured into a delicate bone-china cup." She heard another noise from behind the mask and frowned. "Oh, I forgot. You're a man who prefers drinking Scotch. But surely not for breakfast?"

114

"Of course not, though I prefer the taste of coffee beans to tea leaves, so I'll take your word on the color of this Assam. And what about your eyes? Are they green like the ivy clinging to the sides of the house, or the infernal moss that sticks to the walkways?"

"I believe it's my turn to ask a question. How do you manage so easily?" She hesitated, then said, "You seem to remember so much—you move about your home and the grounds without assistance. As we travel, I notice you seem aware of the placement of each tree and body of water. How do you do it?"

"Being blind, you mean?"

"Exactly." She refused to be cowed by his tone.

He didn't speak for a while. Grace feared their question game had come to an abrupt end. At last, he said, "I told you I spent my childhood summers at Roxwood, so it's more a matter of having memorized where everything is. The contents of the house remain as they were, so I'm not bumping into furniture. And since I've had occasion to visit this area often as an adult, I still recall the proximity of my favorite places."

"What about the hedge maze?"

"I believe it's my turn." But then he capitulated and said, "By the time I was twelve, I could find my way to the fountain at the center of the labyrinth with my eyes closed. I've always had the ability to 'see' without really doing so. Call it a third eye, if you will. Hugh and I often entertained ourselves as boys by wearing blindfolds and competing to see who could reach the fountain first. I always won the prize—a miniature toy soldier we shared between us.

"It became easy for me to navigate with memory instead of with my eyes." A humorless bark escaped the steel veil. "I had no idea the day would come when such an amusement was no longer a child's game."

An unexpected lump rose in her throat. She too had learned

that life could change in the span of a breath. A man loses his sight. A mother dies . . . "They are more like the ivy growing on the side of your house—the color of my eyes," she answered.

"Hmm, much more illuminating than simply green, then. Have you told your father about the changes in your circumstances?"

Again he switched subjects so fast it took Grace a moment to catch on. "I have not." Her cheeks felt warm, and she was glad he couldn't see her. "I thought it best to let him think all had gone according to plan."

"And what plan would that be?"

She glanced at him and saw he'd turned to face her, as though waiting for her to speak.

"I'd rather not say," she hedged.

"But Miss Mabry, I wish to know. You did agree to our little game, did you not?" He edged closer. "You know if it's a secret, you can confide in me. Who would I tell?"

When she remained silent, he retreated and leaned back in the seat. "Of course, if you wish to stop playing . . ." He turned his masked face toward the open window.

"It's just . . . I don't want to tell my father I got fired from the WFC," she said, enjoying their question game too much to have it end.

He turned to her again. "Would he be upset to know you'd been sacked? Is that the plan that's gone awry?"

"There is no plan," she said in exasperation. "But I . . . I cannot afford to fail and return home." Her mouth went dry as she imagined her aunt's disapproving stares, or the lofty Clarence Fowler scrutinizing her suitability much the way a collector of fine china looks for a chipped edge. "Suffice it to say, it would mean dire circumstances to my situation."

"Tell me more."

This time he leaned so close she could smell the spicy scent of his Bay Rum cologne. "No . . . I don't . . ."

"If you cannot be honest with me, Miss Mabry, how is it right I should offer you the courtesy?" He pulled away. "I tire of this game. Please, turn the car around."

Grace eased the car to a halt and scowled. He was always honest with her? Hah! Only until she asked him a question he didn't want to answer. Still, they had barely begun. She wasn't ready to return to the manor. "All right, fine," she said. "If I'm forced to return to London, I'll be placed under the watchful eye of my aunt—the spinster, remember? And if I resist, my only other option is to marry the man of my father's choosing." Staring out the window ahead at a bare-limbed tree amidst a copse of leafy oaks, she felt just as exposed by the obnoxious man beside her.

"Who is he?"

"Does it matter?" She turned to him. "When a woman isn't allowed to marry for love, they're all the same." She flexed her hands on the wheel. "A cage."

"That cage works both ways, Miss Mabry."

He sounded tired. Grace considered him a moment. "Do you speak of yourself?" she asked, forgetting her anger. She'd read about his upcoming August marriage in the *Times*. "Are you being forced to wed Miss Arnold?"

"Of all the cheeky . . . Just drive!" he said.

She gave up any further effort to be civil. With her jaw set, Grace released the brake and eased the car forward. This time she aimed for every pothole in the road.

How could he compare his situation to hers when throughout history women bore the brunt of an arranged marriage? She recalled a suffrage speech that spoke of how women were forced to breed countless children into loveless relationships, "doing their duty" while being confined to home or used as social stepping-stones for their husband's gain.

"A truce, Miss Mabry, please. My insides are churning."

Jarred from her mental tirade, Grace veered the car from an

exceptionally large fissure she'd been driving toward. "A truce," she agreed, though she wasn't certain she would still have a job when they returned.

"Thank you. Now *please* tell me more about yourself. What did you do before joining the WFC? Had you any particular interests?"

His mellow tone disarmed her. "I usually helped Da . . . that is, my father, at Swan's. While he is horribly traditional, he allowed me to update his ledgers."

"Seriously?"

"Are you being impertinent?" She glanced at him.

"Not at all. I merely applaud your ability. Not many women of my acquaintance have such qualifications. You must have a talent for it or your 'traditional' father wouldn't let you perform the task."

"Thank you." Grace was both startled and encouraged by his praise. "My real passion is writing, though I've not sold any of my work. Not yet, anyway. I recently submitted a magazine story to *Women's Weekly*, but it was turned down." She took a deep breath and said, "I refuse to give up, however. One day I plan to write a novel."

"Admirable." Then he asked, "Where are we right now?"

Grace saw only the road ahead, and beyond that, endless green valley. "I have no idea."

"Describe it to me."

She stopped the car and scanned toward the west. "I see a pasture and fences. A few trees and bushes, and I see the road ahead . . ."

"No wonder your story was rejected."

His words stung. "This is *your* part of the country, sir, not mine—"

"And I cannot see it," he reminded her. "You must describe it to me, please."

"Oh, yes, of course," she said, feeling like a dolt. "What would you like me to tell you?"

"Just like an artist captures an image on canvas, a good writer must paint a picture with words. So I ask again, where are we?"

She surveyed the valley once more, taking the time to really see it. "There is much green pasture," she maintained. "But not the type we're working with at the farm. These grasses are red-tipped and only calf-high. I also see an outcropping of gray rock among the grasses that resembles a giant nest of eggs—granite, I believe? And more of the same smooth rocks are scattered in the direction of the morning sun, to the east. Not far from that is a cluster of thin, tall, white-barked trees—"

"Birch," he said. "And from your unusual but accurate description of nesting rocks, we should be close to the turnoff for Tarryton Road. There should be a signpost . . ."

"I see it!"

He turned to her. "Very fine painting, Miss Mabry. You may have the makings of a good novelist, after all."

She beamed, genuinely grateful for his insight. He'd forced her to observe the details in what she was looking at. "There are two . . . no, three bushes to the left of the trees. I'm not much of a gardener, but each has green almond-shaped leaves and is covered in large blue flowers a bit like snowballs."

"Hydrangeas. Hugh and I used to ride our horses out here and pick them when our mother traveled to Roxwood with us. She always enjoyed their beauty."

She caught his somber tone. "Does she live in London?"

"For now, although she keeps to her rooms much of the time. My mother hasn't yet overcome her grief, either from Hugh's death or my accident."

Much like you, Lord Roxwood. "I'm sorry," Grace said instead. She sought to lighten the moment. "What are the white flowers beside the hydrangeas? Roses?"

"Yes, wild roses. Those would be the dog rose." Then he said, "My brother and I spent a lot of time climbing on those rocks. We pretended we were explorers on a mountain expedition to the Himalayas."

"In India," she said.

"You know about them?"

"Only from books. I've read about all sorts of things. You and your brother were very close, weren't you?"

He tilted his head upward. "Not a day passes that I don't think of him."

"I feel the same about my brother. I told you he's in France. I haven't received a letter from him since I arrived, though."

"Perhaps he doesn't know you're here?"

"I sent him a letter posted from Roxwood when I first got here."

"Well, sometimes it can take a while for the Army's mail to find its way to the mainland." He leaned back in his seat, resting an arm against the door's edge. "I wouldn't worry."

She hadn't considered the possibility. His words gave her hope. "I suppose it might take longer for him to receive my letter, as well. That would certainly cause delay in our correspondence."

"It's very likely. How long has your brother been overseas?"

"A little over a year. Colin enlisted in the BEF last April. I miss him terribly, but I am very proud of him. He's doing his duty. 'For God, King, and Country.'"

"You are a staunch supporter of the war, Miss Mabry?"

Grace detected his sarcasm. "I feel we must all be patriotic in whatever capacity we are able," she said primly, reminded again that he was a conscientious objector to the war. "We must win against our enemies and put our country back to rights." She paused. "Surely you must agree?"

"We got ourselves into this war because of a treaty we made

with Belgium scores of years ago," he said. "Yet the cost we've had to pay for that agreement is insurmountable."

He dropped his arm from the door. "The price is too high, in my estimation, with countless lives lost on both sides. And for those who returned home, like my brother . . ." His voice held a tremor. "In the short time Hugh remained with us, he was never the same."

Seeing his hands clench, Grace resisted an urge to reach for him. She knew the devastation of losing someone beloved. "I understand there was an accident . . . after his return?" she said gently. "I am sorry."

"An accidental drowning is what the *Times* reported." He turned to her. "The newspapers print all manner of stories, Miss Mabry. Perhaps you should send them one of yours? Make it outlandish and it will sell."

What did he mean by outlandish? Hadn't his brother's boat capsized? Grace wanted to ask him more, but thought better of it. She said instead, "I do sympathize with your loss, Lord Roxwood. Still, it doesn't change the fact we are in this war and must now fight to win and bring an end to it. Our duty must prevail."

"Ah, Miss Mabry, I've thought of a perfect occupation for you," he said. "Writing propaganda for Parliament. Recruitment posters like the one featuring our departed Lord Kitchener, which still seem to float about London." He paused. "And no one would ever be the wiser as to the truth."

"What do you mean by truth, sir? You think I merely put on an act?" His words cut at her. "You have no right to mock my loyalty to my country or to my brother just because you don't approve of the war."

He was quiet a moment. "Indeed, I do not," he said finally. "Not with regard to your brother. Your allegiance to him is commendable. Now, I wish to return to the house, please."

Grace retraced the direction they had come. Like their other outings, he said little on the return trip. She looked at him from time to time, and whether it was because she could see more clearly the man behind the mystery or she was simply accustomed to his company, the mask no longer bothered her as it had before.

∞

"Milord?"

Jack paused in eating his supper, hearing his steward's voice outside the doors to the dining room. "Yes, Edwards?"

"Excuse me, I do pardon the intrusion on your privacy, but . . . Miss Arnold has telephoned again. She insists on speaking with you."

The unflappable Edwards sounded harassed. Jack could well imagine the earful Violet Arnold had given him. His jaw tightened as he laid down his fork. "I'll be there presently."

"Ah, very good, milord."

A ghost of a smile touched his lips at the relief he heard in his steward's voice. Jack left what remained of his dinner and retied his mask before exiting to the study.

"Violet, good of you to call," Jack said as he took a seat behind his desk. He forced a measure of pleasantness into his tone.

"I've tried to reach you on the telephone several times, as if you didn't know." Her waspish voice crackled through the line. "Have you come to a decision yet?"

Jack sighed. Right to the point, then. "Crying off the engagement? I haven't had time to give it much thought."

"What, too busy scaring off the locals? Or are you still hiding away in your rooms? I would imagine you've had scads of time to think, while I on the other hand want a *life*, Jack Benningham. And I plan to live it."

"So, *you're* breaking off our engagement?"

"Oh, you'd like that, wouldn't you? Then you can paint me as the heartless woman who abandoned her poor, crippled fiancé in his time of need."

"I would hardly call myself a cripple," he snarled, losing the battle to control his temper. "Though being blinded to your beauty is *indeed* a misfortune."

"Spare me!" she snapped. "This engagement was doomed from the start. Surely you can't be so thick as to ignore that?"

"How could I?" *Especially when you remind me at every opportunity*, he thought.

Despite his blindness, Jack saw the issue more clearly than his fiancée ever would. Violet Arnold surrounded herself in the frivolities of fashion, fetes, and following the latest entries into *Burke's Peerage*, but cared little for the crass realities of money, contracts, and the price for a coronet.

"So? What is your answer?" she asked.

"I'll have to think on it a bit more. I'll let you know."

"Oh, you're impossible!" Then she hung up on him.

Jack's heart pounded as he carefully replaced the receiver. He leaned back in his chair, taking a deep breath. By the time Violet had arrived in London with her father, Diamond Princesses—the wealthy, upper-crust American debutantes seeking titles in exchange for money—had become a thing of the past. Still, Jack recalled his stoic father actually smiling when Jack's mother announced a wealthy oilman from America had attended the Sorensens' fete and discreetly asked after Hugh Benningham's marital status.

It had been a last-ditch means to save Stonebrooke and all its lands. Violet and her father soon became regular guests at the Benningham home. A month later, Hugh announced his engagement to Miss Arnold, and her father in good faith advanced the earl an enormous sum to pay off Stonebrooke's pressing debt.

Violet seemed happy and gay back then, and Jack was convinced she'd actually cared for his brother. But then Hugh died, and while she grieved, her father had negotiated the uglier ramifications, reminding the earl of money already paid on account.

Jack had understood his duty. After a proper mourning period, he and Violet were engaged. It was hardly a love match, as she had continued to grieve for his brother and Jack felt no real affection toward her.

He leaned forward, resting his elbows on the desk. He remembered the last time Violet had seen him. Marcus was with him at hospital that day as the surgeon removed the bandages. Jack had remained completely still, sweat running down his back as he prayed to a distant God to give him back his sight. Time froze. He'd felt cool air sting his tender flesh . . . while the darkness remained to crush in on him.

Outside the hospital room, Violet's imperious tone was giving orders to the nurse to speak with him. The door had burst open, and he heard her booted heels clipping smartly across the linoleum floor. The room went silent. Then a guttural cry followed by a sound much like a bolt of cloth hitting the floor. A flurry of commotion and noises ensued. Violet had fainted.

Jack realized then the kind of monster she'd been chained to. Yet despite her pleas to be free of him, it was her father who refused to let go. Mr. Arnold had demanded repayment of his money or the coronet for his daughter. Without sufficient funds, Jack had only the latter to offer, and Stonebrooke must be saved. He and Violet remained trapped.

He returned to the dining room and heard the clatter of dishes. "Oh, excuse me, milord, I was just coming to clear," Mrs. Riley exclaimed.

"That's all right, Mrs. Riley. How about coffee?"

"It will be my pleasure. And if I may be so bold, milord, your

124

appetite is much improved. The fresh air each morning must be doing you a world of good. Now, I'll get that coffee for you."

Jack seated himself at the table. The outdoors *had* improved his appetite for food, as well as providing him with the chance to know Grace Mabry a bit better.

His spirits lifted, recalling their morning outing together. She wasn't one to faint at the sight of him, nor did she allow his looks to affect her many opinions. A smile touched his lips. She'd been ready to do battle for him with the villagers on Saturday.

He considered, too, her proselytizing to him—about God and having faith and any other tidbit she'd gleaned from the good reverend's sermon. Was her piety part of an act . . . or had she meant what she'd said? She'd seemed quite animated as well during their discussion about the war and doing one's duty. In fact, she'd made her views quite clear. Was it all a sham merely to gain his trust?

Jack rubbed at his chin, frowning. He didn't think so. Her passion for both causes seemed genuine enough.

Mrs. Riley returned with his coffee and served him a cup before leaving the room. Once she'd closed the doors, he lifted the mesh of his mask and sipped carefully, the hot, fragrant liquid scorching him. Much like Miss Mabry's temper, he thought, still feeling each and every pothole she'd purposely struck that morning. A chuckle escaped him, a sound rusty and foreign to his ears.

In truth, as each day passed in her company, Jack found it more difficult tying her to any treachery on her father's part. He weighed Patrick Mabry's bribery of a clerk against her candid talk about the doomed choices she faced back in London, much like his own with Violet. And he compared Marcus's theory that she searched out proof, which no longer existed, with that of Grace Mabry's dreams of becoming a novelist. Such contradictions left him stymied. Either she was genuine or she was twice as crafty as Mata Hari.

9

"Where shall we go today, Lord Roxwood?"

Jack sat in the Daimler and deliberated a moment before he said, "I'll let you choose today, Miss Mabry. Once we arrive, you can describe the place, and we'll see how well I'm able to pinpoint our location."

"Margate?"

"No," he said, his pulse accelerating. "I do not know that city well. Choose from one of the country roads closer to the estate. You understand? I do not wish to go to Margate." His insides clenched at the thought of venturing into such a public place. The village had been difficult enough, knowing how they stared at him.

"What if we become lost on one of these country roads?"

Her anxious tone drew his attention. "You had better make certain your powers of description are adequate. Or shall I have Edwards accompany us?"

"No, that won't be necessary."

Jack heard her resolve an instant before the car leaped forward along the graveled drive. He sensed her turning left moments later. Assuming they had passed the gatehouse, away from the direction of Margate, he eased back in his seat.

"I know I would have enjoyed Margate."

Her consuming interest piqued his own. "You seem keen to visit that city, Miss Mabry. Have you ever been there on holiday?"

"No, but I've seen photochromic prints of the harbor and jetty. And London's National Gallery has on display several oil paintings of the coastline by the artist J. M. W. Turner. Margate looks beautiful." She paused, then added, "I expected to go, but now things have changed."

"How so?" Jack leaned forward in the seat. Had he missed a chance to get at the truth? He could still have her turn around, and discover why she seemed so bent on going to Margate.

He wrestled with his discomfort—and lost. Frustration coursed through him. Perhaps Marcus was right to doubt his ability for the task. "What's changed?" he asked.

"The WFC is delivering hay to the train station at Margate today," she said. "I would have been assigned to drive the team, but Lucy's taken my place. It's not likely I'll ever get to go."

"Ah, yes, they move the bales by rail to Folkestone and then ship them overseas." Her reasons seemed innocent, after all.

A dog's loud barking made him grip the door's edge. "We're entering Roxwood?" He could hear a woman hawking fresh bread to his right, doubtless the old crone Maeve, who had been selling loaves from her cart since he was a boy.

"Correct," Grace replied beside him. "But that's far too easy a test for you. We're going beyond the village."

As the Daimler made slow progress along the cobbled main street, Jack imagined all eyes on him. "It truly is a charming little town," she said, and he could tell she tried to put him at ease. "With the prettiest colored shops—apple reds and forest greens, with a few gray structures the color of the sky just before a good rain—"

"Thank you, Miss Mabry. But as I already know where we are, your colorful descriptions, while illuminating, aren't necessary."

"Fine, I won't say another word until we get to our destination. Then let's see how well you do."

Jack smiled as he envisioned her feathers ruffling. "My success will rely solely on the accuracy of your description," he said, releasing his grip on the door. The sounds on the street dimmed, and he perceived the curiosity of onlookers. Even Maeve had stopped her hawking. Only the dog seemed oblivious as it continued to bark.

Freak. No doubt they all gaped at him, just as they had last week. He considered Grace Mabry, how after the first morning she'd questioned him about the mask, she'd never mentioned it again.

The Daimler picked up speed, and Jack knew they had left the village. The car's motion and the warm country air lulled him into a drowsy state. He began dreaming the same nightmare he often experienced—those moments before the man disguised as Chaplin dove over the side of the ship. And Jack, watching in fury, unable to go after him . . . then turning to seek out the captain . . . an explosion, followed by blackness—

A hand touched his shoulder. Jack jerked forward in the seat.

"Are you all right?"

"Perfectly," he said, his voice groggy.

"You fell asleep?"

"Just dozing," he said. "It's a very warm morning and I didn't sleep well last night."

"Did you have a nightmare?"

"Please pay attention to the road, Miss Mabry." He didn't want her prying into his inmost thoughts. "Have we arrived at this destination of yours yet?"

"We have." Her voice came across low and teasing, and Jack found he liked it when she spoke to him that way. "It's a good thing you fell asleep and didn't detect all of my turns. This will prove to be your greatest challenge."

He smiled, enjoying their little game. "All well and good, Miss Mabry, but you must describe our location as though you're writing a story for *Women's Weekly*. I'll pretend I'm the editor and I won't settle for mere trees and bushes."

"Agreed." He heard her car door open. Moments later she opened his. "Would you care to stretch your legs, Mr. Editor?"

He slid from the seat to stand against what felt like hard-packed earth. The sun beat down against his shoulders despite his layers of clothing. Without the car's roof as protection, the mask soon became uncomfortably hot, as well.

"Ready?" she asked. He could imagine her scouring their surroundings for markers.

She cleared her throat and began, "The road is little more than a well-traveled horse track, arcing wide across an endless green pasture. On one side, weathered, crisscrossed timbers hem in dozens of black-faced sheep grazing with their lambs beneath the warm rays of sun. The other side opens out to more grassland, and a smallish, oblong pool of mossy-green water, surrounded by three majestic willow trees. The pool is fed by a narrow creek, stumbling over large white rocks and running off in the distance." She paused. "Well, can you guess where we are?"

Jack was amazed at how much she'd improved on her descriptive passages. She made it almost too easy for him. "You've just described the northeast edge of Miller's farm near Barden. A few minutes ago, we would have passed the gate and a sign that read *Welcome all travelers*. Am I correct?"

"Very good." She sounded equally impressed. "Does this mean you'll purchase my story 'Miller's Farm' for publication, sir?"

Hearing the laughter in her tone, he was pierced with a

longing to see her face. "Most assuredly, Miss Mabry," he said. "I will publish it straightaway."

"Thank you." She did laugh then before adding, "Are you by chance smiling under there?"

How was it she surprised him at every turn? "And if I was?" A sudden desire to show her battled his fear of her rejection.

"I should like to see it, of course." Her voice held a hint of exasperation. "I did catch a glimpse of you in the hedge maze, after all. What I mean is that you have quite a nice smile, when you're not growling at the world."

She enjoyed his smile? Still his fear won out. "I believe I have more to growl about."

"Why is that? When you possess wealth, title, and enough land to start your own country?"

He scoffed at her naïveté. "What is any of it without my sight? Lands, estates, even my prizewinning rose garden. What purpose do they serve when I cannot see them?"

"You can smell your fragrant roses, sir. As for your lands, they provide the good food on your plate at table. You warm yourself by the fire with wood felled and chopped from your forests. And you can do this at any one of your estates. Simply because you're here right now and not in some muddy trench in France is something to smile about, don't you think?"

"Is this the part where I'm supposed to feel ashamed of my attitude?" How dare she minimize his injuries against his greater material wealth! "I hate to disappoint you, Miss Mabry, but I'd beggar myself in an instant to glimpse another sunset or to watch the way the wind and sun dance together like diamonds tossed across Camden Pond. To appreciate the sight of a beautiful woman . . ." His thoughts returned to his goddess in green, so long ago. "I'm afraid living in darkness has obliterated any gratitude I might have felt."

"My intent was not to shame you, sir," she said quietly. "I

only remind you that you do have blessings. And you have gifts—your remarkable sense of direction and the knowledge of your surroundings. I doubt any could navigate as well in the same circumstances."

"Yes, in the same circumstances!" he snapped, breaking the tenuous bond between them. Was he so pathetic, so starved for company and the outside world, he was willing to ignore who her father was and what he'd done? How would she react to the knowledge? Or did she already know? "I hope you never have to endure it, Miss Mabry. Now take me home."

Back at the farm, Grace found Becky waiting for her.

"Are the others back from Margate?" she asked briskly, still frustrated over her outing with Lord Roxwood.

"No," said Becky. "And Clare and Mrs. Vance are mending tarpaulins in the village, so you'll work with me." The red-cheeked woman pointed toward a table and a pair of washtubs beneath the lean-to attached to the barn. Another washtub filled with steaming water sat over a lit brazier just beyond the overhang.

"The gamekeeper's killed the poultry, but the kitchen boy went home sick. Mrs. Riley wants us to clean them." The oolong-colored eyes pierced hers. "Ever plucked a chicken before?"

Grace swallowed and shook her head. The only time she'd encountered chicken was in the form of *coq au vin*, or the *fricassee* that Amanda, the Mabrys' cook, served them at supper. "Aren't the Land Army girls supposed to do that?" Her voice had raised a notch. "When will they arrive?"

Becky shrugged. "They're not here now, are they? So we've been volunteered . . . again." She grinned. "Come on, I'll teach you how."

Grace followed Becky to the table. Her breath caught at the sight of so many dead birds piled high in one of the washtubs.

The other tub held water. "Plucking chickens is easier than you think." Becky grabbed one of the birds by its feet and took it to the tub of simmering hot water. "Just dunk it two or three times to loosen the feathers, like this," she said, illustrating for Grace. She returned to the table with the steaming bird and began removing feathers with ease. "Go ahead. Give it a try."

Grace went to the washtub and gingerly took hold of a chicken. She held it away from her and walked toward the tub of hot water, repeating the process Becky had just shown her. A smell like wet dog rose to her nostrils, and she nearly gagged as she made her way back to the table with the soggy, steaming bird. Taking up the place across from her co-worker, she began pulling feathers.

"Good job!" Becky beamed as Grace held up her first perfectly plucked chicken. "Looks like you've been doing this all your life."

"Why, thank you," Grace said, warmed by her praise. Oddly the smell of the wet feathers wasn't nearly as overpowering as it had been before. She laughed. "This is definitely not something they teach you in finishing school."

Becky showed her how to tie off the bird's feet and hang it from one of the nails protruding from a joist inside the lean-to. "We'll take them to the larder when we finish," she explained. "They need to hang a few days to tenderize the meat."

They continued plucking chickens, with Grace's thoughts returning to her morning with Lord Roxwood—yet another pleasant outing turned sour because she couldn't keep her tongue in her head. Determined to put it from her mind, she glanced up at Becky and asked, "So how did you end up in the Women's Forage Corps? When Agnes and I arrived, you said your family lived near Margate. Did you hear about joining there?"

Becky nodded. "My family lives in the village of Wreston,

but my pa's a fisherman out of Margate. He also works at the train station, loading freight when the fish aren't running. I used to walk into town and bring him supper. While I was there, I'd speak with a few of the locals and that's how I learned they needed women to help with farming and baling hay."

She paused to retrieve another chicken, then took it to the pot. "We didn't live on a farm, but I figured I was strong and could learn to do the work," she called before returning to the table. "I'd also be helping out my family. With nine brothers and sisters, my pa has to work hard to make ends meet, especially with our appetites."

Grace had noticed Becky's second and third helpings at supper. Yet she kept silent. Hadn't her blabbering already gotten her into enough trouble today?

"I do like to eat," Becky said matter-of-factly, reading her thoughts as she grabbed another fistful of feathers. "Working at a farm instead of a factory means better food. Why, I've never seen so much in my life!" She held up the chicken she'd been plucking. "Even the Army rations taste good, and Mr. Tillman gives us all the fresh fruit and vegetables we can eat. I get to go to bed with a full belly each night and send money home." She glanced up. "My younger sister, Ruthie, catches a lift to Roxwood every other Sunday. I meet her after church and give her my earnings to take to our mum."

There was more to Becky Simmons than she'd first imagined, Grace decided with admiration. "Do you have plans for after the war?"

Becky shook her head. "We've been fighting for so long, I hadn't stopped to think about what I'll do when it's all over."

"One day our soldiers will defeat the Germans," Grace said and tried to quell her anxiety over Colin's lack of correspondence. "You'll have to consider your future. You're a smart woman to weigh all the benefits before deciding to join the

Women's Forage Corps." She paused. "You bake the most marvelous yeast rolls and barley bread. Why, your crumpets with butter and jam are the best I've ever tasted. Have you considered owning a bakery?"

"How did you know?" Becky gasped. "I used to dream about having my own shop. I'd bake fresh breads, meat pasties, sausage rolls, scones, even tea cakes just like the bakery in Margate, only my shop would be in my family's village. That way I could be close and take care of them." Determination lit the oolong-colored eyes. "I'd make sure they never went hungry."

"There's nothing to stop you, Becky."

She snorted. "I've little schooling and not a farthing to spare. I can bake, but it won't buy me a shop."

"Women's suffrage will change that," Grace insisted. "Once we win the right to vote, we'll enact laws to help more women like you get the means to start a business. You could go back to school if you wish, or apprentice at the Margate Bakery and one day take over the running of their shop."

When Becky seemed uncertain, Grace added, "Anything is possible, you need only try. With your wits and your fearlessness for hard work, I believe you shall succeed."

Becky smiled. "I hadn't thought about the dream for a long while. But when you put it like that, maybe I do have a chance."

"No doubt about it." Grace reached for another chicken in the tub. "Who would have thought one day I'd be plucking chickens?"

They gazed at each other over the enormous pile of feathers and laughed.

"So, how was Margate?" Grace asked at supper that night. Snatching another one of Becky's delicious rolls from the basket, she broke it apart and dunked it into her soup, feeling freer than she had in a long while. Not only had she plucked dead chickens all afternoon, but now she was being "coarse" while eating her food. Da would have a fit at such vulgarity!

"It's a busy town with miles of seashore," Agnes said, before tucking into another spoonful of Ida Vance's hearty bean and vegetable soup.

"Yes, and we met more WFC women at the station, who re-weighed and loaded our b-bales onto freight cars," Lucy added. "And such sights in the bustling place! There was a kind of amusement park next to the railway, but I didn't get to go in and see it." She glanced toward Agnes. "I had to wait with the horses while Mr. Tillman searched for Agnes."

Grace paused in taking a bite of her biscuit to stare at her maid. "What happened?"

"This will sound silly, miss, but . . . I got lost," Agnes said, her cheeks turning a bright hue. She stirred the soup in her bowl. "Lucy said Merry hadn't eaten this morning and that the mare seemed sluggish on the way to town. She wanted to try giving her some ginger powder, so I offered to fetch it from the Margate chemist while she stayed with the horses."

"Mr. Tillman went to buy a new belt for the steam baler at the hardware shop," Lucy supplied. "When he returned and Agnes was still gone, he went to find her."

"I must have taken a wrong turn outside the chemist's shop," Agnes said. "For about an hour it felt like I walked in circles. I was so relieved when Mr. Tillman finally found me." She shook her head. "I can't believe it. In the last few weeks it seems like we've traveled over half the country, yet I ended up turned around within a few city blocks."

The others smiled as Grace reached for Agnes's hand. "Well, I'm glad all ended well. But surely you must have been fright-ened being gone all that time?" She recalled her own harried experience getting lost in the hedge maze.

Agnes nodded, all humor gone. Grace could feel her maid's

hand trembling beneath her own. "I admit, it was an alarming experience—one I don't wish to repeat."

"Well, Pierpont, you had an adventure today," Mrs. Vance said. "Next time, you must ask directions." She turned to Grace. "Mabry, Simmons tells me you did a fine job plucking chickens today. I think you were meant for farming."

This brought a round of chuckles from the others, and even Agnes smiled.

"I'd hardly make a decent farmer," Grace said before a yawn escaped her. "Though I am learning the meaning of hard work. I don't think I've slept so well in a long time."

∽

Grace couldn't sleep that night. The others had gone to bed an hour ago, while she lay awake in the semidarkness. Already she'd gone over her journal notes twice in her mind, pleased over her colorfully detailed passage about her adventurous chicken plucking that afternoon. She'd also written of Agnes's ordeal at Margate. She embellished her notes a bit for a future story, beginning with how her friend had been kidnapped by pirates, but then changed her mind. Instead she penned how Agnes found her family among the Belgian refugees arriving daily to Britain's shores. They convinced her to move north with them, and no one at Roxwood ever heard from her again.

Her forehead creased. A happy ending for Agnes and her family, perhaps, but what about those she left behind? Grace hadn't forgotten the photograph in Agnes's bag. The knowledge that her friend withheld secrets from her still hurt.

She rolled over and again closed her eyes, yet her mind refused to sleep. The entry where she'd written about her morning outing with Jack Benningham sprang into her thoughts.

Grace smiled into the darkness, recalling his promise to publish her story "Miller's Farm." Even if he had only been teasing, as a novelist one day, she knew his endorsement would most assuredly help.

The harsh exchange they shared afterward came to mind, and her smile faded. He'd been so angry, yet she only meant to point out his life wasn't over simply because he couldn't see. Jack Benningham seemed eaten up by bitterness, his convalescence more a means to turn away from his family and the society of his friends. Perhaps even his faith, if he'd ever had any.

Grace sighed against her pillow. Jack Benningham needed God in his life. She fancied pulling up with the Daimler tomorrow morning and whisking him off to church and one of Reverend Price's sermons. Of course, he would likely fire her on the spot. Well, he couldn't stop her praying for his miserable, pocked soul . . .

The sound of a bed creaking nearby caught her attention.

Someone was moving. Grace turned her head, and with her eyes accustomed to the dark she spied the silhouette of her chicken-plucking companion. Becky Simmons gathered her trench coat and a pair of boots before making her way stealthily toward the bedroom door.

The woman hardly needed her boots to visit the indoor privy. Curiosity burned in Grace as she, too, rose from her bed and grabbed similar clothing. She intended to follow Becky downstairs, but before she reached the bottom step, the front door to the gatehouse had opened and closed.

Shoving her feet into the boots, Grace rushed outside. Becky rode her bicycle toward the farm. The last streaks of light had faded from the sky, the half-moon glowing brightly. Grace hopped on a bicycle and rode in pursuit.

What was Becky doing? Her mind raced, along with her feet on the pedals. Did she have some secret assignation? Perhaps a boy from the village, or one of the young soldiers returning home.

Grace pedaled faster. Becky was going to open her own bakery one day. The last thing she needed was to get into trouble.

Becky stopped at the barn. She leaned her bicycle against the siding and turned to scan the area. Then she walked past the overhang and disappeared from view.

She *was* meeting someone! Grace pedaled up to the barn and abandoned her bicycle. Following past the chicken coops and pigpen, she saw Becky enter a familiar cottage-sized stone structure beyond the vegetable garden.

She was meeting her sweetheart . . . in the game larder?

Grace edged toward the entrance. The door was closed, so she moved around to the side where a window allowed her to see. Even in darkness, she spied the stocky woman removing three of the birds they'd hung earlier.

Dawning struck, and without further consideration, Grace went inside. "Becky, please stop."

She heard a series of thuds as the chickens hit the stone floor.

"Grace?" Panic laced Becky's whisper. "You followed me here?"

"Your sister, Ruthie, comes to town tomorrow, doesn't she?" Grace said by way of an answer. "You're going to send those chickens home with her?"

A sob tore through the dark. "Lord Roxwood has so much," she cried. "And the last time Ruthie was here, she told me Pa hurt his back at the freight station. He can't work. I didn't think anyone would notice three chickens gone."

"God would notice, Becky. And so would you." Grace spoke gently. "Please, don't do this. Stealing is wrong, regardless of how many chickens Lord Roxwood has in his possession. You must have faith. Things will turn around."

"How, Grace?" Becky's tone held a ragged edge. "What I send home barely helps."

"You're being tested right now, don't you see? Is your peace of mind worth three chickens?"

"It is," Becky said in a mutinous tone. "Having peace is fine when your pa is rich. But mine is poor, and you have no idea what it's like to worry if you'll have food enough to eat."

"You're right, I've never gone hungry. But I know what it's like to be frightened. I also know fear can sometimes make us do things we regret." An image of her mother's lovely face, her look of hurt, flashed in Grace's mind. "Afterward we are never the same."

"I can't imagine you having any regrets."

Grace tried to blink away the image. "I'm human enough. I've had my share." Then sensing Becky's capitulation, she added, "Tell me, will you be able to sit in church tomorrow with a clear conscience . . . or not?"

A shadow of movement caught her eye as Becky bent to retrieve the chickens and then rehung them from the ceiling hooks. "All right," she said tiredly. "We'll try it your way. I just hope faith will put food on my family's table."

"You won't regret it," Grace said, relieved. "Now, let's get back before we're missed."

Becky followed her outside, and the two returned to the gate-house and slipped upstairs.

Lying in bed, Grace stared into the darkness a long while before she finally closed her eyes. She smiled, knowing how she might help Becky's faith along.

10

Jack was about to depart the study with Edwards when Knowles intercepted him.

"Pardon, milord, but the new physician has arrived."

More quackery. "Take him into the library," Jack instructed. "I'll be there presently. By the way, have you spoken with Miss Mabry?"

"She called for you earlier, milord. As you instructed, I informed her you had business this morning and wouldn't be available."

Jack gave a jerk of his head, then heard Knowles's retreat. "Who is this doctor, Edwards?"

"Daniel Strom, milord. When Dr. Black went to the Front, he took over his patients."

Jack's jaw tightened as he strode toward the library. He wearied of these sessions, little more than a lecture and a bit of hand-holding over what he already knew—he was blind, and his scars were healing. It seemed a complete waste of time.

"Lord Roxwood. I'm Dr. Strom, from Broad Oak, near Sturry. It's a privilege to meet with you," the voice of an older man called to Jack as he entered the library and closed the doors.

"Dr. Strom." Jack spoke with forced calm. "I apologize you had to come all this way. As you can see, I'm perfectly capable, despite my blindness. Your time is better spent helping your patients."

"*You* are one of my patients," Strom said. "And it's not so far. I'm happy to be here. Why don't you sit on the divan and take off your mask so I can conduct an examination. By the way, is that the new splatter mask I've read about? The one our tank drivers at the Front will soon be wearing?"

Jack nodded. "A prototype." He loosened the ties and removed the mask. The air felt cool against his sensitive flesh. "Having a friend in the Admiralty does pay off."

"Indeed."

Jack heard a chair being dragged across the carpet and then sensed Strom directly in front of him. "Before he left, Dr. Black told me you always wear the mask, though he didn't prescribe it to you. Why is that?"

"He instructed I should keep my skin out of direct sunlight while it heals. The mask was my solution. I was also told to wear a layer of gauze beneath to prevent irritation."

"You're not wearing the gauze now."

"The procedure grew tiresome. The mask no longer bothers my skin."

"But why wear it indoors?" Strom had begun to prod with a finger the tender flesh surrounding Jack's eyes. "Being out of direct light, the air would certainly help you heal faster."

"Because I prefer it," Jack said, pulling back from Strom's examination. He'd endured enough jabbing and poking by doctors while he was in hospital. "And why should I subject my household staff to this?" He pointed at his face.

"Your scars aren't all that ghastly," Strom said gently. "Now, I'd like to examine your eyes. If you'll allow me, I'll add drops to dilate the pupils."

Jack tipped his head back. "Steady," Strom said, and Jack felt him pull back each lid and bathe his eyes in cool liquid.

"I'll be using a lighted ophthalmoscope to examine the retina," the doctor explained.

"I've endured this procedure before. For a country doctor, you seem well versed in optometry."

"With the war on I've found it necessary to broaden my range of medical skills. Now, let me take a look."

He held still while Strom did his work. For a fleeting instant, Jack thought he detected a flash—was it light?—but then it was gone.

"Very good," Strom said when he'd finished. Jack refrained from saying anything. Surely he'd imagined it.

The doctor's bag closed with a snap. "I don't want to give you false hope, Lord Roxwood, but I cannot see any retinal damage. It's possible that with time you might regain your sight."

"You're right, Strom. I don't want your hope, false or otherwise." Jack quelled his anger. "I'm blind and I've accepted it. The price for being a bit too . . . careless one night."

He'd intended the remark to corroborate the Admiralty's cover story, so Jack was surprised when Strom said, "Dr. Black told me about the explosion aboard ship. Your wounds were not caused through carelessness, Lord Roxwood, but because of your duty to king and country. And though the world doesn't know it, for those of us who do, we are thankful and proud for your service to the Crown."

Jack thought of Hugh and how the war ultimately destroyed him. "Sometimes, gratitude isn't enough. And pride can be fatal. Doesn't the Bible mention something about it 'going before destruction, a haughty spirit before a fall'?"

"Proverbs sixteen, verse eighteen," Strom said. "Do you consider your actions that night prideful, my lord?"

Jack let out a rusty laugh. "That night and every other, Doctor. I had a rogue's reputation to uphold, after all. So while I was engaged to one woman, I flirted with another—a bewitching green-eyed beauty whose loveliness distracted me and nearly led to my demise. And the price for that arrogance?" Jack reached for his mask on the divan beside him. "Aside from my present condition, my fiancée wishes to be rid of me, while those enchanting green eyes I spoke about live only in my memory."

"You cannot know the future, my lord," Strom said. "There is always hope."

"Then you can hope for both of us," Jack said. "I'll defer mine until it bears fruit." He rose from the divan. "Please understand, Doctor. Being ostracized because of one's appearance is a difficult burden. I don't care to add to it the weight of more disappointment."

Strom said nothing. Jack then heard the chair being dragged back across the room.

"We're finished here, my lord," Strom said finally, and Jack retied his mask in place. "But please, don't discount yourself. There's more to you than a few scars. I'm certain many appreciate you. Your staff, for instance. Perhaps you simply need to get out and start enjoying life again. Keeping to this house all the time can do more harm than good to the spirit. In fact, on Saturday there's to be a dance held in the village, a welcome-home celebration for the chaps on leave from the war. As the tenants rely on your baronetcy for their livelihood, it would be a good show of support if you attended."

"I appreciate what you're trying to do, Dr. Strom. And for your information, I do not keep to the house. I've hired a chauffeur, who drives me daily into the country. As Miss Mabry's conversation keeps me adequately entertained, I'm in no need of dancing."

"Ah, you've met our Grace, then."

Jack froze. "You know her?"

"I should hope so. Her mother was my cousin, though I haven't seen Grace since last year, and her brother even longer, before he went off to war. The Women's Forage Corps supervisor, Mrs. Vance, tells me she is doing well enough. Would you agree?"

"Yes," Jack said slowly. "Why haven't you been to see her?"

Strom chuckled. "Part of her father's pact with me, my lord. I've been charged with keeping an eye on her. Patrick Mabry is most anxious about his daughter's safety. His concern is warranted, what with all the bombing in and around London in the past few months. Apparently she finally wore him down to allow her some occupation to aid in the war effort. When he dissuaded her from the more dangerous jobs, she settled on leaving home to work at baling hay for horses. He agreed, but arranged for her to work in this county so as to be near family.

"Since I have patients here, I occasionally check in with Mrs. Vance to see how Grace is getting on—without her knowledge, of course. I'm afraid she'd be angry if she knew I was checking up on her at her father's behest. You won't tell her, my lord?"

"Certainly not." Jack felt lighthearted and grinned at the irony. Grace Mabry could hardly be a spy when she was being spied upon. She'd merely been maneuvered to Kent in order to be near her cousin. And Strom's story corroborated Grace's explanation of her father being conventional and overprotective. It all seemed to fit. Apparently even traitors loved their daughters. "Do you plan to avoid Miss Mabry the entire time she is at Roxwood?"

"No, I intend to renew our acquaintance at the dance. Mrs. Vance told me yesterday she'll allow the girls to attend. I hope you change your mind and decide to be there as well, Lord Roxwood. Our boys would appreciate it."

"I'll think on it." After his last drive into the village with Grace, Jack was reluctant to once again confront the gawkers of Roxwood.

"I'll take my leave, then, my lord. You're healing nicely. I'll recheck you in a fortnight, but do try and keep the mask off when you can. The air will accelerate healing."

"Thank you, Dr. Strom." Jack extended a hand, eager to send the doctor on his way.

He planned to fetch Grace, as they still had the entire afternoon at their disposal. Breathing deep beneath his mask, Jack smiled. Perhaps he would surprise her with a trip to Margate, after all. As before, the thought of being seen in such a public place made his insides clench. But for Grace, he would make an exception.

⸎

The women were lunching in the south pasture when they caught sight of Mr. Tillman riding toward them on Merry.

"The ginger powder you put into the mare's feed seems to be working wonders, Lucy," Grace said, seated across from her on a bale of hay. "It's hard to believe Merry was so listless a few days ago."

Lucy dusted bread crumbs from her uniform. "I thought she might be suffering from a sour stomach. My mum used to fix us ginger t-tea, and it always worked."

"You've got a real gift in those hands," Grace said, then winced as she flexed her fingers. "Right now mine are stiff as whalebone after cutting and tying baling wire all morning."

"At least you had those." Seated beside her on the bale, Clare looked pointedly at the handheld wire cutters resting in Grace's lap.

Grace tilted her chin and quipped back, "I could have used my teeth."

Agnes gave a snort of hyena laughter that caused a burst of hilarity from the others. "Oh, miss, that would be a sight to see," she said as the amusement died down. Wiping at her eyes, she was grinning, and it pleased Grace to see her so happy and carefree.

"I wish she had used her teeth," Clare said, winking at Agnes. "Then she wouldn't be able to chew the last piece of Becky's vegetable pie." She gave Grace a playful nudge. "How did you manage to get your hands on it, Mabry?"

Becky sat atop the baler. Grace noticed her apple-cheeked features tense. "The pie was my reward," she said smoothly, "for helping Becky with the chickens."

In truth, she *had* dissuaded Becky from stealing two or three of them. Grace considered it providential that Reverend Price chose yesterday morning to sermonize on the perils of stealing. Becky sat next to her in the pew and kept reaching to squeeze her hand. Grace didn't know if it was due to the money envelope she'd left under Becky's pillow that morning or the ability to sit in church with a clear conscience. Either way, after her younger sister, Ruthie, departed with the funds, Becky had returned to the gatehouse to bake a vegetable pie just for Grace.

"Becky, next t-time you need help, I'm available," Lucy piped up. "And I love your buttermilk scones."

The others chuckled while Becky looked relieved her secret was safe.

"Miss Mabry!"

Grace was still smiling when she turned to see Mr. Tillman swinging down from the saddle. Approaching, he called out, "Mr. Edwards says you're to come up to the manor. Seems his lordship wants an outing, after all."

"Right now?" She quickly tucked the cutters into her pocket and rose from the bale, brushing a few errant pieces of straw from her sweaty uniform. "Do I have time to change?"

"I was told *now*." The farmer frowned, adding, "If I were you, I wouldn't dawdle."

"Go on," Mrs. Vance said. "We'll see you at supper."

Grace said her good-byes and struck out on foot across the field, her spirits lifting with each step. When Knowles sent her away earlier, she hadn't realized how much she looked forward to her outings with Lord Roxwood of late, particularly their guessing game. Perhaps this afternoon they would return to the place he called Eden, his favorite spot. She hoped that she could paint her words well enough to do the wondrous scene justice.

She also intended to unmask him.

Heart thumping, Grace headed toward the garage. The notion had been on her mind for some time. She planned to proceed slowly, of course, but once Lord Roxwood stopped hiding, she felt he could start to accept his situation and begin living again.

Grace soon had the car running and brought it around front. Ascending the steps, she was surprised to see Knowles already waiting for her.

"I need a hat," she told him.

"Pardon?"

"Lord Roxwood will need something with a wide brim. Direct sunlight isn't healthy for his skin. Perhaps you can find something?"

From above the hawkish nose, his rheumy gaze studied her. Finally he stepped back and allowed her entrance. "If you'll wait in the foyer, I'll see what his valet can produce."

Stepping inside, Grace tried to bolster her courage. Getting Lord Roxwood to remove the mask wouldn't be easy, but despite his anger on Saturday, she felt their relationship had shifted. He'd begun to trust her and had revealed more about himself during the past week.

"Will this suit your purposes, Miss Mabry?"

Knowles held out a wide-brimmed straw hat, the same one Lord Roxwood had worn on the day they met in the hedge maze.

"That will do very nicely, Knowles. Thank you." She took it from him.

"Ah, Miss Mabry, you've arrived," Lord Roxwood called from the stairs. Today he wore a loose-fitting brown sack jacket and slacks, with a white shirt and blue-striped tie. Grace thought he looked quite dashing—except for the mask. On his head perched his usual brown felt motoring cap.

"Indeed, Lord Roxwood, and I'm eager to get started plying you with new prose as to our whereabouts on the road," she said in a cheeky tone.

He chuckled behind the steel mesh—much to the butler's delight. Grace noticed the smile forming on the curmudgeonly man's lips. Renewed determination for her mission filled her. The mask was horrid, but more important, it hid the man beneath. She wanted to *see* him smile or frown or look cross at her, scars and all. To feel herself in the company of another warm-blooded human being, and not the cold and creaturely disguise he clung to. She only hoped he would grant her request.

"Margate?" Grace felt a rush of excitement as she turned in the seat to face Lord Roxwood. "You . . . you wish to go there today?"

"I do." Seated beside her in the Daimler, he leaned back against the seat. "Of course, if you don't get this car moving, we aren't going anywhere."

She readily obeyed, and he said, "Turn right and stay on this drive until you see a cross sign for Canterbury Road."

"How long will it take us?"

"The entire trip shouldn't take longer than three hours. I've been told the sky is clear and the wind feels mild, so we'll make a good afternoon of it."

Margate! Thoughts of Eden fled as Grace looked forward

to the drive ahead. She'd never imagined he would grant her wish to visit the place.

Making the required turns, she observed the now-familiar landmarks: rows of plane trees and verdant pastures, the occasional flocks of sheep around a thatched barn or cottage. She made a point to describe what she saw as they drove along, hoping he would tell her more about the meaning each place held for him. He didn't disappoint, regaling her with tales of how he and his brother rode their ponies along the country roads and then stopped to swim in the nearest pond, of afternoons spent fishing or foraging for small game with their bows and arrows.

"Of all your lands, it sounds as if Roxwood holds your happiest memories."

"It does," he agreed. "My grandfather was a kind man. He treated Hugh and me equally, though my brother was eldest and the heir."

"But both of you were his grandsons. Why would he treat you any differently than your brother?"

"You apparently know little about primogeniture, Miss Mabry. The eldest male inherits all, while any siblings are usually left with the scraps."

"I'm aware of that. Still, I find it preposterous your grandfather would barter his affections in such a way. Love isn't governed by wealth or title."

"Lofty ideals," he said. She detected his note of sarcasm. "At least my grandfather agreed with you. The earl, on the other hand, let's just say he's old-fashioned—medieval, to be exact."

"How so?"

"If he could have fostered me out to some distant kingdom, I'm sure he would have leaped at the chance."

"What about now?" Grace asked. "With your brother gone . . . I mean, how does the Earl of Stonebrooke treat you?"

"Stuck with me, I'm afraid. He ran out of heirs." He paused, then said, "You are certainly inquisitive this afternoon, Miss Mabry."

And for a change, you are not, Lord Roxwood. The realization made her smile. Perhaps it would be a good day, after all.

"So how does your father treat you as opposed to your sibling? Is your brother older or younger than you?"

Grace kept her eyes on the road ahead. "Colin is older," she said, feeling a bit of mischief. "And it's true he gets along much better with our father. I'm much more . . . outspoken than what Da would like in a daughter."

His low chuckle filled her with unexpected warmth, and she had to resist an urge to reach over and pull back the mesh to see his laughter. "What's so amusing?"

"Your use of the English language," he said. "You say 'outspoken,' which I suppose serves well enough in polite society. I, on the other hand, would say you bray like a donkey."

Her warmth vanished. "You've got some nerve," she said. "If I bray like a donkey, sir, then you have the manners of a goat!" She clutched at the steering wheel as she imagined her hands around his neck.

Laughter burst from beneath the mask. "I think you've just proved my point," he said, amused.

She opened her mouth to sally a retort—then realized she would only lend credence to his insult. A smile touched her lips. She'd actually made him laugh.

"If you're so outspoken, as you say, I assume your brother is quiet?"

"Yes, he's quite shy," she said amiably. "In fact, my parents were amazed we turned out so differently, though Colin *is* seven minutes older."

"Twins?" He sounded surprised. "Does he look like you?"

"Not really. He stands several inches taller and *his* mustache is black." She was rewarded with another chuckle from behind the mask. "We do share the same nose, I suppose, but with his black hair and hazel eyes, he favors Da's looks." Softly she added, "I've been told I favor my mother."

"You must miss her."

His tone turned quiet, and emotion welled in her. "I do, very much," she said. "Please don't misunderstand. My father and I may not always agree, but I know he loves me and only wants what's best. But his way of showing it is to marry me off to someone who will take over my protection and provide me with a safe and secure life. He doesn't allow that I might be able to take care of myself."

"How did you become so independent?"

"My mother was an early suffragette, despite being married to my traditional father"—she smiled—"or perhaps because of it. Before the war started, she was much involved with winning the vote." Her humor faded. "When she got sick, I wanted to take up the cause, finish what she had started." Grace recalled the words of her beautiful mother. "She taught me to never back down and always stand up for what I believed in. That with courage and God's grace I could become anything I chose in life." *And that I must live with the decisions I make.*

Tears brimmed in her eyes, and she blinked them away. Beside her, Lord Roxwood was still, his mask revealing none of his reaction. It made her long to see his face even more and ascertain his thoughts. She cast a quick glance to the back seat, where the straw hat rested.

"I think you're doing exactly what she taught you, Miss Mabry," he said finally. "You're here working in Kent, charting your own course. I'd say you've come pretty far."

His words pleased her. "Do you also support a woman's right to vote?"

"Absolutely," he said without hesitation. "Most women are by far more intelligent—which is probably why men don't want

151

them voting at the polls." His tone sobered as he added, "Fear tends to breed hatred and dissention, Miss Mabry. It can exacerbate the imagination to the point of becoming ludicrous."

"Like jailing suffragettes?" Grace recalled her mother's indignation when Christabel Pankhurst and Annie Kennedy were arrested for crashing a Liberal Party meeting. She also remembered the ridiculous rumors circulating the village. "Or creating crazy legends about some Tin Man?" she said.

"Exactly." He raised an arm to rest against the top of the seat. When his hand briefly grazed her shoulder, Grace felt her pulse quicken.

He seemed oblivious to the action. "Women have as much to contribute in today's society as any man. They can certainly be as astute when it comes to politics. Look at all the great queens who have ruled throughout Britain's history and you'll have your answer."

"I'm happy to hear you say so. I'm also surprised, since your appreciation for women has previously dealt less with intellect and more with . . . with . . ."

"Physical pleasures, Miss Mabry?" Again his hand brushed her shoulder, and Grace held her breath in an effort to slow her racing heart. "Surely, as you can tell, my days of chasing the ladies are at an end, unless I want to make them scream. Besides, I am also engaged to be married."

To someone he didn't love. *His* cage. "I'm sorry," she said.

"I don't need your sympathy, just your driving skills."

He removed his arm from the top of the seat, and Grace felt a sense of disappointment.

She recalled his notoriety in London, his arrogance and penchant for vice—a man who had spent his days drinking and gambling, his nights destroying the reputation of the fairer sex.

Those exploits seemed distant now. Not for the first time, Grace wondered at his day-to-day activities after their outings.

Instead of attending parties, did he sit alone for hours in the big, empty house, listening to its settling creaks and the shuffling feet of his servants? And at night, did he amuse himself, not with drink and womanizing but with the sounds of the fox and pheasant as he stood at his balcony when he thought no one could see?

She eased out a breath, ridding the last traces of her contempt. His life these days seemed a lonely preoccupation. Despite what he'd been before, no one deserved to fall that far. Was it surprising he volleyed her with questions, living so secluded these past months?

Yes, she wanted to see his smile. She wanted to *make* him smile . . .

The main thoroughfare loomed ahead. "We've reached Canterbury Road," she said, relieved to escape the path her thoughts had taken. She slowed the car.

"Turn left, then straight on until you reach the coast," he said. "We'll follow Margate's shoreline a few miles before entering the city's center. The view is quite nice. You won't want to miss anything."

It wasn't long before an endless expanse of blue-green ocean came into view. "It's beautiful," she said. "I've never seen so much water in my life. Even the Thames cannot compare to the open sea."

"There is as much seacoast in Ireland," he said.

"But I've never seen it. As I told you, my father came here from Dublin when he was much younger and eventually met and married my mother. Colin and I were born in London. We'd each ventured from the city only a couple of times before my brother left for France."

"You still haven't heard from him?"

She frowned. "No, and I've already been here at Roxwood two weeks."

"I'm certain they're keeping him very busy at the Front. I told you how unreliable Army mail is. Worrying about him won't help." He paused. "Instead, describe to me this beauty you see, just as you might write it for *Women's Weekly*."

"All right." She pulled off to the side of the road. He was right. Fretting over Colin wouldn't help to bring her brother's letter any faster.

She set the car's brake and peered out across the coast. "The ocean seems vast, like a country all its own," she began. "Watery arcs, tipped in blues and greens and cresting the surface as far as the eye can see. The warm air is pungent with the smell of brine, while ceaseless waves crash the shore, their foamy tide teasing miles of sparkling sand and scattering strange driftwood, pink and white shells, and bulbous tentacles of dark-brown kelp." She took a breath and continued, "An abandoned boat lies on its side at the edge of the shore, the red-and-white paint chipped away from its hull. Overhead, an azure sky entertains a multitude of gulls wheeling white and brown and gray wings wildly as they call to one another—"

She halted as Lord Roxwood began to applaud. "Nicely done, Miss Mabry. I can see the images quite clearly in my mind."

"Thank you." His approval warmed her. "Shall we drive on?"

"In a moment," he said. "The railway depot should be in the vicinity, along the opposite side of the street. And a place called Hall by the Sea. It's been a dance hall, a restaurant, and most recently a pleasure garden with amusement rides and an animal menagerie."

"Oh, Lucy spoke about an amusement park near the train station," Grace said.

"The very same," he said, a smile in his voice. "As you're a budding novelist, you might be interested to know the Hall's notoriety, as well. A murder was committed on the site a few years ago—a prostitute was killed by the circus strong man."

"Really?" Grace said, fascinated with the possibility of including the detail in her next story. "Oh, there's the Hall!"

Pulling the Daimler back out into traffic, she drove the few blocks to their destination. She parked the car on the shore side. "I don't see many people about."

"I imagine Mondays are slow compared to weekends."

And no doubt he'd chosen today for that reason. "Would you like to go in?" she asked.

"This is not my adventure, Miss Mabry. But if you'll kill the engine, I shall wait while you go inside and survey the sights."

Grace stared at him. "Are you certain?" she said, amazed that he would stay alone in this strange place, unable to see, so she could amuse herself for a few minutes.

"Go ahead, enjoy yourself."

She glanced at his hand now gripped against the leather seat. His other held fast to the inside door handle. Tenderness seized her as she realized the price he was willing to pay for her pleasure. She didn't stop to think as she reached for his hand, hoping to ease his tension.

He withdrew from her touch. "Are you going or not?"

"I cannot," she said, stung by his rejection.

"Why is that, Miss Mabry?" His muscled arms flexed. "I don't require a nanny, if that's your aim. I merely recall your wish to visit Margate. Since I'm in a position to grant that wish, I suggest you make the most of it. Otherwise, we can leave."

"No." She pressed the button to turn off the car's motor. "I . . . I'm just surprised, and very grateful."

"And I am grateful for your service to me." He seemed to hesitate, then added, "I've grown to value your honesty and fortitude during our time together, Grace."

His use of her given name caused a thrill of unexpected pleasure . . . followed by guilt. He didn't yet know the whole truth behind their relationship. Should she tell him now?

"I won't be long," she said. *Coward*.

The weight of her continued deception kept Grace from wholly appreciating the sights within Hall by the Sea. Still, the gardens were beautiful, and she watched how for a few pence an amusement ride, a "Sea on Land" machine, provided customers the experience of a sea-tossed boat ride. The menagerie held a variety of exotic animals, a few she'd seen at the London Zoo. Afterward she wandered through the shops and amusement vendors, her mouth watering with the smells of fried sausages, roasted nuts, and funnel cakes. Pausing at one vendor, she spied her favorite sugary treat—candy floss—and purchased two sticks of the white fairy-spun candy before returning to the car.

"The Hall was fascinating," she called out, alerting him to her approach. She stopped beside his open window. "A bit like an indoor street carnival, only larger."

"I expected you would enjoy the amusements," he said. "And did you see the bear?"

"I saw several animals in the menagerie. Why?"

"Well, if we remain a while longer, you may get the opportunity to watch them walk the bear onto the beach."

"Truly?" Again her imagination blossomed with story ideas. "Then we must stay, for I'd love to see the creature. And I've brought us each a dessert—a stick of candy floss."

"Thank you, but it's quite cumbersome with the mask. Be my guest."

Taking a deep breath, she said, "You know you can remove the mask. We are quite alone along this part of the shore."

"Eager to get another look?" He leaned forward in his seat, hands clasped together between his knees.

"Actually I am."

That caused him to sit up straight.

"You asked me during our first outing what I looked like,"

she said. "You wanted to envision to whom you were speaking. Now I wish the same courtesy. I want to see *you*, Lord Roxwood, not that dreadful mask."

He didn't speak for a long moment, his posture rigid. Finally he said, "We cannot always have what we wish, Miss Mabry. I'm sorry."

He was impossible! Grace swung around to glare at the sea, and the wire clippers she'd pocketed earlier slapped against her thigh. She went still. Would he let her take such a liberty and touch his mask?

She turned back to him. "I suggest a compromise."

11

"What compromise?" Suspicion flooded Jack's senses.

"Hold these, if you please."

Two thin objects—wooden sticks—were thrust into his hands. He could detect the faintly sweet scent of spun sugar. Candy floss.

Jack felt her warm breath tickle the side of his neck as she said, "Now, if you won't remove the entire mask, let me just cut away that awful steel mesh. I'll clip the links—"

"No!" Apprehension twisted his insides. He began to sweat. The smell of the candy floss made him nauseous, and he shoved them at her. "Take these, now!"

"Please trust me," she said softly. "I want to see you. I want . . ."

Her hand settled against his shoulder, and a shudder tore through him. Jack swallowed, barely able to breathe. "What do you want from me, Grace?"

The heat from her touch seeped through his jacket. Jack's pulse pounded in his ears. Why had he brought her here? To grant her wish to see a new place . . . or was it more than that?

"I've seen the man without the mask," she said close to him, evading his question. "He doesn't frighten me."

"I frighten others," he said, recalling Violet's reaction when she'd come to see him in hospital. The revulsion in her tone when they spoke on the telephone.

"I'm not like the others."

No, you're far more, he thought. A woman he enjoyed being with each day, sparring wits with, being angry with. A woman who treated him like a man and not some freak, or worse, a victim.

"Will you trust me?" she whispered.

Jack held his breath. He wanted to—he longed to, in fact. It had been months since he'd allowed himself the touch of a woman's hand, even longer for a kiss or an embrace.

"Jack?" As she said his name, he released the air from his lungs. He tried to imagine himself revealed to her. How would she react to the ragged scar on his cheek? His valet saw it daily, without seeming the least bit squeamish.

Temptation grew as he realized that without the mesh, he'd be able to smell the sea. He could enjoy the mouth-watering flavor of the spun sugar. And Grace . . .

Jack's heart quickened. Would she carry about her the fragrance of perfume? Or smell of the earth, of hay and horses? Did he have the nerve to find out?

"Go ahead," he heard himself say. He tensed as she began snipping away one by one the links that kept the mesh in place. Cool air soon assuaged his dampened cheeks, and he caught the strangely familiar scent of flowers. He edged closer to her, trying to determine the exact smell, but could not place it.

She still said nothing. As the silence ensued, Jack sat unmoving as though paralyzed, regretting his rashness while the seconds ticked off.

Then he felt her gentle touch graze his cheek alongside the

wound, the tips of her fingers soft and warm. He fought the urge to lean into them.

Abruptly she was gone. A moment later, the driver's door opened. She slid onto the seat and closed the door. "I'll trade you."

He felt a stick of the candy floss plucked from his grasp and replaced with the wad of steel mesh.

"Candy floss was always my favorite as a child. Was it yours?" she asked.

She seemed unfazed. Jack eased back into his seat, dropping the steel into his lap before he pulled away a chunk of the spun sugar. "I've always enjoyed it, but my weakness is funnel cakes," he replied. He popped the candy floss into his mouth, savoring the sugar as it dissolved on his tongue.

"I love funnel cakes, as well. There's a vendor selling them in the Hall. Shall I go back and fetch you one?"

He shook his head, pulling away another hunk of the featherlight candy.

"The bear! Jack, I see the bear walking on the beach!"

He grinned and realized how good it felt. "I'd hoped you would get the chance to see Margate's unusual spectacle." He turned to her as he tore away another morsel of the candy. "Tell me, how shall you write about the scene in your novel?"

"Give me a moment," she said.

Jack cocked his head and waited, anticipating her forthcoming narrative. He smiled again. It would undoubtedly be colorful as well as lengthy.

She began, "Breathing labored, the beast ambles along the beach behind his master, the chains around his limbs and neck dragging in the sand. As if he knows all eyes are amused by him, the proud and fearsome creature appears defeated, held captive by his inability to know his strength. He doesn't realize he could break the chains at any time, overpower the one who holds them . . ."

Jack froze, the candy floss like plaster in his mouth. Was that how she saw him—some miserable circus creature? He tossed the confection out the window. "I've had enough, Miss Mabry. Please take me home."

"Are you all right?"

Was the concern in her tone pity? He felt exposed and desperately wished he hadn't let her remove the mesh. "Now," he demanded, wanting only to retreat to the solace of his rooms.

"I didn't mean to upset you." Grace couldn't fathom what she'd said or done to cause his abrupt change in mood. She reached to touch his shoulder. "Are you angry I altered your mask? I only wanted you to enjoy being—"

"Normal?" He shoved her hand away. "Am I your new cause, then, Miss Mabry? Fix the mask and you fix the freak?" His well-formed mouth pulled back, exposing white teeth as he snarled, "I would have thought you got your fill inside the menagerie at Hall by the Sea—" He stopped, and Grace saw his throat work. More calmly he said, "Let us be clear. I do not want or need your pity."

"I do not feel sorry for you one bit," she said, wounded he would misconstrue her intentions. Yes, she'd planned to unmask him on this venture, but not for the reasons he imagined. Pity took no part in her wanting to see his smile or hear his laughter.

He was doing neither at the moment. "Nor do I wish you to be 'normal,' only to be yourself," she said.

"Then your wish is granted." His sarcasm was back in full force. "On both counts."

"Oh, why are you so obtuse?" Grace tired of fencing words with him. "You are not the sum of your scars, sir. You are simply Jack Benningham, Lord Roxwood, warts and all!"

An unexpected smile formed on his lips. "My, my, Miss

Mabry, what would Reverend Price say about that temper of yours?"

"I never had one until I met you." She huffed out a breath. "You do manage to bring out the worst in me."

That produced a chuckle from him, and just as she'd been at the costume ball, Grace was arrested by the beauty of his smile. Her heart beat faster. "You have very white teeth," she said, before she could stop herself. He was still a handsome man, despite the mask covering his eyes. Lean-faced, he had a strong jaw with just the tiniest dimple at its center, directly below the well-sculpted mouth. Her hands had brushed against those lips as she removed the links from his mask, and she'd felt their firmness, her senses teased by the warm scent of his breath as she worked.

She didn't care if removing the mesh made him angry. She preferred this view of him, a man whose features she could readily identify. She then realized he was clean-shaven. "Do you handle your own razor?"

"My valet takes care of it."

"So, you allow *him* to see your face," she said, hurt that he would allow a servant what he'd refused to show her. "Does the sight of you throw him into paroxysms of terror?"

"He sees only what you see now."

The rest of him remained a mystery, then. "The only 'freakish' thing about you is the vile mask," she said. "You could take it off. I've even brought a hat for you to wear, just in case."

Since she'd expected him to rage, his weary tone surprised her. "Why do you insist on trying to save me, Miss Mabry?"

Because you refuse to save yourself. "My reasons merely stem from curiosity," she said instead. "I've been in your employ eleven days already, and as I've told you, I want to see with whom I'm speaking. Do you think it unreasonable?"

"No, not unreasonable." He sighed. "Impossible."

"Why?"

"Miss Mabry, I'd be a liar if I told you I didn't enjoy your company. You've got intelligence and your honesty is refreshing. You're also a good driver. And I'm certain one day you will make a splendid novelist. But you are innocent to the ways of the world and its ugliness. Trust me when I say, you do not want to see this face." He turned away.

"I do!" She reached for him again and felt the muscles of his arm tense. "I have seen you. In the hedge maze, remember? I am not naïve, just curious to know you better. You are not what they say—"

"You don't know what I am." The lines at his mouth conveyed more frustration than anger. "Now, please do not press me further."

Grace felt as though she'd lost some important battle. Heart aching, she threw away the rest of her candy floss and exited the car to crank over the engine.

The ride back seemed to take forever. She was relieved to finally drive past the gatehouse onto Roxwood's estate. He didn't say a word to her once the car halted and he opened the door.

Grace watched him, tears brimming at her lashes. It seemed they must start over again.

❥

The sun was hot as Grace took a break from her raking to stretch her muscles and gaze up at the clear morning sky. Breathing deeply, she imagined tasting the air, fresh and clean, so unlike the sooty odor of London in winter, or the insidious stench permeating parts of the city in summer.

How would she describe it to Jack? *The air tasted of sunshine and freshly mown grass . . .*

As if he would listen, she thought with a pang as she returned to the task of spreading cut hay. After Monday's debacle at

163

Margate, she'd called for him yesterday. Knowles had announced he wasn't up to an outing. The butler actually looked sympathetic, an expression foreign to his rough features.

No, she'd gone too far in removing the steel mesh. He'd been angry with her afterward, believing her attention to him stemmed from pity, the furthest thing from the truth.

Grace paused again with the rake. She *did* like being with him, and more than just a little. She certainly noticed when she was not. And though she enjoyed the company of her WFC sisters, being with Jack made her feel different. Her senses became heightened, her pleasure more intense as they bantered with each other and played the guessing game. The realization that he might never send for her again made her feel hollow inside.

Should she return to the manor and apologize?

"Penny for your thoughts," Clare called to her, manning a rake just a few yards away. "Missing the Daimler?"

Grace looked up and forced a smile.

"He's engaged, you know." Clare bent back to the task of spreading hay.

"I'm well aware of that," Grace said, annoyed at her friend's keen perception. "But I hurt his feelings terribly the other day and I wish I knew a way to make it up to him. Engaged or not, Clare, he's still a human being."

"Be careful, Grace," Clare said.

"Don't worry. Really, it's just that we've grown accustomed to one another. I don't know if you could consider us friends. He's my employer and I'm his chauffeur."

A smirk formed on Clare's lips. "Of course you are." She raked out another pile of hay. "Just don't get hurt."

"A letter for you, Miss Mabry."

Mr. Tillman scowled as he arrived during their lunch to hand Grace a crisp, white invitation. "I've got better things to do

than run messages back and forth for young ladies." He eyed her sharply from beneath bushy brows. "If it needs responding, you can do it yourself." With that, he turned on his heel and strode back across the field.

"I don't think the farmer's going to forgive you, Grace." Becky sat in the grass near her feet, eating one of the buttermilk scones she'd made for their breakfast that morning.

"It's the shovel. Or maybe the pigs. He hasn't g-gotten over either one." Lucy took a bite of her carrot. She was still perched atop the horse-driven tractor mower.

"What's in the letter, miss?" Agnes asked, looking curious from her grassy spot across from Becky.

Grace's mouth went dry as she stared at the embossed linen envelope. Surely he wouldn't fire her with an invitation? She opened it and read the scrawled lines of Jack's steward, Mr. Edwards. "I've been invited to dine with Lord Roxwood. This evening, in fact."

She glanced up and saw Agnes's brow pucker, while Becky waved her arms and cried, "The Tin Man's falling in love with Grace!"

"Nonsense." Grace felt her face heat as she glanced back at the invitation. "We had a row on Monday. He probably wishes to repair our truce."

Grace risked a glance at Clare, seated alongside her in the grass.

"What do I know?" Clare shrugged, then went back to eating her apple-butter sandwich. "But I watched you unpack your bags. At least you have a decent dress to wear to your truce."

❧

The summer sun still shone above the tree line when Grace arrived at the manor for dinner. Knowles answered her summons, and his face brightened at the sight of her.

Grace offered a shy smile. She'd taken special care with her toilette this evening, and while her gown was simple compared to the clothes in her wardrobe at home in London, the embroidered white cotton summer dress made her feel quite pretty.

"My lady." Knowles offered a slight bow and then retreated to allow her entrance. "May I say you look enchanting this evening."

Her smile broadened. "Why, you certainly may, Knowles. Thank you."

He bowed again. "If you'll follow me to the library."

He led her in a direction opposite the study, and she marveled again at the tasteful simplicity of the house. The high ceilings were edged with gilt friezes, while neutral-colored walls enhanced the gold-and-green rugs covering the polished wood floors.

Knowles stopped in front of a pair of heavy double doors and opened them. "Miss Mabry, milord," he said, allowing her to enter.

Jack stood beside a walnut divan covered in soft green-and-beige-striped fabric. The massive Turkish rug at his feet held similar shades, along with reds, blues, and browns. A pair of potted palms in brass urns stood on either side of two floor-length windows draped in dark gold velvet and snow-white sheers.

"Thank you for accepting my invitation, Miss Mabry."

Jack wore standard dinner dress of white tie and tails. Grace admired the way the black jacket stretched across his broad shoulders, contrasting sharply with his white waistcoat and shirtfront. He looked quite dashing but for the mask, though she was pleased he'd left off the mesh. "You're quite welcome, Lord Roxwood."

"Shall I have Knowles pour us a sherry?"

"That would be lovely." Grace glanced at the butler, who

bowed and went to a side table, returning with two amber-filled glasses served up on a silver tray. She smiled at him, taking a glass.

"Milord?" Knowles hovered with the tray.

Jack extended a hand, into which the butler deftly slipped the other glass of sherry. "To good company," he said, raising his glass. Grace lifted hers, as well.

"And may I say, your lordship, the entire staff wishes you a very happy birthday."

Grace paused with the sherry to her lips. "It's your birthday?"

"Another year older." He hesitated. "Though I have grown none the wiser."

Silence reigned for a few seconds before the butler said, "I'll see about dinner, milord." Knowles left the drawing room and closed the doors behind him.

"Please, Grace, take a seat."

She chose the chair next to the divan. "You have a beautiful home," Grace said, her pulse pounding with new awareness of him. They were alone in the same room, although it seemed laughable when she considered they were much that way each day on their outings together. This was different, however. She wasn't being paid to be here. And he'd asked her to dinner on his birthday.

Grace wished she would have known earlier. She could have purchased a gift in the village.

He took a seat on the divan, then a quick sip of his sherry. "I wish to apologize for my behavior on Monday." He spoke without preamble. "I know you had the best intentions, while I . . ." His lopsided smile pierced her with warmth. "I'm afraid I still have difficulty believing anyone sees me as anything other than the village troll."

"But you're not that at all," Grace assured him, moving to the edge of her seat. "You're quite the opposite." Seeing his quick flash of teeth, she added, "While I don't care for the mask, it does lend you an air of mystery—like Erik in Gaston Leroux's *The Phantom of the Opera.*"

His smile faded. "I read the novel when it came out a few years ago. As I recall, Erik was a miserable soul, and the beautiful Christine pitied him."

She straightened in her seat. "Well, as I haven't the slightest twinge of the sentiment in your regard, the comparison is probably inaccurate. Still, I am glad you've left off the steel mesh. You have a nice smile, you know."

He gifted her with one then, and her breath caught before she asked, "Have you spoken with your family today?"

"My mother called earlier to wish me good tidings." He paused. "She conveyed my father's sentiments, as well."

Grace sipped at the amber liquid, enjoying its warmth against her throat. It was a shame Jack and his father weren't able to bridge the divide in their relationship. It made her angry, too. Hugh was dead, while the Earl of Stonebrooke had a remaining son. By allowing his grief of the past to blind him, he missed the love he could have in the present with Jack.

She thought to ask if Miss Arnold had called, but decided against it, enjoying their current equanimity. Grace hadn't forgotten their conversation about arranged marriages.

The drawing room doors opened. "Dinner, milord," the butler said.

"Shall we, Miss Mabry?" Jack rose and approached her chair, offering his arm. Grace stood and tucked her hand into the crook of his elbow. "I hope you have an appetite. Mrs. Riley has prepared my favorite dish—baked salmon."

"One of my favorites," she said.

A moment later, they walked into the dining room and moved toward the elegant table. The white linen cloth held candles, fine bone china, and crystal goblets. Two bouquets of roses garnished the table with their beauty.

Knowles showed Grace to her chair beside Jack, who sat at the head of the table, while an older woman in cap and apron—Mrs. Riley, she presumed—brought in the first course. Grace was surprised a footman didn't carry out the task.

"Carrot soup, milord, and just as you like it." Next, the woman placed a serving before Grace.

"Thank you, Mrs. Riley," Jack said.

"Milord."

She curtsied while Grace inhaled the soup's spicy aroma of ginger and cinnamon. "This smells delicious."

When Mrs. Riley beamed at her, it struck Grace how different the cook's pleasant expression was from that of her brother, Mr. Tillman, who wore an interminable frown.

She retreated, and minutes passed in companionable silence as Grace and Jack enjoyed their food. Knowles had come around to pour a delicate white wine and then removed himself to a discreet distance behind Jack so as to give them a measure of privacy.

"I admit it's much easier dining this way," he said, taking a spoonful of the soup. "Before, I'd have to remove my mask, then replace it after the meal."

Grace glanced toward Knowles. "What about the servants?"

"They have always been instructed to leave the room. I wish my privacy when I eat."

"But you allow me to be here?" Affection brewed in her as she tried to keep her tone light. Grace was thrilled he would trust her enough to share what he considered a kind of intimacy.

"I am still wearing my mask," he reminded her, and her euphoric mood dimmed. "But I wanted you to share in my birthday."

Her spirits buoyed again. "I am honored," she said with sincere warmth.

Mrs. Riley brought in the next course—baked salmon topped

with lemon wedges and served alongside slices of seasoned boiled potatoes and a medley of cooked vegetables from the garden: beans, tomatoes, peas, carrots, and rhubarb. "Everything is set just as you like it, milord." She placed his meal before him, doing the same with Grace.

"I suppose with the war on, you're without a footman?" she asked once the woman had left.

"No, I keep a footman on hand, though Gaines is too old for service overseas."

Grace noticed Jack used his fork to poke at each item on his plate. Seeming satisfied all of his food was sufficiently dead, he began to eat.

"Afraid your salmon will swim off the plate?" she teased. "I see you jabbing it with your fork as if it's still moving."

His cheeks colored faintly, and Grace regretted her remark. Had she blundered again?

His rueful smile reassured her. "I like to know exactly where everything is on my plate. Don't want to bite into any surprises. Meat at seven o'clock"—he stabbed at the salmon—"potatoes at twelve o'clock, green vegetables at three." He indicated with his fork the other two servings. "Always the same, and the reason Mrs. Riley serves my meals."

Grace stared down at her plate. "Lord Roxwood, I didn't mean to pry . . ."

"No harm done. And when we're alone, please, call me Jack. I like hearing you say my name." Then he said, "Knowles, you may go. Leave the bottle of wine."

"Very good, milord." The butler set the wine on the table between them.

"I would like it if you called me Grace," she said when he'd left. Jack answered with a smile and a nod, then speared a chunk of the fish and began eating.

Grace did the same. "I didn't properly thank you the other

day for taking me to Margate. It was all quite fascinating." She darted a glance at him, noting how his strong and capable hands deftly wielded the fork or reached for his glass of wine. If one didn't know he was blind, he could fool even the most critical eye.

"It was my pleasure, Grace. I meant what I said." His tone softened, and he stretched one of those hands along the table in her direction. "I've come to appreciate your company and your honesty."

Grace faltered with a forkful of vegetables to her lips. She hadn't been completely honest with him, had she? Of course, she should tell him about the white feather right now . . .

Seeing his unguarded smile, she hesitated. It was his birthday, after all. It would be heartless to ruin it for him. She took his hand instead, and as soon as she touched him, her heart began pounding like Nessa's racing hooves along the cobbled streets in Westminster.

"I've enjoyed our time together myself," she said quietly. "You've helped me to see things in ways I never could before." *And experience emotions I've never felt before.*

He squeezed her fingers, and the heat from his touch ignited her senses. "And you are my eyes, sweet Grace." His deep voice caressed her like a warm summer breeze. "And so much more—"

"I wish to see him now!"

Their hands broke apart as the doors to the dining room burst open. A fashionably attired woman stood on the threshold, while Knowles, looking distraught, stood behind her. "Milord, I tried to have her wait—"

"It's all right." Jack removed his napkin and rose from his chair. "Good evening, Violet."

Violet Arnold! Grace's fork clattered against her plate. She vaguely recognized her from a newspaper photograph. With her golden hair piled high beneath a stylish plum-colored hat, wearing a smart linen traveling suit of the same shade, she appeared far more beautiful in person.

Ignoring Jack, she cast a derisive glance at Grace. "I have tried calling several times to send a car to meet me at the train station. Each time that man, Edwards, said you were out."

"I was out." Jack's tone sounded lackluster. "I've been in my gardens most of the day."

Miss Arnold finally turned to face him. A flash of distaste crossed her unblemished features. "Whatever for?"

"I wanted to enjoy my roses."

"Wearing that horrid mask?" She quickly averted her gaze.

Fury coursed through Grace. So this was the woman he was to marry next month? No wonder Jack felt so . . . inadequate. It was obvious she wanted nothing to do with him.

"The last time I checked, Violet, my sense of smell was still intact." Irritation colored his words as he fumbled around the table. Grace stood, too.

"You purposely ignored me," she insisted. "And now you're having a cozy dinner with . . . ?"

"Miss Grace Mabry. She's with the Women's Forage Corps." To Grace, he said, "Miss Violet Arnold is—"

"His fiancée," the blonde interjected.

"It's nice to meet you, Miss Arnold." Grace approached to extend a hand to the other woman.

Miss Arnold made no attempt to take it. Instead the dark-brown eyes appraised her. "And I suppose having dinner with the future heir of Stonebrooke is a part of your duty in the Women's . . . what did you call it?"

"The Women's Forage Corps," Grace said. "We harvest and bale hay, then deliver it to a designated station to be shipped overseas to British forces."

"Hay? How tedious." She gave her palm a slap with her lavender gloves.

"I'm surprised you feel that way, Miss Arnold," she said. "I mean, with your own country's recent entry into the war."

Violet Arnold seemed unconcerned as she took in Grace's summer dress. "So why is a baler of hay up at the manor enjoying a formal dinner?"

"Miss Mabry is on my staff," Jack said.

"Doing what?" Grace felt Violet Arnold's second swift perusal.

"She works as my driver in the mornings. In the afternoons she is employed by the WFC."

"Then you should have been there to fetch me hours ago," she said to Grace.

Grace stiffened. Before she could form a proper retort, Jack asked, "Why are you here, Violet?"

"If you recall, we still have important matters to discuss. Privately." She cut a glance at Grace before continuing, "Do you keep a lady's maid here at the house, Benningham? Browne became ill just before we boarded at the station in London, and I had to send her home."

"Violet, I employ only critical staff at Roxwood."

"Which should include a suitable lady's maid," Violet said. She turned to arch a delicate brow at Grace. "I don't suppose that's a part of your job description?"

"Indeed not," Grace said, horrified at the notion of being ordered about by such a haughty woman. She saw Jack's fists clench. "However," she said slowly as an idea formed, "I might offer you instead the services of my own maid." She nearly laughed at the startled look on Miss Arnold's face. "Agnes is here with me, working for the Women's Forage Corps. I feel certain, with the proper incentive, she would act as lady's maid during your stay."

"Will it suit?" Jack asked.

"I suppose, but I wish to meet her first."

"Done." Below the mask, Jack's jaw eased. He unclenched his fists, as well. "Miss Mabry, if your maid agrees, tell her I'll double her wages."

"I wish to speak with her directly—that is, if you've finished your little evening together?" Violet Arnold looked at Grace, then at Jack. "I've had a trying day and I'd like to get settled in as quickly as possible."

With that, she whirled from the dining room, and Grace heard her calling orders to the frazzled butler. Poor Agnes! She had regrets about volunteering her friend to act as the woman's maid. No one should have to put up with such arrogance. Perhaps she should demand triple wages for her friend.

She turned to Jack. "I suppose your birthday party is over."

"I'm sorry, Grace." He left his place beside the table and came to her. "I didn't expect her to arrive."

"You don't need to apologize. I just feel badly because your celebration's been ruined." She noted the blond hoyden hadn't even wished him a birthday greeting.

"It was hardly ruined." He smiled and held out his hand to her. It was a moment before she took it. "I've enjoyed our evening very much."

"It was lovely," she said, wishing she could stay longer. She enjoyed seeing his expressions, his smiles. She wanted to know more about his grandfather and the memorable times he'd shared with his brother; about his unbending father, the earl; and what it was like being a second son and the new heir to Stonebrooke, forced to marry a woman he didn't love . . .

"Jack," she said, wanting some kind of reassurance this new connection between them wasn't at an end. "Shall I call for you in the morning? I need to continue my word-painting lessons, you know. I'm certain the outspoken ones could use more color."

"Not tomorrow," he said, giving her hand a squeeze. "Edwards will let you know when I'm available."

"All right." She struggled to keep the disappointment from her voice. "I'll send Agnes over directly. Good night." She pulled her hand from his and turned toward the door.

"Grace Mabry."

"Yes?" She spun around.

"Thank you." A smile touched his lips. "Being in your company tonight is the best gift I've received in a very long time."

A bittersweet yearning rose in her, touching her heart. "You are most welcome, Jack."

As she exited the manor, Grace found Knowles lugging a large steamer trunk and several portmanteaus inside from the porch steps. Yet despite the proof of Miss Arnold's presence, Grace's pleasure over Jack's words refused to fade.

12

While it was still early evening, Grace found Agnes upstairs, readying for bed. "Wait," she called, bursting into the room. "Would you like to earn extra wages?"

"How is that, miss?" Agnes paused in pulling her nightgown from beneath her pillow.

"Agnes, you really must learn to call me Grace. However, if you take the temporary position I propose, you'll need to re-member your etiquette." She relayed the details of her meeting with the uppity Violet Arnold. "I'm sorry I didn't ask you first, and you're certainly welcome to refuse. I just felt badly for Lord Roxwood. She seemed to harp on him with every other word. Besides, I cannot imagine it would be for more than a few days. He's even willing to pay you double wages for your services."

Agnes brightened. "Why, I'd be pleased to do it. Who would not, for twice the pay? And after hearing your impression of Miss Arnold, it sounds like I'll earn every shilling."

"Every shilling *and* pence," Grace said with a smile. She was pleased her friend had agreed to help Jack sort this mess. "And with all the extra money, you must buy sweets for the rest of us the next time you visit Margate—and no getting lost."

High-pitched laughter escaped Agnes, and she quickly covered her mouth. Grace grinned.

"Certainly not," her maid said after a moment. "When does Miss Arnold wish me to come up to the house?"

"Straightaway, I'm afraid. I know it's late, but she wants an interview. I'm certain she'll give you the job. We'd better first gain Mrs. Vance's approval. We cannot have Lord Roxwood bullying her again." Grace cringed at the possibility.

Mrs. Vance sat in the small parlor, reading the newspaper. The others were in the kitchen playing cards. "Agnes and I would like to speak with you, if you have a moment," Grace said.

Mrs. Vance looked up from her reading. "It's just terrible," she said, frowning. "Our men fight overseas and risk their lives, while this one"—she flashed them the printed article—"sells our country's secrets to the enemy! Well, I don't mean to wish anyone ill, but she's getting her comeuppance, this Mata Hari, or whoever she is. The court just found her guilty of treason. She's to be executed." She shook her head. "A sorry thing altogether, if you ask me."

Folding the newspaper, Mrs. Vance set it on her lap and looked up at them with a curious smile. "Now, what was it you wished to talk to me about?"

Agnes looked pale and anxious. Grace gave her hand a reassuring squeeze and said, "Agnes has been offered a position up at Roxwood Manor," before she too lost her courage.

All pleasantness vanished as Mrs. Vance launched from her chair, knocking the newspaper to the floor. "So, his lordship wants to steal another of my workers. And did he threaten to run us off his lands if I refuse or simply go over my head again?"

"It's not like that at all," Grace said and explained the circumstances of Miss Arnold's arrival. "There is no one at the house qualified to attend her," she finished.

Mrs. Vance looked ready to do battle. Grace regretted her

hasty offer to Jack. Perhaps if she hadn't volunteered Agnes's services, Miss Arnold would have returned to London.

Yet if that were the case, Violet would have remained in the city when her own maid took ill. The woman obviously planned to stay and if possible make Jack's life more miserable.

Grace noted Agnes's crestfallen expression and knew her friend was counting on earning those double wages for her future dress shop. "Please, Mrs. Vance, Agnes would be needed for only a short time, no more than a few days," she said. "Lord Roxwood regrets the inconvenience to you," she added, believing he would echo her sentiments.

Mrs. Vance looked at both of them. "Is this all right with you, Pierpont?"

"Oh, yes!" Agnes nodded vigorously.

"Three days, that's it," Mrs. Vance said, frowning. "After which Miss Arnold can send to London for someone else. Are we clear?"

"Absolutely," Grace and Agnes chorused in unison.

Mrs. Vance turned to Grace. "You've managed to make us shorthanded once again, Mabry. Now the others must work all the harder because you're determined to hire out our workforce."

"Lord Roxwood won't need my services for a while," Grace said with a stab of guilt. "I'm hardly as skilled as Agnes, but happy to work in her place."

"Good," Mrs. Vance said. "You can begin tonight. In the barn you'll find a crate full of chaffing to be loaded into sacks. I was going to ask for a couple of volunteers, but you can have the privilege. We've a good hour of light remaining. Still, take a lantern just in case. After you've finished, we'll go over those section reports and time sheets you've been working on." She eyed Grace's attire. "And I'd change out of those clothes if I were you." She then brushed past them to exit the parlor.

"Well, that went well, don't you think?" Grace spoke with

forced gaiety, trying not to imagine the long night ahead. "I can shovel a bit of fodder into sacks, that's not so bad."

"I think if you let Lord Roxwood steal any more workers, Mrs. Vance will turn *you* into fodder," Agnes said, then loosed another burst of her infectious laughter that made them both smile. "But you did pull it off, miss. And I appreciate it very much."

"You're welcome. Now, you'd better be off."

While Agnes left the gatehouse for the manor, Grace changed and pedaled her bicycle toward the barn.

Inside, she eyed the enormous crate of chaff. She drew a deep breath and lit the lantern, then grabbed a shovel and a burlap sack and began to work.

She'd only labored an hour when a voice called from the barn door, "I hear the future Lady Roxwood's come to call?" Clare stepped inside. "What's she like?"

Grace paused to swipe at a piece of straw stuck to her lower lip. "The word *duchess* comes to mind."

Clare grinned. "I guess she didn't make an impression, then?"

"Hardly, unless one wishes to be in the company of the most rude, ungrateful, and arrogant woman . . ." Grace bit off the rest of her tirade. "I sound like the worst shrew, don't I? Not exactly a shining example of the WFC."

"Well, I'm a fair judge of shrews," Clare said, "and I think I still have you beat. Want some help?"

"I'd love it." Grace handed her the shovel and held the sack as Clare filled it with the fodder.

"You know, Grace, I still feel awful for the way I treated you," Clare said. "And I appreciate you keeping my secret."

"I hope you realize by now I am no aristocrat. Though after meeting Miss Arnold, I can understand why you dislike them." Grace tied off the full sack and put it alongside the others she'd already completed. "Have you heard any more about Daisy?"

Clare shook her head. "Mr. Pittman, the man I hired, is still making inquiries." She pursed her lips, then said, "I confess it's difficult to concentrate on work, knowing my daughter might be so close."

"I can only imagine." Grace met her gaze with sympathy. "When will you hear from him next?"

"Tomorrow or the next day," Clare said. "Then once we find out she's there—"

"I'll drive you myself, as promised." Grace reached for Clare's arm. "You'll get her back, Clare. Have faith, right?"

"I can't afford not to," she whispered, placing a hand over Grace's. "Now come on, let's get this finished up. Becky, bless her, made one of her delicious desserts for supper and saved a helping just for you. And you haven't lived until you taste her raisin bread pudding."

Later, after she'd eaten dessert, Grace pored over reports at the kitchen table with Mrs. Vance.

Agnes entered the house and came to the kitchen door clad in her traveling costume.

"You must have landed the job?" Grace said.

She nodded. "I just came back to get a few clothes and my toiletries."

Hearing her arrival, Becky, Lucy, and Clare came downstairs in nightgowns and robes and dragged Agnes into the tiny parlor. Grace and Mrs. Vance joined them.

"Well? Is Miss Arnold b-beautiful?" Lucy wanted to know. "Does she wear expensive clothes from Paris?"

"She's very pretty to look at, though not as lovely as Miss . . . Grace," Agnes said staunchly. "Her companion, Mrs. Grant, is older and rather plain. Miss Arnold has steamer trunks and boxes filled with the latest Paris fashions. It took me almost two hours to put things away, and another twenty minutes to press the wrinkles from her tea gown for tomorrow."

"How does she act with Lord Roxwood?" Becky piped up. "Does she kiss him with his mask on or off?"

"I wouldn't know." Agnes looked appalled. "And I haven't seen Lord Roxwood, only his steward, Mr. Edwards." Agnes turned to Grace. "Both ladies took a late supper in their rooms and then went to bed. Miss Arnold seemed quite put out when his lordship retired after you left."

Grace felt a spurt of satisfaction, though she knew it wrong. She could only hope in the next few days his fiancée might see beyond the scars to his charming smile, the dimple in his chin . . .

Her heart squeezed as she thought of his wit and sense of humor, his quiet generosity. Would the haughty woman grow to appreciate his true worth? And would Jack share with her his fondest childhood memories, take her to Eden . . . or would she even want to go with him?

"Well, that's a fine thing." Becky jerked on the belt of her robe. "I came downstairs hoping for a bit of gossip, but it all sounds very dull to me."

"And you women will be very dull tomorrow if you don't get some sleep," Mrs. Vance reminded them. "We've a full day in the fields. Agnes, please collect your things and say good-night."

"Yes, ma'am."

When the others had left the parlor, Grace asked, "Is everything all right up at the house? Are they treating you well?"

"I'm fine, miss." Agnes offered a reassuring smile. "And Mr. Edwards seems very kind. I'll see you in a few days."

After she'd left and Mrs. Vance turned down the lights, Grace lay awake in bed, again unable to sleep. Twilight skies had deepened to a midnight hue, and a sliver of moon shone across the bedroom floor. Restless, she rose from her bed and moved to the open window, straining in the meager light to see Roxwood Manor and discover if the man in her thoughts stood on the balcony.

He was there—Jack's tall silhouette poised at the rail. Her pulse pounded. What was happening to her? She found she couldn't wait to see him again, to spar wits with him, exchange ideas, learn more about his life. She loved that he supported her passion for a woman's right to be heard, and believed in her dream of becoming a novelist. And while he'd angered her, frustrated her, and taxed her patience, Jack never talked down to her like Clarence Fowler and even her father had done. He demanded she use her head *and* her imagination, proving to him she could master her words. Yet it was more than that; his confession at dinner resounded in her mind. She had become his eyes.

She should be recording all of this in her journal: her special evening with him and the thrill of being asked to dine with a man who always ate alone. Despite Violet Arnold's unexpected intrusion, they had enjoyed their time together tonight, both of them at their ease. Closing her eyes, Grace savored again his parting words, that her presence tonight was the best birthday gift he'd received in a very long while . . .

"He's engaged." Clare's reminder shot through her. Grace opened her eyes and stared out into the darkness. Jack had been pressured into the arranged marriage, having said as much when she confided Da's ever-pending plans for her own future. She'd seen, too, the way he and Violet barely tolerated being in the same room together, and it saddened her. She wondered if she might feel the same way with Clarence Fowler, and knew it was true.

Turning from the window, she went back to bed. Grace had the fervent wish that Violet Arnold would conduct her business and be gone, so Jack would again call her to drive him about the countryside. She could fill his ears with pictures and perhaps read to him, as well. That way, he would have hours of images to recall and savor. She also wanted to explain to him how she felt and why she'd pressed him into removing his mask the other day at Margate. Not out of pity, but the desire to show him the scars didn't matter to her.

Grace wanted . . . no, she needed to know about the man beneath, to understand his heart.

"I didn't imagine you'd be this surprised by my arrival." Lieutenant Marcus Weatherford, Esquire, sank into one of the leather wing chairs facing the desk. "Especially when you spend your days with Patrick Mabry's daughter."

"I *imagined* you would telephone before showing up on my doorstep," Jack shot back.

Marcus stared at the mask and wondered when Jack had decided to remove the mesh. He felt glad of it—the thing *was* a bit dramatic. His friend had insisted on the splatter mask while in hospital, shortly after Violet Arnold had barged into his room unannounced. And so Marcus acquired it for him.

Now, without the mesh, seated behind his desk, Jack Benningham looked less formidable and more like the lord of the manor. Even the scar on his cheek was healing well.

"I would think you'd be grateful for the extra week I gave you," Marcus reminded him. "I just arrived back from Paris and Mata Hari's trial." He paused as Knowles entered the study with a tea tray.

"Cream and two lumps, Sir Marcus, if I recall," the butler said as he offered tea served in a delicate Sèvres cup.

"Thank you, Knowles." Marcus sipped at the hot brew, savoring its flavor. "There are few things in life that surpass a perfect cup of tea." He was rewarded with the stodgy butler's smile. "And I see you're taking quite good care of our man here, Knowles." Marcus glanced toward Jack while he set his cup atop the desk. "Is Lord Roxwood giving you any problems?"

"Milord is the perfect gentleman, sir." Knowles bowed before backing out of the study and closing the door.

"I believe Knowles is the perfect butler," Marcus said, amused.

"What's so all-important, Weatherford? Have you discovered news on Patrick Mabry?"

"Not much, old boy, though an agent with MI5 did observe a man known to have had dealings with James Heeren lunching at Swan's last week. Mabry sat speaking with him for quite some time. We attempted to shadow the suspect afterward, but he eluded our man. Now the Admiralty's adding pressure to send a Scotland Yard detective here to investigate his daughter. Since I felt certain you wouldn't wish it, I came myself." He paused to eye his friend. "How are you, anyway?"

"So you have nothing on him," Jack said, ignoring the question. "Well, you're wasting your time here, as well." He leaned back in his chair and made a steeple with his fingers. "I found out why Mabry paid the WFC clerk to send her here."

Marcus edged forward, noting Jack's smile. He hadn't seen that look in months. "Why?"

"It seems our traitor, Mabry, is a rather overprotective father. I met with my new physician yesterday, a local by the name of Strom. He happens to be related to Miss Mabry and informed me her father is concerned at her being out here on her own. In fact, Patrick Mabry arranged for her to be in Kent where the good doctor could keep an eye on her without her knowledge."

Marcus wasn't convinced. "Mabry bribed the clerk."

"Yes, but don't you see? He wished only to protect his daughter, nothing else. And I'm convinced Grace has no knowledge of it."

"You believe this relation of hers?"

"Strom's story fits with her description of her father." Jack leaned forward, laying his hands on the desk. "So you can get into your car and return to London."

"Is that any way to treat your best friend?" Marcus said, ignoring the demand. "I haven't seen you since leaving hospital. You fled to this place before I had a chance to say good-bye."

"Good-bye, Marcus."

Marcus laughed. "By the way, I had the pleasure of your fiancée's company at breakfast. Charming as ever."

"Well, toward you at least. Violet's visit was also unexpected, and just as unwelcome." Jack rose from his chair. "Now, I repeat. Good-bye, Marcus."

Instead of being insulted, Marcus looked at his masked friend and felt anger on his behalf. Miss Violet Arnold had turned out to be a disappointment. Wealthy and spoiled, she'd set her cap on becoming the future Countess of Stonebrooke. And while she may have genuinely grieved Hugh's death, she'd also leaped at Jack's offer to salvage her coronet.

Until the explosion. Marcus would never forget her reaction to his friend that day in hospital. Jack had fled to Roxwood afterward, cutting himself off from the world.

Then Patrick Mabry's daughter arrived. Marcus could almost be grateful to her, having unwittingly helped his friend take the first step in rejoining the human race. "So, Benningham, as to my plan . . ."

"Pray tell."

He was relieved to see Jack sit back down. "I wish to meet with Miss Mabry and take her measure." Marcus watched his friend. "Today, if possible. Can you arrange it?"

"If I wish to." Jack's jaw tightened, his hands curling into fists against the desk.

Marcus had anticipated the reaction. He'd gathered enough from their last telephone call to realize his friend was being swayed by the young woman.

Even if her purpose at Roxwood seemed innocent, Marcus wasn't leaving. With the Admiralty's secret project under way and so close to the estate, he had to be sure about Miss Grace Mabry. He would observe her himself—and put her to the test. "And will you?" he asked his friend at length.

"Of course not," Jack said. "And I have my reasons. The first being, I told you on the telephone, my staff watches her constantly. Grace has given no evidence to anyone of suspicious behavior. Secondly, I've interrogated her at length, and she seems all she appears, a somewhat naïve, well-bred young woman who works hard for the Women's Forage Corps. Third, and perhaps most important, is her twin brother. Colin Mabry fights with the British Army in France, and she's quite devoted to him." He relaxed his hands. "I would venture at this point to say Mabry's children are unaware of their father's actions."

"You make a good case, especially if the son fights in the trenches." Marcus rose from his chair. "But there's too much at stake to take the chance. I'd like a meeting with her, Jack."

Jack stood, as well. "I have conditions, Marcus." He spoke with the autocratic tone of a future earl. "I do not want her singled out for your interrogation. You will meet her along with the rest of the WFC women. And you shall simply pose as my friend."

"That shouldn't be difficult, Jack, since I *am* your friend," Marcus growled.

"I'll instruct Edwards to arrange it, at the farm this afternoon."

Marcus eyed his friend pensively. "Will you go along with me?"

"I wouldn't miss it."

Marcus grinned. Yes, Jack was definitely on his way back.

❧

Grace awakened feeling more exhausted than she had the day before. It was surely the nightmare. She dreamed that the

Grimm brothers' Rumpelstiltskin, who strangely resembled the blond Violet Arnold, had locked her away in the bowels of a castle and forced her to turn burlap sacks full of chaff into gold.

Relieved to be in her bed and not in some dungeon, Grace still hoped Jack would summon her for a drive this morning, despite what he'd said the night before.

He didn't, however, and knowing she was being foolish hadn't eased her disappointment. She told herself she had no right to feel anything regarding Jack Benningham, but her heart already knew it was too late.

"You're needed to drive today," Mrs. Vance had announced, giving her hope. "Meet with Mr. Tillman at the barn."

The summons was a far cry from the blue Daimler. "It's an aerator," Mr. Tillman said, walking ahead of Grace. She followed, leading one of the draft horses toward a solitary piece of machinery parked in the middle of the south pasture. It was a cross between a small horse trap and a tractor, with long, rake-like tines attached behind the seat, curving downward to within inches from the ground.

"You'll hitch up Molly and walk her right down the middle of those windrows." He indicated the several long lines of cut hay, raked together the day before. "The tines will sift the straw to dry it faster." He placed his hands on his hips. "Think you can manage the job?"

"Mr. Tillman, I can hitch up a horse." Grace struggled to be civil. He still didn't trust her after the pig fiasco.

The farmer made a grunting noise before turning and walking away. Grace sighed as she led Molly toward the harness. "Let's get you rigged up, girl." Within minutes she had the horse pulling the aerator over the first windrow, sifting hay in their wake.

"Looks like you've got it figured out!"

Grace turned to see Mr. Tillman had stopped to watch her from a distance. She waved at him, grinding her teeth. Didn't he think she could perform the simple task of leading a horse through grass?

When he left, she was grateful for the solitude. The sun remained hidden this morning behind an array of scattered clouds, and though there was no rain, the air felt humid and warm. Still, despite the dreariness of gray skies, she was glad to be out of the direct heat.

Grace encouraged Molly through row after row of hay, occasionally glancing behind her to see the cut grasses flying up in the air. After the first hour passed, she became restless. The job was more than a little monotonous.

"Golden windrows crawl like serpents across a sea of green," she began, reciting aloud as she imagined her next outing with Jack. "And warm air, fragrant with the scent of mown hay, carries the buzz of bees, the chirp of robins, and fluttering finches across my path."

Turning to gaze out across the pasture, she waxed on, "Beyond this valley lies another, then another, all patchworks of yellow, gold, and green that bind the countryside. And edged like lace against the land, trees in reds, browns, and greens crowd one another for the sky."

Her attention darted back to Molly as new inspiration struck. "My dun-colored steed is graceful and steady, fearless as her hooves crush these endless snakes swimming ahead of us. With her long, white tail, my beloved charger banishes other foes—the small winged beasts that arrive on the morning dew, attempting to attack my face and her backside—"

"Grace!"

Lucy waved as she ran toward her. Grace reined in the mare.

"My, you've n-nearly finished!" Lucy eyed her progress with approval. Then she grabbed for Molly's bridle. "I came to fetch you. Mrs. Vance wants us all in the barn. There's a visitor from the manor who wishes to meet us."

Dread filled Grace. "Miss Arnold?"

Lucy shrugged. "Mrs. Vance just said to be quick."

After removing Molly from the harness, she and Grace walked the mare back to the barn. They had just gone inside when the sound of a car's approach caught their attention.

It couldn't be Miss Arnold, unless she knew how to drive. Grace listened to the engine's purr drawing closer. Nor was the car Lord Roxwood's Daimler.

Curious, she awaited their visitor's arrival. Would Jack be with them?

Clare sidled up next to her, meeting her gaze with a look of equal anticipation.

Minutes later, a man Grace had never seen before entered the barn. Like Jack, he was tall and powerfully built, yet his features were more patrician than rugged. He also wore fine clothes, his beige suit of summer linen accentuated by a matching waistcoat and yellow-and-brown-striped tie. As he entered the barn, he removed his straw boater hat.

Grace's breath caught in her chest when Jack entered directly behind him.

"Lord Roxwood, it's a pleasure." Mrs. Vance moved to greet them, seeming composed despite Jack's mask. Grace glanced at her co-workers. Becky's mouth hung open, her soft brown eyes wide with shock, while Lucy couldn't seem to take her attention from him. Even Clare looked stony-faced, blinking several times.

"Madam," Jack said, remaining near the door. "I'd like to introduce my friend, Sir Marcus Weatherford. He expressed a wish to meet the ladies of the Women's Forage Corps and see your operation."

Sir Marcus stepped forward. "I am honored to be in the company of such lovely patriots." His smile flashed beneath a trimmed brown mustache as he gazed at each of them. All

in all, Grace thought he seemed quite fit. She wondered why
he was here and not over in France. Or was he one of Jack's
conchie friends?

Sir Marcus's attention seemed to linger on Clare before he
turned back to Mrs. Vance. "I apologize for any inconvenience."

"You honor us, Sir Marcus!" Mrs. Vance's hands fluttered as
she began introductions. "This is Miss Becky Simmons, one of
our baling hands." She nodded at Becky, who rushed forward to
execute a quick curtsy. "Miss Lucy Young is our horse-transport
driver." Lucy moved to mimic her co-worker. "And Miss Clare
Danner is another of our baling hands."

Clare stood beside Grace, unmoving. Sir Marcus hesitated,
then swiftly closed the distance between them. "My pleasure,
Miss Danner," he said, offering a most charming bow.

Crossing her arms, Clare merely nodded in what seemed a
mandatory gesture. Then she turned from him and moved over
to stand beside Lucy and Becky.

Mrs. Vance shot Clare a reproving look. "And you see Miss
Grace Mabry before you. She acts as our section clerk when
she's not employed by Lord Roxwood."

"Ah, Miss Mabry, I've heard much about you." Sir Marcus
offered another polite bow.

"Shall I take that as a compliment?" Grace darted a glance
toward the tall man standing at the door. Like Clare, Jack's arms
were folded across his chest as he leaned against the doorjamb.
Head cocked as if intent on hearing every word.

"Most assuredly," Sir Marcus said, smiling.

"Then it's a pleasure to meet you." She offered him a gra-
cious nod.

"Your driving skills have impressed my friend," he said,
brown eyes sparkling. "In fact, I believe your morning outings
have become the highlight of his day."

"Why . . . thank you." A flutter rose in her throat as she again looked to Jack. Below the mask his jaw tensed, his lips forming a taut line. What was wrong? Had he changed his mind from the other night?

A thought struck, and her insides ached. Had he reconciled with Miss Arnold?

"They are the highlight of mine as well," she said, still determined to speak the truth. The hardness eased from Jack's face, and he smiled. Grace felt light-headed with pleasure.

"Excellent," Sir Marcus said. "Would you do me the favor of taking Lord Roxwood and me for a ride tomorrow morning? I'd like to observe the WFC's operation, and if I drive, I'm afraid I'll be too preoccupied to enjoy the full experience."

"I'd be happy to," Grace said, pleased by the request. "If Lord Roxwood is agreeable."

"Bring the Daimler around at nine," he called, then abruptly left the barn.

Sir Marcus glanced at the spot where his friend had been and then hastily turned back to Grace. "Until tomorrow, Miss Mabry."

Before departing, he paused in front of Clare. "I am most honored to make your acquaintance, Miss Danner." He held out his hand, and it was a moment before she gave him hers. He raised it to his lips for a light kiss. "I hope we meet again," he said before releasing her.

"Ladies, thank you for your time," he said to the rest.

"Oh, isn't he handsome!" Becky cried as soon as the men had left the barn. They heard the car's engine come to life, then grow distant as their visitors drove away from the farm. "Tall and dressed in such fancy clothes. He even kissed your hand, Clare! Sir Marcus is sweet on you," she sang.

"He is no such thing," Clare said. "Marcus Weatherford is just another conceited man with a title who thinks he can walk on those beneath him."

Grace saw her friend's shaking hands. Was she angry . . . or was it something else?

Clare whirled from them and stormed outside.

"What's with her?" Becky asked.

"You know how Clare feels about the peerage," Grace said. *And rightly so*, she thought with compassion. "She'll be fine. Just leave her be for a while."

Grace considered her own folly with Jack Benningham. How had she allowed herself to care so very much about him? Longing to be in his company, to talk with him, play their games. To be his eyes, filling his dark world with color . . .

An ache rose in her throat, and she pressed her lips together. Especially when there was no future in it.

∽

"Well, what do you think of her?"

Jack sat beside his friend as Marcus drove them back to the manor.

"She's pretty," Marcus said. "So was the other one, Miss Danner. In all, they were quite charming."

"I'd say you were the charmer." Jealousy stabbed at him. Jack had heard enough to know Marcus Weatherford's elegant manners and good looks had dazzled the ladies, including Mrs. Vance, if her animated tone was any measure.

His own entrance had certainly produced the opposite effect. Silence had descended over the barn when he'd followed his friend inside. Jack's lip curled as he imagined the women of the WFC gaping at him, likely wondering when the hunchback Tin Man would start howling.

All except Grace. His heart warmed, remembering her comment. She'd enjoyed spending time with him, as well.

"I was merely being polite," Marcus said. "Besides, it doesn't matter anyway. I'm here on business, not to woo the ladies."

"I thought you did a splendid job at both." Had Grace been smitten with his friend, too? Jack recalled hearing the blush in her voice. In the past two weeks, he'd become well attuned to her inflections of tone—teasing, angry, frustrated, pleased. He could even detect when she was being shy. But Marcus could charm the bark off a tree, and when compared to Frankenstein's monster, likely Grace was just as enthralled by him as the rest.

His hands curled into fists against the seat. "Tell me what she looks like."

It was a moment before Marcus answered. "Pale skin, red hair, green eyes . . . oh, and pieces of straw sticking to every part of her."

"You know, it's hard to believe you're an MI5 agent," Jack ground out. "She gave me much the same information herself. Can you possibly elaborate?"

"Shall I wax poetic for you, Benningham?" Marcus sounded amused. "Milky-white skin, hair like fire, eyes the color of the sea—how's that?"

"Stop or I may become ill," Jack said dryly. "What do you propose for tomorrow?"

"Just a country drive, old boy," he said, and Jack detected his note of evasiveness. "I can get to know her better and make my own evaluation. It might even require hanging on a few extra days."

Jack would have preferred his friend's hasty departure, but it would mean being left alone with Violet. "You're certainly welcome to stay," he bit out.

"That's quite a change from your attitude toward me earlier."

"Yes, well, you're already here, so you can keep Miss Arnold entertained." Gratitude overrode his irritation as he said gruffly, "I appreciate you standing in at meals in my absence."

He was also relieved to postpone his confrontation with Violet.

"So why is she here, Jack? And don't tell me it's because she wants to be close to you."

His friend knew that much, having been with him that day at hospital. Still, Jack wasn't about to disclose any more information until Marcus revealed some of his own. "Why are you here?" he countered. "Aside from wanting to meet Grace and take a drive around the park?"

"Touché, old boy" was all Marcus said.

What was his friend hiding? "Quit playing spy games and tell me what's going on. I have a right to know."

"Do you?" Marcus asked.

"It's my home. Grace is my employee. And you seem to have a reason to doubt my assurances about her. That makes it my business."

"Patience, friend," Marcus said. "All will soon be revealed."

Jack frowned and turned his face to the open window. Patience was a virtue he'd never quite mastered.

13

"Would you like to see the field where the women are baling hay, Sir Marcus?"

"Indeed I would, Miss Mabry. Please, take us where you will."

Grace drove the Daimler along a road past the south pasture where yesterday she'd worked the aerator. This morning the baler was already chugging away as Clare added forkfuls of hay into its maw. Lucy and Mrs. Vance tied off each bale with wire while Becky loaded them off to the side to be weighed. Mr. Tillman was even now assembling the tripod scale.

"Looks like backbreaking work," Sir Marcus said from the back seat.

"Very much so, and it's still morning," she said. "When noon arrives and the sun is directly overhead, it will be twice as hot and the working conditions even more difficult."

Grace felt chagrined seeing her WFC sisters at labor. She'd promised Mrs. Vance to take up the slack from losing Agnes, yet here she was driving Jack and his friend around on a tour.

Still, she had to admit, she enjoyed being with Jack again. He sat next to her, looking quite handsome in a white linen suit that fit snug across his broad shoulders. He wore a smart-looking felt trilby today instead of his usual brown motoring cap.

She wondered if he'd had his "discussion" with Miss Arnold, or if he continued to avoid her. Agnes mentioned he'd immediately retired after Grace left the night of her arrival.

This morning, when Knowles let her in, Grace had caught a glimpse of a dark skirt ascending the stairs before disappearing from view. She couldn't tell if it was Miss Arnold, Agnes, or the companion, Mrs. Grant.

She wondered if Miss Arnold had been invited to come along this morning. Grace was relieved at her absence. Being in the woman's company, particularly while driving, would be unnerving.

"How long have you been with the Women's Forage Corps, Miss Mabry?"

Grace glanced over her shoulder at Sir Marcus. "Well over a month. I've been at Roxwood three weeks."

"And do you like it? The work, I mean?"

She turned back to the road. "I had difficulty adjusting, at first. I got fired when one of the women pulled a prank and left me to chase a dozen pigs around Lord Roxwood's garden."

"Pigs?" She heard him chuckle. "Which woman was it?"

"That is for me to know, Sir Marcus." Grace smiled. "We sisters in the WFC keep our secrets for one another. But it was my good fortune Lord Roxwood changed his mind and offered me a job as his part-time driver. The Corps kept me on, as well." *More or less*, she thought, choosing to omit how Jack had bullied Mrs. Vance into rehiring her.

"I think perhaps it's been *my* good fortune," Jack said beside her. His hand rested against the seat between them, and she smiled as she recalled the evening of his birthday.

"Do you enjoy history, Miss Mabry?"

Grace reeled in her thoughts and glanced back at Sir Marcus. "Why, yes."

196

"Has Lord Roxwood taken you to view the old Roman ruins near Richborough?"

"We haven't yet had the occasion," Jack said in a flat tone beside her. Grace noticed the muscle in his jaw tense. "Is there a particular reason you wish to visit the ruins, Marcus?"

"Merely because I believe Miss Mabry will find them fascinating." Sir Marcus leaned forward and pointed toward an approaching crossroad. "Turn right up there onto Canterbury Road. You'll make another right once you reach Ramsgate Road heading south. The old Roman Road is just a few miles beyond on your right."

She did as he instructed, and soon they were traveling along a good stretch of even road.

"Lord Roxwood tells me you have a brother overseas?"

"Yes," Grace replied, "Colin is with the cavalry."

"You must be proud of him."

"Very much, though I wish . . ."

"Yes?"

Grace hesitated. *I wish I could shake this ill feeling.*

"Tell me, Miss Mabry."

While he spoke congenially, Grace heard the demand in his voice. Why did he press her? "I just miss him, that's all." She looked at Jack, who now sat with arms crossed against his chest. "You and Lord Roxwood share a penchant for asking questions."

"I'm merely curious."

His words irritated her. Jack once offered her the same excuse. "You know what they say about curiosity and the cat," she quipped hotly.

Jack's bark of laughter drowned out any response Sir Marcus might have made. "If you're trying to stir a hornet's nest, Marcus, you've done it," he called back to his friend.

Grace felt her cheeks warm as Sir Marcus said, "I only wish

to get to know Miss Mabry a bit better." To her, he said, "Does he write to you often, your brother?"

"I haven't received any correspondence from him in quite some time." She kept her focus on the road ahead. "Lord Roxwood explained to me how Army mail is often delayed."

"True enough. Do your mother and father write often?"

"Marcus." Jack spoke sharply.

Grace wondered at the underlying friction between them. Jack's expression below the mask had turned to brooding. Was he angry with Sir Marcus? "I haven't received a post from my father," she answered. "And my mother is dead."

"I'm very sorry, Miss Mabry." His genuine condolence appeased her. "Does your father—?"

"What is your profession, Sir Marcus?" she asked abruptly, as she made the next right turn onto Ramsgate Road.

"I beg your pardon?"

She glanced at Jack and saw his grin. Her spirits lifted, and she pressed on, "Well, if you wish to ask me so many personal questions, I think it only fair you answer a few in return. Are you a soldier? Home on leave, perhaps?"

"He's a lieutenant in the Admiralty," Jack said.

"On holiday," Sir Marcus was quick to add.

"Ah, a man with a sense of duty, then," Grace said, satisfied.

"If she didn't approve of you before, Marcus, she does now," Jack said to his friend. "Miss Mabry is quite the patriot."

"Indeed, I am," she said, relieved at their easy banter. "How did you and Sir Marcus first meet?" she asked Jack.

"We were at Oxford together." Grace's heart gave a little jolt at the genuine warmth in his smile. "Marcus was the troublemaker."

Sir Marcus let out a snort from the back seat. It seemed the two men had a lasting friendship after all. "Are you married, Sir Marcus?" she asked, thinking to look out for her friend Clare's interest.

Jack scowled while Sir Marcus said smoothly, "Is that a proposal, Miss Mabry?"

She burst out laughing. "Hardly, I'm merely curious," she said, tossing his words back at him.

Jack's features eased, and he chuckled. "Nicely done, Miss Mabry."

Even Sir Marcus sounded amused when he said, "I am still looking for the right woman."

"Looking for someone who'll put up with you, you mean," Jack said.

Grace noticed his mood seemed to be mellowing the farther they drove away from Roxwood. Perhaps distancing himself from his troubles with Miss Arnold? In any event, it was wonderful to be out enjoying the summer day with a bit of camaraderie. It had likely been some time since he and his friend had had an opportunity to do so. She felt grateful to be a part of it.

"So, Miss Mabry, is your father . . . ah, there's the Roman Road directly ahead. If you'll take it, we should see the ruins on the right."

Relieved to be out from beneath Sir Marcus's scrutiny, Grace made the turn and soon sighted the crumbling walls surrounding what remained of an ancient Roman fort.

"*Rutupiae* was the original name for Richborough," Sir Marcus said as they drew closer. "The fort was built after the Romans landed in England in AD forty-three."

"It's amazing!" Grace forgot her annoyance as she pulled the car to the side of the road that overlooked the ruins. Her mind conjured visions of soldiers clad in red tunics, helmets, and shoulder plates walking the battlements in search of their enemies.

Knowing Jack would wish to be included, she began to describe the place. "Crags of gray stone rise out of a green sea like broken teeth, biting at the warm air as though to grasp and reclaim their history, now lost: Roman soldiers, golden eagles, and the flags of Caesar . . ."

"I am completely enraptured."

Grace looked over her shoulder to see Sir Marcus's smile. Beside her, Jack issued a low, guttural noise. Was he growling?

"You make a great storyteller, Miss Mabry."

She beamed at him. "I am a writer . . . an aspiring novelist, anyway. Lord Roxwood has come to my aid in honing my skills."

"Oh? What skills would those be?"

Grace caught a restless movement beside her. "He's helped me to *see* with my words, to paint pictures with them. We make a game of it."

"Word games, eh? Sounds like you've been extremely productive, old boy."

Jack's mouth tightened. Sir Marcus said, "Did he come up with the game, or did you?"

"Oh, he did," she said. "When we first met, I am ashamed to say I spoke rather unimaginatively. Since then I've practiced every day, even when I bale hay in the fields. I hope one day to write a story about my time here at Roxwood and have it published."

"I imagine there are many tales to fuel the imagination here in Kent," Sir Marcus said. "With so much history, you could write about some mystery or intrigue, perhaps even a spy novel—"

"Leave off, Marcus." Jack ground out the words. "I wish to get out and stretch my legs."

"Of course," Grace said and killed the engine while the two men exited the car.

She came around the Daimler and continued to stare at the ancient Roman fort. "I don't know about writing a spy novel, Sir Marcus, but when I see these ruins, I think of the battles once fought and I'm reminded of my patriotism." She turned to him. "I'd like to write about those who perform their duty to Britain, and the brave women aiding in the war effort while our men fight the enemy overseas." Grace tipped her head. "And don't think you'll so easily put them back into the kitchens and drawing rooms once the war is over, either."

Sir Marcus grinned, and Grace noted the genuine humor in his brown eyes. Perhaps Clare was being too hasty to judge this man. "Such lofty ideals, Miss Mabry, but please tell me you're not one of those suffragettes?" he said with a look of mock horror.

"She is indeed," Jack said.

Grace felt a rush of warmth as he came to stand beside her. "I do support the suffrage movement, though I'm not what one would consider a militant for the cause. I believe women deserve the vote, as they're making such great strides in aiding Britain. Why, they have taken over as policemen, firemen, laborers, and cleaners. They work in agriculture, make munitions, even drive ambulances back and forth from the fighting in order to save lives."

"Those efforts are commendable," Sir Marcus agreed. "But how do they make a woman better able to understand the intricacies of politics?"

Jack's laughter cut into his friend's conversation. "Careful, Marcus, or she'll have you putting her name in for Parliament."

Sir Marcus gazed at her with a look of grudging admiration. "You are a surprise to me, Miss Mabry. Would you care to take a closer look at the ruins?"

"Very much," she said eagerly.

"We won't be long, old boy."

Sir Marcus held out an arm for Grace, but Jack intercepted her first, taking her arm. "Lead the way, Miss Mabry."

At his touch, Grace felt her pulse race. Placing her hand over his, she led him as they followed Sir Marcus a short distance to a place offering perfect visibility of the ruins.

"The fort is built nearly on top of the East Kent marshes,"

Jack said to her once they stopped. "It's probably one of the most important Roman historical sites left in Britain. You can see the natural amphitheater, the series of grass rings surrounding the center of the fort. Near the end of the Roman Empire, Richborough was abandoned and became the site of a Saxon religious settlement."

"It's hard to conceive of these walls being nearly two thousand years old." Again Grace envisioned her Roman soldiers walking the battlements. Sadly, time and progress were slowly wearing away at the stones.

Scanning the distant marsh on either side of the ruins, she caught some activity. Straining her eyes, she could see what appeared to be several tents and men wearing uniforms. "What's going on over there?" She pointed toward the encampment.

Sir Marcus cast a glance in the same direction, but it was a moment before he turned and narrowed his eyes at her. "What do you think it is, Miss Mabry?"

Grace felt Jack tense beside her. "Some sort of training, perhaps?" she said. "But I see trucks, so maybe they're building something?"

"You could be correct," Sir Marcus said.

She frowned. "Well, if they are doing construction of any kind, I hope they do not tamper with these lovely ruins. I would hate to see history destroyed."

"Would you?"

She blinked at him. "What do you mean . . . ?"

"Shall we go back?" Jack gave her arm a gentle squeeze. Once they returned to the car, he commandeered his usual place in front, with Sir Marcus slipping into the back.

"I thought we were to take turns riding in front," Sir Marcus said, and gave Grace a wink.

"You thought wrong," Jack said. "And unless you care to visit a few more old places, I wish to return to the house."

"I've seen enough," Sir Marcus said.

"Very well. Miss Mabry, if you wouldn't mind?"

"On our way." Grace again detected tension between the two men as she quickly restarted the car. Once they returned to the manor, Sir Marcus exited first. "It's been a delight, Miss Mabry." He offered a slight bow. "Thank you for showing me the sights of Kent."

"You're most welcome, Sir Marcus." Grace came around to open Jack's door. "Shall I come around for you tomorrow, Lord Roxwood?" she asked, hoping he would say yes.

"I think not."

She tried not to feel disheartened. Jack must entertain Miss Arnold and Sir Marcus, while she should help her friends in the fields.

"I'll call for you in a few days," he said in a low voice.

She felt a burst of pleasure at his words, looking forward to their next adventure. "Shall I take you as far as Scotland? We will have so many miles to make up for, after all."

"Only if you promise to avoid the potholes." At his smile, Grace's heart melted. She would take him back to Eden and, being his eyes, paint the scene with such words that he might once again relive its beauty.

∞

"You purposely baited her." Jack seethed with fury a half hour later as he and Marcus stood behind the closed doors of his study. "You're telling me the Roman ruins are the site of a secret underground Q port the Admiralty is building, and you took Grace there to . . . what? See if she'd confess to being a spy?"

"Easy, Jack," Marcus said. "I admit, Miss Mabry appears to be all you told me, naïve but refreshingly candid. And I don't detect any evasiveness about her. The bit about her patriotism seems real enough, with her own brother fighting at the Front.

But the Admiralty cannot take risks, despite your feelings or my own. And while she may be pleasing to the eye and quite likable, we must know beyond a doubt her purpose here. I find it hard to believe Patrick Mabry would bribe a clerk merely because he worries about his daughter's welfare, not when construction of a new secret military port is fully under way. It would be a prize for the Germans if they knew about it."

"How pleasing is she, Marcus?" Jack felt somewhat exposed by the question, yet his desire to know more about Grace overrode his pride.

"She is lovely, Jack," Marcus said. "With hair a burnished shade of auburn and the greenest eyes I've ever seen."

"The color of ivy?" He recalled Grace's description.

"More like emeralds, I think."

Jack's heart thrummed in his chest. *Emeralds.* His mind flashed to the other image he kept tucked away, his goddess in green, her luminous eyes lit with passion as she'd slipped him a single white feather. A lifetime ago.

"Is Miss Mabry attracted to you?" he asked his friend.

"I noticed she looks at you a lot."

Jack scoffed. "Haven't you heard, Marcus? In the village I'm known as the Tin Man. They cannot help but gawk at me."

"She wasn't gawking," Marcus said. "Look, even if she had been attracted to me, I much prefer gray eyes to green. And ebony locks to all that fire." He chuckled. "Though Miss Clare Danner does seem to have some of that herself. I'm afraid she wasn't too keen on my attentions. She practically ran from me when I introduced myself."

Jack's tension fled. So Marcus had set his sights on another woman—not Grace. "The famous Weatherford charm not working?" he said, amused.

"She only makes me more determined, not less, old boy," Marcus said. "I shall win her over."

"There's to be a dance in the village tomorrow night for the local boys home on leave," Jack said. "I've been told the ladies of the WFC will attend."

"All of them? Good thing I planned to stay the weekend. I need a day or two just to recover from Paris."

"You haven't told me yet. How did the trial go?"

"Short," Marcus said. "Only two days and they still didn't come up with any concrete evidence. It was shoddily handled, but the jury convicted her as a spy nonetheless. Mata Hari will face the firing squad."

The news left Jack cold. While he was prepared to go to any length to find new proof against Patrick Mabry and bring him to justice, the spy mania spreading across Europe disturbed him. When convictions were handed out because of fear or prejudice instead of proof, that meant no one was safe. "Remind me never to go back to France," he said, half joking.

"Speaking of which, I need to make several calls to London. If you don't mind, I'll use your study," Marcus said. "Meanwhile, you might deal with Violet. She's champing at the bit to speak with you. Can't put her off forever, you know. Care to tell me what it's about?"

"She wants me to break off our engagement," Jack said. "You recall her father shelled out quite a sum to my family before she and Hugh were to marry." He sighed. "If I had inherited a windfall from a distant relation, I could have settled the debt and we wouldn't be in this fix. Stonebrooke would remain solvent and Miss Arnold could have been saved from a 'fate worse than death.'"

"She wants out, does she?" Marcus growled. "Violet Arnold doesn't deserve you."

"I appreciate your loyalty, Marcus. But can you blame her? What woman wants to spend her wedding night with a husband *déguisé*?" He pointed to the mask. "Or worse, without it?"

"I wish I knew what to say."

"Nothing to say," Jack said, keeping his tone light. "Though I do wish . . ."

"I know. But things have a way of working out. It may sound trite, Jack, but have faith. The truth always wins out."

Jack felt the weight of his friend's hand on his shoulder. "That goes for Miss Mabry, as well," Marcus said. "If she's innocent, then nothing will come of today's events at Richborough. If, however, she's guilty . . . she'll bear the full brunt of the law. You understand that?"

Jack pulled away from him. "I lost my sight, Marcus, not my ability to think." Yet as he spoke, uncertainty gnawed at him. Had he lost his edge? Was she a spy, whom he'd allowed to beguile him in his isolation? He didn't want to believe it. "You're only doing your job, Marcus, but I know you are wrong about her."

"Let us hope so, my friend," Marcus said. "For your sake and hers."

❧

"Your butler said you wish to speak with me. It's about time."

Violet Arnold's voice sounded from the drawing room doors. Jack heard her enter the room and settle into the chaise longue directly to his right.

"Tea?" Without waiting for her reply, he rose from the divan and went to the sideboard, where Knowles had placed a tea service and poured a cup before he left.

"You've kept me waiting two days, Benningham. Have you been scheming with Marcus to keep me from my purpose?"

"I apologize for the delay, Violet." He took the cup to her. "And no, I haven't discussed you with Marcus at all. He's working in my study at the moment, so we have the privacy you wished for to 'resolve our issues.'"

She took the cup and saucer from his grasp, and he heard the ensuing rattle as she set them on a table beside her. Jack caught a whiff of lilacs when she rose to stand before him.

"Well?" she said.

"I am here and ready to listen. What do you wish to talk about?"

"Jack, must you be so dull-witted?" He felt her brush past him. The rustle of cloth revealed her pacing the room. "I want you to end this charade of an engagement," she said.

"You haven't told me why." He returned to his seat on the divan.

"We've gone over it countless times. I don't love you. We were ill-suited from the start." Her voice grew nearer as she approached. "I hardly need tell you I'd rather be in London right now, but your obstinacy has forced me here to this rustic . . . hall to speak with you face-to-face."

"Face-to-face, then?" Jack reached behind his head as if to loosen his mask.

"Stop!"

Again he heard her swift retreat. Was she bolting for the door? Maybe she planned to scream or faint into a heap once more, Jack thought bitterly. He lowered his hands. "You say you don't love me and that we're ill-suited." He forced the last, "But many arranged marriages have ended up being quite happy."

"I loathe the idea of marrying you, Jack." Her tone took on a desperate edge. "I could never love you, don't you understand?"

"I know a woman's heart turns fickle once the groom begins to resemble a circus freak." Jack launched up from the divan. "The truth, Violet," he said. "No more games. Your reason for ending this is because you can't stomach the sight of me."

"No," she said. "It's because . . . I've met someone."

He paused, hearing her uncertainty. "Do tell," he said, arms crossed. "Another titled heir? No doubt with a face that doesn't terrify the masses."

"He's the Honorable Arthur Baines of Glennoch." The rattle of a teacup followed the soft creak of the chaise as she resumed her seat. "We met in Edinburgh months ago, when my father and I attended the royal visit."

"I'm being tossed over for the second son of a viscount?" Jack knew of whom she spoke. He'd seen the father, Viscount Moray, in the House of Lords on several occasions. "Then why don't you cry off, Violet . . . or are you afraid your father won't approve of you settling without a crown?"

"Oh, yes, *my father*," she said, and he heard the bitterness in her tone. "Always a man of action and ambition, reaching for the next prize. He started out as a rice farmer in Texas, did you know? Then within two decades he managed to make a fortune in oil. He's traveled the world, been on safari, once he even climbed the Wetterhorn in Switzerland."

He heard the rattle of her cup as she again set it down. "And from the day we first stepped off the ship at Liverpool, he's had his sights set on a royal heir to add to his accomplishments. I was to be his broodmare." He heard her whispered resentment, before she took a deep breath and said, "When I met Hugh, I thought everything would be all right. I cared for your brother, Jack. But now he's gone, and you're . . ."

"Frankenstein?" Jack supplied.

"I didn't say that."

"And you're not thinking it?"

"I know you've never held affection for me, Benningham. What about the redhead in your dining room the night I arrived, your hay-baling chauffeur? You seem to like her well enough."

"Leave Miss Mabry out of this."

"I only meant you must know how I feel. Why not break off our engagement? Everyone would understand *your* reasons."

"Ah, yes, poor Jack Benningham, sacrificing all to spare his betrothed from having to look at his grisly countenance for the rest of her life. And shall I remain hidden away here like Hugo's Quasimodo, so the world can remain a beautiful place?

"Believe me, Violet, I would love nothing better." He clasped his hands behind his back. "But there's the matter of the money, isn't there? We both seem to understand your father's lack of empathy to the situation." He walked to the hearth. "I recall there was a time when you were eager to continue your pursuit as the future Countess of Stonebrooke, so I did my duty and stepped up to take Hugh's place. I will admit after I'd gotten used to the idea of being married, I began to put my trust in you for a relatively happy union."

"But that was before Arthur," she objected. He heard her rise from the chaise behind him.

"I think it was before *this*," he said, turning toward her and touching the mask. "Fate stepped in, and now you've found yourself a shiny new beau, untitled, but no doubt more pleasing to look at." He paused. "Perhaps this new man of yours will pay your father off."

"He hasn't that kind of money," she said angrily.

"And I do?"

"Surely you must have some kind of inheritance or property." He could hear her resume her pacing. "My father would understand if you backed out, perhaps even make a deal with you, under the circumstances. I could appease him by keeping my reputation in town, and Arthur, well, he *is* the son of a viscount." She sighed. "Don't you understand, Jack? I love him."

Jack laughed, and it was a hollow sound to his own ears. "You do sound convincing, my dear. But what else could you say to persuade me, *especially* in my circumstances?" A pause. "I doubt you even know what love is."

The rustle of cloth moved away from him. "I do know"—her

voice carried from across the room—"though obviously you do not. Otherwise you would show a little compassion and set me free."

He heard the abrupt slam of the door as she left the drawing room.

14

"Hurry up, ladies, or the dance is going to start without us!"

"We're coming, Mrs. Vance," Grace called downstairs. She rushed to shrug out of her robe and into the embroidered cotton summer dress she'd worn at the manor.

Clare had also dressed for the occasion wearing a long, blue cotton skirt and flowing white shirtwaist embroidered with tiny blue-and-gold flowers. In her hands she held a narrow straw hat trimmed in matching blue ribbons and sprigs of lavender.

"You look quite sharp," Grace said, tying a bow into the white satin sash, completing her ensemble. "The color goes well with your eyes."

Clare smiled as she donned the hat. "Thanks. Except for church on Sundays, I feel like I live in trousers and boots."

"That's because you do," Grace said. "At least I got the chance to wear this dress for dinner the other night." The memory of her intimate celebration with Jack still warmed her. "Though only Lord Roxwood's staff got to see me in it, and Miss Arnold," she added, recalling the woman's piercing scrutiny.

"Speaking of Her Highness, Agnes said she left in a temper this morning?"

"Yes, I believe Sir Marcus drove her back to London." And if Miss Arnold's abrupt departure was any indication, her visit hadn't gone as planned. Grace was secretly thrilled she'd left Roxwood. "Unfortunate for Sir Marcus, since I think you would have completely swept him away, especially in that darling hat."

Clare arched a brow as she tucked a few errant wisps of dark hair beneath her brim. "Oh, I'd have swept him away, all right—with a good, stiff broom."

Grace laughed, and Clare flashed a conspiratorial grin that produced a dimple in her right cheek. "You clean up nicely, Mabry. That green makes your hair look like fire."

Grace adjusted the emerald gauze framing her wide-brimmed straw hat. "Thanks, *Danner*," she teased. "Green is my favorite color, you know. I'm Irish, after all."

Clare winked. "Won't our dance cards fill up the minute we walk in the door?"

Grace's smile turned wistful. It would be nice if Sir Marcus and Jack could have attended the dance tonight. But Sir Marcus was back in London, and Jack would never consider making a public appearance in the village. Coming under the town's scrutiny once had been enough.

She sighed. At least she would enjoy some leisure time with her WFC sisters, a rare occurrence since they always seemed to be working. Grace wanted to spend time with Agnes, too. She'd returned to the gatehouse this morning after only two days with Violet Arnold. Her friend seemed out of sorts.

Agnes still wore her uniform as she dug through her traveling bag on the bed. Grace finished pinning her hat, then walked to her. She touched her maid lightly on the shoulder. "Agnes?"

Agnes jumped and whirled around. "Oh, miss, you startled me!"

"I'm sorry, I just wondered if you were all right." She noted the tight lines at Agnes's mouth and her high color. "You seem distraught. Did Miss Arnold mistreat you?" Grace felt regret at having tossed her into the horrid woman's path.

"Oh, no, miss." Her features eased. "Aside from helping her dress and arrange her hair, I don't think she even knew I was there."

"Then why aren't you getting ready for the dance? We're all taking our bicycles to the village in a few minutes."

"I . . . want to write a letter first, to my family in Belgium. I cannot seem to find my paper and pen."

Grace was tempted to ask about the photograph she'd discovered in Agnes's bag, but with the other women in the room, she didn't think it prudent. "You're welcome to use my stationery. It's in my portmanteau," she said.

"Oh, thank you." Agnes looked relieved.

Poor dear, she must miss her mother and sister terribly. "Don't be too long getting to the dance," Grace said in an effort to lighten the mood. "It's been a while since you and I have enjoyed time together besides lugging around bales of hay. And wear your new shirtwaist. That shade of pink is so becoming on you."

Agnes paused. Then she shook her head, her brown eyes misting. "You're always so kind . . ."

"Now, that's enough." Grace felt her own eyes begin to burn. "I'm just being truthful."

"Your truth is colored by friendship, miss," Agnes said softly. "And it will always be the most beautiful shade to me." She took a deep breath and made an effort to smile. "I won't be long and I will wear the pink. I'm certain Mr. Tillman will bring me over later in the cart."

Grace nodded. "Mrs. Vance said another WFC gang will be there from the estate of Winton, and rumor has it the new Land Army girls, as well." She winked. "Finding enough dance partners to go around might be a challenge if we don't get there first."

"I'll see you soon," Agnes promised.

Heading downstairs with the rest of the women, Grace thought about her own family. She had yet to receive a letter from her brother, and while Jack's explanation about Army mail had reassured her somewhat, she still worried about Colin.

Nor had she received a letter from Da since she arrived. Grace found she longed to see him, and it hurt to imagine he was too busy with Swan's to think of her.

She halted on the steps as she realized she'd forgotten to post her letter—the one she intended to mail the day she took Jack to the village . . . two weeks ago! She'd changed her mind after seeing how the townspeople gawked at him, then had been so busy traveling or working in the fields that it completely slipped her mind.

Guilt plagued her. She could hardly fault Da when she was so thoughtless. Resuming her descent, she determined to mail the letter on Monday. Tomorrow she could add a postscript inquiring after any news of Colin. Perhaps Agnes would post it with hers, in the event Jack called on her to drive. With Violet Arnold gone, the chances were very good.

The thought buoyed her while she moved to crowd with the other women near the door. All looked their best, laughing and excited at the prospect of a night out. Mrs. Vance looked splendid in a rose-print dress, her straw hat decorated in matching mauve ribbons. "Shall we?" she said, smiling as she opened the door to their resounding yes.

Mr. Tillman stood on the front step. "Ladies," he said in his rumbly voice.

He still wore his work clothes. "Why, Mr. Tillman," Mrs. Vance said in a breathless voice, "are you here to escort us?"

"As much as that would please me, Mrs. Vance, I've still duties to attend to. I came with a message for Miss Mabry."

Grace's pulse quickened as she moved past the others to the front. Was it from Jack? Or perhaps word from Colin? "What message do you have?"

"His lordship has offered to let you drive the ladies to the dance in his motorcar, so that you might arrive 'in style.' I've got the cart here if you'd like me to take you to fetch it."

"Oh, yes!" cried Lucy and Becky in unison.

"Thank you, Mr. Tillman. And thank Lord Roxwood." Grace hid her disappointment. No word from her brother, and any hope she'd held that Jack might decide to attend the festivities was gone, not if he was allowing her to use the car for her friends.

She chastised herself for a fool. How could she think they had any future together? He was engaged to someone else. Grace was his paid driver, nothing more.

Liar. She could still imagine his hand on hers at the table during dinner. The man who ate alone was willing enough then to break his own rules. His words to her, that she was his eyes and the best gift he'd received, burned in her memory and would remain always, no matter what the future held for either of them.

It was dusk when they finally arrived at the dance in the Daimler. Even from the street, the village community hall of Roxwood stood ablaze in light. Sounds of laughter and the quick melody of ragtime being played on a piano could be heard outside.

Parking the car, Grace followed Clare and the others into the hall. Becky was the first to break from their party, cutting a path to a pair of tables heaped with refreshments.

The place was packed with young men and women. A few couples danced while a soldier sat at the piano playing the light, carefree music they'd heard moments before.

"Oh, there's Millicent Foster!" Mrs. Vance waved at a woman

near the refreshment tables. "She's the supervisor for the WFC gang working at the Winton estate. We went through training together at Norfolk."

Millicent Foster, a woman close to Mrs. Vance's age and dressed in a seal-brown skirt and tailored jacket beamed and waved back. She was surrounded by five young and hardy-looking females clad in an array of blue, brown, and gray skirts, white shirtwaists, and straw hats with matching ribbons. Each held a glass of pink lemonade.

"See the woman over there, in uniform?" Mrs. Vance indicated another group along the opposite wall near the piano. "She's with the Land Army girls I told you about."

"Does that mean they'll be coming to Roxwood?" Grace asked.

Mrs. Vance nodded. "I was informed yesterday a gang will start within two weeks. Our haymaking here is nearly done, and then we'll be sent on to the next farm."

Grace felt a jolt as she realized they would all be leaving Roxwood soon. What about Jack? Would she be able to stay on as his driver, or must she go with her sisters to the next farm?

"They're pretty g-girls." Lucy's comment tore Grace from her musings, and she gazed at the Land Army women talking and laughing with a few of the soldiers.

"There seem to be more than enough ladies," Clare observed, though a surprising number of young men in uniform stood in line for refreshments. Grace noted each table laden with mountains of biscuits, floured cakes, mince pies, and tiny cucumber sandwiches. Large punch bowls made of cut glass brimmed with pink lemonade. Given the war's rationing, it was a sumptuous feast.

"It's obvious these folks have scrimped for some time to provide such a bounty," Mrs. Vance said, reading her thoughts.

"Certainly a sign of their patriotism," Grace said, nodding her approval.

"I think it speaks more to their affection for these boys," Mrs. Vance said gently. "When the threat of losing a child hangs in the balance, each moment you're together becomes precious. No sacrifice seems too great for love."

"No, it doesn't," murmured Clare, standing on Grace's other side.

She turned to her friend and caught the flash of pain in the gray eyes. Scanning the crowded room, Grace noted for the first time the uniformed soldiers standing between older couples: fathers, with arms slung over the shoulders of their sons, while teary-eyed mothers squeezed the hands of their boys, who would all too soon return to the Front.

Grace spotted others standing with their families, some wearing uniforms, others sporting bandaged heads, broken arms, or a wooden crutch in place of a leg. A lump rose in her throat as the light of her idealism began to dim. Mrs. Vance was right. Love prompted these families, not duty or allegiance or pride. Again, she couldn't help thinking of her brother, wondering where he was this night.

Did he struggle with sleep in some rat-infested trench? Or stand watch as they waited for the enemy to strike? Would he become like one of these boys, missing an arm or a leg?

Swiftly, images rose in her mind: Grace and her brother shouting wildly at last year's rally, before their mother's death; Colin smiling and looking smart in his brand-new uniform as they both stood beside Mother's bed.

Lillian Mabry's look of devastation as she'd turned to gaze at her daughter . . .

Grace felt her chest tighten. *Oh, Colin, why don't you simply write?*

"My goodness, Sir Marcus is here," Mrs. Vance said. "What an honor!"

The handsome figure of Sir Marcus Weatherford entered

the hall, looking smart in a brown pinstriped suit, matching waistcoat, and hat in hand.

A hush fell over the room as Jack followed closely behind.

Grace drew in a sharp breath. Even with the mask, he looked splendid. His tall frame was encased in a tailored navy-blue suit that fit his rugged form perfectly. In his hand he carried a single red rose.

Sir Marcus searched the room before his gaze settled on them. He turned to murmur something to Jack, and the two men approached.

"Good evening, Sir Marcus, Lord Roxwood," Mrs. Vance said.

"Ladies." Sir Marcus turned to Clare. "Miss Danner, you look enchanting this evening." He offered a polite bow.

Clare seemed frozen in place. Finally she found her voice. "I thought you returned to London."

"Margate." He smiled beneath the dark mustache. "I had to deliver someone to the train station this morning. And while I was there I purchased a new hat. Do you like it?"

Clare pursed her lips, eying the boater as if it might bite.

"Why, it's very smart, isn't it, Clare?" Grace said, moving forward when her friend remained silent.

"Very" was all Clare said, and she cast a wary glance at Sir Marcus.

"Miss Mabry?" Jack had obviously heard her speak and moved closer. With a slight incline of his head, he held out the red rose. "Would you do me the honor?"

Grace's thoughts flew back to the night of Lady Bassett's ball. He'd handed her a rose then just like this one. She'd been angry with him because he'd laughed at her.

He wasn't laughing now. "Thank you," she said softly, taking the flower from him.

"Miss Danner, would you care to dance?" Sir Marcus waved

toward the dance floor. The ragtime had ended, with the piano player leaving in search of refreshments. Now a gramophone and records provided the music, the first notes of the song "Missing You, Dear" echoing in the hall.

Clare shot Grace an anxious look. Grace sympathized . . . then nudged her friend toward Sir Marcus. One could not let fear rule, after all. "It's just a dance," she whispered. "An evening of fun, away from the nasty, loud steam baler. Nothing more."

Her friend's resolve seemed to weaken as she looked toward the couples moving back and forth to the music. "All right." She nodded at Sir Marcus. "One dance."

"Excellent!" Looking pleased, he held out his hand to her, and they headed off to the dance floor.

"Excuse me, Lord Roxwood. I must have a word with a co-worker." Mrs. Vance sketched a brief curtsy and departed in the direction of Millicent Foster. A wide-eyed Lucy followed.

"Thank you for letting me use the Daimler this evening," Grace said when she and Jack were alone. "The ladies were quite thrilled to finally have a ride in the car, and for two of them it was their first experience."

"I am pleased to bestow so much pleasure with such little effort," he said quietly. "And I imagine attending a dance is a special occasion."

"Very much so, especially for these women. Baling hay from farm to farm doesn't allow for much entertainment. It's all rather a quiet, rural existence."

"And does it suit you?"

Grace brushed a finger against the outer petals of the rose. "I love the tranquility and the natural beauty of Kent, though I do occasionally miss being in London with its amusements. I've always enjoyed visiting the galleries and museums. Even the bustling atmosphere at Swan's is to my liking. For the research, you understand," she added. "Patrons always manage to provide me with interesting story ideas."

"Yes, I'm certain gossip must abound in a tea shop filled with women."

"Indeed, it does." Grace wondered if he knew of all the nefarious tales regaled about him.

"What did they have to say about me?" he asked uncannily, and she debated whether or not to tell him.

Grace decided to be truthful. "They said you were quite the reprobate. That you gambled, drank, and had an affair with a different woman each day of the week."

His chuckle delighted her. She was also surprised at his reaction. "Doesn't it make you angry to be discussed in that manner?"

He smiled and said, "In my former line of work, a disreputable reputation was essential."

"What occupation was that?"

He shook his head, and his amusement waned. "I can only tell you the stakes were extremely high"—he turned away from her—"and very costly."

Curiosity burned in her. What kind of work would create such risk? She thought of his notorious gambling in the past. Surely he hadn't made a profession out of it?

Grace wanted to know more, but he seemed reticent. She decided not to press him, at least not directly. She was enjoying his company far too much to risk his getting angry enough to leave. "Was any of it true? The gossip?" she asked instead. He hadn't actually denied any of it.

"I admit to being a bit reckless from time to time." The smile returned to play along his mouth. "But I was hardly the Don Juan they made me out to be."

No, but you made a very believable Casanova. Grace gazed at the rose in her hand, lifting the bloom to breathe in its fragrant scent. "This rose has a lovely smell. Is it from your garden?"

"One of the few your piglets didn't ravage." His teasing voice made her insides flutter. "It's called William Morgan, after my great-grandfather, who created the rose for his garden."

"How can you tell which one it is?"

"By its scent," he said. "I chose it myself."

Pleasure filled her. "Thank you."

"Have you danced yet?"

Startled by his question, she responded without thinking, "Are you asking me?"

His smile waned, and she regretted her words. "I don't dance anymore."

"Why not?"

His jaw set. "You really need to ask, Miss Mabry?"

"Yes, I do," she said, deciding to press on. "Because your legs appear to be in good working order, and with your exceptional sense of direction I'm certain you won't step on my toes. Care to give it a try?"

"Here?" His mouth went slack with surprise before drawing into a thin line. "I don't care to entertain the crowds any more than I have already."

"They have plenty of entertainment," she said softly. "They're dancing, laughing, taking refreshments. They won't even know we're here."

She reached to take his hand. "No." He pulled back from her, his voice low, terse.

"They aren't gawking at you. Please, give me your hand?"

He hesitated for an instant, then relaxed and slowly offered his hand. Grace took it, thrilled over his willingness to trust her. "We'll dance right here, if you like," she said, and felt her heart pounding inside her chest as he closed the distance and ran his hand gently along her side until it settled firmly against her waist. Still holding the rose in her grasp, she placed her other hand against his shoulder as he began leading her gracefully to the soft, somber music.

Glancing toward the other couples on the dance floor, Grace noted a few had turned in their direction. Some made comments between themselves, but no one stared. "I was right," she said in a teasing voice. "You dance well."

"So do you." His tender smile made her feel hot and cold at the same time. "Who taught you?"

Grace hadn't revealed to him that Lady Bassett had sponsored her at Brondesbury, a finishing school in Surrey. Still, she could tell him the truth. "Mother insisted we children learn at a very early age how to maneuver the steps to music. Since Colin and I were of an age . . ."

"He was your dance partner?"

The smile on his face broadened, and Grace was again struck by the strength of his jaw, the beauty of his sculpted mouth. She felt giddy. "Yes, and believe me, I learned to be very fast in sidestepping his cloddish feet!"

Jack's laughter filled the air, and Grace blinked at the wondrous sound. Several people glanced their way, a few wearing faint smiles as though sharing in his amusement. Likely it was a sound they'd not heard in quite some time, and without the steel mesh he didn't look half so fearsome. She felt tempted to ask him right then to remove the mask, but stopped, knowing what his reaction would be. Yet as she turned to scan the room, seeing soldiers leaning on crutches or nursing bandages, she imagined Jack would quite fit in with this gathering of wounded souls. No one need know his injuries stemmed from less than admirable behavior rather than duty. The reasons didn't make his suffering any less painful or real, and likely more filled with regret.

The music ended. Jack released her and offered a slight bow of his head. "Thank you, Miss Mabry."

"You can still call me Grace, if you like," she said, all at once shy. Perhaps he'd already forgotten about their familiarity during dinner the other evening?

"Grace."

His dazzling smile threatened to melt her heart. "I'm glad you joined Sir Marcus here tonight."

"Why is that?"

Flustered, she said, "The townspeople seem pleased you are here, along with the soldiers home on leave."

"And you, Grace?" The sculpted lips settled into a pensive line. "Are you pleased?"

Oh, yes! she wanted to shout, but the reminder of his engagement to Miss Arnold dimmed her joy. "Of course I am. I mean, we all are." She added, "I understand Miss Arnold has departed Roxwood. Shall I drive for you on Monday?"

"She has." His flat tone suggested an end to the subject. "And I look forward to Monday's outing. In fact, you may end up driving me home tonight, unless Marcus can be pried away from the enchanting Miss Danner."

"He seems quite taken with her."

"Do you know how she feels about him?"

"Well, she doesn't really know him yet." Grace considered Clare's earlier remark involving a broom. "But honestly, Sir Marcus could be a barn rat for all the good it will do him."

Jack chuckled. "I did hear she wasn't exactly overwhelmed by his charm."

"That's an understatement." Grace smiled and turned to see the couple had left the dance floor before the start of the next tune. Then moments later Henry Burr's voice blared through the gramophone, singing, "If You Were the Only Girl in the World."

"Clare isn't too impressed with titles or wealth," she said, feeling it safe to reveal that much about her friend. "I think Sir Marcus will have to prove himself mightily before she opens her heart to him."

"Marcus is a good man. Better than I ever was. I hope Miss Danner comes to appreciate his qualities."

Grace looked up at him, a man whose pride had been brought low by his own folly. He'd been humbled by his injuries and existed in a world of darkness, isolation, and fear. Yet he'd risen from his plight to come here now, tonight, and stand in a crowded room, laughing, smiling, and enjoying life, with her . . .

"I am sure she will." She spoke softly, filled with a new, deeper yearning she felt unable to repress.

"Grace?" Jack said in a low voice, seeming to detect in her tone what she really meant.

At that moment, Clare and Sir Marcus rejoined them, each holding a glass of the pink lemonade. The moment with Jack had passed, and Grace felt both relieved and dismayed. She glanced at her friend, and while Clare didn't smile, her color hadn't yet faded.

"Would you like a lemonade, Miss Mabry? Have mine, and I'll get another." Sir Marcus offered her his glass.

"Thank you very much, Sir Marcus . . ." She started to take the glass and saw Jack flinch. Understanding dawned. "However, Lord Roxwood and I were just about to get our own." Leaving her fragrant rose with Clare, Grace slipped a hand into the crook of Jack's arm and led him toward the refreshment tables.

"Why are you doing this?" he hissed.

"Because I have faith in your abilities," she whispered. "Punch bowl and ladle are at ten o'clock, glasses at eight." Grace watched with pride and amazement as he used his fingers to ladle lemonade into two glasses, handing her one of them. "Plates are at three o'clock, and cucumber sandwiches directly to the right of those."

He searched out a plate and filled it with four of the sandwiches. Grace then gently tucked her arm in his and led him to the table, where Clare and Sir Marcus now sat. Once they settled in, Jack passed around the plate.

"Thanks, old boy." Sir Marcus eyed Grace with a thoughtful expression, then reached for a cucumber sandwich. Clare shot her a puzzled frown, but said nothing as she helped herself to one, as well.

"Are you enjoying the dance?" Grace asked Sir Marcus.

"Immensely." He turned to Clare, seated across from him. "And may I say, Miss Danner, you're quite an accomplished partner." He smiled.

Clare's color heightened as she took a long sip of her lemonade. Finally she set down her glass and said primly, "I appreciate the compliment, Sir Marcus."

"Would you care for another dance?"

She raised a dark brow at him. "I agreed to one dance."

"You've not answered my question, Miss Danner," he parleyed in a smooth tone. "Do you care to continue?"

She tipped her head. "If you insist," she said. "But we ladies put in a full day's work before coming to the dance tonight. I'm afraid exhaustion has caught up with me."

"Then we shall wait for another opportunity."

Grace was impressed at Sir Marcus's consideration despite his crestfallen look. He said, "Shall I see you at church tomorrow?"

Clare nodded, and Grace said, "We shall all be there, Sir Marcus." Grace's gaze bounced off Jack. "Perhaps you might even convince Lord Roxwood to attend?"

"Still trying to save my soul, Miss Mabry?" A smiled touched his lips, though it lacked humor. "Don't waste your time." To Sir Marcus, he said, "Since the ladies have tired of dancing, Marcus, how about giving me a lift home?"

"You mean you won't stay?" Grace had hoped for at least one more dance.

Jack slid his hand along the table toward her, and instinctively she reached for it. She ignored the surprised looks from both Clare and Sir Marcus as pleasure coursed through her.

"As much as I would enjoy it, Miss Mabry . . . Grace," he said, giving her fingers a squeeze, "this is a bit more social activity than I've had in quite a while. I'll look forward to our drive on Monday." His smile was genuine. He pressed her hand and rose from the table. His friend also rose.

"Until tomorrow, Miss Danner," Sir Marcus said, then took up her hand and kissed it.

Clare's cheeks bloomed. "Sir Marcus."

The two men made their way past the throng of people, with Sir Marcus casting about several abstract good-byes before he and Jack departed the hall.

"What exactly is going on between you two, Grace?" Clare asked. "I'd hardly call what I just saw a mere truce."

"I could ask the same about you. Sir Marcus seems a decent man. You should consider taking a closer look, Clare, before you tar him with the same brush you use on every other titled and affluent man in Great Britain. Did he tell you he's a lieutenant with the Admiralty?"

Clare nodded. "He does seem very nice," she agreed. "He's quite attractive, too." Her frown returned. "But you've changed the subject. Are you and Lord Roxwood . . . ? I mean to say, do you care for one another?"

Grace couldn't deny her feelings. She bent her head to the rose, again breathing in its heavenly scent. "I think so."

"He's *engaged*."

"I know that," Grace snapped. "But he isn't happy about it, and neither is she."

"It doesn't matter." Clare's tone gentled.

"You're right, Clare." Grace's brow creased. Even though Jack and Violet likely wished to be worlds apart, there remained some mysterious obligation holding them together.

"He's also a member of the royal peerage," Clare added. "Good heavens, Grace. He'll be an earl one day."

"Jack and I are not entirely out of each other's social realm," she said, bristling. "I would imagine my father is just as wealthy as Miss Arnold's, and she is hardly royalty, after all. Times are changing. We're in the midst of a new age *and* a war, with women expanding their roles in society. I believe separation of class will continue to shrink."

Clare snorted. "One of your pretty suffragette speeches?" Then compassion lit her gray eyes when she said, "I live in the world, Grace, and right now it hurts badly. Don't let him break your heart."

"I won't, Clare. I promise." Grace leaned to touch her wrist. "And you should give Sir Marcus a chance. He seems like a good man." She smiled. "Being knighted isn't so lofty, is it?"

Clare's expression eased as she took up her glass of lemonade. "Perhaps not," she said with an offhanded smile.

15

Grace stood at the edge of the dance floor, watching couples sway to the music while Clare went off to find the others.

Already she'd agreed to dance with two young soldiers, yet her enthusiasm waned. She couldn't stop thinking about Jack, or what Clare had said—an impossible situation, though her heart felt otherwise. Closing her eyes, she reveled in the romantic music of John McCormack singing "Roses of Picardy" on the gramophone. She imagined Jack once more leading her smoothly about the floor right in the very spot she was standing, feeling the warmth of his hand against her waist, breathing in the scent of his Bay Rum cologne, and delighting in his smile.

Opening her eyes, she touched a finger to her lips. How would his smile feel against hers . . . or his laughter? The image of his mouth laughing against hers rose in her mind, and she felt another pang of yearning. She would give anything to feel his laughter, his happiness.

When the song ended, Grace headed with her empty glass to the refreshment table for more lemonade. She wasn't surprised to find Becky heaping several ginger biscuits and a wedge of mince pie onto a plate and happily eating away.

It seemed to Grace the young woman was always hungry. Maybe opening a bakery wasn't such a great idea. Becky might just eat all of the profits. Yet despite her stocky build she hadn't an ounce of fat, likely from loading all those bales of hay.

Lucy was nowhere to be found, but Clare stood beside the other food table, nibbling on a slice of strawberry pie. A soldier was trying to strike up a conversation with her. Clare nodded from time to time, but didn't seem at all interested. Grace grinned. Perhaps Sir Marcus had made an impression, after all.

At the sound of hearty greetings behind her, Grace turned to see Mr. Tillman had arrived. The farmer looked quite resplendent in his old British uniform, the vintage red jacket with its badge rank of corporal from having served in the Anglo-Boer Wars. He swept off his cap, and she noticed he'd combed his sparse thatch of salt-and-pepper hair into some semblance of order. He'd even trimmed his mustache.

Grace waited for Agnes to come through the door, then soon realized her friend wasn't with him. Perplexed and somewhat concerned, she intended to ask Mr. Tillman about her, but then he was surrounded by several soldiers, each shaking his hand. Though she and the farmer had yet to make peace with each other, it pleased her that these younger men recognized his contribution from past wars.

"Have you seen Agnes?" she asked once he'd greeted everyone and approached the refreshment table.

"I called back at the gatehouse, but Miss Pierpont said she had an aching head and wasn't up to dancing." He moved to grab a cucumber sandwich and popped it into his mouth.

Grace felt disappointment. She had hoped to spend some time with her friend tonight.

Mr. Tillman reached for a glass and ladled out a cup of the pink lemonade. He began to drink, having neglected to notice hers was still empty.

"Why, I would love some, thank you." She thrust her cup at him. The man simply had no manners where women were concerned.

He blinked, then grunted before snatching up her glass and refilling it from the punch bowl. Grace nodded her appreciation, taking a sip while she surveyed the room.

The next song to play was a slower melody. As couples approached the dance floor, Grace spied Mrs. Vance near the window, casting surreptitious glances at Mr. Tillman.

She sighed. It seemed the farmer lacked insight as well as manners. Having only been at Roxwood three weeks, even Grace recognized Ida Vance's attentions toward him. The look of longing in the woman's face was there for all to see.

Casually she reached for a ginger biscuit from a plate on the table. "Enchanting music, isn't it, Mr. Tillman?" she said, before taking a bite.

He turned from piling a plate with two slices of potato pie and a wedge of apple cake to look at her. "It is indeed, Miss Mabry."

"And you look very fine in your uniform."

His expression turned guarded. "Thank you, Miss Mabry."

"In fact . . ." Grace cast a purposeful glance around the room. "I imagine several ladies here might enjoy a dance with a man in uniform. I see one or two over there in that corner." Her gaze settled on Mrs. Vance, and she waved.

"Maybe," he said without looking and continued to fill his plate, this time topping the apple cake with another cucumber sandwich.

Thickheaded. Grace pursed her lips, tugging at his sleeve. "See Mrs. Vance there, by the window? And my, doesn't she look grand! That rose-print dress is perfect with her skin. What do you think, Mr. Tillman? Isn't mauve her very color?"

The farmer paused in the act of placing a ginger biscuit on top of his already huge pyramid of food to follow her gaze.

Grace took hope as she saw him color faintly. "Perhaps she would care to dance?"

He turned to Grace. "You mean . . . you want me to ask her?"

Grace bit back her exasperation. "I think she would happily accept."

"Why would she give the likes of me the time of day?" Yet he shot another hopeful glance in Mrs. Vance's direction.

"Well," Grace confided, "as it happens, I saw her looking your way a few times."

Blinking, he held on to his enormous mound of food. He darted another glance at Mrs. Vance. Then, as if making a battle decision, he thrust the plate at Grace. He straightened the tunic of his uniform over his slight paunch and marched in her direction. They had an exchange of words, in which her supervisor's rosy features positively glowed, before Mr. Tillman led her onto the dance floor.

Grace looked on as the couple stepped lively to the music of "Daisy Bell," and her heart warmed at the sound of Ida Vance's laughter. She'd lost a husband, and having endured her share of grief it was about time she discovered joy again.

Grace found her own thoughts returning to Jack. Even now he could be standing alone on his balcony. She gazed at the rose still in her hand. Had she been a fool to accept the token from him? And was that all it had been, a commemoration of their truce, or had he meant something more? She sensed he did, yet it didn't change their circumstances. He was bound to another, whether there was love between them or not.

"Enjoying the dance?"

Grace whirled at the familiar male voice behind her. A middle-aged man dressed in a chestnut-brown suit and holding a fashionable straw hat grinned at her.

"Cousin Daniel!" She threw her arms around him. "What are you doing here?"

"I'm glad to see you haven't forgotten this old man." He chuckled and returned her squeeze with a bear hug of his own. "I heard you were at Roxwood, and since I have patients in the area, I decided to seek you out tonight, hoping you couldn't resist such an event."

"You know me well," she said. "And I hardly think after only a year I'd forget Mother's cousin." The last time she'd seen him was at her mother's funeral.

He must have read her thoughts. "How are you and your family doing, Grace?"

She made an effort to smile. "Da works long hours at the tea room. And I'm involved with the Women's Forage Corps here at Roxwood, trying in my own way to support Colin while he fights in France."

"Have you had word from your brother?"

"Not in a while." She fought to keep the concern from her voice. "Though I'm told letters can be delayed from the Front."

"No doubt about it." He offered a smile of reassurance. "You'll get word any day now."

The tightness in her chest eased. "Thank you, Cousin Daniel. It's really so good to see you again." She had been lonely for her family. Thank heaven her cousin had come to Roxwood to be with her. "You said you have local patients?"

He nodded. "I have several regulars in the village and a few temporary workers in the area." He nodded toward the dance floor. "Now, tell me, why aren't you out there breaking hearts tonight? I would have imagined several of these young lads asking for a dance."

She smiled at his teasing tone. "I have danced with a few of them, but none were as enjoyable as my first." She fingered the rose in her hand. "Now he's left, and my heart's gone out of it."

His amused look turned to consternation. "What young man is this? Is he from around here? How did you meet him?"

She laughed. "You sound like Da. Or like Lord Roxwood, who enjoys interrogating me at every opportunity."

"Lord Roxwood?" Her cousin's features relaxed. "Ah yes, he told me you work for him."

Grace blinked. "You spoke with him?"

"He happens to be one of my new patients. I was surprised to hear you've been driving him all over Britain. Does your father know we now have a lady chauffeur in the family?"

Grace ignored his question. "Can you tell me about him, Daniel? Do you think he will ever see again?"

"Now who's asking all the questions?" His eyes narrowed. "If I didn't know better, Grace Mabry, I'd say you had feelings for the man."

Grace's cheeks warmed.

He scratched his head. "Well, I never would have guessed a woman could manage to look beyond his atrocious mask long enough to admire the man beneath," he said, looking nonplussed at her reaction. "Still, his old London reputation aside, he seems a decent enough chap these days, though somewhat reclusive."

"Oh, I believe he's actually quite changed, cousin. I know what he was like in London. I met him once, before he received his injuries, though I'm certain he doesn't remember me," she said, which was true enough.

"When I first arrived here, I thought him quite insolent." She smiled. "He questioned me incessantly about Da and our family, without the benefit of sharing any information about himself. But after much persistence, I did get him to satisfy my curiosity. He told me about his childhood with his grandfather and how he and his brother enjoyed their summers together. Nowadays he has me describe our location to him, and if he can guess correctly, I know I'm improving with my word skills. He even let me take him to Margate. We had candy floss, and I watched a bear walk the beach."

"You've had a grand time of it, then." Her cousin's voice was soft, yet she detected the sadness in his expression. "You know he's to marry soon?"

An ache pierced her, and she nodded. "To Miss Violet Arnold. Though it doesn't change how I feel." She met his gaze. "I would like to know if there is a possibility he will see again. I wish that for him with all my heart."

"Ah, Gracie, you're a good girl." He gave her a tender smile. "As to your question, I examined him yesterday for the first time and I feel hopeful he'll regain his sight. The explosion did no real damage to the retina—"

"Explosion?" Grace eyed him curiously. "The townhouse exploded?" She frowned. "I don't recall reading that in the *Times*."

He shifted as color touched his cheeks. "Yes, well, I mean . . . not an explosion, per se . . . ."

Grace had never seen him so ill at ease. "What aren't you telling me, cousin?"

"I shouldn't say anything. The information was relayed to me in confidence."

"Please, I beg of you." She reached to grip his hand. "I need to know what happened."

He searched her face a long moment. Finally he said, "Come, let's go sit in another room where it's quieter."

He led her to a small office near the back of the hall that housed a desk and a couple of wooden chairs. When both were seated, he took her hand again. "My dear, there was no townhouse fire. The Admiralty kept the real story out of the newspapers. Jack Benningham got those injuries while on duty aboard a munitions ship leaving for the open sea. A German U-boat attacked with a torpedo and blew it up."

Grace sucked in a breath. "I had no idea . . ."

"It's a miracle he's alive," her cousin said, shaking his head. "He was only one of four on the entire ship to survive—and with no more bodily harm than the scars on his face, and of course his blindness."

"When did this happen?" she asked.

"April, I believe."

She closed her eyes. The same month she'd attended Lady Bassett's ball. Images flew through her mind: the white feather she'd given him, his laughter and then his fury, Jack storming from the mansion without a backward glance.

The horror of what she'd done pressed in on her until she felt she couldn't breathe. "Oh, cousin, it's my fault!"

Her outburst garnered the attention of a few onlookers in the other room. "Easy, Grace." Her cousin rose and put a hand on her shoulder. "Explain what you mean."

Grace relayed to him the details of the costume ball. "Afterward, he left in such a hurry," she finished miserably, staring at her lap. "I humiliated him in front of his peers. No doubt he rushed to the nearest enlistment office." She shook her head. "I assumed he was no more than a titled, self-indulgent rogue, a coward who refused to take up the call of duty."

She gazed out at the other room, where several boys in uniform and their partners danced. "I so wanted to do my duty to help win this war," she said. "With the air attacks on London and my brother overseas, I thought if I shamed enough men like Jack Benningham into joining the Army, they would go and fight alongside him to end this thing, and bring Colin home. I feel terrible." Her voice broke. "Jack wears those scars because of my foolishness. He may never see again." She buried her face in her hands. "His life is ruined because of me."

"Grace." Her cousin pried her hands free and held them, forcing her to look at him. "Your patriotism and your love for your brother are admirable," he said gently. "And I understand your fear. But war is brutal and unforgiving, and very different from the propaganda we read about in newspapers and see on posters." He seemed to flinch, adding, "As a physician, I've tended to countless injuries of the men returning home. I can't begin to describe to you the horror—poison gas, mines, and mortars. No one deserves to go through that kind of hell.

"But remember, Lord Roxwood is a grown man. He's wealthy, titled, and if his former reputation is any indication, he does exactly as he chooses without concern for what others might think. The man knows his own mind, Grace. If he decided to get on that ship, it wasn't because of anything you said or did." When she still looked unconvinced, he added, "Do you really think him the kind of man to lay blame for his fate at the feet of a lovely but naïve young woman?"

But Grace barely heard his words, unable to get past what she'd done. She'd ruined a man's life, taken his sight. She recalled their earlier conversation, about heavy costs. Was that what Jack had meant by "high stakes"?

Confusion, shame, and exhaustion threatened to overwhelm her. "I need to leave, cousin," she said wearily, "and return to the gatehouse."

"Shall I drive you, Grace?"

She shook her head. "I must return Lord Roxwood's Daimler to the manor. The walk from there isn't far." At his concerned look, she said, "It's all just a bit of a shock."

"I must leave also." He helped her to rise from the chair. "I'll follow you out."

Grace went in search of Mrs. Vance. "Go and get some rest, dear," the older woman said when she'd made her excuses. "I'll round up the others in a while, and we'll have Mr. Tillman bring us back in the cart."

The farmer returned from the refreshment table just then to hand Mrs. Vance a glass of lemonade and a slice of cake. She accepted with an animated smile.

"Miss Mabry," he said, winking at Grace.

"Mr. Tillman." Grace hid her surprise over his congeniality toward her. If only she deserved it. "I'll see you both later," she said, and was off.

Grace said good-bye to her cousin outside, then drove back to the manor. The evening air had cooled from the day's heat, but in her numbed state she was hardly aware of it.

How could she have been so insensible? She thought back to the young men at the dance, the mothers and fathers clinging to their sons. Many wounded and damaged in unseen ways.

She'd beat the drum with others, keen to make certain every man in Britain did his duty to the Crown. How did that kind of patriotism equate with love, or human kindness?

Despite her wish to bring Colin home, how could she have been so calloused as to humiliate another man, someone else's brother or son, to make him risk his life in the same way?

✎

Grace returned to the gatehouse and climbed the stairs to her room. So as not to disturb Agnes, she left the gas lamp off while she changed clothes. She slipped into bed, wishing she could hide there forever. And yet Monday would come soon enough. How could she face Jack, knowing what she'd done?

A quiet sob floated across the darkness, and Grace rose on an elbow. Not Agnes surely; the sound had come from Lucy's bed. "Hello?"

"G-grace? Is that you?"

"Lucy?" Grace rose and padded toward the lamp. She paused. "I don't wish to awaken Agnes."

"She's not here."

"Did she go to the dance, after all?" Grace lit the lamp and saw Lucy lying on her bed fully clothed, even down to her button-up shoes.

"I haven't seen her."

"Are you all right? Does Mrs. Vance know you're here?"

Lucy sat up, wiping at her tears. "No, I . . . I just left."

"Why didn't you tell her?" Grace said gently, moving to sit on the edge of the bed. "They'll be looking for you."

Lucy shrugged. "I got scared and ran."

"You walked back from the dance?"

Lucy nodded. "All I wanted was to g-get away, to hide from him."

"Who?" She gripped Lucy's shoulders. "Is someone after you?"

Lucy nodded again and began to cry.

"Lucy, please stop that. Explain yourself so I can help you."

"No one can!" She cried harder. "I know God is going to punish me for what I d-did!"

Grace felt uneasy over Lucy's words. She'd been having those same thoughts. Still, she said, "Nonsense. Tell me everything, and we'll get this sorted." When Lucy continued weeping silently, she added, "We're sisters in the WFC and we stick together, don't we?"

Lucy's crying stopped. Grace took hope. "If one of us fails, then we all fail. Isn't that what Mrs. Vance taught us? So if you have a problem, you need to come to us. We protect each other," she added softly.

Lucy's mottled expression twisted as she seemed to wrestle with some inner conflict. Finally, she said, "Remember the day we worked together in town and you asked about my life in London? You said I could be anything in the world I wanted to be?"

Grace offered an encouraging smile. "You told me you wished to become a veterinarian."

Lucy looked away. "We also talked about secrets."

Grace tensed, reminded of her own secret. "Is that what this is about, Lucy? You have something you wish to share with me?"

Lucy turned to her. "I told you I was in service." She spoke haltingly. "But the services I performed aren't the kind a well-bred young lady like you should know about."

Grace understood, and her breath caught. "You mean, you were a . . ."

"Prostitute." Lucy's cheeks flamed. "I don't make excuses for my life, Grace, or how it turned out." She wiped at her face with the hem of her skirt. "I'd met Marie, another woman in . . . that kind of service. I remembered her from school. She was older and, like me, from southeast London. Marie knew my family and how cruel my pa was." The turquoise eyes met Grace's. "She showed me a way out."

Grace pursed her lips to keep from voicing her objections.

Lucy's smile was bitter. "I can see it on your face, Grace Mabry, your look of disgust. But you don't know what I went through." Her words held an edge of desperation. "Marie made it sound so easy to escape all of that.

"There was a man we w-worked for, he set things up. I'd only just started when Marie got real sick." She eyed Grace. "I won't tell you what it was, just that she got it from some of the soldiers home on leave. There's medicine for it, but she hid her condition until it was too late.

"Before she died, Marie gave me a packet. It was money, Grace. Every shilling she'd saved over the years. A miracle I hadn't expected. When I asked her why she didn't use the money for a cure, she said she'd waited too long, she was afraid they would arrest her, or that the man we worked for . . . he was mean." She stared across the room, her expression sad. "There was no help for her. She told me she'd made a terrible mistake with me, and it was time to settle up with God. She wanted me to g-get out while I could. She said it was my only chance."

Lucy's gaze shot back to her. "I took that chance! Between Marie and me, there was enough money so I could move across town, buy myself some respectability. I got new clothes and a flat, and I p-purchased letters of recommendation. I hired on with the WFC to get as far away from that world as possible." Fresh tears filled her eyes. "But now it's f-found me again!"

"Please, don't cry." Grace pulled her close, feeling Lucy's shoulders shake with sobs. The knot in her stomach cinched further. "Was it your father, Lucy? Did he find you at the dance tonight?"

"He's dead." Lucy pulled away. "But the man we worked for, he's still looking for me. There was a soldier at the dance tonight from London. He's here staying with his friend in the village. He saw me, remembered me f-from . . . before. He was drinking . . ."

A cry tore from her. "He threatened to tell everyone in Rox-wood what I was if I didn't go with him. He swore he would telephone London and tell the pimp he'd found me. Grace, I was so f-frightened, I ran all the way back here."

She hung her head. "What can I do? I'll be cast out of the WFC and out of Roxwood, and the horrible man I worked for will come after me and drag me back." She clutched at Grace's hand. "I can't go, I swear, I'll end my own life first."

"You're not going anywhere, do you hear me?" Grace shook her gently. "We will resolve this, I promise." Her mind raced. "In fact, I believe Lord Roxwood will help."

Grace hoped she was right. Despite Lucy's lurid past, Jack's sense of justice would surely prevail. He wouldn't allow anyone to take the woman against her will. "I'll speak to him Monday morning when I take him driving. If you'll allow me to share with him just the pertinent part of your story, I'm certain he'll champion your cause."

"Grace, you're a sweet, innocent girl, but I know d-different. I'll have to leave." Lucy spoke through her tears.

"You must have faith, Lucy." Grace rose from the bed. "Now get some rest. The others will return shortly." She reached to brush at a lock of Lucy's hair. "And don't do anything rash, because we're going to get this sorted. We've got church early tomorrow. I want you sitting beside me during the service, just in case that troublemaking soldier decides to show himself."

"I'm not going to church."

Grace straightened. "Why not?"

Lucy glanced down at her lap. "I'm too ashamed."

"We all make mistakes, Lucy. Thankfully, God loves us in spite of them. Have you never heard the phrase, 'No sin is greater than His mercy'?"

Lucy looked up and shook her head.

"Well, it means you, too. After all, He gave us free will." Grace smiled. "And by leaving that life behind, you've exerted yours admirably."

Lucy's lips curved upward. "I think you must be an angel sent to me. Thank you f-for not hating me because of my past."

"Never," Grace assured her. "Now get some rest."

Returning to her own bed, and the guilt about Jack still weighing on her, Grace's smile faded. *No sin is greater than His mercy.* Why couldn't she take her own advice?

16

Seated in the crowded pew, Grace scanned the opposite side of the church and locked gazes with a young soldier standing with his companion against the wall. He was tall and lean, black-haired with brown eyes. Below his pencil-thin mustache, he had a nice mouth except for the smirk he occasionally shot in their direction.

Her pulse raced as she glanced at Lucy, seated beside her with hands clenched in her lap. Grace reached to pat them reassuringly, then returned her attention to the insolent face across the room.

"You see him, don't you?" Lucy whispered.

"Yes, but don't worry. He won't get near you while I'm here," she whispered back.

The rest of the church was filled with locals. As usual, the six women had to squeeze into a row at the back, along with Mr. Tillman who had brought them this morning in the horse cart.

On the other side of her, Agnes muffled a yawn. She'd returned to the gatehouse late last night along with the others and wore her pink shirtwaist. Apparently she'd recovered from her headache and attended the dance after all, just missing Grace's departure.

As promised, Sir Marcus arrived just after the entrance song. He'd moved to stand behind Clare, and her friend's continual fidgeting made it obvious she was aware of his presence.

Grace hadn't expected Jack to attend and felt worse for it, knowing his anger at God must stem from his inability to see, his wounds—injuries she'd helped to set into motion.

"'Do not bring your servant into judgment, for no one living is righteous before you.'"

The words of Psalm 143 echoed through the church as Reverend Price spoke of pride and the dangers of judging others. Grace felt their impact. She prayed for forgiveness, for the wisdom to stop making assumptions, and above all, to seek the truth.

She also prayed for Colin's safety, jarred by the sight of the injured men at the dance. She couldn't bear to think what might happen to her brother.

The service ended, and the people began filing out of the pews. Grace pressed closer to Lucy as the soldier rounded the last pew and winked at her before exiting with his friend.

"What a horrid man." Grace gripped Lucy's arm, hurrying her ahead of the others to exit the church. "He kept leering at us; I was surprised no one else saw it."

Lucy fought back tears. "What am I to do, Grace? By tonight the entire village will know my past."

Seeing her despair, Grace said, "I'd planned to wait and speak with Lord Roxwood, but as you say, the scoundrel likely won't keep his mouth shut until then."

The pair of soldiers stood across the churchyard, talking with an older couple. Occasionally the young man would turn to them with a mocking grin.

"How I would love to wipe that smirk off his face," Grace

said. "Lucy, we need to ask Sir Marcus for help. He's with Clare." She nodded toward the couple standing beside the hedgerow across the green. "Will you allow me to share your secret with her? I believe she can convince him to help us."

Lucy's turquoise eyes looked frightened. "If you think it best, but I d-don't want to see their faces when you tell them. I'd like to go and sit with Agnes and Becky in the cart."

"Of course." Grace smiled encouragingly. "And don't worry, everything will be fine."

"Miss Danner, I know this might seem sudden, but I'd very much like to call on you," Sir Marcus Weatherford said. "Would you allow me the privilege?"

Clare could only stare back at him. His words were soft, his brown eyes entreating as he gazed at her with hope. Her heart pounded so loud she was certain he could hear it. Just as she had felt the night before when he'd arrived at the dance, her tongue seemed stuck to the roof of her mouth. When she'd first seen him in the barn, she'd felt the attraction between them. It had scared her. She'd also enjoyed dancing with him, his gentle words, his manners. It had been so long since she'd had the attentions of a handsome man.

Sir Marcus Weatherford was all that, and his behavior toward her had been decent. But how long would it last? *He's one of them*, a small voice inside her cried. A titled gentleman of the aristocracy, the type of man who more times than not disregarded the feelings of those he considered beneath him. What could he want with her, other than a dalliance until he got bored?

Painful memories rushed to her mind: being rejected by a man she thought she'd loved but who never considered her good enough; her shame at being sent away to the Magdalene House where she'd been forced to suffer her heartbreak alone and in silence, her only consolation the child she would bear; then the horror of having Daisy stolen from her.

Clare wet her lips, searching his face. There was something about him that drew her, yet she was afraid . . .

"Clare, may I speak with you?"

She turned and let out a breath, watching Grace approach from across the churchyard. "Excuse me a moment, Sir Marcus." She didn't wait for his response as she hurried toward her friend.

She met Grace halfway across the green expanse. "What is it?" she said.

"I'm sorry to interrupt, but I've something to share with you. Lucy's in trouble."

Clare blinked, shocked to hear of Lucy's past, and furious over her being threatened by a soldier at the dance. "Which one is he?" she demanded when Grace had finished her tale.

"He's the young man with the mustache." Grace nodded toward a pair of soldiers standing with a couple she'd seen in church. The one with the mustache chose that moment to glance toward the cart, where Lucy sat with Becky and the others.

Clare saw him smirk. "I'm going over to talk with Lucy," she said, seized with an urge to protect their friend.

"Clare, wait." Grace put a hand on her arm. "Lucy is embarrassed enough as it is. She only gave me leave to speak because we need your help. Actually, we need the assistance of Sir Marcus."

Clare felt a prickle of caution. "How does it affect me?"

"You seem to have a particular influence over him," Grace said. "I'm certain if you ask Sir Marcus to make the soldier desist in his threats—"

"No!" Clare nursed her previous anger. "I'll not be obligated to any man, and certainly not him. Why would he agree to help, anyway? Men like him place reputation above compassion,

245

especially when it comes to a 'soiled dove.' I should know," she added bitterly. "I'm sorry, Grace, but it's hopeless."

Just as it was hopeless for him to call upon her, Clare thought. In the end, he would break her heart. Besides, she had to find Daisy. "He'll return to London tomorrow, and that will be an end to it."

"How can you know for certain he won't help us unless you ask him?"

"Trust me, I know." Clare crossed her arms.

"Clare, I've learned you can't judge people," Grace said, and Clare was surprised at the fleeting sadness in her friend's expression. "Everyone deserves the benefit of the doubt. Sir Marcus *is* different from the rest. And since he's leaving for London tomorrow, as you say, why not ask this one boon . . . for our sister in need? I told Lucy we help one another." She paused. "Don't you agree?"

Of course she did. Grace didn't understand her situation. "He's asked to call on me, you know."

Grace blinked. "You mean it?"

Clare nodded.

"Why, that's wonderful!" Grace clapped her hands, then froze. "You didn't tell him no?"

"I was about to when you interrupted us." Clare scowled, adding, "Though you've put me into a fine kettle with Lucy's problem. How can I tell the man I don't want to see him again and then ask him for a favor?"

"Surely, you can't mean that. I saw you two dancing last night and talking at the table. What's changed?"

"I realized there is no future in any kind of romantic relationship with him."

Grace shook her head. "I think you're just afraid he'll break your heart."

"He doesn't have my heart."

"I think he's fairly close to having it," Grace said softly.

Grace glanced over at Sir Marcus. Clare followed her gaze and felt a pang at seeing him standing patiently, watching them, a small, uncertain smile playing at the edges of his mouth.

"Look, why not just put off your answer for a bit?" Grace said. "Tell him you'll consider his request. After all, the two of you just met. And as this will likely lead to courtship, it's a serious undertaking for any woman. Who knows? You might feel differently later. That way you can ask his assistance in ridding Lucy of this troublemaker."

Clare turned to her. "I don't know . . ."

"View it as a test of sorts," Grace challenged. "See if he's the consummate highbrow you make him out to be."

"You're clever, Mabry, but my mind's made up," Clare said. "I'm not going to court anyone, least of all some 'highbrow.'" She sighed. "I will help Lucy, though. I doubt she's ever met an aristocrat in her life, but she and I both know what it feels like to be ill-used."

Grace beamed. "I knew you would help."

"Don't get your hopes up," Clare warned. "And if I'm right, you'll have to wash and press my uniforms for a week."

"And if I'm right and you're wrong?"

Clare said smugly, "I'll spend the week polishing your boots and lacing your gaiters."

"Deal." Grace held out a gloved hand.

Clare took it. "I'll go and talk to him now."

She walked back toward the handsome man waiting for her, already knowing what he would say. But she'd agreed to try to help Lucy. "I apologize for leaving you so quickly, Sir Marcus. We've a bit of a situation."

"May I be of service?"

At his look of genuine concern, Clare wavered in her assumptions about him. She decided to postpone answering his request to call upon her; she would first see if he came to Lucy's aid. A test of sorts, Grace had said. "Miss Mabry would like a word with you, if you would follow me?"

———

Grace watched as her friend and Sir Marcus talked quietly beside the hedgerow. She prayed she hadn't been wrong about the lieutenant. Jack had said he was a good man, and for Clare's sake, Lucy's too, she hoped he was right.

She held her breath when Clare turned and, along with Sir Marcus, began walking in her direction. Once they'd arrived, Clare said, "Tell him what you told me, Grace."

As Grace disclosed to him the pertinent details of Lucy's situation, his features darkened with fury. He turned to the pair of soldiers across the churchyard. "Which one is he?"

"Sir Marcus, please don't make a scene." Clare darted a worried glance at Grace. "I understand if you're angry with us, but don't hurt our friend—"

"You think I'm angry at you?" He turned a surprised look at Clare, then Grace.

"Aren't you?" Clare said in a hesitant voice.

His features relaxed, and he reached for her hand. "I apologize. I am angry, but it's *for* you and your friends. Now, tell me which one he is and I'll rectify the matter immediately."

Grace felt relieved while Clare's eyes widened. "You'll help?"

"Of course, and I have the power to do it." He flashed a smile. "I'm a lieutenant in the Admiralty, remember? These recruits *will* do my bidding."

Clare turned to her, a dazed smile spread across her face. "Grace, please bring me those boots."

∞

It was all the talk that night. The story of how one particularly rude and mouthy soldier was banished from the village of Roxwood for his alleged ungentlemanly behavior.

Only three of them lying on their beds and brushing their hair knew the particulars: Grace, Lucy, and Clare gazed at each other with conspiratorial smiles.

Grace believed Sir Marcus Weatherford would eventually break down the wall Clare had erected around her heart. His behavior had been heroic beyond measure. In fact, she'd written in her journal how he took the miscreant by the collar and dragged him into the town hall. Most of the villagers just stared while a few followers tried to eavesdrop—unsuccessfully, of course—once the doors closed behind Sir Marcus and the young man.

Emerging a short time later, the soldier no longer smirked; in fact, he looked rather nervous as he called for a cab and made a hasty departure from town.

Sir Marcus returned to Roxwood Manor, then sent his regards to Lucy with the assurance the soldier would cease troubling her further.

"He's still leaving for London in the morning."

Clare's whispered voice beside her broke into Grace's thoughts. Her friend had come to sit on the edge of her bed. With the lights dimmed, the others were settling down for the evening.

"He asked me to write to him."

"Will you?" Grace asked.

Clare nodded. "I still can't believe what he did for Lucy."

"No, Clare." Grace smiled. "He did it for you."

Even in the faint lamplight, she could see Clare's cheeks bloom.

"I still wonder what all the fuss was about this morning," Agnes called from the doorway, fresh from her bath. "Sir Marcus looked ready to take a birch rod to that young man's behind."

A few chuckles sounded, and Grace glanced at her maid. She still felt bad they'd missed each other at the dance. She would have stayed if she hadn't spoken with her cousin and learned the truth about Jack. "I think they call it 'military discipline,' Agnes," she said, smiling.

"The soldier must have done something awful to make Sir Marcus so angry." Becky spoke from across the room as she rubbed her palms together, the oolong-colored eyes bright. "Anyone want to take the first guess?"

"Whatever it was, I'm certain Sir Marcus had his reasons," Grace said, hoping to put an end to the questions and Becky's insatiable penchant for gossip. "He isn't the type to jump to false conclusions."

She didn't dare look at Clare. How could she when she was guilty of the same thing?

∞

The next morning, Grace awoke to the sound of Clare leaving the room. As it wasn't yet time to rouse for breakfast, she lay in bed a few minutes more.

Today she would confess her crime to Jack. She'd even had a nightmare about it. After she told him about having shamed him and ultimately destroying his life, he'd ordered her locked up in London's Tower for attempted murder.

Grace rolled over and covered her eyes with a forearm. She longed to postpone their outing together. Perhaps if she had more time to think . . .

You're waffling, Mabry. Already she'd procrastinated too long in telling him how they had really met. After all her talk of demanding women's voices be heard, what would her WFC sisters think of her continued silence?

The wall clock ticked away the seconds and minutes until soon the others were stirring. Grace arose and began to dress in her uniform, slipping into the boots Clare had polished to a glossy sheen. She sat on the bed and was about to lace up her gaiters when her friend returned and rushed over to help.

"You don't have to do that, Clare. Shining my boots is more than enough."

Clare smiled serenely as she bent to cinch up the laces of Grace's leggings. "I pay my debts, Mabry."

"You seem in a rather good mood this morning," Grace said. "I also know you got up half an hour before anyone else." She arched a brow. "Was it a good-bye kiss that put the color in those cheeks?"

Clare jerked hard at the laces and almost pulled Grace off her bed. "Quiet! I don't need Becky overhearing and making it public." She finished tying off one legging then began on the other. "I'll tell you, though, Grace." She paused and looked up. "Marcus did kiss me, just a quick peck on the cheek, mind you, but . . . I've never felt this way with anyone before."

Clare seemed more bewildered than pleased. Grace smiled despite her own misery. "Perhaps Sir Marcus Weatherford might be worthy of you, after all."

"When I write to him, I'll tell him about Daisy and also my circumstances." She finished tying the other gaiter. "Then I'll likely never hear from him again."

"I believe Sir Marcus has more character than you give him credit for."

"Time will tell," Clare said, standing.

Grace stood too. "Thanks." She took a deep breath. "This morning I'm supposed to take Lord Roxwood on another outing."

"Remember what I said." Clare shot her a meaningful look. "Watch your heart. It's much too tender and easily broken by a man like him."

Grace smiled wanly. "I appreciate the advice, but you needn't worry. After today, I doubt I'll even have a job."

"What do you mean, miss?" Agnes walked over to them, having just finished dressing.

Grace shrugged. "I think I might have stepped on his toes

while dancing Saturday night." She wasn't about to admit to them the real reason he would toss her out. She winked at Agnes. "See, you should have been there with me. You'd have kept me out of trouble."

Agnes dropped her gaze to adjust the belt on her trench coat. "I'm sorry we missed each other."

Grace smiled. "Well, I'm glad you were able to enjoy at least a bit of the dance, anyway."

Clare said, "We'd better get downstairs before Becky eats all the porridge."

"After breakfast, I'm off to post my letter," Agnes said. "Miss, I saw you still had one in your bag. Shall I mail it for you, as well?"

In all the excitement with Lucy yesterday, Grace hadn't written the postscript to her father. "I did want to add a note to Da and ask about Colin," she said. "But Mrs. Vance needs those time sheets finished before I leave for the manor."

"You can always write another letter," Agnes said.

"You're right." Her poor father *had* waited overlong to hear from her. "Please post it along with yours," Grace said, "and I'll start a new letter tonight." *Unless I get fired and end up on tomorrow's train to London*, she thought.

∞

Grace's feeling of gloom continued as she pedaled her bicycle toward the manor. The others were working in the fields today. She envied them as she considered her upcoming confession.

"Chin up, Mabry," she muttered while she brought the Daimler around front minutes later. Taking a deep breath, she mounted the steps to the massive oak door.

"Welcome, Miss Mabry. Fine day for a drive, isn't it?"

She'd never seen Knowles so enthusiastic. "Why . . . yes," she said, perplexed by his jovial mood. "Is Lord Roxwood ready to leave?"

"Indeed!" His chuckle caused Grace to blink. "In fact, I believe his lordship has been most anxious for another outing. Breathing in the fresh country air has been most beneficial."

He reached back behind the door and produced a large wicker basket. "Mrs. Riley has prepared a picnic lunch. If you'll come inside, I shall put this in the car. His lordship will be with you presently."

Bewildered over the butler's behavior, Grace entered the foyer. She heard the familiar sound on the steps before she caught sight of him—long, powerful legs clad in fine gray linen, followed by his lean torso and broad shoulders. Today he sported a single-breasted gray jacket, gray-and-black-striped satin waistcoat, and a blue-striped tie. Shades she knew would have enhanced the color of his eyes . . .

Her mouth went dry when his face and the mask came into view. "Lord Roxwood," she managed to utter.

"Good morning, Grace." He paused on the stairs. "Are you unwell?"

She cleared her throat. "I'm fine. And you?"

"Excellent." A smile played at his mouth, and she felt her breath hitch. Those smiles of his were so rare, each one she received from him like a gift. Yet after today she would likely never see another.

As he continued down the steps, Grace noted that instead of the motoring cap he carried a wide-brimmed straw hat, the same hat she'd requested the day they traveled to Margate. Unerringly he crossed the marble floor to her. "After all, I plan to spend the morning with you and enjoy our picnic lunch in the country. Who could ask for more?"

His gentle tone only increased the ache in her heart. "It sounds wonderful."

He donned the hat. "Shall we go?"

Her anxiety grew as she turned and led the way outside.

"I should like to feel the sun on my face today."

That brought her up short. "But . . . you forbid the car top to be removed."

"I've changed my mind. And I've come prepared." He touched the brim of his hat. "As I no longer wear the steel mesh, the sun's heat won't bake me alive." He added softly, "And I have you to thank for that."

Grace didn't want his gratitude. "As you wish," she said, and with Knowles's help they collapsed the car's top and secured it with straps, leaving the Daimler's interior wide open to the air and sunshine.

Jack opened his own door and slid onto the seat. Grace might have been pleased but for her overriding sense of trepidation. She slowly rounded the car and slipped back behind the steering wheel. "Where shall we go today?"

He cinched the cords holding his hat in place. "Surprise me."

Eden, she thought, comforted. As this was undoubtedly their last day together, why not take him to his favorite place in the whole world? Grace let off the brake and eased the car forward.

"You're very quiet today. I trust you enjoyed the rest of your evening Saturday night?" He propped an arm against the back of the seat as she maneuvered the Daimler around the turn at the gatehouse.

"It was . . . interesting," she hedged, thinking of her conversation with Daniel.

"Such a cryptic word, *interesting*. Am I to take it the townspeople were agog with gossip once I left? Enjoyed seeing the lord of the manor bumping and banging along as he danced to the music?"

"I heard no gossip," she said heatedly, angry at herself as much as at the ignorant villagers. "And I thought you danced beautifully." Despite her inner battle, Grace took solace in realizing Jack wasn't left helpless. With his uncanny ability to discern his surroundings, his innate sense of direction, why wouldn't he be graceful on the dance floor? She remembered being held in his arms, his steady strength guiding her in the intricate steps of the dance. Her toes had been completely safe with him. "It was most enjoyable," she said quietly.

He reached out his hand to squeeze her shoulder. "For me as well, Grace."

His touch pierced her like a blade, and she struggled to focus on the road ahead. They passed the familiar verdant valleys, partitioned only by low stone walls or rows of plane trees, and farmhouses with their dilapidated barns and flocks of black-faced sheep. Hawthorn, alder buckthorn, and hornbeam formed hedgerows like islands amid a green sea, and the occasional majestic oak stood with spiky leaves swaying in the soft breeze. The images only deepened her yearning for this place, knowing all too soon she must leave it.

Harmon Lake came into view, and she turned the Daimler onto the familiar track that ran parallel to it, heading for the place Jack called paradise. She spied the gravel shoulder where she'd parked before. Would her description of Eden do it justice? They no longer played a game—not now, not when she knew the enormity of her mistake, the destruction she'd brought upon him. She must be his eyes, and it was important, urgent, that she get it exactly right. She owed it to him on their last day together.

"We're here," she said, and brought the car to a halt. Grace killed the engine. "We must walk a short way. Will you come with me?"

"Depends." He lifted his face to the sun as though trying to discern its direction. "Is this place a good spot for a picnic?"

Grace couldn't think of a better one. "It's perfect. I'll grab the basket."

"Hand it to me. I'll carry it," he said. "And there should be a lap blanket we can sit on."

Grace reached for the small blanket behind her seat as he exited the car. Then she came around to him and lifted the basket from the back, putting it in his hand.

"Just let me have your arm so you can lead the way," he said.

She linked her arm with his and felt his strength as he hugged her to him. Together they traversed the short distance through the woods. Grace was glad that without the mesh, he too could breathe in the fragrance of ferns growing at the base of trees and the fecund smell of the earth beneath their feet. Birdsong echoed among the leafy limbs, and she reported to him a red squirrel clambering to safety in a tall hazelnut bush a few feet away.

When they came to the clearing, she paused at the spot overlooking the valley. "Do you want to guess where we are?"

"I'd rather you tell me a bit first." He smiled, giving her arm another squeeze.

"All right." She closed her eyes and took a deep breath. When she reopened them, she began, "It's like no place on earth. Where cerulean skies touch down to a palette of green, a canvas tinged with the red berries of hawthorn, the purple of lavender, and Viburnum's white flower. Amidst leafy copses of elm and plane stands a crisscross of gray stone walls, like castle parapets dividing and conquering the wilds. Yet a land not to be defeated, as a glittering ribbon of water from the east quenches the valley stretching out beneath the sun."

She turned to him once she'd finished. Jack stood unmoving, his increased breathing and the pressure against her arm the only signs he'd heard her.

Finally he said, "Thank you for bringing me here, Grace. For only Eden could warrant such an occasion."

He was so close she could see his freshly shaved skin, the

healing scar. Her attention settled on his mouth, recalling how those sculpted lips had questioned her, argued with her, teased her, and smiled gently at her . . .

What would his kiss feel like? Again she wondered and dared to hope, even knowing what was to come. *Tell the truth now and save yourself further anguish.* But the words remained stuck in her throat. Grace was being cowardly, she knew, yet she couldn't bear the thought of losing him.

Jack's pulse quickened, feeling her warm breath fan his cheek. She was so close he could kiss her; all he need do was lean in a bit and capture her mouth with his.

His throat worked. He'd thought of little else since the dance. Never would he forget the way she felt in his arms, her softness beneath his hands. The intoxicating scent of flowers that surrounded her when she moved. Jack felt more human that night than he had in a long time. He'd experienced a sense of the freedom denied him since the explosion.

He wanted more of that same feeling. And after his confrontation with Violet, her admission of love for someone else, Jack began to hope she might sever their ties. Release him from the debt Stonebrooke owed to her father and allow him to pursue the woman who truly held his affections.

But did Grace want him? Had she been truthful about his scars, that they meant nothing to her? Jack tensed as the old fear warred with his desire. He planned to find out.

"Shall we eat here?"

Her voice brought him back to the present. "I'll set out the blanket," she said.

He released her as she took the basket from him. A few moments later, they were both seated on the ground. He'd asked Mrs. Riley to pack them a brunch of sorts, with hard-boiled eggs, fresh bread, cheese, apples, and ripe tomatoes from the garden. His cook had also included a glass jar filled with warm tea.

"Food at three o'clock," she said, and Jack easily found the plate Grace had placed beside him. "Shall I tell you what and where everything is?"

"I'll live dangerously today." He wiped his dampened hands against his trousers. "You haven't given me poison instead of Mrs. Riley's good food, have you?" he teased, hoping to cover his nervousness.

"Oh, I would never do that."

The seriousness in her tone gave him pause. Jack expected from her the usual cheeky response. "I was joking, Grace."

"Oh, of course!" And her spirit seemed to rise to the challenge then when she said, "So long as you don't count the pinecones and rocks I put on your plate. And I'm not too certain about the flavor of that moss."

Jack smiled, reveling in their banter. He found flirting with her intellect quite stimulating, strange for a man who in the past concerned himself only with pleasures of the flesh.

Oh, but he did want her. He longed to feel her mouth against his, to touch and see her face with his hands, learning her features. Jack imagined Grace's skin would be soft and smooth, her hair silky. Auburn, Marcus had said. Like the woman from his distant memory.

Yet one question remained. His mouth went dry like a desert, his heart hammering as he slowly reached to remove the hat, tossing it aside.

He had to know if Grace wanted *him*.

His breath came in short bursts as he moved his hands around to untie the mask. "I've something to show you, Grace," he managed in a voice he hardly knew. "Warts and all . . ."

"Jack . . . you don't have to do that."

Flooded with anxiety, he was only vaguely aware of the edge

in her tone. "Yes, I do," he said. "Only with you." He pushed past the last of his fear, released the ties, and felt the cool air against his tender flesh.

Time stopped. Jack waited for her to say something, reassure him. He felt exposed yet wanting to trust in her completely, even praying she wouldn't reject him, not now—

"No . . ." The anguished cry was followed by a swift intake of breath. "Oh, Jack, I am so very sorry . . ."

Devastation electrified him. He clutched the mask and stumbled to his feet, knocking over the plate of food in his haste. His frantic movements were clumsy as he replaced the covering over his face. His gut churned, making him want to retch. He heard his own rapid breathing and saw only darkness. In that moment, Jack loathed his existence. "Get me out of here," he groaned, and he despised his own pathetic plea, hating his dependence on her to return him to his sanctuary to hide.

"Jack, please." Grace shot up from the blanket. "I . . . I didn't mean to hurt you."

"Take me home. Now!"

Seeing his sightless blue eyes had caused a gasp of pain, as regret pierced her insides like a knife. Such a beautiful man, once healthy and whole, and she'd taken it all from him. In the name of God, glory, and duty—

"For pity's sake, woman, have an ounce of heart and do as I ask," he said hoarsely, standing with arms slack and shoulders bent, waiting. He seemed utterly defeated.

Tears coursed down her cheeks. Had she reduced him to begging? The knife drove deeper. "Please, you don't understand. I need to explain why—"

"Do not speak to me!" he roared, then straightened to his full height, his features fearsome. "Just do what I pay you to do and drive me home!"

Grace felt crushed. Yet despite his coldness, she still thought to explain. But as he stood there with his chest heaving, his mouth working, she was reminded of a caged animal unable to find its way out.

She bit back a sob instead and quickly did as he demanded. Tossing the picnic contents back into the basket, she reached to link her arm with his. He threw it off, however, and instead placed his hand on her shoulder as she led him back to the car.

The return trip to Roxwood was excruciating, as silence drove the wedge between them further with each mile. Grace didn't trust herself to speak. He had ordered her not to, but even so, what would she say to him? That his blindness burdened her with guilt, or should she simply tell him the truth of how she'd humiliated him? Either excuse would sound too much like pity, and Jack would hate her for it.

Upon reaching the manor, he fumbled with the door handle before clumsily exiting the car. Without a word to her, he mounted the steps to the front door. Grace watched in misery, at a loss for how to mend this latest breach.

She'd been a coward from the start, she thought. But his anger and hurt right now seemed preferable to the hatred he would soon feel when he knew the truth.

17

The rest of her day was long and hot as Grace helped Clare in the east field, raking out the hay cuttings Lucy had mown that morning. They had finished up and returned their implements to the barn when Mrs. Vance greeted them. "Mabry, I've a note for you from the manor." She handed over an envelope.

Hope flared as Grace took the letter. Was it an invitation? Had Jack forgiven her?

"What does it say?" Clare asked.

After quickly reading the contents, Grace said, "Lord Roxwood will be in meetings over the next several days, and Mr. Edwards writes to inform me my services will not be needed until further notice." She swallowed past the ache in her throat, then looked at Mrs. Vance. "I suppose it means I'll be working full days now for the WFC."

Mrs. Vance smiled. "We're grateful to have you. With all of us pitching in, we can get this hay cut, dried, and ready to bale by Friday." She got back on her bicycle. "I'll see you both at the gatehouse. I'm off to start supper."

"Care to tell me what's going on?" Clare asked once their supervisor left. "Why is Lord Roxwood avoiding you?"

261

Grace shrugged. "He's obviously busy."

"My foot," said Clare. "There's more to it than that. You haven't said two words since you got back this afternoon. Are you all right?"

Grace offered a wan smile and then retrieved her bicycle from where it leaned against the barn. "I'd rather not talk about it."

Clare grabbed her own bicycle. "Oh, I see. Lucy and I must tell Grace Mabry all our secrets, while she gets to keep her own?"

"I don't *make* you tell me anything. I simply want to help, if I can."

"And we don't want to help you?" Clare flashed a hurt look. "I thought we were friends."

How had she managed in less than a day to trample the feelings of two people she cared about? Clare was right. Grace had adopted the women of the WFC as her sisters. "It's about Jack . . . Lord Roxwood," she began. "I did meet him before—at a costume ball in London."

"I suspected as much." Clare arched a brow. "The day Becky pressed you for information about the Tin Man?"

Grace nodded. "And you cleverly turned her attention to something else. Thank you."

Clare smiled encouragingly. "Go on."

"I'd only read about him in the newspapers, but when I met Jack in person I thought him the handsomest man in the room. I'd also deemed him a coward." She paused. "I was so angry. Poor Colin was fighting at the Front while Jack Benningham and others like him sipped champagne, made jokes, and surrounded themselves with beautiful women."

Clare snorted. "So you used the same tarbrush you warned me about?"

Grace felt renewed shame. "I did."

"What happened?"

She quickly explained to Clare how she and Agnes had slipped into Lady Bassett's ball with their contraband of white feathers and told of her encounter with Jack.

"Wait, you were one of those brazen women handing out feathers of cowardice?" Clare exclaimed when she'd finished. "And you gave him one?"

"Yes, and yes," Grace said. "I felt I was aiding my country and Colin. I didn't know Jack would be at the ball, but he was a known pacifist who had dodged the conscription. How could I resist shaming a man who constantly made the news with his proclivities for gambling, womanizing, and his protests against the war?"

"And now he knows it was you?" Clare looked confused.

"No. He apparently never learned my identity, nor does he recognize my voice." Her cheeks flushed as she added, "This might sound strange, but neither of us spoke a word that night. We just gazed at each other for the longest time. Then he smiled and took my hand to kiss it, and I smiled back and deposited the white feather into his."

Clare burst into laughter.

"It's not funny." Tears pricked her eyes. "Here I thought he'd been injured in the townhouse fire I told you about. But I learned he did go and fight . . . not long after his encounter with me. Now he's blind and scarred and hiding behind a mask all day."

When Clare simply stared at her, she cried, "Don't you understand? It's my fault."

"I don't see how. The man made his own decision to join the war. He's a member of the peerage, and if I've learned one thing, it's that they always do exactly what they want regardless of anyone else." Clare's gray eyes softened. "You've nothing to feel bad about."

Her words echoed Daniel's, but Grace's conscience wasn't

convinced. "If I hadn't gone to the ball, if I hadn't goaded him," she said, "Jack never would have enlisted and taken such chances. He wouldn't have gotten hurt."

"If this, if that," Clare said, mounting her bicycle. "Only God knows what goes through a man's mind, Grace, not you or me. You may regret your actions, but Lord Roxwood, or Jack Benningham, did as he saw fit and that's an end to it. You can't blame yourself."

"I feel cowardly," Grace admitted. "I should at least tell him it was me. Ask for his forgiveness. But it's so difficult . . ."

"You'll just make things worse. He'll still be blind and scarred, and have lost a friend . . ." Clare paused. "Oh, dear, you've fallen for him, haven't you?"

Grace looked away. Clare said softly, "We talked about this, remember? He's not free to marry, and you cannot afford to settle for anything less. Trust me, you'll only get your heart broken, my friend. It's not something you want to go through."

"I'm afraid it's too late, my heart *is* breaking," she whispered. "This morning we went to a place—Eden, he calls it—and Jack took off his mask for me. He wanted me to see him, warts and all . . ." Her voice broke. "I'm afraid I reacted badly."

"Oh, dear," Clare said again, reaching across the handlebars to clasp Grace's hand.

"His appearance took me by surprise. Not because of his scars, they aren't so terribly bad, but his eyes looked right through me. And I knew I did it to him."

"I'm so sorry," Clare offered. "But before you do anything rash, why don't you wait and see what tomorrow brings? If he asks you to drive him in the morning, then you'll know he's forgiven you for your reaction today."

Grace held up the letter. "I cannot imagine he will."

"You don't know for certain. Besides, if he cares about you

as much as I suspect he does, he won't wish you to stay away. Now, come on, supper's waiting. A full stomach will lift your spirits and clear your head in no time."

〰

The next three mornings dawned clear and bright, and Grace would have preferred to be with Jack rather than raking hay cuttings into long rows beneath a hot sun. Still, the hard work eased her aching heart while she tried to sort out her thoughts.

"So my spirit grows faint within me; my heart within me is dismayed."

She made another swipe with the rake at the dried grass, then straightened, stretching her cramped back muscles. The verse, another from Psalm 143, seemed to speak to her misery. She should have told Jack the truth on Monday. Then he would have understood her reaction—that it wasn't him who failed to measure up, but her.

More than once she'd considered going to him, since the moment Lucy came back from the manor yesterday bursting with good news. Jack had offered her a position at Stonebrooke. Sir Marcus felt the banished young man might still cause trouble, so Jack decided Lucy would be much safer in the north at his family's estate. Grace was grateful to him. She'd known he would be willing to help her friend. And hearing of his kindness only made her miss him all the more.

"Grace!" She turned to see Mrs. Vance hailing her from the edge of the field. "Grace, Dr. Strom needs a word with you."

Grace felt her own erratic pulse. Cousin Daniel wanted to speak with her? Pulling off her gloves, she dropped them beside her rake and walked to her supervisor.

"He's waiting for you in the barn. Hurry now." Mrs. Vance's furrowed brow and drawn mouth heightened Grace's alarm, and she moved at a half run toward the large structure.

She found her cousin inside the shadowy confines, waiting for her. "Is it Jack—Lord Roxwood? Is he unwell?" she asked.

Daniel removed his felt cap, his expression sober. "Sit down, Grace."

Was Jack's condition worse than she imagined? Grace bit back her anxiety and sat on a milk crate. "Tell me," she breathed, afraid of his answer.

"I'm not here about Lord Roxwood," he said gently.

Her confusion turned to cold, hard dread. "Colin . . ."

He nodded, and Grace teetered dizzily on her perch. He reached to steady her. "He's . . . he's not dead?" she whispered, unable to believe it.

"As far as we know right now, he's alive. He's been listed as missing."

A cry escaped from her as she launched from her seat, grabbing his sleeve. "How . . . ?"

He held her by the shoulders. "Your father telephoned me at home, and I came here directly. I'm told every effort is being made to find your brother."

Her mind reeled as she thought of the worries she'd been feeling about her twin. Real fear took hold of her. "Where was he last seen?" she demanded. "How long has he been missing? Do you know if he was injured?"

"Easy." He helped her back to her seat. "We have nothing yet, but the Army will tell us when they have information. In the meantime, you must try and stay calm."

"Calm?" she wailed. "When my brother might be lying injured, or dead . . ." She bit down hard against her lip. "We must do something," she said, searching his face. "Anything."

"For now, we must wait," he said in a firmer tone. "Mrs. Vance has agreed you should return to your billet and lie down. I'll give you something to help you sleep. You're already exhausted, and this news has certainly given you a shock." He grasped her hand. "Come along."

She followed him outside. Mrs. Vance stood beside Daniel's car, wringing her hands. The older woman's hazel eyes shone with tears. "Mrs. Vance will accompany us and see you settled. Tomorrow, after you've had a good night's rest, we can decide on how to proceed."

"I must go home." Grace shook off her stupor and pulled away from him. "Da needs me."

"Of course. I'll accompany you to London on the train." He placed a hand on her shoulder. "Have faith, child, and pray for your brother's safe return."

"Pray . . ." She looked toward the fields. "But I haven't told him." She turned back to her cousin. "Jack. The white feather . . ." Her head began to pound, and she felt as though the earth might swallow her up. "I've been so foolish. Now Colin is gone, and they'll never find him."

"It's foolishness, all right," Daniel said. "I know what you're thinking, but God doesn't work that way, Grace. He doesn't make deals, and I don't believe He's punishing you for anything." His aged features softened. "Do you understand what I'm saying?"

She nodded, only half listening. "Good," he said. "Now, I'll drive you both back to the gatehouse."

Grace lay on her bed several hours later, having taken the headache powder her cousin prescribed, but refusing anything stronger. Eyes closed, she imagined all kinds of horrible scenarios: Colin sprawled on the muddy battlefield injured and bleeding, or perhaps he'd been captured and was being tortured even now behind enemy lines . . .

Guilt threatened to suffocate her, and she was again reminded of the torment in her mother's expression as she'd stared up from the bed at her only son—Colin, standing in uniform, looking proud, his gaze burning with his sister's ideals.

Dear Lord, what have I done? Tears rolled down the sides of her face. She recalled the young soldiers at the dance. Some were mangled and maimed, while others, perhaps like Jack's brother, wore their damage on the inside. Even Jack suffered living in darkness. *"War is an ugly business, Grace."*

She knew from Colin's old letters that he slept in muddy trenches and ate stale rations. And while London had received many air attacks, the bombing hadn't been on a grand scale— Grace had never actually seen any of the damage herself. Yet now with her brother missing, perhaps near death, the war had become painfully close.

She didn't sense her twin was dead, at least not yet—but she worried he might never be found.

"Lord, please save him," she cried into her blanket. "I made a terrible mistake."

"Show me the way I should go, for to you I entrust my life." The psalmist's verse penetrated her senses. Perhaps God didn't make deals, but Grace couldn't shake the belief that her wrongs outweighed her desires. *"In your righteousness, bring me out of trouble."*

She threw off her blankets, and with shaking hands she laced up her boots and gaiters. Grace knew what she must do.

Praying for Colin with a clear conscience meant first making peace with God . . . and with Jack.

∞

"Miss Mabry?" Knowles's weathered features registered surprise as he answered her summons that afternoon.

"I must speak with him."

"Is something amiss?"

Grace caught his swift perusal of her. She still wore her dirty uniform from the field. Despite her struggle to stay composed, her voice trembled when she said, "Please, it's important."

"Milord is resting," Knowles said. He wasn't as ebullient as he'd been on Monday, but his look of indecision was a far cry from the usual staidness. "Could you perhaps call tomorrow?"

"I cannot." She reached for his sleeve, tears threatening to blur her vision. "Please, I . . . I just received urgent news. I must meet with Lord Roxwood before I go."

Her voice broke, and his features transformed into a look of genuine concern. "Miss Mabry, I truly hope it is nothing dire?" He cleared his throat, adding, "I will of course notify his lordship." He paused. "But is it quite necessary you must leave us?"

She nodded. "I'm needed back in London."

The butler hesitated, then stood aside to allow her entrance. "Please wait inside."

While he disappeared to make the request, Grace stood in the foyer and tried to imagine her conversation with Jack. Would he even agree to meet with her before she left? She said a quick prayer he would at least give her an audience, allow her to try to make amends to him, for her brother's sake if nothing else.

"Good day, Miss Mabry."

Mr. Edwards appeared from down the hall. "His lordship will see you. Please follow me."

He led her back down the hall to the study. Grace had been inside only once before, when the steward arranged her contract as chauffeur. She recalled that day, and Jack's cold and distant manner toward her—so different from the man with whom she'd shared candy floss at Margate, and danced in a quiet corner of Roxwood's community hall.

That was before she'd let her guilt wound him. How would he behave toward her now?

"Miss Mabry, milord," Edwards announced, opening the

door to the study. To Grace he said, "You may go in," and gestured with a sweep of his arm.

She entered, and the steward closed the door, leaving her alone with Jack. Her nerves stretched as she walked deeper into the room, which was silent but for the soft ticking of a clock on the mantel. Quickly she surveyed the masculine surroundings—the dark wood paneling and oak bookcase lining one wall, and across the room the massive cherrywood desk that now sat empty. She turned toward the unlit fireplace and glimpsed Jack's long legs as he sat with his back to her in a leather upholstered chair near the hearth.

Grace inhaled a shallow breath. "Hello, Jack."

Despite his anger, Jack's pulse leaped at the sound of her voice. Having kept her away already three days, he'd counted the hours he hadn't heard her speak, or felt her touch, or breathed in the faint, familiar scent of her. He missed their conversations, their laughter; regardless of her open rejection of him, he had felt her absence to his core.

You're pathetic, Benningham. The silence was deafening but for the clock, and he rose from his chair, turning in her direction. "Edwards said you had urgent news?"

"I've come to tell you I'm leaving for London in the morning."

He grabbed at the back of the chair. Did she find him so repulsive then, she must abandon her position entirely? His throat ached as he fought for composure. "Miss Mabry, I can understand how I caused you embarrassment the other day—"

"You didn't embarrass me," she whispered. "My own behavior was abominable, and I've come to apologize."

"My mistake," he bit out, as the sound of her pity renewed his anger. "I should have realized how you would react." He let go of the chair and advanced a step. "Is that why you're leaving Roxwood?"

"I received news that my brother . . . he's missing in action."

Hearing her anguish, Jack abandoned all pretenses at salvaging his wounded pride. "Grace, I'm sorry." He took a few more steps forward, closing the distance between them. "How did you find out?"

"My cousin, Dr. Strom. He . . . he spoke with my father on the telephone this morning. I must go home and be with Da while we wait for news from the Army."

Her news struck him like blows. Jack hated the idea she would return to her blackguard of a father. "Is there anything I can do?"

"Cousin Daniel said we must wait."

Bitterness edged her words. His gut tightened. "Marcus might be able to help." His friend had high connections in the Army.

"Thank you."

Jack felt a warm hand clasp his own. "I promise you, Grace, we'll find out what's being done to find your brother," he said.

"Jack, there's another reason I'm here."

She withdrew her touch then, and a sense of loss filled him. A moment later, Jack felt her warm hands along either side of his face. He steeled himself as her fingers grazed featherlight over the scar at his cheek. "To seek your forgiveness."

Her whisper, so close to his lips, tantalized him. Yet he would rather die than become the object of her charity. "I told you, it was my error in judgment."

"No, I need to confess something else, far worse than my behavior at Eden."

What could be worse than her rejection? Unless . . . Coldness swept over him as he thought of her father. "You have a secret to share?"

"I want to see you, Jack." Her hands slid around to the ties at his mask. Jack tried to pull away, but she held tight. "Please, trust me," she said. His heart hammered against his chest as he went still. Soon the air touched his exposed flesh, and the room fell silent except for the sound of their breathing. Why was he allowing this torment? He imagined her repulsion, knew he couldn't stand her rejection a second time—

Her gentle touch startled him. "I thought you so handsome that night at the ball, with your midnight cape and your red rose." She spoke softly as she trailed a finger over the uneven skin of his scars. "Women flocked to you as they once must have done with the real Casanova."

His body stiffened, her words hitting him like a shock wave. "You?" he breathed. "You were at the dowager's party?"

Warm hands cupped his face. "I was so angry with you," she said, ignoring his question. "You and your pacifist friends lazing about, while my brother fought in the trenches and the enemy's bombs fell on London. The war had to be won." She paused. "I thought to shame you in front of your peers and gave you the white feather—"

"Pandora?" Stunned, he reached for her hands against his face.

"Yes. It was me." Tears edged her voice. "And in my effort to teach you a lesson, Jack Benningham, I nearly destroyed you." Her breath shook. "It's my fault you cannot see."

He felt dazed. "I can't believe . . . Jasmine," he said, recalling the scent of flowers surrounding her at the ball. And when Marcus had described her auburn hair and green eyes to him, he'd imagined the beautiful goddess in green who had captured his attentions that night.

It now seemed perfectly reasonable Grace would be the same woman.

"I was just as surprised as you when we met in your hedge maze," she said. "You were this Tin Man the villagers spoke of. I'd read in the *Times* about your injuries. I chose to believe you'd gotten drunk and set your own house ablaze." Her voice dropped. "I assumed that you deserved your fate. Oh, Jack, I'm so ashamed."

She tried pulling away from him, but his grip held her firmly. Finally she quit her struggle and said in a sad voice, "I kept my secret at first, not because I regretted my actions, but I feared you would be furious and banish me from Roxwood. I didn't want to return home, to what awaited me there. Ironic, isn't it?" Anguished humor colored her tone. "Now I *am* leaving, and of my own will."

"Grace, you don't need to do this."

"Please, let me finish." Her breath trembled between them. "When I learned the truth, that you were injured in the line of duty and not by some house fire as everyone thought, I realized how badly I'd misjudged you. I felt horrible for having shamed you into enlisting. And the other day at Eden, when you took off your mask, I . . . I couldn't bear knowing what I had done to you. Please forgive me."

"Forgive?" Jack's confusion cleared the second he realized Grace felt she was to blame for his injuries. She couldn't know her effect on him the night of the ball, or how the feather had amused him—until Chaplin made his escape. He released her hands and dug into his waistcoat pocket, retrieving the talisman he'd kept with him the past few months. "I believe this once belonged to you?"

Shocked, Grace stared at the white feather in his grasp. "You kept it?"

He twirled it between his thumb and forefinger. "Amazing, but when they fished me from the Thames, your token of affection managed to remain with me." He smiled. "This feather and your lovely image have haunted my dreams for months."

"But the memory, it . . . I . . . was responsible for you getting hurt."

"Grace, I was already in service to the Crown the night I met you." He returned the feather to his pocket. "Your boldness provided me a pleasant diversion, nothing more."

The knowledge eased her conscience considerably. Then she recalled his words at the village dance, his "high stakes" job. "Did you work with Marcus at the Admiralty?"

"Yes, I'd been working at . . . my position for some time," he said. "I knew the risks, so there is nothing to forgive. You would have felt much better had you told me sooner."

"I thought you would despise me."

"Never," he whispered. He reached out to her, and she again put her hands in his.

"I did consider baring my soul to you once or twice," Grace admitted. "But I was afraid to take the chance. Then news came about Colin, and I worried . . ."

"About what?"

She hesitated, then said, "We've already discussed your views on the subject of God and religion, so you'll think me silly. But I desired a clear conscience . . . to pray for my brother."

"Clear conscience or not, the Almighty does what He likes and we have no say in it. But if it makes you feel better, Grace," he said, smiling, "I forgive you."

"Thank you." Impulsively she rose on tiptoe and pressed a kiss to his scarred cheek.

He gripped her hands. "What was that for?"

The mantel clock chimed the hour. "I should go," she said instead, unwilling to reveal her true feelings. "I didn't tell any-one I was leaving the gatehouse. I don't want them to worry."

"Will you ever come back to Roxwood?"

Tension colored his tone. Grace's heart ached at the thought of leaving him. "I don't believe so," she said truthfully. "The Women's Forage Corps will finish work next week and then move on to another estate. I'll likely remain in London until word arrives about my brother." She stepped back, and he released his grip. "Thank you for offering to help, Jack."

He nodded. "Will you call me?"

"You wish me to?"

"What do you think?" Jack again reached for her and this time pulled her into his arms. Grace hesitated, but then relaxed against him, feeling comforted by his strength. She rested her head against his chest and felt his heart beating as fast as her own. "Do you have any idea how much I'm going to miss you?" he whispered close to her ear.

His breath tickled her skin, and she tilted her face upward. "How much?" she whispered back, knowing the danger of such a question.

His sculpted lips smiled at her irresistibly. "Kiss me and I'll show you."

His gentle voice caressed like the rustling grasses of the field. Grace gazed at him, mesmerized, longing to feel the touch of his lips against hers. But she resisted. "We haven't the right." Yet as she spoke, she gave into temptation and reached to trace along the edge of his mouth. "And I don't want my heart broken."

He caught her hand, kissing her fingertip. "I won't break it." He leaned to touch his head against hers. She felt his warm breath on her cheek. "I promise."

There were so many reasons she shouldn't kiss him. She would likely never see him again after today, and Jack must marry and eventually lay claim to his title as earl. He'd be provided with a legion of chauffeurs at his disposal and would have no further use for the daughter of an Irish tea man.

As she mentally cited all the reasons against it, Grace pressed close and touched her lips to his. Let this be their parting then, she thought, surrendering not to reason but to her heart.

But as he deepened the kiss, drawing her ever tighter into the circle of his arms, passion unfurled between them like the petals of his most prized rose. His fingers grazed lightly over her face as he put to memory each and every line of her features. She sensed in him a longing, tasting the loneliness he would face in the days to come. Surrounded by him, she breathed in the spice of his Bay Rum cologne mingled with a touch of aged leather and the scent that was uniquely Jack Benningham— Lord of Roxwood, Viscount of Walenford, heir to the Earl of Stonebrooke.

A man she could never have, and one with whom she'd foolishly fallen in love.

18

Jack roused himself from the dregs of sleep the following morning, first to the sound of a crow cawing loudly in the English elm beyond his balcony . . . and then to the brightness permeating his closed eyelids.

At first the sensation seemed natural, one which had instinctively been with him since birth. But as he gradually became fully conscious, his heart pounded as he opened his eyes and squinted against . . . light.

Foggy, indistinct shapes loomed around him: bedcovers, his dresser, the chaise in the far corner. He turned his head toward the blurry image of partially opened French doors, the fine fabric sheers fluttering in the soft breeze.

He blinked rapidly and observed the objects in the room becoming more defined. He recalled the day Strom had checked his eyes, when he'd imagined he'd seen a flash of something. Was it possible he was seeing . . . or was he dreaming?

Jack's breathing came fast, his excitement warring with disbelief. He tore away the bedsheets and swung his feet onto the floor. Light played against the polished hardwood, and he wiggled his toes. Though blurry, he could make them out.

No dream! He leaped up and rushed to open wide the French doors and step outside. Gooseflesh rose along his skin with the chill morning, yet he barely noticed. Shading his eyes, he drank in the light and colors surrounding him.

Jack continued to blink while the images became clearer. Minutes later, he could make out the detail of his intricate hedge maze and the differing shades of green in his sprawling lawn. Looking off to his gardens, he saw for the first time in a long while his pink hydrangeas, the rainbow-colored dahlias, and purple lavender—even his grandfather's roses.

A joyous laugh rose in him at seeing the red, yellow, and bright orange blooms, reminding him of Grace's adventure with the pigs . . .

Grace. Jack spun around and returned to his room. She was leaving this morning. He had to see his Pandora! Memories of yesterday and holding her in his arms crowded his thoughts. Had that been real, as well?

He walked across his room toward the pull, intending to ring for Townsend. Nearing his dresser, he caught sight of his reflection and stopped.

For a long moment he stared at the stranger looking back at him. He reached to touch the wrinkled flesh at his brow and temples. His eyelids looked well enough, but the scarring around them gave him pause. No wonder Violet had rejected him. He was hideous to behold.

Jack hesitated. Should he send for Grace? Now that he knew what he looked like, would he see her pity, her revulsion?

He recalled again her gentle touch, her sweet caress. He'd kissed those soft lips, and she'd returned the kiss, passionately.

Reaching for the mask on his nightstand, he hesitated. Then he donned the guise and moved to ring the bell for his valet. Grace would be the first to learn of his news, to see him looking back at *her*. She had accepted him, all of him, he realized, and he wished more than ever that she could stay with him.

Townsend arrived, and within half an hour Jack was dressed and descending the stairs. "Edwards!" he called, and soon he could see his steward from behind the slats in the mask.

Battling his excitement, Jack was tempted to reveal his secret to the man who had been with his family for years. Instead, he said, "Miss Mabry is returning to London this morning. I wish to meet with her before she goes. Tell her . . ." He paused, then smiled. "Tell her I wish to settle her wages. And I want her to take me for one last turn around the property."

Jack's smile broadened at Edwards's startled look. "Bring her to my study once she arrives. Now, I'm famished, and something smells very good."

Without further regard for his steward, Jack strode to the breakfast room, where Mrs. Riley stood as she did each day, waiting to fill his plate from the sideboard. Today, he thought to surprise her, taking the plate to get his own food.

Again he stopped himself. Grace would be the first to know. "The full breakfast today, Mrs. Riley, if you please."

Her look of astonishment delighted him as well, and it struck Jack that his melancholy over the past few months had affected his staff. He vowed to improve his mood, and started by thanking Mrs. Riley for the steaming hot plate she laid before him.

"I'm glad your appetite's back, milord. Shall I bring you coffee, then?"

"I think tea today, Mrs. Riley."

"Very good, milord," she said with another dazed look before leaving the room. As he tucked into his breakfast of eggs, beans, tomatoes, black pudding, sausage, bacon, and toast, she returned with a tea service and poured him a cup before placing the set on the table near his reach. "I found some lovely Assam, milord. Will it do?"

"Perfectly. Thank you, Mrs. Riley."

She flushed with pleasure and departed, reminding Jack of how difficult it must have been for his staff to endure his sullen reclusiveness these past months.

Jack heaved a sigh. He would try to make it up to them, he vowed. Meanwhile, he eyed the contents of the cup, and a smile played along his lips. *"Like Assam tea, steeping in the cup."*

Weeks ago, Grace had used those words to describe the color of her hair. Now, knowing she was Pandora, her depiction seemed quite apt.

He took a sip of the tea, breathing in the fragrant brew. A low chuckle escaped him. Here he was, a conventional coffee drinker, sipping at tea. It was Grace's doing, he realized. He wanted to please her.

After breakfast, Jack took more tea in his study while he awaited her arrival. He pulled the white feather from his pocket, turning it over in his hands. He tried to imagine her exquisite features just as he'd seen her the night of the ball: the riot of fiery curls, and large deep-set eyes the color of green jewels . . .

A knock sounded lightly at the door. "Milord, a visitor?"

Grace. Jack rose from the desk and moved from behind it. "Come," he called, feeling like a schoolboy in his nervous excitement to finally set eyes on her after so many months.

"Sir Marcus Weatherford, milord."

The butler bowed before stepping aside to let Jack's friend enter.

"Jack." Marcus stood at the threshold.

"Marcus." Having recovered from his surprise, Jack quelled his impatience. He had hoped it was Grace. "You're up early, old man."

"And you seem rather chipper this morning," Marcus said as he entered the room.

"Why not? It feels like a beautiful day. Even the crows sang outside my window this morning."

"Jolly good for you." Marcus seemed irritable. "I awakened to a ringing telephone."

Jack noticed Marcus was in uniform, and that he carried an official-looking satchel. He resisted remarking upon either, determined to keep his secret. "What brings you?" he said instead.

"Thank you, Knowles." Marcus excused the butler, then turned to Jack once he'd left. "Is that coffee or tea you're drinking?"

"Tea, and help yourself."

Marcus poured a cup and moved around to sit behind Jack's desk. Jack strode to the hearth where a fire was laid to remove the morning's chill. Turning around, he continued rolling the feather between his fingertips while he assessed his friend.

Marcus Weatherford looked much as he had months before, though his features held a few more haggard lines around the eyes and mouth. Doubtless he worked long hours at the Admiralty. "I'm waiting, Marcus. Aside from enjoying my hospitality, why are you here?"

"I've a bit of surprising news."

Jack's fingers went still on the feather as he caught the grim look on his friend's face. "And . . . ?"

Marcus set down his cup. "We've arrested Patrick Mabry for treason."

∽

"I still can't believe you're leaving us today."

Clare sat on the edge of Grace's bed and watched her finish packing. "I understand, though. I'm sure your father longs to see you. Right now you're the only family he has."

Grace paused in stuffing the last of her petticoats into her bag. "I'll miss you too, Clare." She smiled. "Whenever I hear the word *duchess*, I'll think of you."

Clare gave a misty-eyed smile and said, "Whenever I see a woman driving a cartload of pigs to market, I'll think of you."

Grace lifted a brow. "An experience I won't forget." Her humor faded as she reached for Clare's hand. "Take care of yourself, Danner."

"Godspeed, Grace." Clare hastily wiped at her eyes. "Look at me, will you? I've got to get down to the barn. We're baling the south field today. The others are waiting around downstairs to say their good-byes."

"I still need to go up to the manor." Grace had received Jack's urgent request and continued teetering between delight and dismay. She longed to see him again, but knew a second parting would be as painful as the first. "It seems Jack wants one last outing."

Clare eyed her knowingly. "Prolonging the agony, if you ask me."

Grace nodded, and Clare rose and enfolded her in a tight hug. "I've got to dash. Good luck up at the house. And I'll pray for your brother's safe return."

Grace felt her eyes burn. "I'll be praying for you and Daisy, as well."

Clare released her and stepped back. "Who knows? Maybe one day you and I can meet in London. We'll have tea at Swan's, and I'll introduce you to my little girl. You can introduce us to Colin."

Grace did smile then. "That sounds perfect." And as she watched Clare depart, she realized what a wonderful friend she'd made at Roxwood.

Turning her attention back to packing, Grace added in the last of her treasures—her journal. It contained the details of her adventure, including the dear women she'd come to accept as sisters in the WFC.

Grace had also filled pages describing the places she and Jack had traveled: Camden Pond with its colorful ducks; the seashore at Margate and Hall by the Sea where she and Jack shared candy floss as she described the bear on the beach; Eden's beautiful valley and glistening river and their picnic the day Jack removed his mask.

The book held so many memories—painful, precious, and life-changing. Loving memories as she recalled his tender kiss and the way he'd held her in his arms. He'd promised not to break her heart, yet even now the steady beat inside her chest felt fragile, as if it might crack wide open with the knowledge they would never be together.

Grace took a deep breath and fastened the last leather clasp on her portmanteau. She left it beside her haversack on the bed while she went downstairs.

The others sat quietly around the table, awaiting her appearance. Mrs. Vance looked up and beamed. "Are you off to the manor, then?"

"Very soon," she said, her insides still fluttering over the prospect of seeing Jack.

"Things won't b-be the same without you." Lucy offered a sad smile. "What time does Dr. Strom arrive?"

Grace checked the small watch pinned to her shirtwaist. "Not for several hours. There's a one o'clock train out of Canterbury."

"You will write to us?" Becky asked as she munched on a leftover biscuit. "Let us know how you're getting on?"

"Of course, and each of you must come visit me. London isn't so far away." Grace turned to Agnes. "You're certain you wish to remain here?"

Agnes nodded. "Just until we finish the hay, miss, if it's all right with you. I so enjoy the peacefulness of the country."

Grace smiled. Agnes had been much happier here than in London. "You are a free woman, Agnes. You should chart your own life as you see fit."

"Is that another saying in the suffrage movement?" Lucy asked.

"Yes, I believe it is." Grace looked around the small kitchen. "I'll miss you all very much," she said before her gaze resettled on Mrs. Vance. The woman had been as close to a mother as she'd had since losing her own. "Thank you for giving me a second chance."

"Oh, posh!" Mrs. Vance said, blinking back tears. "It was Lord Roxwood's threat hanging over our heads. And your hard work. I did nothing."

"But you did. Even when he overrode your authority, you still treated me well." She arched a brow. "Maybe you're happy now you bent those rules?" Grace recalled how much Mrs. Vance enjoyed dancing the night away in Mr. Tillman's arms.

"Perhaps." Ida Vance smiled, reading her thoughts.

Grace said to Becky, "I don't know when we women will get the vote, but remember, no one can take away our dignity. You've a great sense of humor, Becky, and you're one of the hardest workers I've had the privilege to know. I predict great things for you one day, like that bakery you've been dreaming of. Or perhaps even our first woman prime minister!"

The others laughed while Becky smiled, chewing on her biscuit. She swallowed and said, "Thanks all the same, Grace. I'd still rather open a small shop in my village and help Pa take care of our family."

"What? No grand pastry shop?" Lucy asked, and more laughter circled the table.

"A bookshop," Becky said, surprising them. Her eyes shone with gratitude. "For when Grace writes her novel. I want to sell lots of her books."

Grace smiled at her with watery eyes. "That's wonderful, Becky. Thank you." To Lucy she said, "And you—leaving soon for the north to work for the Earl of Stonebrooke!"

"Now who's going to be a duchess?" Becky said, and they all laughed.

Lucy nodded, despite a worried look on her face. "I'm grateful for all you've d-done, Grace, but I'm not sure I can do this."

Grace pinned her with a firm look. "Lucy, God gave you a special gift. You must believe in Him, and yourself too, and you'll accomplish whatever you set out to. I have every faith that one day we'll be standing in the midst of Britain's first woman veterinarian."

Lucy's eyes glistened. "I hope so."

"I know so," Grace said with a wink.

"Grace, I leave for Stonebrooke next week. Will you c-come and see me?"

"If I can." The idea of another chance meeting with Jack—and his new wife—at Stonebrooke was too painful at the moment to consider. Speaking of which . . .

"I need to go and perform my last duty as chauffeur." Again she eyed each of them. "I know you all need to get down to the farm, so I'll say good-bye."

Each woman rose and came around the table to embrace her, with tears flowing freely, smiles, well-wishes, and the promise to pray for her brother.

Grace pedaled her bicycle along the graveled drive toward the manor and thought of her WFC sisters. When the war was over, she planned to put on a grand tea party at Swan's and invite them all. Perhaps by then Clare and Daisy could join them, and surely Lucy could leave Stonebrooke long enough to travel down from the north.

Her pulse quickened as she neared the house. Spending a few more precious hours with Jack was a temptation impossible to resist, despite the heartache she knew would follow once she left. Would he take her in his arms and kiss her one last time before she departed forever?

Sir Marcus's Pierce-Arrow sat parked alongside the front steps, and Grace was seized with affection as she realized Jack had already contacted his friend to help in finding her brother.

She knew Clare would be pleased to see Sir Marcus and felt a bittersweet ache, happy for her friend despite her own circumstances. He was not only a kind man, having helped Lucy, but Grace believed Sir Marcus would accept Clare Danner for what she was. Her friend just had to believe in love again.

Grace decided to postpone fetching the Daimler and instead rang at the door. She was anxious to learn of any news about her brother.

Knowles answered her summons. He seemed surprised, but then a look of warmth crept over his crusty features. "Miss Mabry. You look quite fit for your journey."

She surveyed her tailored blue traveling suit, the same clothes she'd worn on her arrival to Roxwood. "Thank you, I think," she said, smiling.

"Indeed." He cleared his throat. "You have been like a ray of sun in this dark place, my lady." His rheumy eyes gleamed. "And you will be missed."

"Thank you, Knowles. I shall miss you, too."

The old butler stood back to allow her entrance. "His lordship awaits you in the study."

∞

"Patrick Mabry . . . arrested?" Jack swayed on his feet. His first instinct—to crow with delight—was tempered by the knowledge that Grace would be devastated. He tightened his grip on the feather. "You've got proof?"

"Irrefutable," Marcus said. "We intercepted a letter yesterday. Our Room 40 people found a coded message using invisible ink inserted between the written lines. The code breakers were able to decipher information about the port at Richborough—"

"Not possible!" Jack pushed away from the hearth. Cold dread shot through him. "Grace is innocent, Marcus."

"You've been deceived." His friend stood from behind the desk. "Look, Jack, I didn't want it to be true, either. I'd hoped you were right and she was merely an innocent victim." He withdrew an envelope from his tunic. "I've got a warrant—"

"Give me that!"

Jack strode to the desk and snatched the envelope from Marcus's surprised grasp.

"What the devil . . . ? You've got your sight back?"

"Just this morning." Jack dismissed his friend's look of shock as he opened the envelope. "Though I think it might have started to return when Strom was here."

"That's incredible. And welcome news, old boy," Marcus said softly.

Jack was already scanning the arrest papers. The happiness he'd felt upon waking had begun to unravel. "This states she wrote the letter. You're absolutely certain it's Grace?" He looked up, already knowing the veracity of his friend and the Admiralty.

Marcus nodded. "I'm sorry, Jack. I know this isn't what you wanted."

"Where is the letter now?"

"New Scotland Yard has the original, but I managed to get a photograph of the last page," Marcus said. "Knowing your feelings for her, I thought to at least give Miss Mabry the chance to verify ownership before . . ."

"Before you arrest her and throw her into prison?" Jack said. "Let me see it."

He wanted to laugh at the irony of his own words. Through some miracle he hadn't asked for, he was given back his sight.

And what did he demand but to view the evidence condemning the woman he loved.

Marcus withdrew from his satchel a large photograph. Jack studied the picture of the letter, easily recognizing the insidious dark brown code written above the elegantly scribed words. The words sounded so much like Grace, regaling her father with tales of her success in the WFC, digging ditches and sewing tarps. She wrote of the women she worked with and their kindness to her. She also mentioned the mysterious Tin Man and the rumors surrounding him, and Jack's face heated.

"None of this makes sense," he said. "Grace came to me yesterday and confessed to being at the ball the night of the explosion. She apologized for giving me this." He held up the white feather. "She seemed to feel responsible for my injuries."

Marcus narrowed his eyes. "Why didn't you tell me you'd met her before?"

"I didn't know it, not until yesterday. She arrived at Lady Bassett's costume ball dressed as Pandora." He grimaced. "I thought her the most beautiful creature, and when she surprised me with this feather, I was so amused I lost track of Chaplin for a few moments. He was leaving the ball when I realized I'd missed the exchange of information." He glanced at his friend. "It didn't occur to me in hospital to tell you I'd bungled my assignment."

"I think 'Pandora' was there for that reason," Marcus said. "Her distraction allowed Patrick Mabry to make contact with Chaplin without being seen."

A chill coursed through Jack at his friend's logic. It would have made for the perfect scheme. Had he been so swept up in passion yesterday, and with finding her again, that he'd missed the signs? "If that's true, why did she tell me her part in it, and beg my forgiveness?" Jack was still unconvinced. "Why not simply remain silent?"

"Perhaps she learned of Mabry's arrest yesterday and panicked," Marcus surmised. "Grace Mabry is an intelligent woman. Telling you her version from the night of the ball might induce you to champion her cause, in the event she's implicated with her father. As heir to Stonebrooke, you would be a powerful ally in court."

"Yes, but she's returning to London today. Why . . ." Jack let his voice trail off and stared at his friend. "Grace told me she was contacted by her cousin, Dr. Strom, the physician I told you about. He received news her brother is missing in action."

"It's possible," Marcus said. "And I'll gladly check it out. But if she is aware of Mabry's arrest, it could just be a ploy in order to make her escape."

Jack swore under his breath.

"Jack, it is possible that Grace Mabry was entirely manipulated by her father, from giving you the white feather on the night of the ball to writing this letter." He pointed to the photograph in Jack's hands. "However, it doesn't lessen her guilt." He paused. "Have you any idea where she is?"

"I sent for her." Jack's gut ached. "But if what you say is true—"

A knock at the study door brought them both around.

"Miss Mabry, milord." Knowles's muffled voice sounded from the hall.

"Send her in," Jack barked. Then to Marcus, "Say nothing of my improvement." He thrust the photograph back at him. "I prefer to remain blind awhile longer."

Marcus nodded. "Keep your advantage for as long as possible."

What advantage? Jack had begun to believe that despite the difficulties of his betrothal to Violet Arnold, he might have a chance at happiness, to share his life with someone who saw past the scars to the man he wanted to be.

Instead, he'd become more of a laughingstock—the Tin Man Grace wrote about in her letter. A creature so desperate for love, he'd allowed himself to be duped by Mabry's daughter.

Jack strode back to the hearth while he struggled to shore up his pride and reconstruct the shield around his heart. The future seemed darker than even his blindness had been. Each day as he resumed the dismal monotony of his life, he would know the cost of surrendering his trust.

Grace entered the study to find Sir Marcus behind the desk. Then her gaze sought the blond, broad-shouldered man standing by the mantelpiece. Her pulse leaped at the sight of him. "Jack?" she called softly.

He didn't answer. Instead, he turned away from her to face the small fire burning in the grate. Dread filled her. Was it Colin, then?

"Miss Mabry, come in."

Sir Marcus stood beside Jack's desk. Grace noted his uniform and his grim expression. "What's wrong?" She darted a glance back at Jack. Why didn't he acknowledge her?

"Please take a seat." Sir Marcus rounded the desk and offered her one of the leather wing chairs.

She refused. "Do you have news about my brother?" Alarmed, she clasped her hands tightly together. "Is Colin hurt?" Panic seized her as she considered the worst. "Please don't tell me he's dead!"

"I wouldn't know, Miss Mabry. I am here for another reason entirely." Sir Marcus's features remained implacable. "Now, please, sit."

This time she did as he asked, perching on the edge of the chair. She glanced to see Jack had turned around, standing with feet braced apart. He remained still and distant; the only sign he wasn't made of stone was the hand at his side, fingering the white feather she'd given him.

"Jack, what's going on? Why am I here?"

"The matter involves your father," Sir Marcus supplied. "And you."

"Me?" Grace turned to him, rising from the chair. "Something has happened to Da?"

"Did you know Patrick Mabry was arrested yesterday on charges of suspected treason?"

The room seemed to shift. Grace fell back against her seat. "What?"

Sir Marcus handed her a photograph. "We've also discovered his accomplice."

"No . . ." she whispered. What was he saying?

"Do you recognize this?"

She took the photograph from him with trembling hands.

It was a picture of a written letter. Grace felt the hair rise along her nape as she recognized the handwriting. "This is part of a letter I wrote to my father." She observed a series of stained numbers and letters above her written words. "What are these marks?" She glanced up at him. "And why do you have it?"

"I've a warrant, Miss Mabry." Sir Marcus ignored the question and took back the photograph. His brown eyes hardened like flint. "By order of the Admiralty and New Scotland Yard, you are under arrest for treason."

Treason? Hysterical laughter rose in her throat, followed swiftly by outrage as she launched from the chair. "I am no traitor, sir, and neither is my father!"

Sir Marcus seemed unmoved by her speech. She turned to Jack, still at the hearth. "Jack, what's going on? Please tell him this is all nonsense!"

At his continued silence, Grace bit her lip to keep from crying.

Wouldn't he speak up for her? She turned back to Sir Marcus. "What proof do you have for this ridiculous accusation?"

"As you can see, we found your code in the letter." He indicated the brown-stained marks, and Grace felt sickened. "You were exposed to confidential information, and as expected, you passed it on to your father and his agents."

"I don't know what that code means," Grace sputtered. "And I don't have any confidential information."

"You've forgotten the Roman ruins?"

She blinked. "The stone ramparts we viewed at Richborough?"

He nodded. "You saw the activity going on there because you mentioned the workers and trucks to me. Training, you called it. Then you used this letter to try to report it to your father."

"This is insane . . ." Her voice died at the implication of his words. She turned again to Jack, noting his fierce expression. "Jack, please say something! Did you know about this . . . this test?"

"I did," he said coldly. "And you failed, Miss Mabry. Apparently the axiom is true that the apple doesn't fall far from the tree."

Miss Mabry. His chilling formality lashed at her. This couldn't be the same man who held her in his arms only yesterday, the man who had vowed not to break her heart.

Grace went to him. "You think me some kind of spy?" She'd bared her soul to him, begged his forgiveness and he'd given it, or so she thought. With his tender kiss and the soft words he'd spoken to her of love and regret . . .

But he hadn't mentioned love, she realized. He'd been too busy laying his trap. "Did you ever trust me?" she whispered.

"I did once." Jack felt as though he'd been physically beaten. He'd hoped, *believed*, she would deny having written the letter, that perhaps it belonged to someone else.

He'd been a fool.

She stood so close, he could smell the scent of her flowers. It was painful to look at her. Despite her guilt, she still was the most beautiful creature, the same vision in green whose image haunted his dark world those long months. He recognized the lovely auburn hair, tucked beneath her fashionable straw hat, a few fiery tendrils curling gently along her nape. Her skin, like translucent silk kissed by the sun, revealed the same rosy cheeks, the same full mouth he remembered. And her eyes, emerald pools he'd nearly drowned in the night of the ball . . .

"That was before you lied to me," he said, hardening his heart.

"But I told you everything yesterday—"

"I'm talking weeks ago." He'd only just recalled the conversation they had during one of their earliest outings together. "When I asked if you attended Lady Bassett's ball, you denied it."

A flush crept into her cheeks, and the knife in his gut twisted. "You asked if I was invited, and I told you I would never receive that kind of invitation. As it was, I attended the ball without one. I did not lie to you, Jack. I only let you keep your misconception."

"You've become quite adept with your words, haven't you? Twisting and turning them to your liking." How could he have been so gullible? "I trusted you, even when I knew your father to be a traitor, the man responsible for this." He jabbed a finger at his face. "I wanted to believe you innocent, untainted by his treasonous blood."

Pain flashed in her eyes, but he made himself continue to look at her through the mask. "And when you came to me yesterday, I believed you. I thought your apology"—he raised the feather for her to see—"stemmed from misguided patriotism. But patriotism had nothing to do with it." He crushed the feather in his fist, wanting to hurt her the way he ached inside. "You intended to distract me while your father passed British secrets off to a German agent."

Grace reached out and laid a hand on his chest, and Jack gritted his teeth against the sensation. "You think my father responsible for your wounds? That's not possible."

The reminder of Patrick Mabry's treachery made him seethe inside. "There was no doubt," he ground out, removing her hand. "I found his letters aboard ship that night, proof of his guilt. They were destroyed in the explosion. And I nearly died."

"That's absurd! My father would never do that," she cried.

"Wouldn't he? How about a bribe?" He ignored her look of shock. "When you arrived here of all places, seeming innocent of any wrongdoing," he mocked. "You knew your father had paid off a clerk in the WFC to ensure you were posted at Roxwood."

Her face whitened. *Guilty*, he thought, and then delivered the final blow. "Did you really wish to enlist my help with the Admiralty to find your brother? Or is that a lie, as well? Perhaps he's not missing at all, merely gone over to the side of the enemy."

"How dare you!"

Before he could react, she slapped him across the face. "First you accuse my father, and now my poor brother. Are we all traitors, then?" she snapped.

"You tell me." Jack stood like a stone, numb inside.

"You've suspected me from the first, haven't you?" she accused. "All those questions, prying into my father's life, our family . . ." Her green eyes glittered. "That's why you kept me on. You were interrogating me in truth!"

"Now it seems it was prudent." His tone sounded hollow to his own ears. "You wrote the letter to your father about Richborough."

"I'm no traitor, nor is my family." She sounded desperate. "You're making a terrible mistake."

"No, you're the one who made the error, Miss Mabry." He raised the crushed feather in his fist and tossed it into the flames. "You should never have come to Roxwood," he said, ignoring her stricken look. "Perhaps then you wouldn't have been caught."

"Jack," Marcus cautioned.

"I'm finished now, Marcus." Jack turned from her to face the fire. "Get her out of here."

19

Clare Danner had just tossed another forkful of dried hay into the steam baler when she spotted Mrs. Vance running toward them across the field, waving frantically.

"Someone turn the engine off, will you?" Clare yelled.

Becky off-loaded the last bale, then went to the front of the baler and killed the engine. The sudden quiet was interrupted by Mrs. Vance's cry. "Girls, come quickly!"

Her note of hysteria caused alarm as Clare, Lucy, Agnes, and Becky rushed to meet her.

"It's Grace," she said, breathless and clearly distressed. "She's been taken by force to London."

"What!" they all cried. Clare said, "Who took her?"

"Sir Marcus—or should I say, Lieutenant Weatherford—arrived at the manor and took our Grace away. Her bags are still at the gatehouse where she left them." Beneath her hat, Mrs. Vance's features lined with worry. "Mrs. Riley came to the barn with the news."

A shiver coursed through Clare, and she crossed her arms. "I don't understand . . ."

"I do, and it's just awful." Mrs. Vance bit her lip and eyed each of them. "Grace has been arrested for treason!"

A cry sounded among their collective gasps. The women turned to see Agnes collapse in a dead faint to the ground.

"Oh, dear, she's had a shock!" Mrs. Vance rushed to her and started chafing her wrists. Agnes began coming around with an agitated moan. "Quickly now, Becky, Lucy, let's get her into the cart. Hitch up the team, and we'll take her back to the gatehouse."

Clare stood by, feeling stunned and angry, while the others helped Agnes to the cart. Marcus had seemed so different from the rest; she hadn't detected arrogance or the subtle air of self-entitlement so many men of his upper class seemed to share. Just those soft, brown eyes, looking at her warmly, and a smile so tender that it made her breath catch.

When he'd done the unthinkable and championed Lucy, she'd actually entertained the notion of being courted by him, imagining he would accept her past, help her find Daisy . . .

A bitter lump rose in her throat. In the end, he was like the rest. Had he cozied up to her simply to learn more about Grace? Why would he arrest her friend on such a ridiculous charge, then whisk her off to London?

"Agnes will be fine once she has a lie-down with a cold compress," Mrs. Vance said, moving up to stand beside Clare. They both watched Lucy harness the horses. "The lieutenant, Sir Marcus—he paid you marked attention, Clare. Did he mention anything to you?"

Clare reared at the question. "What do you mean? I'm as surprised as you are."

"Of course." Mrs. Vance's brow creased. "We've all had a bit of a shock, and poor Agnes has received the brunt of it. She was so devoted to Grace."

"You speak of Grace as though she's dead!" Clare said. "She's very much alive and she needs our help." All at once the anger went out of her. "There's got to be some explanation, Mrs. Vance. I cannot believe her guilty."

"What can we do about it?" Lucy had finished harnessing the horses and approached with tears in her eyes. "Grace has done so much for me. I c-can't stand by and do nothing. Once she's in London, the bobbies will lock her up. If she's found guilty of treason, they'll have her shot—"

"Let me think, will you?" Clare said, still struggling with her own devastation over Marcus, and the fact her friend was in dire trouble. "I don't yet know how we'll manage it," she said finally, "but Grace is our sister, and we're going to get her out of this mess."

❧

Seated silently beside her jailer, Grace seesawed between fury and fear as Sir Marcus drove them the distance to London. Already she'd tried to argue with him, but he insisted she save her excuses until they arrived at New Scotland Yard.

Staring out at the acres of hay ready for harvest, Grace wondered about her WFC sisters. They would be baling the south field right now. Did they know yet of her fate? She still felt dazed trying to make sense of the morning's events. News of Da's arrest, then the photograph of her letter and the outlandish accusations against her. The defamation against Colin was the worst, as Jack, in a monumental stroke of cruelty, suggested her brother wasn't missing but had instead gone over to the enemy.

Pain and humiliation cut through her anger. He'd simply used her from the beginning, making her a pawn in the game he'd orchestrated the moment he learned she was Patrick Mabry's daughter. He'd asked his annoying questions, not out of mere curiosity but to try to extract from her some kind of incriminating evidence against her father—evidence that didn't exist! He had thought her a spy as well, never trusting her . . .

But then memories of their shared laughter rose in her mind, and she recalled his gift to her, the beauty of Eden, and the moment he'd allowed her to remove the mesh from his mask. He'd spoken with honesty when he shared with her the love he felt for his grandfather, the pain of losing his brother. He'd been brutally candid when he spoke about being the second son of a man still blinded by grief over losing the first.

She remembered being in his arms, and reaching to touch her lips she imagined she could still feel the warmth of his kiss. Those moments had been real enough. In her heart, Grace knew he *had* trusted her.

Until Sir Marcus had brought him the letter.

She turned toward her jailer, wanting to hate him for it. But already panic was setting in, and her heart hammered as she remembered the newspaper story about the spy, Mata Hari. The woman had been convicted by the French to die.

Would Grace and her father end up at the Tower in front of a firing squad?

The vise of fear within her tightened with each mile as cottages, barns, and pasturelands gave way to the concrete buildings and traffic of more populated communities, and finally to the congested streets of Westminster.

The city bustled with the sounds of life. An ambulance with its siren blaring roared past the car, followed by the clopping of horses' hooves pulling a cart loaded with vegetables, and a man shouting, selling newspapers on a street corner. But the noise quickly faded as Grace stared up at the brick building of New Scotland Yard—and realized the enormity of her situation.

"Miss Mabry."

She jumped as her door was yanked open. Sir Marcus offered his hand. With shaking limbs, she allowed him to lead her from the car. Never before had she been to such a place. And here she was now, being incarcerated, a prisoner with a looming death sentence . . .

As if in a dream, she watched as they booked and processed her. Then an MP led her off to a room located in the bowels of the building and locked her inside.

Grace shivered, hands clenched together in silent prayer. Electric lamps mounted high along one wall revealed a bare room with a rectangular wooden table. A pair of uncomfortable-looking ladder-back chairs had been placed on either side. The austere quarters offered no other accoutrements—no bed, washstand, or chamber pot—so it couldn't be a cell, could it?

The room held the faint stench of body odor, and Grace felt her knees weaken in fear. She eased down onto a chair. Did they plan to keep her here until she expired of hunger and thirst? Or would they do something worse to her?

She looked at the walls, then under the table, relieved to find no hidden implements. Was Da in a similar room, or had he already been taken to the Tower? Fear blossomed into panic. Was he being tortured?

The door unlocked, and she emitted a low cry. Her heart threatened to explode in her chest. Sir Marcus entered first. Grace crossed her arms to keep them from shaking.

"Miss Mabry, I've brought Inspector Cromwell with New Scotland Yard. He wishes to ask you some questions."

Cromwell? Grace straightened as a uniformed man followed Sir Marcus into the room. He removed his hat, revealing a head of thinning black hair slicked down with tonic. His waxed mustache was just as dark and quivered above a thin-lipped smile as he scrutinized her.

Was this to be an inquisition? she wondered as he took the chair opposite hers. Sir Marcus stood off to one side.

"Miss Grace Elizabeth Mabry," Cromwell began, dropping a sheaf of papers onto the table, "do you know why you're here?"

She raised her gaze to him, swallowing her panic. "I haven't the slightest idea," she managed, pleased that her voice didn't waver too much.

"Indeed?"

He shot a look at Sir Marcus, who eyed her with impatience. "Miss Mabry, you are aware that you've been arrested for suspected treason?"

"Of course, I know *what* I've been arrested for," she said, resurrecting her anger at him. "I just don't know *why*. I'm not guilty."

"The letter, Miss Mabry," Cromwell said, shuffling through his stack of papers.

"You mean the letter everyone insists I added some secret code to? Well, I didn't."

Cromwell slid two sheets of stationery across the table to her. The brownish symbols above her writing were identical to the photographed copy Sir Marcus had shown her. "Code written with this type of invisible ink is common," he said. "With a bit of heating, in this case using an iron, we were able to detect its presence."

Feeling his shrewd eyes on her, Grace forced herself to look at him. Cromwell continued, "As Lieutenant Weatherford probably told you, we arrested your father yesterday, after we intercepted the letter and discovered the contents of the code."

It must have been shortly after Da had telephoned her cousin Daniel about Colin. Grace seethed inside. How much could her poor father withstand? "Where is he now? Can I see him?"

"Perhaps," Cromwell said, leaning back in his seat. "It will depend on your cooperation. So far, Patrick Mabry hasn't been forthcoming. If you provide us with the information we require, I'll make certain you get your visit with him before he's taken away."

Grace gripped the edge of the table. "Taken where?"

"Again, that all depends on what you have for us."

The probing look he gave her caused a fresh stab of fear. "I don't know what to tell you. I don't know how these"—she pointed to the brown-inked symbols between the lines—"got there in the first place." She cast a desperate look at Sir Marcus. "Really, this has to be some sort of mistake."

"Mistake, Miss Mabry?" Cromwell leaned forward. "Who else could have written this letter to Patrick Mabry? Or signed your name to it?"

"No one," Grace sputtered. "But that doesn't mean I put those . . . those marks on it!"

"Then how do you suppose they got there? Magic?"

"Of course not. But I can't tell you, because I don't know!"

"Fine." Cromwell snatched back the letter and placed it on top of the stack. He rose from the table. "Since you mean to be uncooperative, perhaps you'd like to sit here awhile and consider your options. Confess the truth, and because of your young age and the undue pressure your father must have exerted to make you betray your country, you may receive leniency from the court.

"Keep silent, however," he added, eyeing her gravely, "and you'll suffer the consequences. Do you read the papers at all, Miss Mabry?"

Mata Hari. She wet her lips before she whispered, "Yes."

"Good. Then I trust you know what happens to traitors. We'll continue this conversation later." He turned to Sir Marcus. "Lieutenant?"

"I'll be with you presently, Inspector."

Cromwell left, and Sir Marcus came around the desk to face her squarely. "Miss Mabry, please. For your friend Clare's sake, if not your own, tell the inspector what you know. I promise I'll do everything I can to help you get a lesser sentence."

Grace searched the face of the man who had captured her friend's heart. She abandoned her anger. "Lieutenant Weatherford . . . Marcus," she pleaded, "why won't you believe me? I haven't betrayed my country, and neither has my father. This has to be a mistake."

Her pulse sped as the honey-brown eyes flickered with a trace of compassion. His words, though, cut like a blade. "We have the proof, Miss Mabry. I only want to help you."

"Then find out who is responsible," she said in a flat tone, "because it wasn't me."

❦

If God existed, then He definitely had a twisted sense of humor.

Jack removed his mask and dropped it onto the bed before he strode out to his balcony. In less than twenty-four hours he'd gotten his wish: Patrick Mabry behind bars. Then this morning the thing he'd dreaded most—discovering the betrayal of Mabry's daughter.

Leaning against the marble rail, Jack struggled with the disappointment of being betrayed. He peered out at the manicured lawns forming a smooth blanket of green, while in his garden red, pink, yellow, and white roses thrived beneath the warmth of an azure sky. So much beauty to behold. Why had the Almighty gifted him with the return of his sight, only to rob him of the only woman he'd ever loved?

Jack could still hear her laughter, an honest sound coming from deep within, and Grace's uninhibited nature, expressing candid views or showing her temper as they spent hours in each other's company. Had it all been pretense?

Painfully he recalled their time at Margate when she'd ambushed him with a pair of wire cutters and removed the mesh from his mask in order to see him. Nudging him back into the real world. Yet he'd been willing with her. She had accepted him, brought him back from the darkness.

"Lies, all of it," he breathed aloud, gripping the rail. Still, he couldn't forget her enormous green eyes, glistening with tears as Marcus led her from the study. For an instant, Jack's convictions had faltered, and he'd fought the desire to banish Marcus from the house and take Grace into his arms, beg her forgiveness, and forget it all happened.

But it did happen. And Marcus held the proof of her guilt.

"We have to live by faith, Jack, not by sight." Words she'd spoken to him, saying faith was discovered with the eyes of the heart rather than by what the world sees. True enough, he thought bitterly. Grace Mabry had deceived him into believing she was innocent, as if she knew all along he suspected her. And Jack did suspect her at first, until he foolishly began to ignore the signs: her omissions to his questions, her anger, and her father's use of bribery to place her at his estate. Even Marcus had been skeptical, while Jack had argued in her defense.

Self-recrimination filled him. What an actress! She'd had him completely convinced. Perhaps she'd found their situation amusing, gathering information for her father. Writing to him those dirty little letters about secrets—Q ports at Richborough and any other tidbits a defunct agent of MI5 might let slip in his weakened state. Perhaps mocking Jack's pathetic situation altogether—

"Milord?" A sharp rap at the outer door to his rooms brought him back to the present.

Jack returned inside and stared at the mask lying on the bed. For a moment he was tempted to leave it off, permanently. Whether it was his mood, however, or perhaps some innate sense of preservation, he grabbed it up and covered his face, postponing his revelation a while longer. "Come," he said tersely.

"Excuse me, milord." Edwards entered and offered a cursory bow.

"What is it? I specifically asked not to be disturbed."

"I do apologize, your lordship, but you're needed at the gate-house."

Jack straightened. "Why?"

"I'm afraid the hay balers have gone on strike."

Jack paused, then said irritably, "And why is that my problem? If they wish more pay, let the Army Service Corps deal with them."

"It's . . . not about money, milord," Edwards said hesitantly.

"Then what *do* they want?"

His steward shifted. "They wish to see you specifically, milord, and discuss terms."

"What terms?"

"They won't say. But if you'll only meet with them in the morning, milord—"

"Fine," he snapped. Jack sensed they wanted more from him than to discuss terms. "Have Tillman come around at eight o'clock."

After Edwards departed, Jack removed his mask and tossed it back on the bed. Returning to the balcony, he continued staring out at his gardens, wondering what he would have to face in the morning.

Lying on a bed in her cell, Grace felt too exhausted and heartsick to sleep. Since her arrival at New Scotland Yard hours before, Cromwell and his detectives had barraged her with the same questions, over and over again a hundred times. Where was her father the night of April fourteenth? Did he attend the British Red Cross benefit with her at the home of the dowager countess, Lady Bassett? Was his costume that of the film star Charlie Chaplin? Had he planned any trips, purchased passage aboard a ship? To Ireland, perhaps, or even farther abroad? Who were his associates, his friends? Did she have any other contacts outside of her father? Where had she hidden the code book?

Grace felt further humiliation when detectives returned from Roxwood with her bags. They made her watch as they pawed through her most intimate things, including her journal, which Cromwell kept for himself before allowing her a change of clothes.

They'd found nothing, of course. But their frustration only made them more demanding, causing her unending hours in the interrogation room, seated in that torturous wooden chair as more detectives were sent in to bully her for information she didn't have.

She tried in vain to convince them Da was honest and hard-working, and as loyal to the Crown as she was. Grace reminded them that *she'd* been working hard for the war effort, and Colin had been fighting for his country in France.

Her words fell on deaf ears. Cromwell, heading up the investigation, even had reservations about her brother, echoing Jack's callous assumption that Colin had likely gone over to the Germans.

She lay in the dark, hands fisted at her side, trembling. Tears streamed down the sides of her face, and a sob tore from her throat. What would they do to her? How much longer would they flog her with questions before taking action? Would she and Da be sent to the Tower?

"Oh, Colin, where are you?" she cried into the darkness. Closing her eyes, she took deep breaths while praying fiercely for his safe and swift return. He was proof of their loyalty to Britain; his homecoming would exonerate both her and Da and disabuse the belief he was a traitor to his country.

Her brother would be a hero they could not ignore!

Inside the cramped parlor, Jack surveyed the occupants through the slats of his mask. They in turn gaped at him. He'd met the women of the WFC only once before, at the barn, prior to regaining his sight. Until they spoke now, he wouldn't be able to identify one from the other.

Mr. Tillman had entered behind him and moved to stand beside a uniformed woman slightly older than the others. Jack surmised she must be Mrs. Vance, their supervisor.

"Speak!" he said, growing impatient at their gawking.

His order seemed to shake them from their stupor. A young, very pretty woman stepped forward from the group. "Thank you for meeting with us, milord."

Clare Danner. While she hadn't spoken the last time, Marcus had seemed most taken with her midnight hair and gray eyes. Jack felt a pang of envy, knowing his friend was in love and had a chance at happiness. He, on the other hand, would marry a woman who loathed the very sight of him. And the one he'd come to love, Grace, was lost to him forever.

The familiar dull ache in his chest made him angry. "Out with it. Why have you asked me here?" Though he suspected he already knew the answer.

Clare Danner moistened her lips and wiped her hands against her uniform. "It's about Grace—Miss Mabry."

Jack admired her courage. She would need it, coping with Marcus's line of work. Still, why should he make this easy on any of them? "Miss Mabry left," he said. "I don't know what you think I can do about it."

"She didn't *leave*, milord." The gray eyes flashed. "We know she was arrested."

"And . . . ?" He waited.

"She's not guilty."

Hope flared for an instant before Jack willfully quashed it. "Can you prove it?" he demanded. "Have you any information?"

She took a step back. Jack eased out a breath. "I appreciate your intent, but there is substantial evidence—"

His words were cut off by a muffled burst of laughter—a brief, high-pitched cackle echoing around the cramped confines of the parlor. Jack raised his head and tried to determine its source.

"Agnes, please hush."

Clare Danner had turned her remark to a short brown-haired woman barely visible at the back of the room. Then her gaze swung back. "What evidence?"

"It's confidential. And I still don't understand how it affects your work at the estate."

"Grace would never commit treason, Lord Roxwood."

Jack recognized the voice of Lucy Young, the woman with whom he'd met recently. She came forward to stand beside Clare Danner. "She's not only a p-patriot, but her brother fights in France."

"So we've been told." Jack recalled his accusation against Colin Mabry and the way Grace had reacted. Even now, his belief wavered.

"You doubt it, milord?"

As soon as she spoke, Jack confirmed the woman beside Tillman was Mrs. Vance. Her features suffused with indignation. "I was there when Dr. Strom told Grace the news about her brother. I saw her reaction. She's no traitor. You must be mistaken."

Her words gave him pause. Jack remembered how distraught Grace had been when she'd come to him, telling him she must leave for London. And Strom seemed legitimate enough . . .

No, he'd been taken in once already. Grace Mabry kept secrets from him, and perhaps she would still but for her family's situation. "Obviously, there are things you don't know about her," Jack said.

"And many things you don't about her either, milord. If you'll pardon me for saying."

A stocky red-cheeked woman came to stand beside Lucy Young. By process of elimination, Jack deduced she must be Becky Simmons. Her look of outrage impressed him. If the proof were not so final against Grace Mabry, he might believe she'd been wrongly accused.

"Grace has been the truest friend. She's helped all of us in one way or another." Becky Simmons glanced to the others in the room, who all nodded before she said, "We'd like to tell you about it."

"And if I listen?" he asked, longing to end the meeting and return to his sanctuary.

"We will return to work and bother you no more," said Clare Danner. "Will you promise at least to consider our words?"

He let out a heavy sigh and nodded, taking a seat in the worn Sussex chair near the door. "Proceed."

Two hours later, Jack sat on the bench inside his hedge maze, considering what he'd just heard. While he'd suspected Grace was the reason the women insisted upon meeting with him, he'd nevertheless been stunned by their unfailing allegiance.

Becky Simmons had started off by confessing her attempts to steal his chickens from the meat larder. Grace had saved her from a life of crime by stopping her with a few inspiring words, plus extra shillings from her own purse to aid Becky's family.

Mrs. Vance had come forward next, linked arm in arm with Tillman. Jack hid his surprise as both sang Grace's praises, not only for recognizing their growing attraction to one another, but for acting as a sort of matchmaker during the village dance.

He was already familiar with Lucy Young's circumstances, yet she made certain to underscore to all present that it was Grace who had taken the first step to come to her aid.

Clare Danner's revelation was perhaps the most shocking. Jack recalled the ride to Richborough when Grace refused to tell him and Marcus the name of the woman responsible for setting the pigs loose in his garden. It was for Marcus's own love that Grace had kept silent, taking the punishment so that Miss Danner could remain at Roxwood and continue her search for a missing daughter. Jack wondered if she'd informed his friend about the child.

Finally, there was Agnes Pierpont, the woman with the odd, vaguely familiar laugh who had assisted as Violet's maid during her brief stay. Miss Pierpont claimed to owe her very life to Grace and told of a husband, Edgar, who abandoned her without means. Grace found her begging outside Swan's and took her in, giving her a position in the household and treating her more like a companion than a domestic. The small woman's expression was teary-eyed and pale as she related the story; she seemed a devoted servant.

Their testimonies unsettled him. Jack found it increasingly difficult to reconcile the motives of a traitor with the generosity and kindness Grace had allegedly bestowed upon her friends. Their loyalty to her seemed unquestionable as they shared their stories, some at the expense of their reputations, in order to prove her innocence. In fact, all that goodness made yesterday morning's arrest seem ludicrous.

It was at that juncture Jack had made an impossible promise—to help free Grace Mabry.

He sighed, digging at the soft earth near the base of the fountain with the toe of his shoe. Then he gazed at the clear stream of water bubbling up from its moss-infested stone. If only Grace's motives were as transparent, he thought. He wanted to believe in her innocence. At the least, he wanted to be convinced she'd been coerced to do her father's handiwork the night of the ball while he traded Britain's secrets.

But Jack had seen the proof with his own eyes.

He reached to cup his hands beneath the fountain's cool liquid and bathe his heated flesh. He'd been in the middle of this same act when she first happened upon him in the maze. Hearing her relief at finding help, she'd soon gone silent, doubtless at having seen his horrific scars before he covered his face. He didn't sense in her then any artifice or guile, merely a woman lost and in need of rescuing, trusting he would be the man to do it.

How had his instincts been so wrong?

His foot hit something hard against the dirt, and Jack caught the glint of metal as he reached for a small object lying half buried in the mossy ground.

A wistful smile touched his lips when he retrieved the metal toy soldier that he and Hugh once used as their prize. He must have left it here the last time they competed together in the hedge maze.

Brushing away the dirt, he noted the painted uniform long chipped away. He recalled telling Grace how he'd always won the contests, navigating the myriad twists and turns of the maze, better with a blindfold than using his eyes . . .

"Not by sight." Again the words she'd spoken to him rose in his mind. Yet instead of feeling resentment, Jack rested his arms against his knees and closed his eyes, allowing his heart to navigate the past: the mornings Grace had been frustrated with his questions or pleased when she'd bested him with some witty remark; showing her temper as she made certain to hit each and every pothole in Great Britain, then candidly sharing with him her dream to become a novelist. She'd been gentle in removing his mask, touching his scars. And he'd felt her softness relax against him when he pulled her into his arms. Her passion as they shared a kiss.

All real enough, Jack realized. The blindness may have taken away one sense, but he'd managed to hone the others. Hearing the smallest inflection in tone, feeling tension and pleasure. Smelling fear and deceit. Now that he could see again, why did he abruptly abandon those gifts?

Grace's reactions with him had been genuine. And her friends believed in her enough to disclose their secrets. Jack was beginning to feel his own compulsion to share that faith.

He opened his eyes, clutching at the toy soldier. Regardless of how he felt, this was not some contest to be won or lost. Mata Hari had been found guilty of treason, and Marcus said there wasn't sufficient proof. Even so, the woman would face execution.

How could he possibly help Grace when there was concrete evidence against her?

Jack stared into the clear water of the fountain. Nothing made sense, he thought as confusion warred with his aching heart. Nothing but that blasted letter.

20

"How is she?" Jack asked, having returned inside to his study to telephone his friend.

"Tired, but holding up," Marcus said through the line. "I'd forgotten how thorough Cromwell's investigations can be."

Jack leaned forward in his chair behind the desk. "How thorough, Marcus?"

"Easy, old boy. The inspector's only asking questions."

Jack didn't miss the gravity in his friend's tone. "Any progress?"

"Not beyond what we already know. I did verify with the Army that Colin Mabry is still reported missing, though no one is certain yet if his departure from the regiment was intentional. They're still conducting an investigation into his last whereabouts. As far as Patrick Mabry is concerned, detectives have combed through his offices, his residence, and his personal effects, but so far they've found nothing. He's been questioned about the suspect he was recently seen talking with at Swan's. He has nothing to say other than he visits with most of his customers. I'm afraid his daughter's letter is the only thing connecting him with treason. And despite our being at war, there is still a slim possibility he'll get released."

"Oh, that's beautiful!" Jack clenched the phone as rage tore through him. After getting this close to the truth of Mabry's actions, they might let him go? The injustice made him grind his teeth. "What about Grace?" he demanded.

"I think you know the answer to that," Marcus said.

Dread filled Jack. "Have we missed something, Marcus? I ask because, as ridiculous as this is going to sound, I'm not certain she's guilty." He then recounted to his friend the stories Grace's co-workers had shared with him earlier. "They make a persuasive argument as to her character, despite the letter. It's hard to believe someone so selfless could simply turn around and betray her country."

"A good spy goes to great lengths to remain undetected." Marcus spoke matter-of-factly. "Miss Mabry has obviously done the same."

"Is she that calculating? I know in this business we've met all types, but usually even the most experienced agent slips up in some way—with a word, a look, a nuance." Jack hesitated, then said, "I've spent the past three weeks with her. In that time we've shared so much together . . ." He cleared his throat. "In spite of her father's treachery in April, every instinct still tells me she's innocent."

"Jack, I understand what you're saying," Marcus said. "Even I admit that Grace isn't what I'd first expected. And she did help me along . . . with Clare. I'm sorry."

Jack wasn't in the mood for commiseration. "What's happens now?"

"Cromwell will end the questioning soon and send her to await a court-martial."

Jack felt the air leave his lungs. "They'll find her guilty, Marcus," he whispered. "The firing squad—"

"I know," Marcus said with equal gravity. "I'll do what I can."

"I'm coming to London." Jack shot up from his seat behind the desk. "I want to see her."

"Impossible. Both Mabrys are under New Scotland Yard's jurisdiction. No visitors. Not even you, Jack." He paused. "And to be honest, I don't think she wants to see you right now."

Of course she didn't. "Keep me posted hourly" was all he managed before ringing off.

Moving away from the desk, he walked to the hearth and gazed into the empty grate. Any remnants of the white feather had now turned to ash.

Grace had been devastated by the action. Yet Jack was so angry, he hadn't really seen it. He'd only wanted to lash out at her for betraying him that night months ago, and for the hundreds of poor souls killed on the Thames. For allowing him to hope for the first time in months, and then taking it all away with the simple ease of a letter—a letter much like the one he'd found aboard ship. Patrick Mabry's letter. Ironic that the traitor might go free while his daughter would not.

He turned and slumped down into the chair across from the hearth. The women at the gatehouse believed in Grace, and he had promised to help. But how?

"Look to your heart, Jack." Closing his eyes, he recalled the morning Grace had spoken those words to him. He leaned forward in the chair and clasped his hands together, as close as he'd come to prayer in a long time. If she was right, if indeed God did exist, then he hoped the Almighty would show him where to start.

Jack awoke in the early hours of the morning, sitting straight up in bed, his body covered with sweat. He'd had a dream; it was the night of Lady Bassett's ball when he'd dressed as Casanova and glimpsed the mesmerizing figure of Pandora approaching him, her gown flowing around her like angel's wings.

He'd known even then he could love her. The emerald eyes smiled at him while her kissable mouth parted and she whispered, *"Not by sight, Jack,"* as she drew nearer, carrying with her the little gold box.

In his dream, Jack felt his eyes close for a moment, and he heard the sound—a high-pitched cackle from across the ballroom.

Laughter . . .

Grabbing up his robe from the bed, uncaring of the mask on his nightstand, he went downstairs to telephone Marcus.

∞

Agnes was terrified.

Seated in the pew beside her co-workers at church the next day, she clutched her songbook and prayed silently while the others sang. The past two days had been a grueling nightmare—first, with her mistress being arrested for treason, then yesterday having to be in the same room again with Lord Roxwood.

She'd tried to remain obscure, standing at the back of the parlor. But then she'd laughed—it always happened when she was excited or nervous—and Lord Roxwood seemed to stare right through her. Agnes had to remind herself he was blind. He couldn't possibly know it was her at the dowager's costume ball that night long ago, or that she'd exchanged information with the man disguised as the American film star, Charlie Chaplin.

That Agnes was a spy for the Germans.

She'd listened while her co-workers bared their souls, shocked at some of the secrets they harbored. Agnes had hoped to evade telling her own, despite wanting to help Grace. Before long, however, it seemed all attention was upon her.

Even the lord of the manor had turned his masked countenance back in her direction.

And so she'd started spinning her tale of woe for her audience. How she'd met her British husband, Edgar, overseas, and he'd brought her here to his homeland before the war. How she'd married a coward who abandoned her once conscription laws were enforced.

All of which was true. Yet Agnes hadn't told them Edgar was also a traitor to his own country, leaving Britain and his Belgian wife to return to Germany, where Agnes had lived with her mother and younger sister, Renee, as Belgian nationals. That he'd never really loved her but merely used her as part of his cover, doing his spy work in Britain.

"I was at loose ends," she'd said. *"It wasn't long before I ran out of funds. I became desperate."* True enough, as Edgar had left her almost penniless. Agnes then relayed to her co-workers and Lord Roxwood how months later, Grace found her begging outside Swan's and took her in. That part of her story still filled her with shame. Not the begging, which was just a ruse, but having manipulated Grace Mabry's sympathies. By then Edgar's Dutch agent, Alfred Dykes, had made contact with her. He informed Agnes that her mother and Renee had been moved to a concentration camp at Holzminden in Lower Saxony.

If she ever wished to see them again, she would do as she was told.

"She took me in, Miss Mabry did. It was luck that her lady's maid suddenly quit, running off to elope. I was offered the post." Agnes wondered if there really had been an elopement, or if Dykes disposed of the maid to allow Agnes access to Mabry's household. Swan's, he'd said, provided the perfect cover—"hiding in plain sight" with its steady stream of clientele. Just days before, he'd taken up position as Swan's floor manager,

317

replacing an employee killed in an automobile accident. Agnes wondered about that "accident," as well.

"*I became more like Miss Mabry's companion than her maid.*" Also true. Her relationship with Grace Mabry allowed Agnes the freedom to meet with various contacts during their outings together. In fact, the night of the ball, she'd met with Chaplin under the ingenious guise of handing out white feathers, which Grace had unwittingly suggested in her determination to enlist every able-bodied man to the Front.

As Dykes had access to Mabry's posts, it was easy for Agnes to obtain letters written to certain shipping personnel who were also on Germany's payroll; she would steam open the seals and insert coded messages using invisible ink, just as Dykes instructed. The letters would then be resealed and sent on their way, with Patrick Mabry none the wiser.

"*I owe Miss Mabry everything.*" Agnes had meant those words. Even now it grieved her to be the cause of Grace and her father's arrest. But what choice did she have? Each time she looked at the photograph she'd been sent, of Mama and Renee standing beside the barbed wire, she feared for their lives. Agnes hated spying. There was one hope to cling to, though she knew it was likely a foolish one—that with Grace Mabry in jail, Alfred Dykes might finally leave her in peace.

"Aren't you c-coming, Agnes?"

Lucy's voice jarred her from her reverie. She was startled to realize the service was over and most of the villagers had already vacated the church.

Rising from her seat, she followed the others outside. Despite the calm day and clear skies, Agnes felt a storm of emotions assail her. *I'm a murderer* . . .

"Enjoy your day, ladies," Mrs. Vance said. "Tomorrow we'll

finish up in the south field and by Wednesday deliver the last cartload of hay to Margate."

"I hope I'll get to go this time," said Becky, and despite her own troubles, Agnes caught the note of worry in her co-worker's normally cheerful voice. "I need to see my family."

"Your sister, Ruthie, was just here. Is anything wrong?" Mrs. Vance asked.

Becky's cheeks reddened, and she quickly shook her head.

"Ah, you're just suffering a bit of homesickness," Mrs. Vance said. "But the assignments have already been handed out. And since we've only a few days before we head to the next post, I suggest you make the best of it, Simmons."

She scanned the rest of them. "I seem to recall Grace telling us about a place, Camden Pond I think it was." Her attention settled on Becky. "Why don't you ride your bicycles over and go for a swim? It's a beautiful day and you'll feel better."

The notion seemed to lift Becky's spirits. She smiled, then turned to Agnes. "Will you come with us?"

"I'm not much of a swimmer," Agnes lied. How could she possibly think of going off to enjoy herself while Grace languished in prison?

Lucy read her thoughts. "I know you're worried about Grace, but Lord Roxwood p-promised to help, didn't he? And I'm sure he'll talk to Clare's friend."

"Marcus Weatherford is no friend of mine," Clare said. "And he won't help. He's just like the rest of them. Good for drinking and dancing, and little else."

"Oh, Clare, that's not true," Lucy said. "Look what he d-did for me."

"Yes, he helped you. Then he dragged our friend off to jail without saying a word to me or anyone else." Clare turned to Agnes, her gray eyes full of compassion. "I believe Lord Roxwood still has feelings for Grace." She sighed. "But he'll need a miracle to exonerate her."

Indeed, Agnes thought miserably. "If . . . if you don't mind, I'll stay on at church a few minutes more. I'll meet up with you later."

Mrs. Vance offered a sympathetic smile. "Of course, take all the time you need. Being alone with God can bring comfort to a troubled mind." She touched Agnes on the shoulder. "Take heart, my dear. We're all praying for Grace."

"Thank you," Agnes said. Oh, how she longed for that comfort! After the women departed, she returned to the cool interior of the church and sat in the pew she'd vacated just moments before. Bowing her head, she clasped her hands together and closed her eyes.

What should she pray for? Grace would only be released if Sir Marcus discovered it was Agnes who had written the code into the letter. How was she to pray for both Grace and herself at the same time? It would indeed require a miracle . . .

"Morning, Agnes."

She started, turned, and sucked in a breath. "Dykes!"

The devil himself sat next to her. Agnes quickly scanned the empty church, then turned to him. "Why are you here?" she whispered.

"I figured to find you here on a Sunday. You didn't go with the others." Eyes the color of amber pierced her. "Guilty conscience, maybe?" He smiled thinly. "Still, it's good we got a bit of privacy. And Roxwood's an easier distance than Margate."

Margate. The others thought she'd gotten lost, but Agnes had been meeting with Dykes. He'd been angry, demanding her immediate return with Grace Mabry to London.

"You should have come back to the city when you had the chance," he said, reading her thoughts. "I had a feeling it was you and not Miss Mabry who wanted to leave in the first place. And now look at what you've done to her."

Agnes's insides cramped with guilt. In Margate, she'd managed to stall for more time, telling him of Lord Roxwood's identity—Chaplin's pursuer, and a man of whom they both had knowledge. "You were interested enough in Jack Benningham at the time to have me see what I could find out."

His features hardened. "And you promised me information."

She reared back. "I kept my word."

Fortune had smiled on her when Violet Arnold arrived without a maid. While up at the manor, Agnes had eavesdropped on a conversation between Roxwood and Sir Marcus about a secret Q port at Richborough.

"Did you now?" he asked, arching a golden brow at her.

"I did send you her letter." The night of the dance when the others had left, Agnes found inside her mistress's bag the letter Grace had started to her father. She coded it with the information she'd learned and posted the letter on Monday. "Miss Mabry's in jail because of it," she added. "Isn't that proof enough?"

"Maybe, but it doesn't matter." He withdrew from inside his jacket a small, wrapped parcel. "Take this."

Agnes eyed the package with apprehension. How could she have been so stupid to think that even after Grace's arrest, this man would leave her alone? "What is it?"

"New instructions," he said in a low voice. "Since your last letter was snatched up by the bobbies, you'll have to send another."

"But . . . Miss Mabry is in jail. Whose letters can I use to send the message?"

"You write it this time."

"Me?" Panic squeezed her chest. "Why don't I just tell you what I know," she said quickly. "Then you can be on your way."

His low chuckle echoed inside the church. "You know that's not how we do business, Agnes. *You* put the information in writing so *I* can send it on to our friends."

"And your hands stay clean," she said bitterly. "Where do I send this letter? I have no one back in London save Miss Mabry."

"Write to me at Swan's. Since both the father and the daughter are in jail—"

Agnes gasped. "Patrick Mabry's in jail, too?" She didn't think the others knew.

He nodded. "Anyway, no one will notice if Miss Mabry's maid writes to Swan's floor manager asking for wages." A pause. "His business seems to be going sour with the scandal, so your letter won't cause suspicion. In fact, I'm already handing out notices. So just code your letter like before and send it to me."

"But what if you're wrong? The police might decide to check my letter."

He indicated the package. "You'll be using a different kind of invisible ink. Sodium nitrate. Unlike lemon juice, it can't be detected with heat. And it's fairly new, so the Admiralty won't be looking for it."

"Don't make me do this." Agnes didn't care that she sounded desperate.

"You've come too far, lovey," he said coldly. "You not only have your mum and sister to worry about, but your own neck, too." He rose from the pew and eyed her sharply. "Don't keep me waiting too long, or you'll find yourself standing with your mistress in front of the firing squad."

Dykes left the church while blood pounded in Agnes's ears. With a sob, she got down on her knees and prayed fervently to God, begging to be released from the burden. Yet it seemed hopeless, for Dykes had been clear.

Agnes would lose her family—and her life—if she failed.

∾

"Good morning, Miss Mabry."

Grace glanced toward the door of her cell. "Sir Marcus." She raised herself to a sitting position on the bed. "Why are you here?"

"I thought to give you a bit of company this morning." He entered and grabbed up the only chair the cramped space afforded and placed it next to the bed.

"I'd prefer the company of my father. When can I see him?"

"When you provide the information Cromwell wants."

Dear God, please help us. Grace blinked back tears of exhaustion. She'd been locked up three days and they had yet to give her news about Da. "Can you at least tell me if he's well?"

Sir Marcus nodded. "He seems to be coping with his confinement."

His words gave her little relief. Standing, Grace asked, "May I be allowed to attend church? It is Sunday, after all." She longed to be free of this cage.

"Unfortunately, no," he answered. "However, I can send for a chaplain, if you wish."

"Last rites?" she snapped. When he didn't react, she felt a chill ripple through her. The past few days had been all too real. Cromwell grew more impatient with her each day. Soon she feared a trial, and then . . .

"I'm innocent, Sir Marcus." Impulsively she reached for his sleeve. "Please believe me." Her voice broke and she let go, looking away from him.

He cleared his throat. "How well do you know Mrs. Agnes Pierpont?"

She turned back, surprised at the question. "Why do you ask?"

"Tell me about your maid" was all he said.

Curious, Grace returned to her place on the bed. "I discovered Agnes outside my father's establishment back in January," she began. "It was cold and she was hungry and seemed desperate for funds. She told me she'd been a lady's maid in her homeland of Belgium. She'd met and married a British national, Edgar, who brought her to this country just before the war. He disappeared when Parliament enforced the conscription laws. As my own lady's maid had departed unexpectedly, I gave Agnes the position. She's been with me ever since."

"Have you always treated her more as a companion than a maid?"

"Did she tell you that?" Grace straightened and stared at him.

He nodded. "You have friends in the Women's Forage Corps, Miss Mabry. Each has come forward to share her personal story about how you helped them, in order to vouchsafe your character."

Grace fought tears, and her heart swelled with a fierce love for her sisters. "I cannot believe they would go to such lengths for me," she whispered.

"It seems you did the same for them," Sir Marcus said. "I know you helped Lucy."

"Did you speak with them then?"

He shook his head. "Tell me more about Agnes Pierpont."

What was he getting at? She held on to her patience. "Yes, Agnes was more my friend than a servant. We went everywhere together—shopping, the museums and art galleries. And after learning how Edgar had mistreated her, I encouraged her to join me at the suffrage rallies. I wanted her to realize her value and know she needn't be dependent on anyone else, save God, to find happiness."

His honey-brown eyes shone with admiration. "I take it she attended social functions with you, as well? Did she also attend the costume ball where you first met Jack?"

Grace nodded. "Agnes showed me the announcement in the paper. Lady Bassett was hosting a ball to benefit the Red Cross. The reporter mentioned that several persons excused from duty at the Front would be attending as a form of community service." She looked down at her lap. "Agnes and I had gone to a rally just the day before, so we decided to sneak into the party and hand out white feathers of cowardice."

"Were you with her the entire time?"

She blinked. "Yes . . . I mean, we arrived together, but then separated to pass out our feathers. Once Jack departed, the butler escorted Agnes and me from the house. Why are you asking me these questions?"

"Has Mrs. Pierpont at any time had access to your personal things?"

"I . . . suppose." She glanced up at him in shock. "You don't think Agnes had anything to do with this? All of us kept our bags beneath our beds at the gatehouse. Anyone could have snooped." Her cheeks warmed. "I confess I did that very thing."

He arched a brow.

"The day the pigs got out, I'd gone upstairs to fetch my heavy gloves. When I couldn't find mine, I thought to check and see if Agnes had a pair. There was a photograph in her bag, of her mother and sister, I think. She'd never shown it to me."

"What did you do with the picture?"

"I put it back," she assured him. "And I didn't mention it to her. I'd hoped Agnes would eventually trust me enough to show it to me herself."

Sir Marcus's brows drew together. "She never mentioned having a family to Jack."

"Jack?" Grace's heart thudded in her chest. "He spoke with her and the others?"

He hesitated, then nodded. Grace hardly dared breathe. "Does he believe I'm innocent?"

"I cannot say." His expression turned guarded. "But he's promised your friends to help if he can. And when he called me yesterday, I gave him my word to look out for you."

"He called you? Then he's changed his mind about me! Does he realize my family is innocent, too? My father, my brother—"

"Hold on. One thing at a time," Sir Marcus cautioned. "There was proof against your father on board the ship that exploded the night of the ball, so his guilt or innocence is still being determined. As far as your brother is concerned, the Army has no word yet on his last known whereabouts." He paused, his expression grave. "But Grace, there is still the letter . . ."

"Stationery!" Grace shot up from the bed. "Agnes had access to my letter. She borrowed my stationery the night of the village dance. She wanted to write to her family and couldn't find her own. I'd forgotten to mail my letter to Da, and so she took it along with hers last Monday to the post office." She stared at him, swallowing, then said, "It must have been her!"

Sir Marcus rose from his chair. "I certainly plan to check it out." He offered a smile for the first time. "I must leave now. May I get you anything?"

Grace searched his face, excitement coursing through her at the prospect of clearing her name, and her father's. She also felt anger and hurt over the possibility Agnes had betrayed her. How could she have been so wrong about her maid . . . her friend?

But through the tangle of her emotions, hope emerged, flooding her heart. Jack believed her innocent, or at least he wanted to. "Yes, Sir Marcus. Freedom," she said softly. "Please, I beg of you, get me out of this place."

21

Clare felt the late afternoon heat against her back as she pitched more hay into the noisy baler's chute. A few feet away, Agnes tied off the bales with wire while Becky, Lucy, and Mr. Tillman off-loaded and weighed the bundles before stacking them onto the cart. Tomorrow was the last day of haymaking, and everyone pitched in, except for Mrs. Vance, who had taken over Grace's duties of record keeping.

"That's the last of this batch," Clare called, tossing in a final forkful. "We'll finish baling the dried windrows over on the west side tomorrow and then take the last shipment to the station on Wednesday."

"Lucy is leaving for Stonebrooke that day, so who gets to go to Margate?" Becky shouted over the baler. "I want to see my family before we go south to the next job."

"Mrs. Vance is sending Clare," Lucy said, after turning off the baler's motor. "I'll be taking the t-train out of Canterbury, so Mr. Tillman is going along with her and Agnes."

Clare leaned the pitchfork against the baler and removed her sweat-stained hat. She walked to the drinking barrel set up beside the cart. "Could it get any hotter than this? I'll burn like morning kindling if this keeps up." She wiped at the perspiration beaded along her brow and slapped the hat back into place.

"I really wanted to go this time," Becky continued to complain as she moved another bale around. "I need to see my—"

"Your family. Yes, we know, Becky," Clare said crossly. "Just be glad you have one."

"Clare? Are you all right?" Lucy asked.

Clare shot her a hostile look, then ladled a cupful of the water. "Daisy's not in Canterbury, after all." She'd met with Mr. Pittman, the private investigator, that morning in the village. He'd given her the news he'd received bad information. Her daughter wasn't anywhere near the area.

Without looking at them, Clare took a drink, then said, "It seems I have to start a new search."

"Oh, Clare, I'm sorry," Agnes said as she and Lucy approached. Clare saw Mr. Tillman offer a sympathetic nod, though he remained back and removed his hat. Becky stood off in the distance, sulking.

"Daisy could still be here in Kent," Lucy said. "Grace would t-tell you to have faith and you'll find her."

Clare took another drink of water, then sighed. "She would, wouldn't she? Has anyone heard anything?"

"We were going to ask you." Lucy took her turn at the ladle.

Clare glanced at Agnes. "I saw you at the post office this morning, Pierpont. Did you receive any news?"

Agnes had removed her gloves, scratching at her fingers. When she looked up again, she wet her lips and said, "I mailed a letter, but not to Grace. I wrote the assistant manager at Swan's. Since Mr. Mabry has been arrested, I—"

"Grace's father was arrested, as well?" Clare's gaze narrowed. "How do you know?"

Agnes tilted her chin, and Clare could swear she looked

afraid. "I'm sure Lord Roxwood mentioned it on Saturday. Anyway, I wished to find out about my back wages."

Clare eyed her with disgust. "I'm surprised at you, Agnes Pierpont. Poor Grace *and her father* languish in prison, their very lives hanging in the balance, and you're worried about a few shillings owed to you as maid?"

"A woman's got to live, doesn't she?" As Agnes spoke, she turned a bright hue while she continued scratching at her hands.

"Come on, ladies, let's finish weighing these bales and get them onto the cart. I'm ready for some supper." Mr. Tillman put his hat back on and released a bale from the scale before moving to set another in its place. "We'll cover the whole thing with a tarp and start again first thing in the morning."

Clare glanced at Lucy, then to Becky, who seemed over her brooding now. Each of them shook their heads, clearly disappointed. Of all people, they would have thought Agnes most loyal to Grace, particularly after the maid shared her story with Lord Roxwood. She practically owed Grace Mabry her life.

Then Clare recalled being chided by Grace for being too quick to judge others—like Sir Marcus Weatherford. And just look what had happened!

She frowned as she went to help the others weigh the last of the bales. It seemed her friend had been wrong about Agnes Pierpont, too.

∽

"Let's have a look, shall we?"

Jack sat on the divan while Dr. Strom flashed the ophthalmoscope in front of his eyes.

"Remarkable, simply remarkable," Strom said after a moment. He leaned back in his chair across from Jack and pocketed the instrument. "When I examined you before, Lord Roxwood,

I didn't detect any damage to the retina, but the speed at which you've recovered is amazing. Congratulations."

Jack drawled, "Yes, now I can look in the mirror and see the brute staring back at me."

"I said before, your wounds are still healing. You will have scars, but the swelling and coloring will fade. And those injuries were hard won," he added quietly.

"I imagine with you being a relative of the Mabry family, New Scotland Yard put you through your paces?" Jack said.

"I was a guest at the precinct in Westminster over the weekend, Lord Roxwood." His tone was sharp. "Fortunately, they weren't too interested in a country doctor who has spent most of his years living in rural Kent. Thanks to some, they have more important suspects to torment."

Jack took a deep breath. "I am sorry about Grace . . . Miss Mabry. But the proof is undeniable, as I'm sure you're already aware—"

"I don't believe it!" Strom launched from his chair to pace the carpeted floor. "That girl is as sweet as her mother ever was, and more heartsick than I can tell you about her brother's disappearance." He spun to face Jack. "Why in heaven's name would she risk Colin's life by selling out secrets to the enemy? Why would her father, for that matter?" He began to pace again. "I'm no detective, but something else is at play here."

"If it makes you feel better, I agree. In fact, I have my friend at the Admiralty looking into it." Marcus had called him back yesterday, and Jack felt relieved Grace was still in one piece. He'd even been optimistic to learn Agnes Pierpont had borrowed her stationery and posted the incriminating letter. Yet they lacked any real proof to connect her to the deed.

"Strom, how well do you know the women working for the WFC? I'm particularly interested in Miss Mabry's maid, Agnes Pierpont."

Strom looked surprised. "I don't know her well at all, though she is a patient of mine." He held up his palms. "She's got some kind of rash on her hands. The skin is irritated, and she's scratched at them so much they've begun to bleed. I bandaged them for her this morning before I came to see you. Why?"

"What did she get into?"

"She said she was handling fertilizer without gloves." Dr. Strom shrugged. "It doesn't have the look of stinging nettles or gorse, although I can't rule it out."

"Did she say when she contracted this rash?"

"Sunday, I believe."

Jack shook his head, perplexed.

"Sorry I'm not much help." Strom moved to grab for his black bag. "You're healing well, Lord Roxwood. I can call on you again in a couple of weeks, but I think at this point it's unnecessary, unless some problem arises."

"I appreciate you keeping the news about my sight confidential," Jack said. He stood and extended his hand. "I'm not yet ready to publicize it."

"I don't understand your reasons, your lordship, but I will respect your wishes." The two shook hands.

"Thank you," Jack said. "You once told me to have faith my sight would return. I didn't want to believe it."

The physician arched a brow. "And now?"

Jack smiled. "I'm beginning to." Then he sobered and said, "I'll do everything in my power to help Grace. I just don't know how—"

"With faith, son," Dr. Strom said. "In the end, the truth always wins out."

"Now I know where Grace gets it from."

The doctor shook his head. "Lillian Mabry was my uncle's daughter and had a faith to rival the angels. I'm sure Grace inherited that good trait from her mother."

Jack watched as Strom departed before he replaced the mask and went into his study to telephone Marcus. "How is she today?" he asked his friend.

"She's doing rather well, given the circumstances. I think her temper holds her in good stead with Cromwell. I tell you, Jack, except for that confounded letter, even I'd believe her innocent."

"She didn't write that code," Jack said, his jaw set. "We just need to prove it. Did you learn any more about Agnes Pierpont?"

"I didn't want to get your hopes up, but after talking with Grace on Sunday, I started censoring all mail going in and out of Roxwood," Marcus said. "A letter postmarked yesterday from Agnes Pierpont was being sent to the attention of Mr. Alfred Dykes at Swan's in London. In the letter she asks about her back wages."

Jack leaned against the desk. "That sounds a bit cold, wouldn't you say? A far cry from the teary-eyed performance I witnessed at the gatehouse. What do you make of it?"

"I agree, it's odd," Marcus said. "But we used heat on the letter and didn't come up with anything other than what she'd written, so it seems legitimate."

Jack scoured his mind for inconsistencies. An idea began to form, and he asked, "Marcus, aside from lemon juice and the like, are there other types of invisible ink? Before my accident, I remember a report about the enemy starting to use chemical-based substances."

"Correct," Marcus said. "Room 40 recently began using spectroscopy to decipher some of those inks." He paused. "What are you thinking?"

Jack relayed to him the conversation with Strom about Agnes Pierpont's rash. "He says she claims she got it from fertilizer, but why wouldn't she have worn gloves?"

"We recently heard the Germans are using sodium nitrate, though it's relatively new." Marcus's tone took on an excited edge. "It's soaked into clothing—a tie, a scarf, a handkerchief, so it can be transported without detection. It reactivates with water. The person need only wet the cloth and wring out the moisture to be used as invisible ink. Sodium nitrate *can* irritate the skin, and it's found in fertilizer. When did the rash occur?"

"Sunday." Jack's pulse raced. "Marcus, do you suppose . . . ?"

"Very possibly," his friend said. "Got to ring off now, old boy, I've some investigating to do. I'll get back as soon as I can." Then he abruptly hung up.

Jack carefully replaced the telephone's receiver, seized with a rush of excitement. Grace might be exonerated.

He strode from his study with new purpose. He planned to do some investigating of his own.

∞

"I still don't understand why I'm not allowed to go to Margate," Becky Simmons complained as the women dressed for their last day of work.

"Not another word, Simmons." Clare shot her a warning glance while she cinched the belt at her trousers. Shrugging into her trench coat, she added, "I'm tired of listening to you go on. We can't all have what we want, you know."

Becky glared at her while Lucy flashed a look of sympathy that only fueled Clare's anger. She was sorry she'd ever mentioned Daisy to any of them. She didn't need their pity. "What are you two looking at? We've got work to do."

"Easy for you to say, Danner," Becky said. "You'll get to go right past my family's village, while I have to stay here . . ."

Clare was surprised to see tears in Becky's eyes. "What's wrong with you? Are you still homesick?"

The woman shook her head and continued dressing. Clare relented and said, "Look, if it were up to me, Simmons, I'd let you go. But Mrs. Vance is our supervisor and she gives the orders."

When Becky said nothing, Clare sat to lace up her boots. She glanced over at Agnes, who scratched at her hands through her gloves. "Still have that rash, Pierpont?"

Agnes nodded. "I changed the bandages, but the sulfur the doctor gave me doesn't seem to be working."

"I've never had such a reaction before." Clare scrutinized her. "You must have very sensitive skin. What were you doing handling fertilizer on Sunday, anyway? It was our day off."

Agnes paled. "I . . . I met with Mr. Tillman. He asked if I wanted to make extra, taking care of Lord Roxwood's rose garden." She tipped her chin. "I could use the money."

"Yes, a woman's got to live, right?" Clare said, tossing Agnes's words back at her. She thought again about the letter Agnes had mailed on Monday and fumed. In truth, she would rather go to Margate with Becky. At least Simmons was grateful to Grace for her help, unlike this one who seemed more interested in getting paid her back wages than in the fate of her mistress.

"Breakfast!" Mrs. Vance poked her head through the bedroom doorway and beamed. "I cooked up eggs and a bit of sausage for our last day, ladies. So let's make the most of it."

Once the women finished dressing, they headed downstairs. Seated at the kitchen table minutes later, Clare looked over at their supervisor and wondered what the future held for Mrs. Vance. If they were all to move south, what of her budding romance with Mr. Tillman?

She soon had her answer. "I suppose I should tell you all now." Mrs. Vance's features had taken on a glow. "I'll be staying on at Roxwood . . . as Mrs. George Tillman."

Several gasps rose from the table before the kitchen echoed with a resounding cheer and a flurry of congratulations. Mrs. Vance laughed and suddenly seemed years younger. "Yes, he's asked me to be his wife," she said. "My friend, Millicent Foster, is in need of a few extra hands in her gang, so you'll meet with her at the Mortimer estate tomorrow and take up the task of showing those women how it's done." Her eyes held a suspicious gleam. "I've already told her how proud I am of all of you. Not only have you done exemplary work, but you've shown each other respect and teamwork. I couldn't have asked for a finer gang of women in all the Corps."

Less than a half hour later, hugs were exchanged and a few tears shed before Clare and Agnes made their way outside and down to the barn, where the horse cart was loaded and waiting.

"I think congratulations are in order," Clare called as she spied Mr. Tillman adjusting the tack on the horses. He looked up and colored, but his broad smile spoke volumes.

"You will take good care of our supervisor, won't you?" she asked once she and Agnes climbed into the cart.

"For the rest of my life," he said solemnly.

His words pierced her. In her heart of hearts, Clare had hoped one day to share that with Marcus . . .

Mr. Tillman eased the team forward. Clare let go of the thought as she looked back to see Lucy and Becky walking toward the barn while Mrs. Vance stood near the doors. They all waved, and she raised a hand to them in return. She'd said her good-byes to Lucy, who would be gone by the time she returned. Clare realized how much her WFC sisters had come to mean to her and was thankful for their support and encouragement. Like her, they believed Grace would soon be free. They also believed Clare would find Daisy.

She turned back to face the road ahead, feeling renewed determination. She must keep that belief also.

Jack remained concealed between two lilac bushes growing alongside the gatehouse wall and waited nearly an hour until the last of the women left.

Entering the women's quarters, he climbed the stairs and proceeded to make a search of the bags and boxes beneath each bed. Fifteen minutes later, he found what he was after. Having learned about Agnes Pierpont's family from Marcus, he plucked a photograph from the bag beneath one of the beds near the window and surmised he'd found her possessions.

He emptied the rest of the bag's contents onto the bed, but after an extensive search through various articles of clothing, toiletries, and stationery, he came up with nothing.

Had they been wrong? So far, Agnes Pierpont had turned out to be exactly what she seemed: a domestic who put on a good show, but in the end worried more about wages than her mistress; a citified fieldworker who had forgotten to wear gloves before handling fertilizer.

The woman who had been Grace's one hope.

He stared at the empty bag, and for the second time he prayed for a miracle, some shred of evidence he'd overlooked. He was no magician to pull a rabbit out of a hat, though, unless Agnes Pierpont was a well-seasoned spy . . .

He plunged his hand inside the bag, his fingers searching for a false bottom or hidden compartment.

A moment later, he smiled.

Jack took off at a half run back to the manor with his proof in hand. He'd no sooner closeted himself into the study and picked up the telephone than Knowles rapped at the door. "Sir Marcus Weatherford has arrived, milord."

"Excellent! Show him in." Jack waited until his friend entered the study. "I was about to call you. I've found something." He bent down to retrieve Agnes Pierpont's bag from the floor.

"I'll go first." Marcus closed the study door and moved toward the desk. "After I spoke with you last night, I contacted our people in the War Office. We've this remarkable woman who has a real knack for deciphering various mediums used in making invisible ink. Maud was able to detect the sodium nitrate and make visible the code used in Agnes Pierpont's letter to Alfred Dykes. Early this morning, New Scotland Yard sent two detectives over to Swan's." He eyed Jack with barely concealed excitement. "And guess what?"

"I'm on tenterhooks," Jack said, his heart hammering in his chest.

"They searched the floor manager's rooms and found code books, also maps of our Naval Yards, directives written in German and Dutch, and a healthy supply of sodium nitrate. When he was confronted, Dykes confessed all. It seems he and his agents have been using Patrick Mabry and Swan's to transmit classified British naval secrets to the enemy. Mabry couldn't have known the people he was corresponding with were put in place by the Germans for precisely that reason. His letters would be unsealed, coded with invisible ink, and resealed to be forwarded on to those contacts."

Marcus's brown eyes gleamed. "The letter to James Heeren you found aboard the *Acionna* is just such an example. And it was Agnes Pierpont who gave that letter to Chaplin the night of the ball, not Grace. She's innocent, and so is her father."

Jack felt as though the sun had just come out. Relief and elation filled him. He grabbed the bag and thrust it at Marcus. "Take a look."

Marcus peered into the bag, then reached in to remove a code book, several sheets of stationery, a photograph, and lastly a neatly folded handkerchief.

"Agnes Pierpont's possessions," Jack said. "I took the liberty of searching their quarters. As you can see, those sheets of stationery have brown markings—lemon juice. No doubt she was practicing her craft. The code book speaks for itself. But you'll see in the photograph what appears to be barbed wire behind the women."

Marcus nodded, looking grim. "According to Alfred Dykes, these two are Agnes Pierpont's mother and sister. They're being held at a concentration camp in Germany. It would explain why she felt compelled to spy for the enemy. I feel certain she was being blackmailed." He held up the handkerchief. "And this?"

"I would guess it contains the sodium nitrate she used in her letter to Dykes."

"I need to get her back to London," Marcus said, replacing the contents in the bag. "Any idea where she is?"

"Down at the farm, I imagine."

"Let's take my car."

Minutes later, Marcus's Pierce-Arrow pulled up alongside the barn. Mrs. Vance came outside and appeared shocked when Jack, still wearing his mask, strode directly up to her and addressed her. "We're here to see Agnes Pierpont."

"She . . . she's not here, milord," the woman stammered. "Agnes is with Clare Danner and Mr. Tillman. They've taken the last load of hay into Margate and should be at the train station by now."

"Let's go." Marcus led the way back to the car.

Once they were on their way to Margate, Jack said, "When will the Mabrys be released from New Scotland Yard?" He wondered if Grace could ever forgive him. Perhaps once she learned of his help in bringing Agnes Pierpont to justice? He had treated her father abominably, though all indications at the time proved Patrick Mabry's guilt.

Would Grace understand? Jack didn't dare to hope.

"They're still at the precinct in Westminster, but I'm certain with the new evidence, it will be only a day or two before they're free to go," Marcus said. "I will tell you I'm relieved about the turn of events, more than you can know. I haven't seen or spoken with Clare Danner since the day after the dance, and frankly I've been afraid to."

He shot Jack a grimace. "She and Grace are close, and no doubt I'm being blamed for taking her friend off to jail. I hope once we've sorted this business and Grace is released, Clare will still be amenable to my courtship."

Jack turned to him. "You really are keen on her, aren't you?" he said softly.

"Enough to imagine a future with her," Marcus said. Then he flashed a humorless smile. "But one step at a time, old boy. I haven't exactly won her affection yet."

They had just passed through the village of Wreston a couple of miles from town when overhead Jack heard the whine of plane engines. "Marcus, do you hear . . . ?"

Marcus slowed the vehicle and glanced up. "Dear God, no," he said. A formation of German Gotha planes was flying up from the south and heading into Margate. They began dropping bombs. Marcus floored the accelerator. "Clare!"

Moments later, explosions rent the air. Black smoke rose against the horizon.

Scant minutes later, the Pierce-Arrow entered town, and the two men witnessed the devastation and destruction. The enemy planes had disappeared, having dropped their bombs. Buildings lay in rubble. Fires burned out of control in various places. Cars had been overturned. And the bodies . . .

"Marcus!" Jack pointed toward the train station, where a huge inferno blazed. "The hay, it's on fire!"

The road was blocked with debris. Marcus braked the car, and they exited, rushing forward on foot. Unconcerned for their safety, the two approached the station to search out the three from Roxwood.

Others who had managed to remain safe now rushed from houses and buildings and began rescuing victims of the attack. A dozen men—railway personnel and a few shopkeepers—hauled buckets of water to try to douse the flames while shouting for the fire department.

Jack and Marcus found Mr. Tillman first, his leg crushed beneath a large timber several yards from the burning cart.

"Where is Clare?" Marcus grabbed the injured farmer by the collar.

"Easy." Jack pressed a hand to his friend's shoulder. He'd never seen Marcus look so wild with fear.

"The blast," Mr. Tillman groaned. "Over there." The farmer pointed to a cratered outbuilding near the station.

Marcus started to leave, but Jack said, "Quick. Let's get this beam off of him."

They freed the farmer's leg just as two other men approached to offer their assistance.

"Come on. Let's go!" Marcus urged. "They'll take care of him."

Jack followed his friend as they ran to the outbuilding. "Clare!" Marcus shouted, and Jack caught a glimpse of black hair amidst the rubble.

She sat on the ground behind a foot of debris, leaning against the building's one undamaged wall. Though her midnight hair was discernible beneath the concrete dust, the rest of her looked disheveled.

"Clare!" Marcus leaped over the pile of wreckage and knelt down beside her. Jack moved to her other side. Agnes Pierpont was there as well, her head lying motionless in Miss Danner's lap.

"She saved me." Clare Danner blinked at Marcus, looking dazed. Tears streaked her dusty cheeks. "Agnes . . . jumped in front of me when the block flew at us." With a shaking hand, she pointed to a cinder block that had once been part of the building. "After the bomb . . . she saved me."

She pursed her lips and looked down at the woman in her lap, who appeared to be sleeping. Gently she brushed back a tendril of the dusty, dark hair. "She said to tell Grace . . . to tell her she was sorry."

She began to cry. As Jack reached to gently remove Agnes from her lap, Marcus swept Clare up into his arms. "Oh, sweetheart, I was so afraid I'd lost you," he groaned against her hair. "When I saw the hay burning, I thought . . ."

Marcus pressed Clare close, and Jack realized what he wanted. Love. Passionate, steadfast, unending—love that could see beyond his scars to the heart of the man within. The joy he felt whenever he was with Grace . . .

He carried the body of Agnes Pierpont to a cart set up to take the dying and injured to hospital. While Mr. Tillman's leg was being tended, along with Miss Danner's cuts and bruises, he and Marcus spent the next several hours doing their best to help the townspeople of Margate clear away debris and put out fires.

It didn't occur to Jack until later that no one remarked on his mask or gave his appearance a second glance. They had more important issues to deal with—life and death.

22

Filled with anticipation, Jack stood at the rail of his balcony the next afternoon and considered his options. Like the iridescent green of the labyrinth stretching out across the grounds below, his future now seemed fraught with twists and turns and traps. How should he proceed?

Last evening, after returning with the others from Margate, he'd decided to abandon the ruse of remaining blind. His announcement received a hug from Mrs. Riley and cheers from the remaining women at the farm, while Edwards, Knowles, and Townsend had yet to quit smiling.

He still felt reluctant to remove the mask, however. Reemerging into life's stream after being immersed for so long in his quiet pool of darkness would take time. Jack was thankful to Grace for helping him take the first plunge. It amazed him to realize he'd had more social interaction in the past twenty-four hours than in the last several months. Many in Margate were grateful for his and Marcus's efforts after the bombing, aiding with the injured and helping search out those who were unaccounted for.

Jack hoped the experience had bolstered his confidence enough to reenter society on a more long-term scale. Once news of his recovery reached his father, he would certainly be made to return to London. The thought made his heart race. As Stonebrooke's heir, he must look to the future of the estate. Even if that future now seemed like the labyrinth, difficult to navigate unless one knew the way.

He gripped the rail and took a deep, cleansing breath. His telephone conversation with Violet less than an hour ago had been quite surprising. In fact, he couldn't recall a time when she'd been that nice to him, going so far as to tell him he didn't look so fearsome, after all.

One corner of his mouth lifted. He was sure her unexpected benevolence had everything to do with his calling off their engagement. Now that he understood what real love felt like, he refused to settle for less. And if Violet loved this Arthur Baines enough to give up an earldom and spend her life with the second son of a viscount, he wouldn't stand in her way.

The consequences of his actions would likely reach the earl before long, and of course, Mr. Arnold. Jack had evaluated his assets. His grandfather had left Roxwood to him and his brother jointly; with Hugh gone, it was solely his decision. As much as it tore at him to sell the estate in order to repay the debt to Violet's father, Jack would do it—not only to save Stonebrooke but to give himself the freedom to marry Grace.

Edwards knocked at his outer door. "Sir Marcus is on the telephone, milord."

Jack returned inside to his rooms. "Tell him I'll be with him directly," he called as he retrieved his mask from the nightstand beside his bed.

The painted toy soldier lay beside it. Jack thought of Hugh and their childhood game in the hedge maze, and his confidence in always being able to win against his older brother.

Now he felt uncertainty. He'd said some terrible things to Grace. Despite his having helped her, she might not be willing to forgive him. He recalled the stories her friends had shared and how she had forgiven Clare Danner.

Jack's offenses were far worse than letting a few pigs loose in the garden.

His heart pounded. He had risked all for love. Would Grace be able to return it?

Taking a deep breath, Jack closed his eyes. He recalled how in the study he'd asked for God's help in finding a way to save Grace. Now he needed another favor—her forgiveness. "For faith," he whispered, before bending his head to pray. Then he snatched up the soldier in his fist. "And for luck," he said before heading downstairs.

∞

"Grace is gone." Marcus spoke in a grim tone over the line. "They were released from New Scotland Yard this morning. Mabry left with his daughter on the first ship for Ireland. He's got a brother with a farm just outside Dublin."

Standing beside his desk, Jack felt the floor beneath him shift. He gripped the telephone as if it might steady his feet. "Did she say anything?"

"I didn't speak with her, but I heard it was a solemn event. Mabry was barely civil to Cromwell and his detectives, and I can't say as I blame him. Swan's is barred shut and closed for business. The father wasn't about to remain in town and subject himself or his daughter to any more humiliation."

Guilt stabbed at Jack's insides. "Did Mabry indicate when they would return?"

"No." Marcus let out a sigh. "The scandal has ruined him. I understand before the war, he put up the bulk of his wealth as collateral to expand his tea room franchise. Now, because of the manpower shortage, building progress has been slow. And with these latest events, the bankers have backed out entirely."

Mabry ruined. Jack recalled the accusations he'd hurled at Grace about Patrick Mabry, and knew she would likely include him in the blame for destroying her father's livelihood. He replayed their last conversation in his mind, the ugly words he'd spewed against her family. She'd been telling him the truth, yet he hadn't believed her. Grace had come to him, welcomed his embrace, shared the passion of his kiss . . . and he'd destroyed it all with cruelty and suspicion.

He cleared his throat. "What about her brother?" Jack eyed the painted soldier he'd placed on top of the desk. Never would he forget Grace's devastation when he accused Colin Mabry of defecting to the side of the enemy. "Does the Army have any new information?"

"There was a mistake in paper work, so Colin Mabry wasn't at the post he'd been assigned to. Once the problem was sorted, they discovered he'd been working with our sappers—the men excavating a new line directly underneath the German tunnels in order to lay explosives." Marcus paused, then added, "Not much time for letter writing, which explains why Miss Mabry wasn't receiving his correspondence."

"So they found him?" Jack asked, relieved.

"It gets worse," Marcus said. "Often the enemy ends up digging a parallel tunnel within a few feet of our own. The Germans must have heard our racket and beat us to it, setting off their own explosives. Our line collapsed. We had four inside, all of whom are listed as missing."

"Colin Mabry." Jack grabbed the toy soldier and clenched it in his fist. "Is there any chance they're still alive?"

"More than a week has passed since the explosion, and our tunnel rats still haven't been able to pinpoint the exact location. Without food, water, fresh air, it's unlikely. No one's notified

Patrick Mabry yet, since he's still traveling. I'm sure the Army will contact him in Dublin once he arrives. I hate to think of how this news will affect Grace."

Jack couldn't speak for the knot in his throat.

"Well, I've got to get back to work. The war goes on," Marcus said. "Will you be all right?"

Jack released a bitter laugh. "I'm hardly the worse off, Marcus. I still hide away here at Roxwood, nursing my scars." His voice turned hollow. "And, it would seem, I am still blind."

"You can't blame yourself, Jack. Alfred Dykes and Agnes Pierpont were the real cause of the Mabrys' downfall. And while we seemed harsh at the time, we possessed concrete proof of her guilt. If it had been anyone else, you and I would have proceeded in the same manner."

But I would not have felt this miserable. "As you say, Marcus, duty calls."

Jack rang off before his friend could argue.

He felt sick inside. Grace and her father would be forever altered by Colin Mabry's death. He recalled his own devastation when the authorities arrived at his father's brownstone in London with the news Hugh had died in a boating accident. But Jack knew. He may have been the best at navigating the labyrinth, but his brother had been an excellent sailor. The war had taken some integral part of him, leaving it behind in France. What remained of him when he returned had eventually given up.

He thought of his own isolation and of his mother in London, who barely managed her social affairs as she remained in mourning. The earl, his father, continued to grieve in the only way he knew how, with the punishing inflexibility he demanded of himself and tried to perpetrate upon his only remaining son.

Their family had never been the same.

Despite his friend's logic, Jack felt responsible for ruining

Patrick Mabry's life. He'd also fallen in love with the man's daughter. He'd kissed her, held her in his arms, and then proved his fidelity by calling her brother a traitor.

Marcus had said the odds of finding Colin Mabry alive were unlikely, as it had been over a week. Without food and water and clean air, Grace's brother would need a miracle.

Jack gazed at the painted soldier in his hand. The prize he'd always won . . .

"Edwards!"

His roar brought the steward rushing to the study. "Milord?"

He owed it to Grace and her father. He owed it to his brother, Hugh. "Get Townsend in here. I'm driving to London."

23

Ireland was as green as she'd imagined.

Grace straightened and peered out at the forested hills beyond Uncle Brian's farm. Though the land was more mountainous than Kent, Dublin's outlying countryside with its varying shades of green, clear-running streams, and crisscrossed stone fences seemed much the same.

She returned to her task, lifting another forkful of hay and loading it onto the back of a small cart. Nearby, the horse, a black-and-white Irish cob called Bea, grazed lazily. While the sky was overcast, the air felt warm, filled with the sweet scent of clover. Grace was grateful to be outside, not only for the chance to repay Uncle Brian's generosity, but the hard work acted like a balm to ease her wounded soul.

Her father had yet to recover. After two weeks, Da still sat beside the picture window of her uncle's house, staring out at the fields for long hours. She'd overheard him talking to Uncle Brian shortly after their arrival, telling him they had lost everything—not only Swan's but the franchise tea rooms her father had hoped to complete in the coming year.

With the Mabry name mired in scandal and suspicion, she and Da had only his generosity to see them through.

She and her father hadn't spoken of Colin, either. When word came from the Army about the explosion, Grace felt her heart cut in two. The report had been vague, some kind of tunnel accident, and they hadn't found his body. Colin Mabry was listed as a casualty of war.

Grace didn't want to believe her twin dead. Wouldn't she feel it inside if he were?

Tears brimmed at her lashes, and she ground her teeth, stabbing the pitchfork into the mound of hay at her feet. She'd prayed constantly to God to bring him back, but it hadn't changed anything. Colin was gone. Grace didn't think she could ever forgive herself. *Mother, I'm so sorry . . .*

Grace flung another forkful of hay onto the cart. She ached for her brother, and after receiving a letter with news about the girls from Mrs. Vance, she missed the comfort and camaraderie of her sisters in the Women's Forage Corps.

On a whim, Grace had written to her supervisor at the farm and received a reply yesterday. She'd been thrilled for Mrs. Vance and her upcoming wedding to Mr. Tillman, and shocked to learn Becky went home abruptly when it was discovered both of her parents were gravely ill and two of her youngest siblings had contracted rickets.

The Simmons family was starving.

Grace recalled the envelope of money she'd given to Becky after lecturing her on the perils of stealing and felt new shame. While it was true, stealing wasn't the answer, providing a one-time handout hadn't solved the dilemma for Becky's family, either. To think she'd actually felt smug over having solved Becky's problem! Now, with her and Da in such dire straits, she could only pray the Simmons family would survive.

With Becky's news came other doubts plaguing Grace. It

seemed Lucy Young had gotten off to Stonebrooke all right, but what would her new life be like in such close quarters with all those gossiping servants? Would her secret remain safe? *Had* Grace done the right thing by involving Sir Marcus and Jack?

Jack . . . She straightened to lean against her pitchfork and gazed out across the field. He had wounded her deeply with his accusations the day of her arrest, yet Grace realized he'd had ample reason to be suspicious. Not only because she'd seen the secret Q port at Richborough firsthand and asked about it, but before leaving New Scotland Yard, Inspector Cromwell had explained to her and Da the depth of Agnes's treachery.

Heat climbed her cheeks. It seemed *she* had been the blind one, allowing herself to be taken in by Agnes Pierpont. Mrs. Vance had sketched details about the bombing in Margate and how Agnes had died saving Clare's life. Yet Grace struggled with forgiveness, not only for Agnes but for herself, as well. She'd hired the maid without references and brought a spy into their home, one who ultimately caused Da's ruin.

She'd also let Agnes manipulate her into attending the ball that night, playing on Grace's fears and righteous sense of duty. Grace may not have set out to target Jack, but her association with the woman nearly cost him his life. He had every right to think her a complete simpleton.

Still, she missed him. Certainly Jack must be married to Violet Arnold by now. At night, after working in her uncle's field, Grace found comfort lying in bed and reading back through her journal, rediscovering her time with him. Amused at first over her written irritation at his incessant questions, her heart was eventually moved, reading the ways in which he'd begun to share himself with her, his childhood memories and the happier times with his brother, Hugh. Taking her to his special places and allowing her to be his eyes.

He'd helped her with her dream of becoming a writer, as well. And despite her pain, Grace had already started writing her first novel—not about the Tin Man or the glories of aiding the war, but simply about a few brave young women. Women who, despite their own difficulties, came to trust one another with their secrets, their dreams, and their friendship while helping their countrymen . . .

A car's engine sounded in the distance, pulling Grace from her reverie. The black Ford turned onto the long, dirt driveway heading toward her uncle's house.

Unaccountably, she felt her heart race and she dropped the pitchfork she'd been holding and started for the house. She was still a few hundred yards away when the car stopped. A man in uniform exited the passenger side and pulled out a bag from the back seat. Even beneath his cap, she could see the crop of black hair, the unmistakable tall frame—

"Colin!" she screamed, breaking into a run, her hat flying as she took a shortcut toward the house.

He turned to her, hearing her cry. Grace was close enough to see him smile before her eyes blurred with tears.

Soon she was in his arms and sobbing his name.

"Oh, Colin, they told us you were dead, but I didn't believe it. I would have known . . ." She clung to him, weak with relief as she babbled on, dazed and euphoric to see him again.

"Easy, Grace." He pulled back gently, and she spied his left arm in a sling. He was also much thinner and pale, almost ghostly.

"Colin . . ." New tears crowded her lashes. She turned and shouted at the house, "Da! Uncle Brian! Come quickly!"

Colin had dropped his bag to the ground and was paying the cab driver when Patrick and Brian Mabry strode out onto the porch. Da whitened. "Son?" he said hoarsely.

Colin saluted. Her father stumbled down the porch steps and

gently embraced his son. "It's a miracle," he cried. "I thought I'd lost you, too."

Colin hugged his father and then it was Uncle Brian's turn. Grace looked on, smiling, swiping her cheeks with the heels of her hands. Her brother looked weather-beaten, but he was here with them and safe. God had answered her prayers.

Once the cab drove away and Da grabbed up Colin's duffel bag, they entered the house. Uncle Brian went to fetch Bea and the cart.

Reveling in Colin's safe return, they enjoyed a special celebration supper that night, with roasted mutton, potatoes, carrots, and bread fresh from the oven. Grace even tried her hand at making an amber apple pie, which didn't turn out too badly.

It wasn't until hours later that Grace and her twin had a private moment to speak together.

"How did you get injured?" she asked him. They sat together on a bench outside the small barn. The air cooled while the evening light faded to dusk. A chaffinch sang in the apple tree several yards away, while cicadas chirped in the tall grasses beyond. The scent of sweet clover floated on the breeze.

As Colin turned to face her, Grace felt a new rush of gratitude toward God. The endearing presence of the brother she'd worried about for so long was now with her again, sitting beside her. She could hardly believe it.

Then as he withdrew his hand from the sling, she sucked in a breath to see only a bandaged stump at his wrist. "I didn't want to tell Father just yet," he said. "Let the good news of my return content him for tonight. He's been through so much. Tomorrow is soon enough."

Grace wanted to weep. "Oh, Colin, what have I done?" she whispered. "I have been so foolish. You cannot know the consequences my actions have caused." She touched the bandage. "I never should have insisted you go with me to that suffrage rally." Again she envisioned her mother's look of devastation.

"It wasn't your fault," he said gently, laying a hand on her shoulder. "I know what you're thinking—that because Ma didn't want me to go with you that day, you feel responsible. But I'd already enlisted in the BEF days before the rally. It was my decision, and nothing you could have said would have changed that."

Grace blinked. "Why didn't you tell me?" she asked. "Did Da know of this?"

Colin nodded. "With Ma so ill, he and I decided to say nothing about it."

"But she found out a few days later," Grace said, "and she blamed me for your leaving." Her gaze dropped to her lap. "I blame myself, too. I was so eager at first to take up the call to arms with my fellow suffragettes, I had no idea of the realities of war. I thought only about the glory of victory, and despite Mother's disapproval, I believed my cause was the right one."

She looked up at him. "After she died, and your letters began arriving, I read about the difficult conditions you endured and how lonely you sounded. I began to have doubts. And I was afraid, I think; with the air attacks in London, I grew even more self-righteous. I eventually convinced myself that if I shamed others into joining you in the fighting, it would bring victory that much sooner. And you, my brother, could come home to us safe and sound. So I handed out white feathers of cowardice. I am ashamed to think of it even now. I even misjudged a man . . ."

She fought back tears and continued, "This man, I thought him a coward at first, but later I learned he was fighting for Britain all along, in less obvious ways. And at Roxwood, I encountered other young men returning home from the Front. Many were injured, some on the inside as well as out, but I hadn't yet realized how naïve I was about war, not until I learned you were missing."

Impulsively she reached to hug her brother. "I'm so relieved to see you again. You said little when Da and Uncle Brian asked about your being recovered by the Army," she said, searching his face. "Will you tell me what really happened?"

He gazed at her a long moment before he said, "It was a miracle, Grace."

When he fell silent, she reached to touch his shoulder. "Please, I want to know."

Colin stared out toward the fields. "We were dismounted cavalry, and they'd asked for volunteers to help excavate a tunnel very close to one the Germans had built," he began. "But the enemy decided to blow their own tunnel first, before we got the chance to finish our work. Suddenly four of us were trapped, buried beneath several feet of earth." He released a shaky breath. "Cleese, Ames, Richards, and myself. Cleese was an older chap. He died in the collapse."

Colin rubbed at his forehead. Grace longed to ease his grief.

"I'd broken a couple of fingers, so Richards and I tried pushing with our feet through the rubble," he went on. "When it finally gave way, we discovered a hollow the enemy had dug out to store their cache. As both of Ames's legs were crushed, we had to drag him through the opening we'd made." He looked at her. "It amazes me still. There we were, thinking ourselves done in, when in the next minute we ended up in this space underground. The Germans had it stockpiled with water and rations and ammunition. They'd even crafted a series of hoses through the ceiling to the surface, so we had air to breathe.

"We held on, waiting for rescue. Hours turned into days. I still had my wristwatch, otherwise I couldn't have determined morning or night. We were in total darkness, except for a few flashlights. And aside from the distant shelling, we heard nothing except our own breathing and Ames groaning in pain."

He eyed his bandaged wrist. "My fingers had started going sour, until eventually my hand got infected and swelled up.

Richards showed me how to use my belt as a tourniquet. I kept applying pressure to the wrist, hoping to keep the infection contained." He glanced up at her. "But in the end, they had to take the whole hand. Still, I was better off than Ames."

Grief lined his expression. "He died on the fourth day. From the pain, I think. His legs were so broken up there was nothing we could do." He swallowed. "On the seventh day we ran out of food and water. By the ninth day, Richards had begun raving. I felt close to it." He reached to touch her cheek. "But I thought of you and our father. With Ma gone, I couldn't bear the idea you might lose me, too. I remember closing my eyes and praying, praying so hard to hang on a bit longer. I called out to God to help me, and then He answered."

Colin's smile was tinged with wonder. "He called me by name—several times, in fact. At first it was very faint, and I thought I must be going mad like Richards. But the voice grew louder, and then the rubble where we'd pressed our way into the cache crumbled away and I saw my savior. It wasn't God, but a soldier. At the time I didn't know if he was a friend or a foe, but I didn't care."

"Who was he?"

Colin shook his head. "I haven't a clue. The mission was top secret. I did learn from the commanding officer he'd come for the sole reason of finding *me*." His voice shook. "And for that I will be forever in his debt."

"As will I," she whispered, and reached to embrace him once more. He'd been through so much. He could have become raving like Richards or died like the others, but thanks to his angel, her brother had lost a hand instead of his life. She said a silent prayer of thanks to God and His emissary for bringing her brother home. "I wish I could thank him myself."

Her brother nodded. "Once they brought us up to the surface and took us to a field hospital, I spent the next week and a half in and out of consciousness. The doctor told me my savior stopped by to ask about my condition several times. He must have been a tank driver." Colin pointed to his face. "Because he wore a mask, you see. He hadn't taken it off."

Grace sat forward on the seat, hardly daring to breathe. It couldn't be . . .

"While I was in hospital, my C.O. did reveal to me how the rescue came about," her brother said. "He was quite impressed. Seems this secret soldier had an uncanny sense of direction, having once been blind. He studied our maps of the tunnel thoroughly, then descended into an existing shaft closest to where we'd been working before the explosion. In a matter of minutes, he was able to pinpoint our location. They began digging and found us."

Grace's heart pounded. Jack! It had to be Jack. And he could see again? Mrs. Vance hadn't mentioned that in the letter.

Joy filled her while a thousand questions burned in her heart. Where was he now? Did he return to Roxwood or had he gone on to London? And . . . had he married Violet Arnold?

Grace had her answer the next day when a private courier arrived with a post for Da.

Taking the letter into the main sitting room where her father sat across from her brother, she felt another rush of gratitude toward Jack. Grace had no doubt he was Colin's savior.

"For you, Da." She handed the letter to her father.

Brother and sister watched as their father opened the missive. When he scanned the lines and his rounded face turned pale, Grace rushed to kneel beside his chair. Her brother leaned forward from his seat on the sofa.

"Da, what's wrong?" Hadn't her poor father already suffered enough? "Is it Aunt Florence?" she asked. "Cousin Daniel?"

He dropped the letter to his lap and eyed both of them. "It's

Swan's." A slow smile spread across his face. "It's reopened for business."

She snatched the letter from him—only it wasn't actually a letter. She stared at a clipping from a newspaper advertisement for the tea room. *Want a Bit of Tea and Intrigue?* the headline read. As Grace scanned the contents of the article, her heart swelled with love for the man she knew must be responsible.

Swan's was now heralded as a place of heroism, not scandal. The advertisement described the tea room as being the scene used in cutting down a notorious espionage ring. Patrick Mabry was being hailed as the man who had saved the countless lives of British soldiers and sailors.

As the owner, Mabry had been instrumental in aiding New Scotland Yard in their ruse to catch the traitors and bring them to justice. Now fully staffed, with the doors reopened for business, Swan's awaited his return from a well-earned sojourn to take up the helm once more.

"Incredible," Patrick Mabry whispered. "Who could have done this?" He rose from his chair and paced with nervous excitement. "Children, we must leave for London immediately. There is much I need to do. My investors!" His hazel eyes gleamed. "I should be able to recoup what I lost and continue construction."

He turned to his son. "Colin, now that you're home, you'll help me build up the franchise." He glanced at Colin's bandaged wrist. "You've paid your dues, son. It's time to look to your future."

"Father, I'd like to stay on with Uncle Brian. For a while, at least. It's peaceful here." He turned to Grace, and she noted his haunted look. "I could do with a bit of that before I return to the world."

"Take as much time as you need," Grace said. She understood. Even Jack had sought his own refuge at Roxwood. To her father, she added, "Da, I'm coming with you. Colin will join us once he's healed." Her brisk tone allowed no room for argument.

Her distracted father merely nodded his agreement. "Grace, my girl, get your things packed. We're off to London on the steamer at first light."

She nodded, feeling pensive. Jack would likely be in London by now, no longer convalescing at Roxwood.

Grace had been thrilled and relieved to learn he'd regained his sight. She hoped Violet Arnold was just as pleased for him. Once he'd returned from the Front, Jack had no doubt married her as planned, with the wedding scheduled for mid-August—last Saturday. How could it be otherwise? Grace knew it was his duty as Stonebrooke's heir.

A familiar ache pierced her. She'd come to learn Jack Benningham understood all about duty. She thought, too, of what it had cost him. He'd risked his life for her brother and then restored her father's livelihood. That made her love him all the more, and despite the hollowness in her heart, she vowed to seek him out and thank him for all he'd done.

∞

Back in London, business at the tea room was brisk as Grace and her father returned to find Swan's overflowing with customers. Da was lauded as a hero and received a standing ovation from the patrons when he walked through the front door. His bankers arrived soon after, profuse in their apologies and eager to resume work on the Mabry tea room franchise that would extend to several areas of the city.

With Alfred Dykes arrested, the only man reasonably qualified to act as Swan's floor manager was a frazzled waiter who had nearly wept upon seeing the Mabrys' arrival. Thereafter,

Grace assumed the role, and she was relieved no one who visited the tea room objected to a woman holding the position. Even her father's chief patroness, the elegantly dressed Lady Bassett, gave her an approving nod from a table where she sat with a few of her close friends.

"Mabry!"

Grace turned at the sound of the chime above the door and Clare Danner's familiar voice. She entered the tea room with several other patrons and waved.

"Clare!" Grace rushed to her, embracing her friend. "I cannot believe you're here."

Grace turned in time to see a disapproving frown from Lady Bassett. "We're being watched," she said, grinning. "Come, sit here in the alcove by the window where we can talk. I'll order us tea."

Once she'd seated the other patrons and their tea was on the table, Grace sat with her friend and reached for Clare's gloved hand. "Well?" she demanded. "How are you?"

"That was my question." Clare arched her pretty dark brows, leaned forward, and whispered, "How was prison?"

Grace made a face. She'd forgotten Clare's candidness. "It was horrible, and I have no wish to see the place *ever* again." She paused. "Mrs. Vance wrote to me about what happened . . . in Margate. Are you all right?"

Clare nodded, a shadow crossing her face. "I've never been so afraid. And poor Agnes." Her gaze met Grace's. "I know what she did to you, but she saved my life."

"And I am grateful to her for that." Grace gave Clare's hand a squeeze. She'd finally managed to forgive Agnes. "If my own family was threatened in the same way, I cannot say what I would have done," she admitted. "I know how sorry she must have felt for her actions. In the end, I'd like to think she made her peace with God."

"I don't imagine I would have acted differently if it were Daisy's life at stake."

"Any new developments?" Grace asked gently.

"I'm meeting Marcus here in an hour." Tears brimmed in her gray eyes. "I told him everything, Grace. About me, and my past. About Daisy. He was furious."

"What!" Grace leaned back, surprised. Sir Marcus had been stern at New Scotland Yard, but she'd never seen him full of wrath. "Tell me what happened."

"He suggested I should learn how to trust again," she said, "or I would never find happiness. Marcus also said if I had told him earlier, he could have found Daisy in half the time it took that overpriced 'idiot' to try." She smiled. "Then he told me he would help me. We would first find Daisy, and then he wants to begin courting me properly so he can prove his love."

"And you said yes?"

Clare grinned, and Grace blinked back tears. "I'm so happy for you."

"Once Marcus gets here, we're leaving to go to fetch my daughter," Clare said, positively glowing. "Marcus located her at an orphanage next to the workhouse in Medway. Do you believe it, Grace? She *was* in Kent all along!"

"This is such good news." Grace beamed. "I cannot wait to see your new beau and thank him myself."

"Did you hear about Becky?" Clare said, her smile fading. "I still feel awful for having scolded her, always talking about going home to see her family."

Grace nodded. "I felt badly when I got Mrs. Vance's letter. I thought I'd helped Becky, but I didn't do a very good job. However, I intend to correct that situation."

"How?"

"Have you ever read *Mrs. Dymond*?" When Clare shook her head, Grace said, "In the story, there's a turn of phrase, 'If you give a man a fish, he is hungry again in an hour. If you teach him to catch a fish, you do him a good turn.'" She smiled. "I've already spoken to Da. Swan's is going to hire Becky to make all our baked goods. That way she'll earn more than enough money to send home to her family."

Clare clapped her hands. "Oh, Grace, that's wonderful news! Becky will be thrilled and relieved."

"I'm just thankful to be able to really help her this time, now that we've been put back to rights here," Grace said. "I feel I owe it to her."

"What's next for you?" Clare reached for her teacup and took a sip. "Have you forgiven Jack?"

Grace nodded. "There is nothing to forgive. Bringing Agnes and the damage she caused into our lives was my fault, not his."

"So you haven't heard from him?"

"No, but we've been back in London only a few days. Still, I doubt he wishes to speak with me." She paused. "Is he in town?"

Clare smiled. "He's got his sight back, you know. It was quite marvelous the way he and Marcus helped the townspeople of Margate after the bombing."

"Yes, he's done many great things," Grace murmured, thinking of all he'd accomplished in secret for her family. "How was the wedding?"

Clare eyed her in confusion.

"Jack's wedding to Miss Violet Arnold? It was to have taken place last Saturday," Grace said, trying to quell the familiar ache in her heart. Though it would be painful, she needed to see him. She owed him that much. She would even brave the haughty new Mrs. Benningham in order to thank him properly.

"He never married."

Grace stared blankly at her friend.

"Didn't you read a newspaper in Ireland? Jack called off their engagement," Clare said. "Then the *Times* reported Miss

Arnold rushed off to Gretna Green and married the second son of the Scottish Viscount Moray. I believe her father was quite put out."

Jack . . . not married? A tendril of hope took root. Why did he not go through with it? "I had no idea," Grace said.

"Well . . . ?"

"Well what, Clare? He must know I'm back in town, yet I haven't seen or heard from him." She bit her lip, then said, "If he was interested in seeing me . . ."

"Grace."

Clare's gray gaze leveled on her. "When we were all at Roxwood together, you told us time and again about suffrage and how with the war women's roles were changing. But more important, you instilled in us a belief that nothing was beyond our reach. We women, each of us, could become whatever we wished to be." She paused. "Do you still feel that way?"

"Of course I do."

"And do you love Jack?"

Grace felt her skin grow warm. "Very much," she said softly.

Clare flashed a broad smile. "Then go to him. Tell him what's in your heart." The gray eyes sparkled. "Be the duchess we all know you were meant to be."

24

Sounds of Mozart played by a string quartet echoed inside the Countess of Lindham's cavernous ballroom. Jack nabbed another flute of champagne from a passing liveried waiter and eyed the character across the room. It was a sign of the times to see most of the servants abovestairs were older men; still, with the war raging on, there was the chance many of them would be pressed into service. He hoped for their sakes the day would never come. God willing, the fighting would soon be at an end.

Meanwhile, there were spies to catch. Jack sipped his champagne while he scanned the room for possible culprits. A very short man dressed as Napoleon looked promising. Out to defeat the British Crown yet again. And like the former tyrant, he kept a hand tucked inside his uniform jacket. Was he hiding something?

He also looked quite full of himself. Jack sighed. When would they learn?

For his own costume, he'd chosen carefully. Tonight he wore the mask of the disfigured Erik from Gaston Leroux's *The Phantom of the Opera*. Jack thought of Grace and smiled, recalling his birthday dinner with her.

He was not to be Christina's pitied Phantom, however. After being at the Front and witnessing bravery, as well as carnage, Jack was proud of his wounds. He had come by them honestly in defending his country. And he would hide them no longer. It was a tribute he owed, not only to himself but to every man who had experienced war. To his brother, Hugh . . .

A commotion at the ballroom entrance drew his attention—a crowd of newcomers. Jack glimpsed a swatch of green cloth, and his pulse quickened. Grace . . . ?

Robin Hood. His hope deflated as a man clad in the green tunic and tights of the legendary forest prince entered through the elaborate double doors.

The champagne felt stuck in his throat. He'd been foolish to think she would come here tonight. He'd written to her twice while she and her father were in Ireland, but had received no response. And yesterday he'd telephoned Swan's and left a message with one of the employees, but had yet to hear back. Likely, Grace never wanted to see him again after the way he'd treated her. Still, he felt grateful for the chance to find Colin Mabry. He'd also worked tirelessly to rectify the damage done to her father, and in that regard, fortune had smiled on him. Just days after Violet sped off with her Scots groom to Gretna Green, he'd received a telephone call from her father, canceling Stonebrooke's debt and apologizing for his daughter's scandalous behavior.

Mr. Arnold had been surprised when, instead of being angry, Jack talked about forgiveness. He pointed out to him that Violet had already mourned the loss of one man, Jack's brother. There was no reason she should lose the love of her father, too. Mr. Arnold should simply take comfort in the knowledge his daughter was at last happy and in love.

Jack had only recently started learning to apply forgiveness to his own circumstances. He had learned at the Front that life was too brief to harbor grief and resentment. He'd finally come to terms with accepting Hugh's death and dealing with his own injuries.

Faith was a new concept to him. He believed God had answered his prayers, and since his return from France, he'd visited Roxwood and met with the Reverend Price. After several hours of lively theological debate, Jack was beginning to read the Bible for the first time.

He still grappled with the concept of suffering, but the reverend had maintained its purpose was to hone the spirit and make one fully reliant upon God, trusting He would see them through.

Would God see him through this? Jack wondered. His heart felt heavy as he again looked toward the door. Was he meant to suffer for some greater good, or was he meant for Grace?

The blue gauntlets and capes of several musketeers appeared, like a flock of bluebirds in their white-plumed hats as they laughingly ventured forward.

Again Jack thought he caught a flash of green before it disappeared. His gut ached, and he turned away. She had given up on him, after everything . . .

He turned again and caught a splash of auburn behind the musketeers before a beautiful woman in emerald pushed through the crowd. She clutched a gold box and slowly approached. Jack felt as if he were in a dream. "Grace," he said hoarsely as she came to stand before him.

Her emerald eyes gleamed, and Jack drank in her presence— from the riot of red curls bound in green ribbon to the beautiful eyes, her perfect nose, and her rosebud mouth that now quivered with mischief.

With a gloved hand, she opened the small gold box and held it out to him. When he finally tore his gaze from her, Jack glanced into the box.

A single red rose lay at the bottom.

"'And after she'd wrought all manner of trouble on the earth,'" Grace said softly, her words reaching to the depths of his heart, "'what remained in the box was hope.'" She moved close and reached to touch his cheek. "Hope for a better future. Hope for us."

He grasped her hand in his. "And faith?" he asked.

She smiled, and it was beautiful and filled with love. "We live by it, Jack."

He smiled back at her. Then, taking her in his arms, he kissed her with all the love in his heart.

Author's Note

Dear Reader,

I hope you've enjoyed reading Grace and Jack's story. As a writer of historical fiction, I'm fascinated with Britain and the time period surrounding WWI. So much was happening—not only the war but Ireland's Easter Rising, women's suffrage, and the dawn of mass production in automobiles, food, clothing, and technology. Women left their homes and domestic service to work in factories and fields and commandeer positions formerly held by men as the war years dragged on. It was a time of wonderment and change, and sadly of loss.

While *Not by Sight* is wholly a product of my imagination, I included a few factual people and places I'd like to share. First, the Women's Forage Corps (WFC) did exist and was a precursor to the Women's Land Army of WWI, the latter better known for their service during WWII. While information about this group seems to be scarce, I did come across this article from the April 1919 issue of the British publication *Land and Water Extra*. "The foundations of the Women's Forage Corps, R.A.S.C. (Royal Army Service Corps), were laid in 1915, but the Corps did not come into being as a whole till March 1917. They [WFC] work in gangs of six, headed by a Gang Supervisor. . . . Some help to bale hay and work with a steam baler, while others act as transport drivers in charge of the horses; these are responsible for the carriage of the hay from the stacks to the railway stations. There are other interesting branches of forage work, such as chaffing, wire-stretching, tarpaulin sheet mending, sack making . . ."[1]

Espionage was also a fact and a real threat during WWI involving German and Dutch spies, the use of invisible ink, and Britain's MI5 constantly on the hunt for domestic traitors. The woman Maud in my story is based on a real person who worked in Room 40, cracking codes and convicting spies. "Mabel Beatrice Elliott uncovered secret messages written in invisible ink between the lines of letters she inspected while working as a deputy assistant censor for the British War Office. Her role remained largely unknown because she gave that evidence under the false name Maud Phillips."[2]

The exotic dancer Mata Hari is best known to the world as the femme fatale spy of WWI. Her Paris trial on July 24, 1917, ended with her conviction and subsequent execution on October 15, 1917. Recent evidence suggests she may not have been a German agent after all. Research reveals an intriguing picture of the German and French intelligence services inadvertently working together to achieve a common goal—the elimination of Mata Hari—and a trial in which the prosecution never called (and the court never allowed the defense to call) two witnesses who could have proved or disproved the case against her. After about forty minutes, the court found Mata Hari guilty, for which no evidence was presented.[3]

The port at Richborough was also a real place, near the town of Sandwich in Kent. During the war, a secret Q port by the banks of the River Stour was the starting point of a ferry service for troops and munitions to France and to Flanders. The chosen spot for the hidden port was under the Roman fortress of Richborough.[4]

Lastly, I admit to embellishing somewhat the destruction wrought by German Gotha planes on Margate, August 1917. Though enemy planes did bomb the area on the twenty-third of that month, the damage was minimal and caused few deaths.[5] A more horrendous attack occurred in that part of the city on September 30, 1917, resulting in many losses of both servicemen and civilians.

—KB

Notes

1. http://www.scarletfinders.co.uk/160.html.

2. http://www.cbc.ca/news/technology/world-war-i-spies-caught-by-woman-who-read-invisible-ink-1.1113118.

3. http://ic.galegroup.com/ic/suic/MagazinesDetailsPage/MagazinesDetailsWindow?zid=c59c508e24676db9e2868469013eac6c&action=2&catId=&documentId=GALE%7CA4224553&userGroupName=clea26856&jsid=dce44fb4bf2c07c6504558e16cb019ca.

4. http://www.open-sandwich.co.uk/town_history/richborough_port.htm.

5. http://paperspast.natlib.govt.nz/cgi-bin/paperspast?a=d&d=FS19170823.2.33.2.

Discussion Questions

1. Seeing Jack Benningham at Lady Bassett's ball, Grace has already formed her opinion of him, based on the newspapers and gossip from Swan's. Can you think of an instance, past or present, where a public figure was maligned by the press or a group of people, and then later exonerated?

2. Women's suffrage was strengthened during the war as women took on more men's roles. They worked in munitions and as tank builders, ambulance drivers, policewomen, and forestry workers, just to name a few. If you had lived in that time, what occupation would you have chosen, and why?

3. When the two women arrive at Roxwood, Grace finds herself the target of Clare's animosity. Have your first impressions ever been wrong? If so, what did you do about it?

4. Agnes spies for the Germans to keep her imprisoned mother and sister alive—actions that betray the country fighting for her Belgian people and likely cause the deaths of countless British sailors, and have the kindhearted

Mabrys arrested and facing execution. What would you have done in her circumstances? Do you think the enemy would have kept their word?

5. At the village dance, Grace coaxes Mr. Tillman into taking a turn around the room with Mrs. Vance, and romance blossoms. Have you ever played matchmaker for someone? Set up a blind date or invited to a party two singles you thought well-suited to each other? What was the outcome?

6. Violet Arnold comes across as a rich, spoiled, and shallow heiress in want of a coronet. Yet as she confronts Jack, her harshness seems more out of desperation than hatred. She feels caught in the net of her father's agenda and frustrated by Jack's unwillingness to end the farce and repay Stonebrooke's debt. Do you feel she was sincere about loving the Scottish viscount's son, or as Jack suspected, did she want out once she saw his horrible wounds at the hospital?

7. Grace's coded letter to her father results in her being suspected as a spy. Yet Jack has doubts after hearing the testimony of her friends. Have you ever had an instance where your instincts conflicted with your reasoning? How did you proceed?

8. A budding writer seeking publication for her stories, Grace keeps a journal of her adventures with the WFC and her outings with Jack. Have you ever kept a journal or diary? What key observations did you notice when you reread the entries later on?

9. Jack teaches Grace to "paint with words" so he can envision the places they visit during their outings. Among her colorful descriptions, did you have a particular favorite? Did it remind you of a place or an event you've seen before?

10. When Jack rescues Colin Mabry in France, he gains new understanding into the cause behind his brother Hugh's death after returning from the war, how "shell shock" is as much a wound as missing limbs or being blinded. In *Masterpiece*'s *Downton Abbey*, Mrs. Patmore's nephew, Archibald, suffers from a similar condition and deserts. With today's return of so many soldiers from places like Iraq and Afghanistan, do you have thoughts on how we can help those with PTSD make a better transition back into society?

11. At the end of the story, Jack has come to terms with Hugh's death and his own injuries. He begins to rediscover his faith in God and to understand the concept of suffering. Do you feel his circumstances in the story better enabled him to help Grace? If so, in what way? And how did Grace help Jack?

12. Who was your favorite secondary character in the novel, and why?

Acknowledgments

I don't believe in coincidence but instead that everything happens under God's Watchful Eye. He has a plan for each of us, and despite the choices we make, He is always there to offer guidance, encouragement, and if we accept it, His strength to see us through.

The title for this novel, *Not by Sight*, is no exception. While I did not choose it, the corresponding passage from Scripture (2 Corinthians 5:7) was meant for me. The verse was ever on my mind as I wrote these pages, oftentimes my mantra before deadlines or while laying down a particularly difficult passage in the story. Reminding me to look with my heart, to my faith in God, and not to what I was seeing on the raw page. I feel this novel is a testament to the veracity of those words.

I would like to thank my husband, John, for his love and patience, especially those times when the pressure was on. My deepest gratitude also to my critique partners, Anjali, Darlene, Elsa, Krysteen, Lois, Patty, Rose Marie, Susan, and Sheila, whose generosity of time and expertise helped to make this story that much better. To my agent, Linda S. Glaz, and to my editor, Raela Schoenherr, and all those at Bethany House, I cannot express enough my appreciation for your graciousness and unwavering support in this endeavor.

About the Author

A Florida girl who migrated to the Pacific Northwest, **Kate Breslin** was a bookseller for many years. She is the author of the highly acclaimed novel *For Such a Time*. Kate lives with her family near Seattle, Washington. Learn more at KateBreslin.com.

More Fiction From Bethany House

A powerful retelling of the story of Esther! In 1944, blond-haired and blue-eyed Jewess Hadassah Benjamin will do all she can to save her people—even if she cannot save herself.

For Such a Time by Kate Breslin
katebreslin.com

At Irish Meadows horse farm, two sisters struggle to reconcile their dreams with their father's demanding marriage expectations. Brianna longs to attend college, while Colleen is happy to marry, as long as the man meets *her* standards. Will they find the courage to follow their hearts?

Irish Meadows by Susan Anne Mason, COURAGE TO DREAM #1
susanannemason.com

When a family tragedy derails his college studies, Henry Phillips returns home to the family farm feeling lost and abandoned. Can he and local Margaret Hoffman move beyond their first impressions and find a way to help each other?

Until the Harvest by Sarah Loudin Thomas
sarahloudinthomas.com

You May Also Enjoy...

When a librarian and a young congressman join forces to solve a mystery, they become entangled in secrets more perilous than they could have imagined.

Beyond All Dreams by Elizabeth Camden
elizabethcamden.com

Rose McKay has plenty of ideas on how to make her family's newly acquired pottery business a success—too many ideas, in long-time employee Rylan Campbell's opinion. But can these two put aside their differences and work together to win an important design contest?

The Potter's Lady by Judith Miller
Refined by Love
judithmccoymiller.com

When a new doctor arrives in town, midwife Martha Cade's world is overturned by the threat to her job, a town scandal, and an unexpected romance.

The Midwife's Tale by Delia Parr
At Home in Trinity #1

BethanyHouse